KALEIDOSCOPE EYES

"Karen Ball offers an intriguing story that kept me turning the pages and guessing the truth right up to the end. Recommended reading for anyone who enjoys suspense and romance."

—TRACIE PETERSON, bestselling author of *What She Left for Me*

"This is my kind of book! Intrigue, suspense, search and rescue…and romance! Karen Ball delivers with a story that is perfect for a snowy weekend in front of a cozy fire. Well done!"

—SUSAN MAY WARREN, author of *Expect the Sunrise*, a Team Hope search and rescue romance

SHATTERED JUSTICE

"Karen Ball speaks to the heart. Readers will fall in love with her realistic characters and gripping story line in *Shattered Justice*. A surefire hit!"

—KAREN KINGSBURY, bestselling author of *One Tuesday Morning* and *Beyond Tuesday Morning*

"*Shattered Justice* is for anyone who has ever known grief or asked God, 'Why me?' Karen Ball paints a beautiful picture of redemption and regeneration and shows that even our suffering sometimes has a greater purpose. Keep a box of tissues handy, because you're going to need it!"

—TERRI BLACKSTOCK, bestselling author of *River's Edge*

A TEST OF FAITH

"Anyone who has ever struggled in a mother-daughter relationship will identify with *A Test of Faith*. The story is as real as the evening newspaper. It was as if I was reading about my own mother, my own daughter, and perhaps more profoundly, reading about myself."

—DEBBIE MACOMBER, *New York Times* bestselling author

THE BREAKING POINT

"*The Breaking Point* is compelling and strikingly honest. This story touches the heart and gives hope for struggling marriages. Karen Ball writes with clarity, depth, and power. It's a pleasure to recommend this engaging and memorable book."

—RANDY ALCORN, bestselling author of *Safely Home*

"Gut-wrenching in its honesty and passion, *The Breaking Point* packs a powerful message of obedience and God's healing."

—BRANDILYN COLLINS, bestselling author of *Brink of Death*

~

NOVELS BY KAREN BALL

FAMILY HONOR SERIES:
Kaleidoscope Eyes
Shattered Justice

A Test of Faith
The Breaking Point
"Bride on the Run" in the *3 Weddings and a Giggle* anthology

A NOVEL

KALEIDOSCOPE EYES

FAMILY HONOR SERIES BOOK 2

KAREN BALL

MULTNOMAH
BOOKS

KALEIDOSCOPE EYES
Published by Multnomah Books
© 2006 by Karen Ball

International Standard Book Number: 978-1-59052-414-5

Cover design by Kirk DouPonce, DogEareddesign.com
Cover photography by PixelWorks Studio, shootpw.com
Interior design and typeset by Katherine Lloyd, The DESK

Scripture quotations are from:
Holy Bible, New Living Translation © 1996.
Used by permission of Tyndale House Publishers, Inc.
All rights reserved.

The Holy Bible, Today's New International Version (TNIV) © 1973, 1984 by
International Bible Society, used by permission of Zondervan Publishing House
The Holy Bible, New International Version (NIV) © 1973, 1984 by
International Bible Society, used by permission of Zondervan Publishing House
The Holy Bible, King James Version (KJV)

Published in the United States by WaterBrook Multnomah, an imprint of the
Crown Publishing Group, a division of Random House Inc., New York.

Multnomah and its mountain colophon are registered trademarks of Random
House Inc.

Printed in the United States of America

For information:
MULTNOMAH BOOKS
12265 ORACLE BOULEVARD, SUITE 200 • COLORADO SPRINGS, CO 80921

Library of Congress Cataloging-in-Publication Data
Ball, Karen, 1957-
Kaleidoscope eyes / Karen Ball.
    p. cm. -- (Family honor series ; bk. 2)
    ISBN 1-59052-414-4
    1. Domestic fiction. gsafd I. Title II. Series: Ball, Karen, ád 1957- Family
honor series ; bk. # 2.
PS3552.A4553K35 2006
813'.54--dc22

2006001516

09 10 — 10 9 8 7 6 5

For Jackie Darby and Rogue.

Some of my earliest memories of search and rescue
include you, Jackie. Your boundless energy, your humble
confidence, your heart for finding the lost…You epitomize
the heart and soul of K-9 search and rescue. Courage.
Determination. Compassion. Skill. Wisdom.
And, ever and always, a great sense of humor.
Thank you for giving of yourself, for sharing your
amazing ability and your remarkable dog with so many.
You and Rogue were a wonder, finding those that others couldn't.
And though you can't be out there now, doing what you love
so much, you're still a wonder. The battle before you is huge,
but know that you have countless people pulling for you.
Because we know that even this won't keep you down.
We believe in you, Jackie.
And we love you.

AUTHOR'S NOTE

This was an especially fun book to write because of my love for both dogs and search and rescue. Annie's Kodi is real. Well, sort of. She's based on my dad's black German shepherd, Kodi. And while Dad's Kodi isn't a skilled K-9 rescue dog, her personality is exactly what you see in this book: a big, too-smart-for-her-own-good, lovable moose who thinks ninety-five pounds is the perfect weight for a lapdog. So thanks, Dad, for loaning me Kodi for the story.

A multitude of thanks to the Rogue Valley K-9 SAR (search and rescue) members Frank, Jo, Mike, Gary, and Karen. They let me follow them and their dogs during a training session. Not only did I learn a lot; I got a great workout. Tell you what, those dogs are some kind of athletes. My respect for them, and for their handlers, is boundless. So thanks to Karen Mihaljevich in particular, who read this story to make sure I got the SAR details right. And pats on the head and an extra treat to Rio, Raven, Holly, and Abby, search dogs extraordinaire. If I'm ever lost, I hope you're there to bring me home!

A big hug and thanks to Michelle Yarborough, a talented stained glass artist. I saw Michelle's work last fall at a home show and knew she was the kind of artist I wanted Annie to be. Michelle's work is stunning. Creative and unique. She may not have synesthesia, but I think she sees things others don't. Beautiful things. I went into this book knowing nothing about the art of stained glass, and Michelle welcomed me into her studio, walked me through the procedure, and read the manuscript to ensure accuracy (and forgave me for the liberties I took with Annie's window). She was an invaluable resource and a delight.

I'm especially grateful to Clay Jacobsen, fellow novelist and

TV director, who shared his expertise on the workings of network TV with me. His credits are impressive, though too numerous to mention (but you can check them out for yourself at www.clayjacobsen.com).

Finally, thanks to my dear friend Lori Benton for sharing from her own life. Lori has synesthesia. I remember the first time I heard about the condition. My weekly coffee group was meeting, and Lori commented that she'd changed the date in which she'd set her most recent novel because "the colors were better." Now, Lori just went on talking. But all of us in the coffee group are writers, so you can imagine how we put on the brakes and demanded to know what she meant. We listened amazed as she explained how she saw colors in letters and numbers, that her sister has synesthesia as well, but "her colors are different."

Thus began my exploration of a condition I didn't even know existed. But the more I studied it, the more I wished I had it! And I knew, without a doubt, that Annie Justice did have synesthesia. So with Lori's permission, I incorporated her colors into the story, both through Annie's point of view and in the color descriptions of the dates. (If you'd like to see Lori and Annie's color chart, visit my website at www.karenballbooks.com.)

Many thanks to Lori for sharing what I believe is a special gift from God. To see colors where others don't, to have that added dimension of beauty, seems a rare blessing. Which is fitting, because Lori's friendship is that as well.

Blessings to you!

Karen

"For you are a holy people, who belong to the LORD your God. Of all the people on earth, the LORD your God has chosen you to be his own special treasure. The LORD did not choose you and lavish his love on you because you were larger or greater than other[s]... It was simply because the LORD loves you... his own special treasure."

DEUTERONOMY 7:6–7

"O LORD, you are my light; yes, LORD, you light up my darkness."

2 SAMUEL 22:29

PROLOGUE

*"If we have no peace, it is because we have
forgotten that we belong to each other."*

MOTHER TERESA

*"Have compassion on me, LORD, for I am weak.
Heal me, LORD, for my body is in agony.
I am sick at heart.
How long, O LORD, until you restore me?"*

PSALM 6:2–3

It's over.
She sank to the ground, not caring that it was frozen. Not caring that the cold seeped into her body. Into her very bones. The ache gave her something to focus on. Something other than the terrible truth.

Everything she'd started to believe, started to trust...

Gone.

Annie pulled her knees to her chest, circled them with her arms, and buried her face.

She would not weep. She refused. But while she could hold the tears at bay, she couldn't stop the questions that assaulted her mind and soul.

How did this happen? How did she end up here?

Because you're a fool. Because you believed his lies. His promises.

She turned her face to the night sky. Promises? He didn't promise anything.

Not in so many words. But you saw it in his eyes. That he cared. That he accepted you. That you belonged.

She belonged…

Annie squeezed her eyes shut against the pain and lifted her face to the sky. She forced her eyes open, searching the blanket of stars. Was He there? Was He listening? Did He care that her world was collapsing around her?

"God…please…"

The prayer floated onto the frigid night air in a puff of white, her plea frozen in space, suspended for a heartbeat between heaven and earth before disappearing.

Why, Lord? Why couldn't You leave me as I was? Alone, yes. But content. At peace.

But even as she flung the questions at the sky, Annie turned her face away. She couldn't face heaven because she knew.

It was a lie.

She hadn't been at peace. Not then. Not ever. Not in what mattered most. She'd spent most of her life searching, longing.

Is that so bad, Lord? All I wanted was to fit in. To belong somewhere. To someone.

Her fingers curled into a fist. He'd made her so sure she'd finally found that…

Fool! Stupid, trusting fool.

Annie pushed herself to her feet, the cold that had seeped through her body and heart embodied in two fierce words: "No more!"

Her words filled the night around her, shivering with the intensity of resolve. He'd played her for a fool. But that was over. She knew what she had to do, and she'd do it. As quickly and completely as possible.

And then, when her task was finished, she'd walk away. Go back to who she used to be, to where she was safe. Protected. Guarded against the pain wracking her.

She'd been a fool once. She'd never be that again.

Not for him.

Not for God.

Not for anyone.

ONE

"From childhood's hour I have not been
As others were—I have not seen
As others saw..."

"Alone," Edgar Allen Poe

"May the God of peace...equip you with all you need for doing his
will. May he produce in you...all that is pleasing to him."

Hebrews 13:21

Two Months Earlier
August 24—A Red Clover Day (Green and Rose)

The woman in the mirror was dressed for a wedding.

If anyone had told her a year ago that she'd be standing here, dressed like this, ready to walk down an aisle, flowers in hand—

"You look beautiful."

She turned and felt the joy in her smile as she faced her brother. She was so used to seeing him in his deputy uniform— either that or jeans and a T-shirt—that the sight of him in a tux nearly took her breath away. "So do you."

Dan arched one brow and came to stand beside her, slipping his arm around her waist. "I, my dear sister, am *not* beautiful. Stunning. Handsome. Debonair. Drop-dead gorgeous, yes. But beautiful?" He flicked the end of her nose. "I think not."

A low, offended rumble drew their attention down, and Annie giggled. "I believe Kodi is still miffed at us."

Dan shook his head. "I still can't believe Shelby let you talk her into using your German shepherd for the flower girl."

Annie knelt beside her dog and adjusted the flowers woven into the shepherd's collar. "Hey, it wasn't my idea. It was hers. She knows Kodi is part of the family." Annie angled a look at her brother as she stood. "Does Shelby know she's marrying such a hunk?"

His grin was equally playful as he tugged at the front of his tux. "Why do you think she said yes?"

"Well, I thought it had something to do with you wearing a gun…"

"Brat." He nudged her with a hip and stepped away. "So where's the other bridesmaid?"

"You mean our beloved Sister-Mommy?" His lips twitched at her nickname for Kyla. "She's making sure everything is running smoothly, of course. And by the way, she's not a bridesmaid. She's the maid of honor."

"Of course." He looked out the window at the back yard. "You've really done a great job, Annie. It looks great down there."

She joined her brother at the window and nodded. Rows of chairs had been arranged in two sections beneath a large canopy. A long white runner ran down the middle aisle between the chairs, leading to front. Cascades of fresh flowers adorned the front, providing the backdrop for the coming ceremony.

It was perfect. "Kyla oversaw most of it, of course."

"All except the flowers."

Annie squeezed Dan's waist, then let him go. "All except the flowers. Well, I'd better go down and see how your bride is doing. Kyla would never forgive me if she found out I was up here twiddling the morning away."

"Go to it, then. Since I'm just the groom, I'll go hold up a wall someplace."

She laughed. "See there? You're getting back into the swing of married life already."

Annie hurried down the stairs, Kodi at her side, doing her best to avoid anyone as they made their way across the yard to her studio, which had been turned into the bride's dressing room. Annie had been delighted when Shelby and Dan asked to have their wedding at her home.

"Your garden is just so beautiful," Shelby said. "I'd love to be surrounded by all those flowers as we're saying our vows."

Annie couldn't argue. Her garden was her pride and joy. Well, one of them. And the flowers had outdone themselves this year—almost as if they knew they were going to be part of something special.

That's what this wedding was. Special. She could hardly believe it had been just over three years since Dan's first wife, Sarah, died. Annie hadn't been sure he would recover from that loss.

She opened the studio door and stepped inside. The sight that met Annie stopped her in her tracks. Shelby, in all her bridal glory, stood in front of a full-length mirror.

She turned to look at Annie as she drew close, and when their eyes met, Annie saw such joy in Shelby's gaze. "Do I look okay?"

"Okay?" Annie's laugh was choked with emotion. "You look amazing." She embraced the woman God had used so wonderfully in Dan's life and heart. "I'm so happy for you. And for my brother."

Shelby returned the hug.

"What are you doing? You'll wrinkle the dress!"

The two women jumped apart and turned guilty gazes to Kyla, who stood there watching them. It took a second for Annie to realize the sternness in her sister's eyes was teasing. "Oh, you!" She swatted at Kyla, who laughed and came to join the hug, careful not to squash the two bouquets she held.

Kyla stepped back. "Everything's set. The place is packed. Dan's standing up there looking all excited and nervous. Jayce is at his side, looking particularly dashing in a tux."

"The flower girl is ready." Annie patted Kodi's head and met Kyla's bland stare. Annie knew it took all of her sister's self-control not to protest again. And from the wink Shelby sent her, her sister-to-be knew it too.

Kyla handed one of the bouquets to Annie, then lifted the large, beautiful bridal bouquet and extended it to Shelby. "So, what do you say, Miss Shelby? You ready to join this crazy family?"

The warmth of Shelby's smile enveloped Annie and Kyla. "Just try to stop me."

Annie eased into her office chair, glad to be out of the bridesmaid dress and back into jeans.

The wedding had been wonderful. But she couldn't deny she was glad it was over, that everyone was gone. Crowds just weren't her thing.

She glanced at the calendar. August 24. A day of joy for Dan and Shelby. A day of green and rose.

The warm colors shimmered behind the twenty-four on the calendar, shading the day with a rich, contented mood.

Annie leaned back in her chair, eyes closing as her thoughts drifted.

Green...

She liked green. It was friendly, alert, vibrant, and alive. Green had a way of infusing Annie—and the day around her—with excitement. As though something good was coming.

Anticipation.

Yes, that was it. Green was the color of anticipation. How appropriate for her brother's wedding day.

"Daydreaming again, Annot?"

Annie stretched and looked at the elegant woman standing at the end of her bed. "Don't you know it's rude for a houseguest to wake the hostess when she's dozed off?"

"I'm not a guest; I'm family."

Annie grimaced at her older sister. Everything about Kyla, from her perfect thick hair to her oh-so-coordinated clothes to her insistent use of Annie's proper name, proclaimed her controlled outlook on life.

Hard to believe they were related.

Where Kyla was tall and willowy, Annie was short and athletic. Where Kyla's eyes shared the pure green of emeralds, Annie's were an odd mix of gold and brown. Kyla called them hazel; Annie called them indecisive. Then there were their personalities. As different as night and day, white and black, relaxed and obsessive—

A grunt beside Annie drew her attention to the large black form lying on the floor next to her. Annie reached out a hand to pat her dog's broad head. "You have to admit it, Kylie, our flower girl here did a great job."

"I'll give her this: she was the most obedient flower girl I've ever seen. Of course, she's also the only flower girl I've ever seen who sheds." Kyla sniffed. "Do you know that it takes me *weeks* to get rid of all the dog hair that adheres to my clothes after I've visited you? I thought German shepherds didn't shed."

It was on the tip of Annie's tongue to say something sarcastic, like, "Yeah, and I'll bet you still believe in fairies too." But it would be a waste of breath. Kyla hadn't ever believed in fairies.

"Now shut that silly computer down and come eat. I've called you twice to let you know dinner was ready."

Annie straightened in her chair. "Okay, okay, Sister-Mommy, I'll be there in a minute."

Kyla's generous mouth thinned. Amazing how stern her sister could look when she wanted to. She must make contractors shake in their steel-toe boots.

"How many times do I have to tell you not to call me that?"

"You don't have to *tell* me at all." Annie leaned her elbows on her computer desk. It never ceased to amaze her that Kyla could be so...hard-edged at times when her color was such a soft, warm rose. "I'll stop calling you Sister-Mommy when you stop acting like one."

"Hmm. I'll stop acting like one when you stop needing someone to do so." Kyla eyed Annie's wrinkled clothes.

Annie had changed as soon as the limo bearing her brother and his new wife was out of sight. She hung up the bridesmaid dress with careful attention, then grabbed the clothes she'd dumped on the floor earlier that day. So what if they were wrinkled? The wedding and reception were over. It was time to relax.

Kyla's clothing, of course, wouldn't dare sport a wrinkle. Poor things were pressed to within an inch of their lives.

"It was a beautiful ceremony, wasn't it?"

Annie nodded. "It's been a while since I've seen Dan that happy."

"He deserves it."

No argument there.

"So, are you coming downstairs?"

Drawing in a breath of patience, Annie took hold of her computer mouse. "Just let me finish what I'm doing here."

"Which is?"

"Checking my e-mail to be sure there isn't something I need to deal with. You know, something from search and rescue or Killian."

"Annot, when are you going to realize there's more to life than that dog and your work?"

Annie ran her hands through her short-cropped hair. "Meaning?"

"You need a man."

Oh, please. Not again. Today of all days. Annie had been so sure Kyla would be too focused on Dan and Shelby and the wedding to get into this again.

Idiot.

"Kylie—"

"I don't want to hear it."

"Hear what?"

"Whatever excuse you've come up with." Kyla's tone was as forceful as her stance. Hands planted on slim hips, trim shoulders cocked in a don't-argue-with-me-young-lady stance, chin jutted out.

The picture-perfect Sister-Mommy.

Fire sparked in Kyla's eyes. "Don't."

"Don't?"

"Don't you dare call me that horrendous nickname again. Just because I care about you doesn't mean I'm pushy."

Annie eyed her sister. "You? Pushy? Why would I *ever* think you were pushy?"

"Ha ha. Now come on and eat."

Rather than point out how Kyla had just proven her point, Annie followed her sister out of the bedroom and down to her kitchen. At least, she *thought* it was her kitchen. It was hard to tell, what with everything so sparkling and spotless.

Kyla strikes again. "I take it you've eaten already?"

"Of course." Kyla poured coffee into a mug and handed it to Annie then grinned. "But I can always have some wedding cake and coffee while you eat dinner."

Kyla turned toward the fridge, almost taking a nosedive over Kodi. "*Must* your monster be in the *middle* of the kitchen?"

As though sensing Kyla was talking about her, Kodi jumped up and leaned against Kyla's leg, looking up at her with those big puppy-dog eyes. Kodi adored Annie's older sister.

Pity Kyla didn't return the sentiment. She peered down at Kodi. "Listen, beast, I am not your leaning post."

Kodi's thick tail whomped against the kitchen cabinets. Annie took a sip of her coffee. "I keep telling you, Kylie, if you don't want Kodi lovin' on you, don't talk to her. Attention is her favorite treat."

Kyla didn't reply. Just kneed Kodi away and opened the refrigerator to pull out a plate of food. She set it on the table in front of Annie. "Now, what were we talking about?"

No point trying to avoid it. "My need for a man. Of course, I don't see *you* waltzing down the wedding aisle, and you're considerably older than I am. So which of us, me at my tender age, or you at your ripe ooold age—"

Kyla spun, piercing Annie with a glare.

"—should be more concerned about finding a man?" Annie delivered a smile so sweet it would choke a honeybee and blinked her wide-eyed innocence.

Kyla managed to hold the glare for another few seconds, then dissolved into laughter. "Annot, you are incorrigible."

"Spell that." Annie pulled the plastic wrap from around her plate.

"I-n-c-o...rrigible."

"Close enough." Annie played with her fork. "So how 'bout you give me a break on the 'go get married already' speech? Just for today."

Kyla opened her mouth, resistance in her features, then clamped her lips together. "I only talk about it because I care."

Annie sat back with a sigh. "You know I'd love to get married, but there's this little detail of finding a man I actually like, let alone love."

"It might help if you tried this really fascinating little thing called dating."

Annie grimaced. "Fascinating. That's another word for revolting, right?"

"Annie."

"I *have* tried it." She lowered a hand to scratch Kodi's head. "Remember Frank?"

Kyla had the grace to bite her lip. "That really was a disaster, wasn't it?"

"How you could ever think I'd be interested in a man like that?"

"Frank is a nice man."

"He hates animals." 'Nuff said. But Annie went on anyway. "*Especially* big dogs."

"But I didn't know tha—"

"And then there was Bruce. I believe he was another one of your setups."

"What on earth was wrong with Bruce? He loved animals—"

"Sure, if their heads were mounted on the wall of his den. Besides which, he had no sense of humor, was barely an inch taller than I am, and was just this side of bald—unless you count that oh-so-manly comb-over." Annie held her hand out to her sister. "Would you care to bless this feast, or shall I?"

Kyla took Annie's hand and closed her eyes. "Father, thank You for the blessing of food and shelter and for the blessing of family. Let our time together please You."

"Ame—"

"And show Annot she's being far too picky about men. Amen."

Annie's glare went unnoticed as Kyla focused on stirring the perfect amount of cream into her coffee.

"You know I only hound you because I care about you, Annot."

"I know."

"I look at you and see someone with so much love to share, so much talent and passion…"

Annie set her fork down. "You know what *I* see when I look at me? A warm marigold. Know what I see when I look at you? A rich rose. And Dan?"

Kyla leaned back in her chair. "Marigold." She sighed. "I'm your sister. Heavens, I helped you plant your garden with flowers and plants that have your colors. I know about your condition."

"You know about it, but you don't really understand it. You don't understand what it's like to see shadows of a person's color when you look at or think of him. That even though I'm not always conscious of it, I see pink whenever I look at you."

"Well…" Kyla cupped her hands around her coffee mug. "No, I guess not."

"Don't you see? That's the point. I'm different." Annie looked down at the food that had seemed so mouthwatering moments ago.

"Just because you have synesthesia…"

"No. That's only part of it." Annie crossed her arms, hugging herself. "Yes, I have synesthesia. Yes, I perceive things others don't—"

Kyla rested her chin in her hand as she chewed. "Colors in numbers and letters. I'd really like to see that."

"Don't be so sure. It's not always fun, Kylie. Remember grade school, when the teachers thought I was just this side of crazy because I told them I didn't like the number one?"

Kyla's lips twitched. "Oh, right. It was too arrogant."

"A total snot, to be exact. Thinking it was all that just because it's first—" Annie caught herself, then offered a sheepish grin.

"Okay, so I still don't like the number one much. And therein lies my problem. I see things others don't. I *feel* things others don't. And it's not just the synesthesia. I'm thirty-six and I still cry when I see an animal dead on the side of the road."

"A tender heart isn't a bad thing."

"Maybe not, but people think you're weird when you see a squashed cat or raccoon—"

"Or possum. Or squirrel. Oh, and there was that snake once." Kyla's brows drew together. "At least I think it was a snake. I couldn't really be sure."

"—and the tears start flowing."

Her sister speared a mouthful of cake. "I still can't believe you cry over possums."

"*See?*" Annie waved her fork in the air. "You're my sister and even *you* think I'm odd."

Kyla caught Annie's wrist and lowered the fork back to the plate. "Well, of course I do. It's in my contract as big sister."

"Be serious."

"You think I'm not?"

"And then there's my art. And my search and rescue work with Kodi—I mean, it's like I live in two totally different worlds, and yet I need them both. How schizo is that?"

Kyla laid her hand on Annie's arm. "It isn't. Annot, you do both because you excel at both. You're a wonderful artist, and you've helped so many people through search and rescue. It would be a loss, for you and for others, if you quit either."

Annie swallowed hard and her voice came out in a hoarse whisper. "I know that. But sometimes…I wish I could just settle into one world and stay there. Belong." She brushed at her eyes. "There has to be *some*place I fit in, Kylie." She looked away, staring at nothing, fighting the longing that snaked through her, coiling around her heart, squeezing…

"You belong with us, Annot. With me and Dan. Our family."

Annie lifted her coffee, let the hot liquid sear her tongue and throat as she took a gulp. Kyla believed what she was saying, but the sad truth was that Annie didn't fit there either. Not really. Dan and Kyla thrived on being in crowds; Annie found more than two or three people suffocating. She far preferred the company of animals and silence. Kyla and Dan were so organized, so logical and in control. Annie? All her life she'd been called the flighty one. Miss Emotional.

"This is my sister," Dan loved to say about her. "The woman who's never met an emotion she didn't express."

Her siblings loved her. Annie knew that. But understand her? Hardly. And if her own family didn't, what made Annie believe some stranger out there would be able to? In all her life she'd found only one person who seemed to get her. And though she loved him, he wasn't...well, "the one."

Oh, grow up, Annie! There is no knight in shining armor. And even if there was, he's not going to ride up and sweep you off your feet.

"He's out there, Annie."

She almost choked on her coffee. "What? Who is?"

"The right man for you."

Annie set her mug down. Was her sister reading her mind?

"He's out there. I know it. I feel it, deep inside."

What was this? Miss Practical getting sentimental? Annie couldn't remember the last time she'd seen Kyla get emotional.

Oh. Yes, she could. When they stood beside their brother as first his wife, then his two children, were buried.

But since then? Not even close. Kyla was as stoic as a woman could be. But there she sat, eyes actually glistening with unshed tears as she patted Annie's arm. "When the time is right, God will bring him to you. You just can't give up."

"I won't."

Annie squeezed her sister's hand, asking God to forgive her for the lie. Because what she hadn't told Kyla—couldn't bring herself to admit out loud—was that she'd already done so.

A long, long time ago.

By the time Annie got back to her computer, she was so tired her eyes would hardly stay open. Good thing she only had one more e-mail to check. She just couldn't decide whether to open it. It seemed to be from her nephew, but it wasn't Jayce's usual address.

It was probably nothing. Jayce was forever opening new accounts. No reason to think it was another…

She shook her head. Enough. The more she thought about it, the more tense she became. She steadied her fingers on the mouse and clicked. *Just open the stupid thing and be done with i—*

Shock. Dread. Revulsion.

They coursed through Annie as she read the ugly block letters in the post. The message was short and anything but sweet:

I KNOW WHAIR U ARE.
I CN GET TO U.

Shivers tripped along Annie's skin as she studied the words. Not again.

She'd received two others like it last week. But something about this e-mail stood out. This time there was a picture.

Of her and Kodi.

That fact alone was disturbing enough, but there was something more. Something that made Annie's stomach clench.

A big red *X* slashed across the picture.

Annie's fingers trembled as she slid the cursor to *Delete*. One click, and it would be gone. Just one click…

She let go of the mouse and pushed her chair back. As though sensing her mistress's alarm, Kodi stood from where she was lying next to the desk and used her long snout to nudge Annie's hand onto her head.

Annie scratched her worried dog's ears. "It's okay, girl."

Pity she didn't sound too convincing, even to her own ears. She stood and paced to the window, peering out at the street, studying the parked cars. But she couldn't tell if anyone was inside them.

"Knock it off, Annie!" She grabbed the cord to the blind and jerked on it; the blind dropped like a guillotine, blocking the window. "Nobody's out there. You're being paranoid."

Yeah, well just because I'm paranoid doesn't mean someone's not out to get me.

Kodi's whine cut through the silence, and Annie settled back into her chair, leaning over to bury her face in the shepherd's soft black fur.

Okay, fine. The e-mails gave her the creepy crawlies. Who on earth would send such things to her?

A crazy person.

Well…yes. But where did said crazy get her private e-mail address? *AJnK,* for Annie Justice and Kodi. She reserved that e-mail address for her family and closest friends. They knew better than to share it with anyone, which meant this address never got spammed.

Which was why although she hadn't recognized the return address on the first e-mail—Dan@hostmail.com—she'd opened it without a second thought. She figured her brother had gotten a new e-mail address and was letting her know about it.

The second the large, bold letters had appeared on her screen, she knew she'd figured wrong. That message had been equally short—and equally chilling.

I'M WATCHNG U.

Her brother would never send something like that, not even as a joke. She had configured her account to block the person's address, then deleted the e-mail, figuring it was a tasteless prank from someone who had too much time on his hands. Nothing to worry about.

Then the second e-mail showed up.

This one was from Kylie@questor.net. Again, not an address she recognized, but she only hesitated for a moment. No stranger could know that *Kylie* was her nickname for her older sister. It had to be okay.

Wrong again.

THAIR R WORST THINGS THEN BEING LOST. U'LL SEE. SOON.

Annie considered forwarding it to her brother. After all, one of the perks of having a sheriff's deputy for a brother was that he was there when things got weird.

Or frightening.

But she didn't want to get him all worked up just because of some anonymous twit. Better to just save it and then wait to see if any more messages showed up.

Well, apparently the old saying is true: Third time's a charm.

When she'd opened her e-mail account a few minutes ago, she saw the suspect message right away. At the sight of Jayce's misspelled name in the address, an increasingly familiar dread skittered through her. She grabbed the mouse. She'd just forward the message to Dan with an explanation. Let him deal with it...

Yeah, nice welcome-home-from-your-honeymoon gift.

Right. Well, then, she'd just keep it in her mailbox and talk with him when he got home. That decided, she peered at the picture again. It looked like the one the local paper had used for an article on search and rescue several years ago. Anyone could have found that, made the *X* with a marker, then scanned it in.

But why? Why would someone want to do this?

It's Dan's job to figure that out. Just leave it alone until you talk with him.

Good idea. She clicked the *close* button, then just about jumped out of her skin when a hard rap sounded at her door.

"Annot! Turn off that stupid computer, and go to bed."

Annie gritted her teeth and powered down her computer. She loved her siblings. She really did. But as she slipped the laptop into its case, she thought she'd had about all the sisterly mothering she could take.

And then some.

TWO

"'Because of God's tender mercy,
the light from heaven is about to break upon us,
to give light to those who sit in darkness
and in the shadow of death,
and to guide us to the path of peace.'"

LUKE 1:78–79

"Step within His light and keep following."

ELSI DODGE

SEPTEMBER 8

Time had lost all meaning.

Torture had a way of making that happen. And if standing here being badgered by these two women wasn't torture, Dan Justice didn't know what was.

"I can't believe I let you two talk me into this. Do you know what time it is?" He lifted the phone from its base, ready to dial.

"Your sister won't mind, Sheriff. I just know she won't."

Dan's fingers tightened on the phone. "Aggie, how long have we known each other?"

Agatha Hunter pursed her lined lips. "Sheriff, do you *really* think now is the time to reminisce?"

"Agatha, how long?"

"Howl on?" Doris Kleffer, Agatha's best friend and constant companion, tugged at the taller woman's sleeve. "What's the sheriff

27

talking about? Did you howl? I didn't hear you howl."

Aggie batted at Doris's veined hand. "How *long*, Doris. He wants to know how *long* we've known him."

"Well!" Doris huffed. "This is hardly the time to discuss *that!*"

"That's what I said, but he wants to know."

"Wants to go? Go where?"

"*Know*, Doris. He wants to *know!* Turn up your hearing aid!"

His head was going to explode. Dan was sure of it. Just blow, right then and there, into a million throbbing pieces. He *knew* he should have taken two weeks for a honeymoon instead of one.

He gripped the phone so hard his hand ached. "Ladies! *Please!*"

The two elderly women nearly jumped out of their skin at Dan's bellowed exasperation, but he didn't really care that he'd startled them. "All I'm saying is we've known each other long enough for you to remember that I. Am. Not. A. Sheriff!" He ground out each word with precise—and increasing—emphasis and volume. "Got it?"

"Well, fine, Sher—*Deputy*," Aggie amended at Dan's murderous glare. "Why didn't you just say so before?"

"Why didn't…?" No point saying he'd been telling them that from the day they met over two years ago. They wouldn't listen. Yup. His head was definitely going to explode.

Sighing his surrender, Dan punched in Annie's pager number. *Sorry, Sis. But I need reinforcements.*

SEPTEMBER 8—A CATTAIL DAY (AUBURN)

Annie was dreaming.

It was a nice dream too. No, make that a great one.

She'd had the same dream off and on since she was a teen. A tall, handsome man riding a white horse. The breeze ruffled his short brown hair. Approval twinkled in those Belgian chocolate eyes as he studied her. The faintest tinge of raspberry shimmered around him as he reached down from the height of the horse's back and held out his hand. Annie laid her palm in his—the fit was perfect—and his fingers closed, nestling her hand in warmth and strength. He was just about to lift her to the saddle behind him, and Annie was poised and ready…

Her dream self frowned.

What was that noise? Something sharp and piercing…

Someone needed to make that noise stop.

Her knight's face lifted in a warm smile—a smile as familiar to Annie as her own. He pulled her onto the horse, and as she settled against him, he looked back over his shoulder. "Will you…?"

She strained to hear the rest of his question. Longed to hear it. But that noise tugged at her.

Ringing. Something was ringing.

"Will I?" She laid her cheek against the back of his shoulder, so at home.

His fingers brushed her face. "Will you…?"

What *was* that ringing!?

She gritted her teeth, ignoring the annoyance. "Yes? Go on."

He blinked. Then turned around and frowned. "Will you answer that darned pager?"

Annie jerked awake, sitting bolt upright, heart pounding. She blinked as her knight's image faded, then tried to focus on the bright red numbers of the clock on her bedside table.

2:00 a.m.

Not that that bothered her. Annie was used to pages or phone calls in the wee hours of the morning. Nor was it Kodi's sudden restless pacing next to the bed, as though the dog knew before Annie answered who was on the line. Because she probably did.

Calls at this hour usually meant one thing.

Someone was lost.

As much as Annie hated to think of someone wandering in the darkness, frightened, possibly injured, that didn't really bother her either. Because she and Kodi were good at what they did. The best, some said.

And what they did was find people. Bring them home.

But what *did* bother Annie as another ring split the silence was one simple thought: *Killian's gonna kill me.*

She pushed clear of the last vestiges of her dream—though she *really* didn't want to—and freed her legs from the bedsheets. Perching on the edge of the bed, she grabbed her pager and read the callback number.

It wasn't search and rescue. Well, then who on earth was it?

She considered ignoring it, but something about the number looked familiar. She grabbed the phone and dialed. Someone answered on the first ring.

"Hello?"

"Hi, this is Annie Justice. Someone paged me—"

"Annie? It's Dan."

She frowned. Why was he paging her at this time of morning? She grabbed the clock and peered at it again. Yep. She'd read it right. 2:00 a.m. "Dan, you're my brother and I love you, but you woke me out of a dead sleep—"

"Is she there? Will she come?"

Who was talking in the background? Annie set down the clock and rubbed a hand over her eyes. It sounded like…but no. No way she'd be awake this time of morning—

"Hush!" This from Dan, kind of muffled, as though he'd turned away from the phone. Then he came back on the line. "Look, sis, I know this is unusual. But—"

The background voice broke in again. "Ask her if she'll help us, Sheriff."

"I'm *not* the sheriff!" Dan's terse reply sounded like it forced itself through gritted teeth. Only one person could make Annie's brother this crazy.

"Ask her if she's *jealous?*" A second voice chimed in. "Why on earth would she be jealous?"

"*Help us,* you twit. Not jealous!"

Annie held back a laugh. Okay, make that two people. No mistaking those voices—Agatha Hunter and Doris Kleffer were not only awake, but in rare form.

Her brother groaned. "Annie, I need your help."

"Obviously." Kodi pawed at Annie's arm, begging a scratch,

but she shooed the dog away. "What's up?"

"Have you heard about the Alzheimer's patient who wandered off up here?"

She stifled a yawn just as Kodi lifted that huge paw to whap her arm again. She held the receiver away. "Fine, you monster." She patted the bed beside her, and Kodi gave one powerful leap. Annie braced herself for impact, but the bed barely moved under the dog's gentle landing. Amazing how such a large animal could move with such grace. Always made Annie think of a linebacker doing ballet. She leaned against Kodi as the shepherd snuggled close and settled down.

Right on Annie's pillow.

Over her shoulder Annie eyed the dog; Kodi turned her head to stare at the wall.

Coward.

"Annie? Did you hear me?"

"Sure. It's been all over the news."

Just after dinner several nights ago, an eighty-five-year-old woman with Alzheimer's had apparently walked out of the senior foster home where she lived. The home was situated on the outskirts of town, backed by a clearing, a stand of woods, and a ravine.

Not a brilliant place for a foster home, but options were limited in Sanctuary, Oregon.

Since Dan lived in Sanctuary, she'd known he'd be involved in the search. Shelby was getting a taste of being a deputy's wife right off the bat. But as much as Annie felt bad for Shelby, she also knew Dan would be an invaluable resource for the search teams.

"In fact, I figured that's what this was, a callout for me and Kodi to come join the search." She slid her feet back under the covers, pushing back against Kodi. The dog didn't budge. "But I can't say I'm sorry it's not. I could use the slee—"

"Actually—" there was a cringe in Dan's tone—"it is."

Annie lay against her dog for a second, then pulled her feet free of the sheets and sat on the edge of the bed again. What was going on? Dan didn't issue callouts for K-9 search and rescue. She glanced over at Kodi. The dog was still sprawled on her pillow, but her brown gaze was fixed on Annie, and those giant bat ears were perked.

Yeah, you can tell something's up, can't you, girl? "Oh?"

Dan released a heavy sigh. "Look, sis, I know this isn't following protocol—"

"Not even close."

Kodi's large paw reached out and batted at her. She batted back, giving the dog an exaggerated frown. This was no time to beg for attention.

"—and that I should let you wait for an official request to join the search—"

Another paw. Another frown. "But?"

"But I'm a deputy, so you could consider this official." Dan's voice dropped to a whisper. "And these two women are driving me absolutely bonkers!"

Annie couldn't restrain a laugh, and Kodi jumped up, pacing behind her on the bed. Annie looped an arm around the dog's neck.

"Friend of theirs, I take it?"

"Not just a friend. A 'bosom buddy,' as Aggie says. Woman's name is Bertha Norris."

"She lives at the adult foster home with Aggie and Doris?"

"She does."

"The search teams haven't had any luck finding her?"

"No. They haven't found any sign of Bertha yet. Doris and Aggie have been all but glued to my side since Bertha wandered off."

"Lucky yo—"

"Day and night."

"I get the pict—"

"Right here. With me."

Annie swallowed another laugh. Clearly now was not the time to tease her beloved brother. "Do Doris or Agatha have any idea where she might have gone?"

Silence met her question, then another heavy sigh. "They think she's been abducted."

"Let me guess, by aliens?"

He snorted. "I wouldn't put it past them to think that. But no, they think she's been nabbed by—"

"Did you tell her about the reprobate who was hanging around the home, talking with Bertha?"

"For heaven's sake, Doris, you're standing practically on *top* of the sheriff. Did you *hear* him tell his sister about that?"

"Did I *what?*"

"*Hear* him. Did you *hear* him tell—"

"*Knock it off!*" Dan's voice barked over the phone lines with such force that Kodi yelped and jumped away even as Annie jerked the receiver from her ear. A second passed, then, "Annie? You still there?"

She nestled the receiver close again. "Oh, yeah."

"Sorry about that. I'm just at the end of my rope. I mean, I know you've got a big showing today—"

"Don't worry about it. We'll be there."

"Killian's gonna take my head off."

Yeah. Dan really sounded worried. Not.

Little wonder. Killian was matchless when it came to dealing in contemporary art. And his gallery, Expressions, was arguably the most respected in the region. As evidenced by the fact that he was rapidly becoming the darling of home makeover shows, being flown hither and yon as a consultant.

But take Dan's head?

He couldn't even *reach* Dan's head.

Annie stood. "Let me worry about Killian."

"Better you than me, that's for sure. I don't think I could be nearly as patien—"

"Well?" Agatha's voice was so clear that it had to be right in Dan's ear. "Is she coming?"

"Humming? Who cares if she's humming? Is she *coming?*"

"Oh, for—! That's what I *said*, Doris. I said coming. Didn't I say coming, Sheriff?"

"How many times do I have to tell you two—" good thing the

ladies were hard of hearing, or Dan's furious growl would surely send them scampering for cover—"I'm *not* the sheriff! I'm a deputy!"

Agatha was having none of it. "Oh, piddly-poof! You're as good as any sheriff in our book."

"Better!" Pure glee overflowed with Doris's agreement. "Sheriffs make you do things *their* way, like they're the law or some silly thing."

"The nerve!"

"Indeed!"

Annie was almost choking on laughter when Dan's hoarse whisper came back on the line. "Annie, for the love of heaven—hurry!"

She stretched. "Kodi and I will be at your office within the hour."

"Thanks, sis, I owe you."

"Yes, you most certainly do."

Annie hung up, fingers tapping out a mindless rhythm on the phone as she gathered her thoughts.

Killian loved her, quirks and all. She knew that without a doubt. He'd found out about her condition in high school, when they teamed together for a world history report. Killian wanted to do the Revolutionary War, but Annie preferred the history of the Eiffel Tower because, she told him, the colors were better.

At Killian's stare, she explained. "I see colors, okay? It's called synesthesia, a condition where actual physical perceptions get crossed. Letters and numbers have their own colors. And when you combine them, the shades mix, even change a little depending on the color of their neighbors. Whatever letter or number comes first has the most impact…kind of shades everything else. So some dates, some words, they're nicer than others."

She'd waited for him to laugh, to make fun of her. Instead, he cocked his head. "What color am I?"

No one had ever responded with such acceptance.

"Well, the letters in your name are a mixture of colors, but *k* is a bright pink, so that kind of overshadows the rest."

He blinked. "So you're telling me I'm...pink?"

Annie laughed. "I know, not too masculine, huh? But it's a very nice color. Friendly and warm." She touched his arm. "Just like you."

She didn't mention that his pink clashed a bit with his red hair. It would only upset him. Besides, Killian was a smorgasbord of conflicts—caring and demanding, supportive and sarcastic, understanding and impatient. So the clash fit.

From that point on, Killian delighted in hearing about her condition. And any time she whined about being different, he'd shake his head. "Annie, your ability to see colors where others don't? It's a gift." He peered at her over those round, wire rim glasses that made him look so wise. "I'd love to see life the way you do."

Even her own family hadn't made her feel as comfortable with herself, her differences, as Killian.

Lately, though, Killian was stressed to the max. He'd been working long and hard to get ready for today's showing. Of course, that was only right since the whole thing was *his* idea. One he hatched the moment he saw her most recent completed window.

"A grand unveiling, that's what this calls for. We'll feature this window and your other works. It will be huge! Now—" he'd pulled his large desk calendar toward her—"what day in September has the best colors for a showing?"

When she chose the eighth, he fingered the date on the page. "Why that one in particular?"

"It's an auburn green day."

"An auburn green day..." Killian took a green marker from his desk drawer and circled the date. "That's good. Green Auburn is rich and alive, earthy. A good day for creativity."

"Exactly."

Killian snapped the cap back on the marker. "Perfect choice."

Too bad he wasn't as enthusiastic about her involvement with search and rescue.

He'd never liked the idea of her spending time away from her art. When she and Kodi earned a reputation for finding people when others couldn't and the demand for them increased, Killian hadn't said a word. He didn't need to. Annie could tell he didn't like it.

Not even a little.

But it wasn't until her stained glass art started gaining notice that Killian actually suggested she give up search and rescue. The first time he did, Annie just patted her flamboyant friend on the head.

"Don't be silly, Killie."

"Oh. Fine. Now you think you're a poet."

The last few months, though, any good humor on his part had faded. He'd brought it up again just a few days ago. "Annie, please, this search and rescue thing is too disruptive. You never know when you're going to get one of those call ups—"

"Callout, Killie. You get called up in the military."

"Whatever. And they're almost always in the middle of the night."

"Because people don't call for help until they've spent hours trying to find the lost person themselves. Then it gets dark and they get scared."

Killian brushed imaginary lint from his sleeve. Like lint would *dare* land on his immaculate clothing. Killian was as *GQ* as it got—stylish to a fault. Always had been.

"All I know," he went on, "is that it's time away from your art. And that's not good for you."

"It's about balance, Killian. Not one involvement taking over another."

Unfortunately, Killian and balance weren't terribly well acquainted. Which made her that much more hesitant to risk upsetting him. After all, this showing was featuring her art. He'd expect her to be there.

On time.

Ah well…no point putting off the inevitable. She lifted the phone, punched in the number, and listened as the phone rang once, twice—

"Good morning."

Annie smiled. Leave it to Killian to sound wide-awake at

almost two-thirty in the morning. "Killie, it's Annie."

"No. Don't you dare."

She bit her lip. "Now Killie…"

"Annot Christine Justice—"

Ouch. Her full name. He really was peeved.

"—don't you *dare* tell me you're going to miss your own showing and reception! Not after all I've put into this event. Good grief, woman, I've practically sweat blood for you, and if you think…"

She knew better than to interrupt one of his rants, so she stood there, waiting. Killian knew how to show any medium to its best advantage and delighted in taking virtual unknowns and introducing them to the art world. No, he did more than introduce them.

Killian made stars.

But the very creativity that made him a master in his chosen vocation made him mercurial at best, explosive at worst. Do or say the wrong thing, and Killian proved that he came by that red hair naturally. The man was painfully adept at exhibiting the ugly side of creativity.

Good thing she knew how to handle him.

When he finally paused his tirade long enough to draw a breath, Annie broke in. "Killian, calm down. Yes, there's been a callout. And yes, Kodi and I are going. But I'll be at Expressions right on time. The showing doesn't start until three this afternoon, and you know how hot it's been."

Killian's sniff did his disdain—and his outrage—proud. "Hot? What does the heat have to do with anything?"

"It's too hot to work Kodi after eleven. So if we haven't found the woman by then, I'll pack Kodi up and head home."

There was a moment's silence. "By eleven? Then you'd be at the gallery by two, which should give us time to prep before the showing. I'll have Ryan get everything ready so all you need to do is clean up and show up."

Oh dear. Sounded as though Killian's poor assistant was going to bear the brunt of this change in plans.

"Swear you'll be on the road back to town no later than eleven?"

Annie's lips lifted at the grudging mollification in his tone. "Scout's honor."

He snorted. "Yeah. That might sway me were you ever a Scout. But we both know you weren't."

"Yes, well, and whose fault was that?"

"Oh, please. Haven't you guilted me about that for long enough?"

"*Your* mother was the Scout leader. *You* told her I hated the Scouts and only wanted to join, how did you put it, to 'foment rebellion.'"

"You've got to admit I was precocious as a kid."

"Precocious? Is that another word for lying pinhead?"

Killian's teasing drifted over the phone lines, easing the tension between Annie's shoulder blades. "Look, Killie, you know I'll do my best to be there today—"

"Do your best?" The amusement vanished from his voice as quickly as it had appeared. "Not good enough. You *have* to be there, Annie. This is important."

Enough was enough. She matched her tone to his. "So is a woman's life."

Silence. Then a weighted sigh. "You're right, and I'm a worthless pile of humanity."

"Well—" Annie allowed a hint of humor to soften her response—"not entirely worthless."

"And so I'm condemned with faint praise. Go on, then. You and your beast—"

"Dog, Killie. Kodi is a dog."

"—go and find the poor, lost soul. I'll send good thoughts your way."

"Thanks."

"And expect to see you no later than 2:00 p.m."

Annie eased the receiver back into the cradle. Killian tried to be understanding. He really did. And Ryan helped a lot. He kept reminding Killian that Annie had never missed a deadline or a showing. But Killian had always taken her art more seriously than she did. Even in high school he'd been the one to submit her work for contests and awards, not Annie. When she won every one, he all but glowed with delight. For her. No doubt about it, Killian believed in her and her stained glass art before anyone.

Even herself.

He was so certain she belonged in the art world. That art was her home. Annie wanted to believe him, but she knew better. She didn't fit in the art world. Any more than she fit anyplace else...

She pushed the thoughts away, going to the closet and pulling out her search and rescue clothes.

Okay, Annie girl, knock it off. Stop feeling sorry for yourself. Besides, what have you got to be all morose about?

It was true. She really did have the best of all worlds. She loved working in stained glass. Killian was spot on about that. And yes, people paid her very good money for what she created. But she was more than an artist.

Search and rescue was as much a calling as her art.

And, for the moment, that calling was considerably louder.

She jerked on her boots and fastened the gators snug. From what Dan had told her, she would be walking through a good deal of brush, so the gators would protect her ankles and calves.

"Let's go, Kode."

She didn't have to speak twice. Kodi was out the bedroom door and waiting at the front door, her tail thumping a steady beat on the hardwood floor. Annie grabbed her keys and Kodi's leash off the hook. The dog watched her every move, ears perked, brown eyes wide and expectant.

"You ready, girl?"

Kodi's excited bark split the night, and Annie opened the front door. "Okay then, let's go to work."

THREE

"The truth, even though I cannot feel it right now, is that I am the chosen child of God, precious in God's eyes, called the Beloved from all eternity and held safe in an everlasting embrace."

HENRI J. M. NOUWEN

"Even in darkness I cannot hide from you."

PSALM 139:12

SEPTEMBER 8
3:00 a.m.

Get to work, Andy! Move it!"

Jediah Curry pressed a hand into his cameraman's back. "We're losin' 'em!"

"Are you *nuts?* I am not following those guys up ther—"

"Look out!"

Jed didn't have time to respond. One minute he was standing there, directing Andy to follow the firefighters up the stairs of the burning two-story home; the next he was grabbed by powerful hands, jerked backward, and dragged from building. The excruciating heat that chased them out the door told him just how close he'd come to being fried.

He struggled free of what he now realized was a firefighter's grip, wiped at his still hot face, and stared with stinging eyes into the smoke billowing from the open doorway. "Andy!"

Dread sliced through Jed's gut. He'd done it now. He'd really

40

done it. He'd gotten Andy killed! His best friend. And for what? *TV ratings?*

Jed passed a hand over his eyes. How was he going to live with thi—?

"I oughta knock you flat."

He spun, and relief so strong it made his knees weak swept through him. Not even the furious glare under the black smudges on Andy's face tempered Jed's joy. "Oh man!" He threw his arms around his friend.

"Whoa, you big jerk! Look out for the camera."

Jed stepped back. "You're alive."

"No thanks to you." Andy gave a rasping cough.

"But how?"

Andy shrugged. "You said you picked the guys from this station for the show because they're good. Well, you were right. One minute I'm standing there; next minute a couple guys grab me and haul me out. My feet hardly touched the floor." He patted the camera on his shoulder. "Good thing I had a solid grip on this baby, or it woulda gone flyin'."

"They must have taken you out another door."

"No way were we going out the way you did." His voice grew rough. "I've never seen fire like that before." His gaze narrowed and fixed on Jed. "You know you almost got us both killed."

Jed nodded, turning to look at the house. "'Who's more foolish: the fool, or the fool who follows him?'"

"Now?" Andy's outrage sent his voice up an octave. "You're quoting Shakespeare *now?* What did I tell you about that? Huh? No more Shakesp—"

Jed held out his hands. Most people got a kick out of his propensity for the bard's words. But Andy? He'd hated it from the minute they met, a few months after Jed hit LA. "Hey, it's not Shakespeare."

Doubt settled on Andy's brow. "Yeah? Then who?"

"One of your heroes, ol' buddy. Obi-Wan Kenobi."

"Oh, no you don't. You're not getting around me on this by quoting someone who actually makes sense."

Now that was too much. "Shakespeare makes perfect sense—"

"Nah, man. I'm not getting into this with you. No rabbit trails. We're gonna talk about this. Right here, right now." Andy squared off. "What happened just now? It's exactly what I've been saying, Jed. You're taking way too many risks. The captain *told* us to stay outside. But no, you gotta get the action shots. Well, *we* got 'em. I just hope it was worth it."

Jed kept nodding, even as he studied the still burning house. The alarm roused the firehouse just after midnight, setting the well-orchestrated team into action. It never ceased to amaze Jed how quick and efficient these men were, even in the face of such pressure. Within fifteen minutes they were on-site, and the battle with the blaze had begun. Now, two hours later, the fire was finally showing signs of surrender.

The building was an old warehouse, a portion of which had small apartments in it. Smack-dab in the nastiest part of the city, the place had been a pit. Reports circulated that the police had just been there a few days earlier, investigating a possible meth lab. And the people congregating beyond the fire trucks watching the place burn weren't exactly your high-society brand of folks. In fact, Jed was glad he was on the *fire* side of the police barricade.

So yeah, Andy was right. Being here was risky. But Jed hadn't made *Everyday Heroes* one of the top-rated new shows of the season by playing it safe.

"I mean, I know you're about to make it big, Jed. There's no denying this new series of yours is a hit, and the network execs are taking notice, but it's a little hard to enjoy success when you're dead."

"Uh-huh." Jed frowned. What was that?

"Of course—" Andy's sarcasm intensified—"knowing you, if we got killed, you'd just have me film our trip to the other side."

"Right." Jed squinted, staring hard at a window on the ground floor. Was that what he thought it was?

"I, of course, would go to heaven. You, on the other hand, would need some seriously heat-resistant equipment to shoot your little journey beyond."

It was!

"Curry, are you listening to m—"

Jed spun toward the firefighters working by the truck. He gestured to the window. "Hey, guys! Someone's still inside!"

The firefighters jerked to follow Jed's pointing finger, then jumped into action. Jed grabbed Andy's arm. "Come *on!*"

For a second he thought Andy would refuse, but then years of working together must have kicked in, because he fell into step beside Jed. They ran, feet pounding the ground as they followed the firefighters racing toward the window. As they drew closer, Jed almost did something he'd sworn never to do again.

Pray.

Almost, but not quite. Because that part of his life was gone, buried so deep inside him that not even the heat of the fire reaching out to chafe his face could touch it.

No, prayer would stay where it belonged.

In his childhood, with the rest of the fairy tales.

FOUR

"Don't waste life in doubts and fears;
spend yourself on the work before you,
well assured that the right performance of this hour's duties
will be the best preparation for the hours and ages that will follow it."

RALPH WALDO EMERSON

"'Who makes people so they can…see or not see?
Is it not I, the Lord?
Now go, and do as I have told you. I will help you…'"

EXODUS 4:11–12

SEPTEMBER 8
3:30 a.m.

"You know, once upon a time I had a doggy just like you."

"Just like…? For heaven's sake, Doris, don't be a nit. Your dog was about as big as that dog's head, and you know it."

Annie glanced over her shoulder to where Doris was lavishing hugs on Kodi, ignoring Aggie's outrage. She leaned toward her brother. "They almost sound like they don't like each other."

"I wish."

Annie started. "You do?"

Her brother snorted. "Sure. Because then they wouldn't talk to each other." He tossed a glance their direction. "No such luck though. Just pretend they're not there."

"Does that work?"

"Not yet." Dan's pained look was almost as comical as the two women. "But I'm willing to work at it till it does."

Annie turned back to the map in front of her. She'd reached Sanctuary about ten minutes ago and found Dan ready for her, a topographic map rolled out on his desk. Within minutes he was giving her a quick rundown of the situation, highlighting where the searchers had looked so far.

Doris piped up again. "I wish I'd brought Half-Pint with us. You two would have had such fun together. Don't you think so, Aggie?"

"What I think is that that huge beast would think your silly little Chihuahua was a walking hors d'oeuvre." Ignoring Doris's wide eyes at such a horrific thought, Aggie went to peer over Dan's shoulder. She'd listened to his briefing, adding tidbits here and there and driving Dan to distraction. Now she reached an arm around Dan to point at a spot on the map, then glared at him when he swatted her hand away.

Annie covered her smile under the guise of a cough. The two women had to be at least in their seventies, maybe older. But something about them, a kind of gleaming mischief in those time-worn eyes, made them seem more like teenagers than senior citizens.

It was fascinating to Annie that the two shared the same color. *A* and *d* both shimmered in happy marigold yellow. A color that fit these ladies to a *t*.

The same color as Dan.

Annie's eyes widened, and she almost laughed out loud. How had she missed that? No wonder the three of them always seemed to blend together so well.

Of course, she knew better than to say such a thing to her brother.

As though sensing Annie's thoughts, Doris looked at Annie from where she hugged Kodi, and there was no denying the concern in her clear eyes. "Where are you going to look for dear Bertha now?"

"I wish I knew." Dan rolled his shoulders, and as he stared down at the map, Annie took in the sag of his shoulders and the stubble on his face. Unless she missed her guess, he hadn't slept much the last few nights. This kind of situation was stressful on anyone who understood the implications.

But with most people who were lost, you could count on patterns of behavior, things that helped in formulating a search plan. Most people, when lost, tended to travel in a straight line. If they found any kind of path, they'd stick to it, no matter what. Often they climbed to the top of the closest hill to get a better view—though the trees on top of hills could obstruct any view. Lost people seldom reversed direction on a trail and tended to travel downhill or downstream. But most helpful of all was the fact that lost people seldom moved around randomly. They usually moved with conviction, with a dogged hope that they were heading in the right direction—whether they were or not.

Then there were the unpredictable victims. Children didn't have any concept of being lost. They just walked and wandered, their attention caught by whatever they encountered. Fortunately they tired easily and couldn't roam as far afield as an adult. Older children were a little better. But people like Bertha, who suffered from a mental condition such as Alzheimer's?

That could be a searcher's nightmare.

It was bad enough that people with dementia didn't follow any of the usual patterns—in fact, they didn't follow any pattern period. But an added complication was the fact that so often they were caught in the past, and they might not even know what was happening or where they were. If someone was in fairly good physical shape, she could wander a long way…miles, even.

A soft hand on her arm drew Annie's attention from her increasingly depressing thoughts. Doris was beside her, her lip trembling slightly. "You will find her, won't you?"

Annie laid her hand over Doris's thin fingers. "I'll do my best."

Of course, with each passing hour, Bertha's chances dropped. The odds of finding someone alive were best in the first twenty-four to forty-eight hours. They'd been looking for Bertha for nearly thirty-six hours. But no reason to point that out to Doris.

Annie focused on her brother, listening as he indicated areas on the map where she and Kodi could start. She frowned, catching his hand as he pointed at one particular spot.

His brows drew together. "What?"

"You've come back to this spot at least four times in the few minutes we've been standing here." She tilted her head, studying the coordinates. "That's actually in the ravine, right?"

Dan ran his hand through his hair. "Yes. The search teams looked there a number of times, but the trees and brush are so dense. I don't know..." He lifted one shoulder. "They did grid searches and were thorough. They always are."

That her usually unruffled brother was troubled could not be denied. In fact, his vexation was so pronounced that it moved over Annie, seeping into her, setting her nerves on edge as well. "But?"

"But something keeps pulling me back there." He traced a finger across the map. "Maybe if you work the ravine edge, just in case? I don't know...I just can't shake the feeling that she's there somewhere."

Annie didn't argue. She'd learned a long time ago to trust her brother's hunches. "You got it. We'll start there." She started to signal to Kodi to follow her when Dan caught her arm. She turned back to him.

"About that e-mail you forwarded to me."

She'd waited until a few days after he got home from his honeymoon before finally telling him about the e-mails. He had her do two things: send the posts to him and set up a new e-mail address without letting anyone else know about it. He'd monitored her old account so he could deal with anything that looked suspicious.

She studied Dan now. If her nerves hadn't already been on edge, the caution flickering in her brother's eyes would have put them there. "Did you figure out who sent it?"

"I handed it over to a friend who works in cybercrime investigations. Unfortunately, whoever sent it knew what he was doing. He did something called remailing, which makes it next to impossible to trace the source."

Cybercrime? That sounded so…serious. "But it's nothing to worry about, right? Probably just some kid fooling around?"

She waited for him to reassure her, but instead the silence between them grew tight with tension. "Dan?"

"Look, Annie, I don't want to worry you—"

"Too late."

"Just…be careful. Okay? You might be right. It could be some kid acting stupid. But you and I both know the cost of doing high-profile work. People find out about you. Most of the time that's not a problem."

She noticed her hands trembling and slid them into her pockets. "But you don't think this is 'most of the time'?"

He put an arm around her shoulders and turned her toward the door. "I don't know one way or the other. What I *do* know is that you've got Someone looking out for you who is more powerful than any nutcase with a computer."

Ah, there it was. The comfort she'd needed from her big brother. She managed to dredge up a smile out of the anxiety bogging her down. "Right you are. If God is for me, who can be against me, right?"

"Right." He squeezed her shoulders. "Just hold on to that, and don't worry."

Annie leaned against him, his solid presence as comforting as his solid faith. If God could carry Dan through the tragedy he'd endured and bring him out whole, He could certainly help her deal with a few stupid e-mails.

"Well, ladies—" Dan straightened—"Annie and I are going to head out."

Clearly, he'd hoped the two women would stay behind. Clearly, he was in for a disappointment.

Doris stepped up to him. "We're going with you."

Dan angled a firm look down at her. "Now listen, you and Agatha really need to go home. Get some sleep."

"With dear, sweet Bertha still lost out there?" Doris stood her ground, as immovable as the floor beneath their feet. "I think not!"

He wasn't giving in. "It's pitch-black out there. You won't be able to see a thing."

Doris's already thin lips compressed, leaving her mouth a disapproving slash. "We don't need to *see* anything to pray, Sheriff."

Dan turned to Aggie, but the little woman's arms were planted across her chest, and her chin jutted out like a prizefighter's. He'd find no help there.

"Face it, Dan—" Annie motioned for Kodi to follow her to the door—"you've been outvoted."

He grabbed his keys from the desk, muttering as he followed Annie. "See what happens when you give women rights?"

Neither Doris nor Aggie rose to the bait. Instead, they padded along behind Dan, bestowing sweet smiles upon him as he jerked to a halt and held the door open for them.

Doris patted his cheek as she waltzed past. "Ever the gentleman, Sheriff."

Annie didn't hear her brother's reply, but the grins on Doris and Aggie's faces—and the dark cloud on Dan's—were enough to tell her it had been a concession speech.

FIVE

"Adversity...usually takes us by surprise....
To us it often appears completely senseless and irrational,
but...God...has a purpose in every pain
He brings or allows in our lives.
We can be sure that in some way
He intends it for our profit and His glory."

JERRY BRIDGES

"I have sent them into captivity for their own good....
I will give them hearts that will recognize me as the LORD.
They will be my people, and I will be their God,
for they will return to me wholeheartedly."

JEREMIAH 24:6–7

SEPTEMBER 8
3:30 a.m.

"Okay, fine. You win. This is going to be the best episode yet."

Jed whooped and looked back over his shoulder. "You'd better believe it is." The firefighters were almost to the window. "Are you getting this?"

"Of course I am! You think I'm stupid?"

No, if there was one thing Andy was not, it was stupid.

Which is probably why he stopped before Jed did. He stood there, a few feet behind Jed.

"Come on, Andy. Up here. Just a little closer and it will be like the viewers are right there."

His friend's head tipped from behind the camera, and he glared at Jed, lips compressed. Though he could hear Andy's muttered comments consigning him to a very unpleasant place, the cameraman came to stand beside him.

Perfect! They were only about fifteen feet from the house. The heat was almost unbearable, but that didn't matter. They were getting the footage!

"Over there!" Jed pointed at the window, but Andy was already filming. Jed peered close, trying to see who was inside, and his blood ran cold. There in the window, framed by the raging flames behind him, was a little boy of no more than five or six. His screams were muffled by the glass, but the terror on his face was clear. So much so that Jed's pulse kicked up a notch.

The firefighter nearest the window was a big man. Though Jed couldn't see his face, only one of the guys at the station was that big—Ken Hall, who had two little boys of his own. Jed watched as Ken radioed to the men inside the house, yelling for them to direct the hoses to the room the boy was in. After two weeks with these guys, Jed understood the fury in Ken's voice.

They hated fire. And they loved it.

Had to love it to understand it.

Had to hate it to kill it.

And he understood how angry they got when the fire tried to win.

The little boy clawed at the window, and it took all of Jed's control to not run over there and start slamming his fists on the glass. How could they stand it? How could these guys go through this emotional wringer day after day after day?

As though in answer to Jed's agonized question, Ken lifted one of his huge gloved hands and pressed it to the glass. The little boy wiped his face, then reached up and held his own small hand opposite Ken's.

At the contact, Jed's breath caught in his throat. He knew what was happening. Ken was talking to the boy, trying to calm him, telling him what he needed to do. And he knew the man was doing something else.

Praying. Big time.

Though Jed had talked with all the firefighters in the station, he and Ken had spent the most time together these last two weeks. Jed wasn't sure why. They just seemed to end up in the same places all the time. Ken loved to talk about his family, which Jed didn't mind.

And God.

Which Jed did mind.

Andy used to try to talk to Jed about God too. When Jed made it clear he wasn't interested, Andy backed off. But he still carried his Bible with him wherever they went. Even read the thing. That was fine with Jed, as long as he didn't have to hear about it.

But when Ken turned out to be a Bible thumper, Jed kept his mouth shut. He didn't want to insult the man, so he just listened as Ken talked about God's provision, about the way God walked beside him, helping him help others.

"That's the business He's in, you know. Helping and healing."

Jed forced himself to agree. And to ignore Andy's smile behind the camera.

But some of it was good. Or—to be more accurate—it made good material for the episode. Like the conversation they'd had just last week. Ken was telling Jed how prayer kept him focused and calm. Jed listened and was just about to challenge Ken when Dobin, one of the other firefighters, grabbed a chair, flipped it backward, and plopped down beside them.

"You really believe that stuff, Kenny?"

Ken studied him. Dobin was younger, maybe in his late twenties, and full of what Jed's mother used to call "spit and vinegar." After a few moments, Ken relaxed.

"Yeah, I believe it."

"That God works miracles and prayer makes a difference?"

"Absolutely."

Dobin crossed his arms, leaning them on the back of the chair he was straddling. "How can you? I mean, look around you, dude. The world's gone crazy. What good does prayer do in a world like this?"

Jed wanted to add a resounding "Amen," but the viewers weren't interested in what he had to say. So he just kept his mouth shut. Or would have, if Ken hadn't pulled him into the fray.

Ken tilted his head at the sarcasm in Dobin's tone and slanted a look at Jed. "I suppose you agree with him?"

Jed held out his hands. "Hey, I'm just listening in. This isn't my fight."

"That's where you're wrong."

They'd all turned to stare at Andy.

"Well, whaddya know." Dobin slapped his leg. "You do have a voice. I figured you was a mute, boy. You never say anything!"

Andy shrugged. "I'm a cameraman. It's my job to stay in the background."

Dobin waved his words aside. "Well, you're in the spotlight now. Why do you think ol' Jed's wrong?"

"Because it's everyone's fight. Why do you think the world's in such bad shape to begin with?"

Dobin snorted. "Because people are basically jerks, out for themselves, and that's life?"

Ken shook his head. "That's what people *think* life is, but it's not."

"How can you say that?" Jed knew he should just shut up and let the others talk. He'd just have Andy edit him out later. "I mean, just look at the things people do and say."

"So we judge humanity by the lowest common denominator?" Ken's slow smile was almost paternal. "I think your buddy Bill pegged that kind of thinking."

Jed frowned. "Bill?"

"'That way madness lies; let me shun that.'"

"Shakespeare, right?"

When Ken nodded at Dobin, Andy groaned and disappeared

behind the camera again. But Jed could hear him mutter, "I *hate* Shakespeare."

"Shakespeare's good, but I've got a better one." Ken stretched his legs out in front of him. "'When you go through deep waters and great trouble, I will be with you. When you go through rivers of difficulty, you will not drown! When you walk through the fire...you will not be burned up; the flames will not consume you.'"

"Now that's cool!" Dobin pounded out his enthusiasm on the back of his chair. "Who wrote that?"

"God—" Jed caught Ken's surprised glance—"supposedly. Through a prophet. Guy named Isaiah."

"Isaiah 43:2 to be exact. Very good, Jed. I'm impressed."

Jed's lip curled. "Don't be. I've got a brain that doesn't let go of much of anything I've memorized. No matter how long ago I memorized it."

"It's not bad to have the Bible stuck in your brain."

"So you say."

For a second Jed thought he might have offended the big man, but Ken just smiled. "Know what else I say?" He turned to Dobin. "Life is more than being out for yourself, brother. A lot more." He reached into his pocket and drew out a worn photo. Jed had seen it a number of times—it was a great shot of Ken and his wife, Amy, with their two boys. He held it out to Dobin. "Take a look."

"I've seen your family, Kenny."

"I know, but look anyway. 'Cuz *that's* what life is about, Dob. Love. And legacy. And reaching out to pass on truth."

"So you think you got a corner on truth?"

Ken's smiled. "Nah, man. I don't." He took the photo and slid it back into his pocket. "But God does. And I know that as sure as I know my own name."

Jed couldn't help it. He had to ask. "What if you're wrong?"

Ken pinned him with a stare, and slight apprehension slithered through Jed. Sure, Jed was athletic and fairly well built, but this guy had arms like tree trunks. He could break Jed in half if he wanted to.

Instead, the firefighter just shrugged. "I don't believe I am. But just for argument's sake, let's say I might be. So okay, I've spent my life following what God says. Raised my kids to love God and trust Him. Helped others when I could." He eyed Jed and Dobin. "You tell me, who's the real loser? Someone who lives life with integrity, who knows true joy and love and has added good to the world, or someone who's just out for himself?"

He had a point. "Okay, I'll give you that. But prayer? Come on, Ken. You live in the real world. How can you think it changes anything?"

"I don't *think,* son. I know." Ken tapped his fingers over his heart. "In here. And so will you one day."

Jed stiffened. "Don't count on it."

Ken stood, reaching out to lay one of those big hands on Jed's shoulder. "I don't count on anything, but God and my brethren." He eyed Jed, that small smile on his face. "Neither one has ever let me down."

Jed wished he could say the same.

"Get down, Benny! Pull the blanket over you!"

Ken's bellow brought Jed's attention back to the drama unfolding in front of him. He glanced at Andy. "What's going on?"

"I'm not sure—" Andy shifted the camera on his shoulder— "but I think they're getting ready to break the windo—"

The shattering of glass split the air, and Jed watched Ken knock the window glass out of the way, then vault inside. In seconds, he was leaning out the window, passing the boy, wrapped in the blanket, to another firefighter. The man hurried the bundled boy past Jed and Andy to one of the waiting ambulances.

"Come on, Ken…get outta there…"

As if he heard Jed's muttered urging, Ken looked up. His gaze met Jed's, and a grin broke through the black smudges on his face, triumph a banner across his features. He said something, and though Jed was too far away to hear it, he was pretty sure he understood.

He took a step closer. "Forget the gloating, you big ox! Just get out of there."

Ken laughed, then planted his hands on the windowsill, ready to jump out—

The explosion came out of nowhere.

It seemed to shake the world, the concussion hitting Jed dead center, a shock-wave battering ram that sent him flying backward. He lay there, sprawled on the ground, ears ringing, watching debris rain down on him from the sky.

"Oh man…"

The groan came from his right, and Jed pushed up on one elbow, peering at Andy, who was curled in the fetal position on the ground beside him. "You—" Jed choked on the smoke billowing around them—"you okay?"

Andy straightened, then sat up, the camera in his lap. He must have curled himself around it when he fell. Now that was a great cameraman. Save the camera at all costs.

Andy wiped at his face, then glared at Jed. "I quit."

Chuckling, Jed struggled to his feet, then held a hand out to Andy. "Whooee! Now that's what I call a ride. We must have flown ten feet!"

"Twenty." Andy took his hand and pulled himself to his feet. "But at least we're still in one piece."

Jed frowned at the odd sound in Andy's words. He studied his friend's grim features—and understanding slammed into him as hard as the explosion had. Jed spun back to the house.

The whole side was gone. What remained was engulfed in flames and roiling black smoke.

Ken was nowhere to be seen.

"I got it all."

Jed turned back to Andy, whose deadpan voice went on.

"I had the camera trained on him, on a close-up of his face, when the place blew." He shook his head, his eyes reflecting the shock in his tone. "He was smiling, Jed. And he looked right at someone. Someone right next to us."

Sickened, Jed swallowed. "He was looking at me."

"You?" Andy stared at him. "Last thing the guy ever said, and it was to you?"

Jed closed his eyes as questions flooded him. Questions he couldn't have stopped if he tried. *God...where were You? How could You let this happen?* Bitterness seeped through him as Jed turned to walk away.

"What were they?"

He hesitated at Andy's low question then spoke without looking back. "What?"

"Ken's last words. What did he say to you?"

Jed didn't answer; he just started walking again. Away. He had to get away. As far and as fast as he could. Because Jed had a good idea what Ken had said. He was almost certain the firefighter had spoken four words. Four simple words.

Never lets me down.

But Ken was wrong. Horribly wrong. And as long as Jed lived, he knew he'd never forget those words.

Or forgive the God who'd made Ken Hall a liar.

SIX

*"There are always uncertainties ahead,
but there is always one certainty—God's will is good."*

VERNON PATERSON

*"'I am the LORD, the God of all the peoples of the world.
Is anything too hard for me?'"*

JEREMIAH 32:27

SEPTEMBER 8
4:00 a.m.

People thought darkness was the same everywhere.

It wasn't.

Nothing compared to darkness in the woods. There, it was thick, unbroken, dense. A heavy blanket that cloaked and suffocated. No residual light from streetlights or homes or businesses...and even the bit of light offered by the moon or stars was swallowed in the branches of towering trees.

Annie studied the woods around them, just beyond the clearing.

This was where she belonged. Out here, in the quiet of the wilderness, with Kodi. They worked with easy comfort, each aware of the other, focused on the task at hand. And as they worked, one overwhelming sensation filled Annie.

Contentment.

She loved being out here, doing this. Helping people. Bringing them home.

Unfortunately, Bertha probably didn't share her feelings. Out there in that blackness the poor woman was probably terrified. It was bad enough when you knew what was going on. But with Alzheimer's clouding her perceptions and understanding…

It would be like living a nightmare. One you couldn't escape.

At least right here, in the clearing behind the ladies' foster home, the moon and stars gave a little light. Annie turned back to her Jeep, pulling equipment for her and Kodi from the drawers she'd set up in the back. Her Jeep wasn't the newest vehicle on the road, but it was dependable. And since Annie kept it loaded for searches, all she and Kodi had to do was hop in and take off when they got a callout.

Annie and Dan had just returned from walking to the ravine across the clearing. She didn't see how a woman Bertha's age could make her way down that incline, into the ravine—let alone up out of it—without hurting herself. But Annie had seen stranger things. Besides, if the woman was down there, at least she'd be somewhat contained. If she'd reached the woods beyond…there was no telling how far she might have wandered.

Annie looked at Kodi, who sat in the backseat of the Jeep, ears perked, ready to go. "Well, let's just hope she's somewhere in the ravine, eh, girl?"

Kodi barked, and Doris came padding up beside Annie. "Oh! She's barking! Does that mean she smells someone?"

Annie smiled. "No, that just means she's talking to me."

Though Annie hadn't yet put on her headlamp, she had no trouble seeing the disappointment on Doris's usually cheerful features. She touched the woman's arm. "Don't worry, Doris. We'll find your friend."

Though the woman's smile was clearly forced, it held a definite sweetness. "I know you will, dear."

Annie let Kodi roam around a bit while she got the dog's gear ready.

"How on earth do you keep track of this sweet animal in the dark? Why, with that black coat, she almost disappears."

In the light of her headlamp, Annie saw that Kodi had come to sit in front of Doris. Annie grinned. Kodi knew a pushover when she saw one. Sure enough, Doris leaned down and planted a resounding kiss on Kodi's snout.

The dog was in heaven.

Her big tail pounded the ground, and she lifted her snout for another smack.

Doris was about to comply when Agatha chirped up. "Doris, for heaven's sake, be careful. That dog is nearly twice your size."

"Oh, he wouldn't hurt me."

"She." Annie pulled Kodi's shabrack and search collar out of the back of her Jeep, looped them over her wrist, then knelt beside the shepherd.

"She. Even better." Doris bent over and pressed her cheek to Kodi's. "We girls need to stick together."

"And to answer your question, this is how I keep track of her." Annie set the bright orange vest on the tailgate of her vehicle, then turned and fastened Kodi's collar in place.

"What's that?" Doris fingered the vest, tracing the large gold SEARCH DOG embroidered on the sides.

"It's Kodi's shabrack."

Doris frowned. "Her what?"

"Shabrack. Her search vest."

"Well, it's certainly bright enough."

"That's the idea." Annie pressed a small button at the back of the shabrack, lighting up the reflective strip lining either side.

Doris clapped her hands. "Why, she'll be all lit up like a Christmas tree."

"As I live and breathe, she's even got a bell." Aggie flicked the bell hanging from Kodi's collar.

"Yup, so I can keep track of her when she's out of sight, and to scare off any wild animals long before we encounter them." As Annie leaned over to slip the vest onto the dog, Kodi gave her face a quick, sloppy lick.

Annie wiped her face and eyed the shepherd. "Thanks a lot,

you moose." Kodi's only reaction was a panting grin. Annie chuckled, fastening the shabrack firmly in place. She stood, then turned at Doris's light gasp.

"Well, my goodness! Kodi looks so…serious all of a sudden."

"She is." Annie slipped her own vest into place. "She knows when her shabrack goes on that it's time to work."

Dan joined them, holding a radio out to Annie. "Here you go, sis." He turned to the two women hovering beside them. "Okay, ladies, back to the cruiser."

"Oh, but we want to watch—"

Dan shook his head. "Aggie, you don't want to be a distraction, do you?"

Annie had to turn away so the ladies wouldn't see her smile. Dan knew full well that the women wouldn't distract Kodi. Not once she was working. But his ploy to get them out of the way worked. They bowed their heads and trudged back to his cruiser.

"Clever boy," she muttered as he made sure their radios were on the right frequency.

"Hey, got them out of your hair, didn't I?"

"My hair?"

His lips twitched. "Yeah, well…anyway, it's a little after 4:00 a.m. You good to go by yourself?"

Dan knew it was highly irregular for Annie to go on a search without at least one person as backup. But the two of them had realized that with the ladies along, he'd have to stay at the vehicles with them. And neither of them wanted to lose any more time while waiting for another SAR member to arrive. "I'm fine."

"Check in at regular intervals, say every half hour or so?"

Annie nodded, clamping the radio into her chest pack then clipping the small bottle of powder she used to check wind direction onto her belt. "You got it." She lowered her hand to Kodi's head. The dog stood so tall that Annie didn't even have to bend over to scratch her ears. "Come on, girl."

She led Kodi to the edge of a clearing just before the ravine, then stepped back a few paces so she was behind the dog. Lifting the container on her belt, she squeezed a puff of powder into the air at Kodi's nose level. It fell almost straight down. Not much wind—just a hint blowing due east. Which meant Kodi would work across it, zigzagging north and south, nose in the air until she hit human scent. Then she'd follow the scent rafts as they were carried on the wind into the subject or any other person who might be out there.

Annie often wondered what it was like to be able to pick up scents like that. To draw in the air and scent discriminate, finding any human scent out of all the scents floating by. Like the saying went, when a dog walks into a bakery, she doesn't smell cake; she smells eggs, flour, sugar, and vanilla. Add the training Kodi had received in air scenting, and there was just no stopping that nose.

Which was why air scenting dogs like Kodi were in such demand. They were trained to follow *any* human scent, unlike trailing dogs, which were scent specific, meaning they trailed one particular human's scent. To do that, they needed a point of origin—the last known location and an article worn by the person who'd gone missing.

As amazing as it seemed, given the time and conditions, wilderness air scenting dogs could find almost anyone. It didn't matter if the person was dead or alive—though, of course, alive was always the hope—or if she was out in the open, hidden, or even under water.

Thank goodness they didn't have to worry about water on this search. There weren't any lakes or rivers out here that Bertha might have fallen in. That was a blessing anyway.

Father, go with us. Help us find the lost.

It was the same prayer Annie sent heavenward every time she and Kodi started a search. Annie leaned over, took firm hold of Kodi's collar, and issued the order. "Kodi, find her!"

The dog shot forward, nose to the ground, ranging one way then the other. She lifted her nose to the air, sniffed, then dropped back to the ground again. And so it went, Annie griding behind Kodi, tracking on the map Dan gave her as the shepherd ranged back and forth. Annie kept her steps slow and easy, letting Kodi find her pace. But she couldn't help glancing at her watch.

4:30 a.m. Lately the thermometer started climbing around ten. By ten-thirty, odds were good that it would be too hot for Kodi to work. That gave them roughly six hours.

Please, Father, let it be enough time.

SEVEN

> *"I can't say as I was ever lost,*
> *but I was bewildered once for three days."*
>
> DANIEL BOONE

> *"O LORD, you have examined my heart*
> *and know everything about me....*
> *You chart the path ahead of me....*
> *You both precede me and follow me."*
>
> PSALM 139:1, 3, 5

SEPTEMBER 8
5:30 a.m.
Cold.

It permeated everything, making Annie's muscles tense and ache. She nestled her hands in her pockets. Unless she missed her guess, the temp was in the low forties. Cold enough to set her shivering despite her insulated clothing.

Cold enough, she acknowledged, foreboding curling deep in her gut, to kill poor Bertha.

Annie couldn't remember the last time the temp had dropped so low this early in the year. Man! It was bad enough to have time working against you. But when the elements joined in, merely hazardous conditions power-shifted straight to deadly.

Annie's lips compressed.

She'd really hoped they would be done by now. Hoped they

wouldn't have to spend hours out in this cold. Because if *they* had to, so did Bertha. And while Annie and Kodi were ready for whatever the elements chose to throw at them, Bertha was not.

Not by a long shot.

Bertha's age and dementia were enough of a detriment. They'd work against her, keeping her confused, possibly even making her hide from Annie and Kodi if she heard them. Then there was the fact that, when last seen, all Bertha was wearing was a light robe and fuzzy slippers.

Not exactly adequate protection against this kind of cold.

The tinkling of a bell drew Annie's attention, and she peered into the dark morning surrounding her, squinting.

It was a little after five-thirty, so the sun had just begun to climb out of bed, and the moon and stars were playing hide and seek behind dense clouds. Still, the lights in the sky peeked out just often enough for Annie to discern the tops of the trees below her in the ravine.

Kodi ranged back and forth, up the incline and then back down. More than once as she followed the dog—Kodi's halo of pink, the same shade as Kyla's, dancing in the layers of darkness—Annie wished she had the dog's energy and sure footing. Four legs were definitely better than two in terrain like this.

Since at night wind currents moved downhill, she and Kodi had been griding the hill from the bottom of the ravine, working their way to the top. When the sun came up, it'd be a new game. Wind currents would shift, going uphill, so she and Kodi would have to shift as well, starting at the top of the incline and griding back and forth down to the bottom.

Annie had just started back down the incline into the ravine again when she caught the sound of the bell. She listened, holding her breath—then released her disappointment with a sigh. From the sound of the bell, Kodi wasn't running, which meant she wasn't coming back because of a find. The shepherd had been working her heart out for the last two hours, and still there was no joy in Mudville.

The jingling bell drew closer. Any minute now…

There.

Fairy lights danced through the forest, zigzagging in a pattern as familiar to Annie as breathing. The lights moved with deliberate ease, each jog up and down accompanied by the light tinkle of the bell.

Annie squinted, watching the shades of black and blue-purple that were the night shift and fold in on each other. She tried to focus, to see the animal moving through the trees below, toward her. But with that black coat, all she could see at this distance was Kodi's lighted collar.

And just the suggestion of pink.

She heard paws pounding, sticks breaking, brush scraping along Kodi's sides as she ranged. Then, finally, Annie made out Kodi's form as the shepherd cleared the woods and came loping toward her.

If not for the lit collar, Kodi would be as invisible as a panther in the African night. Like the big cats, Kodi was a study in controlled power. Body relaxed as she trotted along, her strong legs moved with ease and purpose. Mouth set in a typical shepherd grin, Kodi's panting sent tufts of fog circling into the air, trailing behind her like steam from a locomotive.

Annie waited where she was, bracing herself. Kodi's steady stride didn't break until she reached her mistress. Then she leaned forward, poking that cold nose against the collapsible water bowl hanging from Annie's belt.

"Good girl, Kode." Annie kept her tone upbeat, encouraging. She couldn't let her growing concern bring Kodi down. The dog drew alongside Annie and poked her snout at the water dish again, all business. No begging for ear scratches now. Like all search dogs, when Kodi was working, nothing mattered but finding the subject.

"Thirsty, huh?"

An enthusiastic bark filled the morning stillness, so Annie unclipped the dish and filled it with water. Many handlers just tipped the dish, keeping it attached to their belts as they filled it, then held it for the dog to drink.

If Annie did that, she'd get a bath.

Kodi might be one of the best wilderness air scenters in the country, but one thing she was *not* was dainty.

Annie watched until she was done drinking, then shook out the bowl and clipped it back in place. Kodi started to turn, then stopped when Annie touched her neck.

"Hang on a minute, girl."

Kodi turned those soft brown eyes up to her. Was anything more soulful than a German shepherd's gaze? Annie knelt, draped an arm around that powerful neck, closed her eyes.

Breathed in the fragrance of the woods, the heady scent of dirt and pine.

Be still.

Listened to the whisper of life around them. The chorus of chirruping insects. The song of birds greeting the day…

Be still.

Kodi leaned against Annie, resting her chin on her mistress's shoulder. Annie stroked the dog's long ears. *Help us, Lord. Help us to see…*

A breeze kicked up, brushing Annie's face and lifting her hair with invisible fingers. A tremor shuddered down her spine, but not because of the breeze. Annie opened her eyes.

The sun was coming up.

Rays of light slipped through the clouds, spilling onto the trees, the bushes, the grasses. Colors and light shifted, blended, reflecting all around them like diamonds in the dew. All around them…except…

There.

About twenty feet away, near the bottom of the ravine. Something about the grass, the bushes, was different.

Annie's heart tripped and she stood, walking with slow, careful steps, keeping her eyes on the subtle difference in sheen. When she reached the spot, she knelt and studied it more closely.

Yes. Someone had walked here. And not that long ago. The grass was bent, pressed down. Dew was wiped away from a section of branches on the bush, as though someone had brushed against it as she hurried past.

Annie glanced at Kodi. The dog had straightened, ears perked, her eyes flitting from Annie to the area beyond them, then back to Annie. She felt it too. She had to. That sudden quickening inside, the feeling she needed to catch her breath.

Standing, Annie gripped Kodi's collar. "Bertha's out there, Kodi. *Find* her, girl!"

Kodi was off like a shot. Annie followed, heart pounding. They were going to find Bertha. She knew it as surely as she knew daylight was coming.

She watched Kodi range back and forth, and even the jingling of her bell sounded more assured.

Doris was right. Kodi was beautiful. Annie never tired of watching her work. Growing daylight filtered through the trees around them, sending rays of gold and rose across the ravine, making Kodi's black fur shine as she zigzagged with that easy, comfortable gait, her nose lifted to the air then lowered to the ground as she sought the elusive scent cone. Those strong legs and immense feet moved with determined grace. She was in her element, on task, and loving every minute of it.

As the shepherd headed farther down into the ravine, Annie followed, eyes and ears alert. She was so absorbed in studying the area that the crackle of the radio startled her. She lifted it from the chest pack, talking as she walked.

"This is Annie."

"Everything going okay?"

She could hear the doubt in Dan's voice. Time was running out. "We're still looking, bro."

"And we're still praying. Keep me posted, sis."

"Will do."

She was about to sign off when a sound caught her attention. She turned her head, and her pulse rate jumped. "Dan, hold on!"

"Annie, say again?"

She didn't reply. Instead she waited, listening, then burst into a grin. Kodi's bell was jingling like a Salvation Army bell ringer gone wild. That could only mean one thing.

Kodi was running!

"Dan, I'll be right back. I think Kodi's got something."

No sooner had she slipped the radio back into the chest holster than the dog burst out of the woods. Annie braced herself as Kodi ran to her, then lifted both front paws off the ground midgallop and planted them on Annie's thighs.

An alert!

"Good *girl,* Kodi! Show me. Thatta girl, show me!"

Annie scrambled through the woods, on the heels of her excited dog. Kodi disappeared around a large fallen tree. Her exuberant barks filled the air—then fell silent.

Normally when Kodi found a victim, she almost wore herself out with the excitement of it, jumping and barking, letting her celebration fill the air. Alarmed at the silence, Annie ran after the dog, rounded the tree—and jerked to a halt.

Kodi sat there, her rapid panting and thumping tail the only external signs of her jubilation.

Beside her, seated on large stump like a queen on her throne, was an elderly woman. Her disheveled snow white hair bore a crown of twigs sticking out this way and that, and her wrinkled face, though smudged and scratched, held no fear or anxiety.

She seemed...peaceful. Almost as if she belonged out here, in the middle of the wilderness. A bemused smile touched those pale lips, and she directed an adoring look down at Kodi as one veined hand scratched the shepherd's ears.

Annie took a step forward. "Hello, Bertha."

The woman looked up, and a beautiful smile blossomed on her face. "Do you like my wolf?" Her eyes were wide and innocent.

Annie smiled back. "Yes, Bertha. I like her very much."

Kodi turned her head to give Bertha a quick swipe of her tongue, then stood and nudged at the tennis ball hanging in a net bag from Annie's belt. The payoff. In the dog's mind, the search was always a game. And the payoff for finding the subject? A dog's favorite thing: play!

Annie slipped the ball free from the bag and handed it to Bertha. "How would you like to throw out the first pitch?"

Bertha clapped her hands, then took the tennis ball and threw it. Barking out her joy, Kodi bounded after it.

As Bertha and Kodi played, Annie pulled her radio free and keyed the mic. Dan must have been waiting because his response was immediate.

"You found her."

What beautiful words, spoken with such confidence. But then, her brother knew they weren't out here on their own. "We found her. And she's fine. A little disoriented, but fine."

She gave Dan the coordinates from her GPS, then knelt beside Bertha and checked her out. The old woman was weak from hunger and dehydration, but other than that she was no worse for the wear.

God must have held the dear lady in His pocket.

Annie gave Bertha water, and they settled in to wait for the cavalry.

Two hours later, Bertha was safely ensconced back at the adult home. Much to Annie's dismay, reporters were waiting for them when they emerged from the ravine. Even a few TV cameras. She shot a look at her brother, but he denied culpability.

"I didn't call 'em. I know better."

Indeed he did. He was well acquainted with his younger sister's dislike for the spotlight. Unfortunately, there was no avoiding the hordes as she and Kodi and Dan walked outside. And since she was a member of the K-9 SAR unit, she had to behave.

So, one hand on her dog's collar, Annie stood next to Dan,

listening as he answered a barrage of questions. He knew she wasn't allowed to deal with media; that was his responsibility. But Annie couldn't escape the flashing cameras.

She endured it as long as she could, then looked at her watch. "We have to go, Dan."

"Sheriff?"

Dan turned to look at Agatha, and she signaled him inside the house, then held a hand up to Annie. "Would you please wait just a moment?"

Annie nodded, fidgeting as Dan went back inside. When he came out Bertha was with him, leaning on his arm. He shrugged. "She wanted to say good-bye to her wolf."

When Dan and Bertha reached Annie, the old woman patted Dan's arm, and he helped her lean over to hug Kodi.

Bertha looked at Annie, then reached out to wrap her soft, wrinkled fingers around Annie's hand. "Will you bring my wolf to see me again?"

Annie squeezed her hand. "Of course."

Dan led Bertha away, and Annie slipped Kodi's shabrack off her, opening the Jeep door. Kodi jumped in, circled twice on the seat, then settled down, uttering a contented groan. Annie put a hand on Kodi's head, loving the way her colors blended with Kodi's—marigold and pink, shifting and mixing to create a combined shade of warm peach.

"You done good, girl." She touched her forehead to Kodi's. "I'll bet you liked being a wolf, huh?"

"Arrooow-roow-rooo!"

Annie chuckled. Not exactly a wolf howl, but that was okay. It was the sound of pure contentment. And that was music to Annie's ears.

She glanced around at the crisp Oregon morning. It was going to be a beautiful day. She'd much rather spend it outside.

Kodi lifted one of her paws to bat at Annie's arm, and Annie sighed. "I know, I know. I promised Killian I'd be there."

She shut the passenger door and climbed into the driver's seat, then glanced at Kodi. "You can't blame a girl for just thinking about ducking out, can you?"

The dog's ears perked and she tilted her head, eyes wide and focused. Annie got the message.

Kodi wouldn't blame her, but Killian certainly would. No escaping it.

Time to face her fears.

EIGHT

*"We are not necessarily doubting that God will do the best for us;
we are wondering how painful the best will turn out to be."*

C. S. Lewis

*"Whether we like it or not, we will obey the Lord our God....
For if we obey him, everything will turn out well for us."*

Jeremiah 42:6

September 8
3:30 p.m.
You can do this.

Annie peered through the branches of a potted ficus tree almost as tall as her at the people milling about Killian's art gallery. This was her showing, for heaven's sake. She should be out there. Mixing it up with the crowd. And she would be. In just a minute.

Or two.

Or twenty...

Lord, Kylie said You'd send my knight when I needed him, right? Well, now would be a good time. Really. Couldn't you just send him along to carry me away from all of this...this...

"Now *this* is what I call a party."

Annie drew in a gulp of oxygen before answering her older brother. "Funny, I was just thinking *torture* was a better descriptor."

He joined Annie in leaning against the wall, not looking at her but fully aware of what she was feeling. He'd talked her through being in crowds ever since they were kids.

"Too many people for your taste, huh, sis?"

"Where did they all come from?"

He slid his arm around her shoulders. "All over the place. You're quite the sensation, or didn't you know?"

She wasn't sure if that was good news or bad.

"So...how are you doing?"

Annie faced Dan. "Other than the obvious, I'm fine. Why?"

"I just wanted to be sure you wouldn't...you know, worry about the e-mails."

Ah yes, the e-mails. Annie turned back to the crowd, even more uneasy than before. "Any more show up?"

"Not a one."

So why didn't he sound happy about that?

"Any luck finding out who sent them?"

"Not a bit. I'm hoping my buddy from the cybercrime unit will be able to figure something out soon." He leaned over and nudged her with his elbow. "Annie?"

She sighed. "Yes, I'm being careful."

"Locking the gate to your property? Securing the house at night?"

"Filling the moat with alligators and piranhas."

At his pointed silence, she turned to meet his gaze—and hesitated. Her brother actually looked worried. "Dan, just this morning we talked about all this. I know you think I forget things, but I promise. I'm being careful."

"Where *is* the artist? I thought we were going to get a chance to talk with her?"

At the stringent voice right in front of them, Annie peeked around the leaves of the ficus and saw a well-dressed woman, crystal glass of iced tea in hand, scanning the room. Just as she was about to turn Annie's way, Ryan Evans stepped in, taking the woman's arm and turning her so her back was to Annie's hiding place. He caught Annie's eyes for a moment, then focused on the woman.

"Miss Justice will be available soon, I assure you."

"Well! I should certainly hope so. I've purchased one of her pieces—not an inexpensive one—and I should think that entitles me to speak with her." She snatched her arm away from Ryan. "*Not* the hired help."

Despite the woman's increasingly rude demeanor, Ryan's tone stayed calm and unruffled. "Of course. But I wonder—" he leaned in close to the woman—"have you seen the room with Miss Justice's more…exclusive works?"

Dan and Annie exchanged a glance.

"More exclusive works?"

Annie shrugged. She didn't know what Ryan was talking about. But it made an impact on the overbearing woman. She immediately lowered her voice to a conspiratorial whisper. "No. Where is it?"

"Just come with me. I'll show you."

Annie released a breath as Ryan led the woman away.

"You gotta admit it: The guy's good at what he does."

"Definitely."

Within minutes Ryan was on his way back across the room, heading for Annie and Dan. She touched his arm when he joined them. "Thanks for that, Ryan."

"No reason you should have to deal with some pushy woman who fancies herself an art expert." He ducked past the low-hanging leaves of the ficus. "Irritating creature."

Annie studied the man beside her. Ageless. That's the word that came to mind when she first met Ryan, and it still applied. With his smooth features and lean frame, he could be anywhere from twenty to forty. True, his short cropped hair had silvered at the temples, but rather than age him, it just gave him a distinctive air.

Killian had hired Ryan as his assistant a little over three years ago. The two not only shared a similar artistic temperament, but they looked enough alike to be brothers. They even wore the same kind of glasses, much to Annie's amusement. But where Killian loved the spotlight, Ryan was far more comfortable backstage. Which made him more understanding of Annie's distaste for crowds.

He glanced at her. "Does Killian know you're hiding back here?"

"No. I've been careful not to let him see me."

Ryan lifted one lean hand to brush at the ficus branches. "Good hiding spot." His gaze drifted to Dan. "But I'm afraid it's not big enough to hide your brother as well as you. And if Killian sees him here—"

He didn't need to finish. If Killian saw Dan, he'd know Annie was hiding out there as well.

Dan held up his hands. "Say no more. I've been wanting to visit that buffet since I arrived."

Annie laughed. "You'd better hop to it before Jayce eats it all."

Dan turned, eyes wide. "He's there already? We just got here!"

"Are you kidding? Your son has the most effective food radar I've ever seen. Now go, you big oaf."

She didn't have to tell him twice—well actually she did—but she didn't have to tell him thrice.

"I'd probably better get back to our guests." Ryan studied the throngs spilling from this room into the next. "I'm guessing we've had close to twice the attendance Killian anticipated." He grinned. "Should make him happy."

"It should make him ecstatic, but you know Killian."

Ryan's grin faded a fraction. "Yes, I know Killian. He's not exactly easy to please."

Annie tipped her head. "Yes, well, if he neglects to say anything, I want you to know I appreciate all you did for this showing. It's your advertising and promotion ideas that sparked people's interest."

He looked at the crowds again. "I imagine your beautiful art had something to do with it too."

She shrugged at his wry tone. "It's just a window, Ryan. I mean, it's not like I cured cancer or anything."

But despite her protestations, she *was* glad. Glad all these people were here. For her work. For her.

And that irritated her to no end.

"Face it, Annie. You're good at what you do—" his gaze drifted to the large stained glass window beyond them—"make that *great* at what you do. At finding people like you did this morning—"

"Kodi finds people. I'm just along for the ride."

He ignored her. "And at your art. So it's not a cure for cancer. It's still beautiful. And people appreciate that."

She supposed he was right.

"Well, back to work." He glanced around the ficus. "I don't see Killian, so you should be safe here a while longer." He patted her arm. "Just relax and bask in the moment, okay?"

Annie watched him move away, then she caught sight of Dan from across the room. In one hand he held a large plate heaped with goodies, in the other a punch glass. When he spotted her watching him, he grinned and held up his punch, the crystal glass looking miniature in his massive paw as he toasted her.

Jayce, who stood beside Dan, reached under his raised arm and snatched something off Dan's plate. Dan's responding yelp made Annie laugh. She loved watching those two together.

"They've come a long way, eh?"

The words were accompanied by the gentle pressure of a shoulder against hers. Annie leaned back, slanting a look at the man beside her. She should've known she couldn't hide from him much longer.

"Hey, Killie."

"Hey there." He linked his arm in hers, tilting his head. "Explain to me, will you, why my star artist is hiding behind a potted plant at her own showing?" His red brows climbed up from behind those round glasses. "Her very successful showing, I might add."

Annie flicked a finger at the earpiece of his glasses, then tugged at his short, curly hair. "Honestly, Killian, why do you wear those things? You know you don't need them."

He waggled a finger at her. "Ah, ah, no you don't. I won't be distracted."

Annie knew that wasn't true. In fact, she was counting on it. Sure enough, he reached up to adjust the glasses.

"Besides, Ryan says they make me look...academic. Scholarly even."

She leaned her head close to his. "Ryan's just trying to get on your good side."

"Pity I haven't got one, isn't it?" His sardonic tone was a perfect match for his expression. "Well, I'd best get back to your adoring fans. I mean, *one* of us has to."

"You do have Ryan out there, you know. And he's better than four of me."

"He's better than four of most anyone. Don't know what I did before I hired him."

Annie's lips twitched. "Good thing you were smart enough to do so."

"Indeed. Just don't tell him that. He's not going to be happy until I make him a partner in my gallery."

"He *has* worked hard, Killian."

"Three years of hard work does not a partner make. *I* built this place, not Ryan. It's *my* reputation, not his, that draws people here. When he's survived ten years in this business, *then* I'll think about it." He delivered a peck on her cheek and headed for the crowd.

Annie settled back against the wall, watching him go. Poor Ryan. Did he have any idea just how far away that partnership really was? She doubted it. Killian might be arrogant, but he wasn't stupid. He wouldn't take a chance on losing Ryan to someone who'd actually give him his due.

Nice thoughts about your friend, Annie.

She shrugged. Hey, she loved Killian. But she didn't have any illusions about him.

Her glance drifted back to her brother, and she saw that Shelby, his wife, had joined him and Jayce at the buffet table. Annie's heart smiled as she watched her brother and his family. Their colors were so different—marigold for Dan, raspberry for Jayce, and emerald green for Shelby—and yet they fit together so well. As Annie watched them now, the colors shimmered and blended, creating a warm, harmonious rainbow outline. No doubt about it, those three belonged together.

Annie could hardly believe it had been nearly a year since Jayce came to live with Dan. The teen had been so good for her brother, helping him get through the deaths of his son and daughter, Aaron and Shannon. And Dan had been great for Jayce, helping the boy overcome a troubled past to blossom into a really great kid.

As for Shelby…well, she just kept those two in line and had a blast doing it.

Three women moved past Annie's hiding place, and she caught bits and pieces of their conversation—words like *beautiful, creative, genius*… Words they were using to describe her.

No, not me. My window.

She'd known the floor-to-ceiling stained glass window she'd created for the new Central Point city library was something special. Even now, as she studied the way the sunlight played in the rich colors and varied styles of glass she'd chosen, she could hardly believe she'd made the window.

A wealthy businessman in the valley had commissioned her to do the piece for the library. He had lived on the Oregon coast most of his life, and when he talked with Annie about the window, he told her he had only one request.

"Can you put something in it…I don't know, a scene or something, that makes me feel like I'm back on the beach, watching the waves?"

He sounded so hopeful, so wistful, that Annie couldn't refuse. Of course, she hadn't been at all sure she could pull it off. She'd spent days—weeks—sketching, matching colors and textures of glass, leaning back and letting words run through her mind. As they did, their colors shifted and blended, showing her what belonged in the piece.

Ocean…the snowy white of the *o* flowed through the rest of the letters.

Beach…*b*'s deep red tones warmed everything around it.

The rust of *waves*, the deep blue of *tide*, the green of *sand*, the yellow of *gulls*. Slowly but surely they coalesced, creating a sense in Annie's mind of the colors and images she should use.

The window was only half finished when Killian came to her

studio to see how it was going. He'd walked in and stood there, watching her work. She was so immersed in painting gold accents on one of the pieces of glass that she hadn't noticed him at first. Not until he started clapping. Then she jumped and spun—and found him staring at the window, tears in his eyes.

"It's stunning—" His voice cracked, and he drew a deep breath.

She turned back to the window, its pieces laid out on the table before her like a giant puzzle, and let his words wash over her. The scene was a young boy sitting on the beach, the ocean spread out in front of him, a book in his lap. And above him, as though being brought to life in his imagination, were characters and scenes from well-known books.

"It really is, Annie." Killian lay one hand on the window. "It's the best work you've ever done."

She'd thought so too but had been afraid to say so out loud.

Annie had discovered stained glass in high school—and immediately knew she'd come home. Her stained glass art was one of the few places her synesthesia really fit. She never felt funny about it in her work—in fact, it helped her. Seeing colors the way she did, in letters and numbers, when music was playing, enabled her to create windows with added depth and dimension. She spent several years as an apprentice to an established artist, then took the plunge and branched out on her own.

Now, almost seven years later, she was at a place she'd never imagined. Though she tried not to think about it too often, Killian said she was one of the most sought-after stained glass artists in the country. All she knew was that she never lacked for creative challenges, and her art gave her the freedom to stay as involved as she wanted with K-9 SAR. Which left Annie feeling abundantly blessed.

Now if she could just figure out how to do what she loved without having to endure showings.

Shame on you, Annie! You should be grateful for all Killie has done for you.

Yes, of course. That was true. And she was grateful. Not to mention—she glanced around—a bit astonished. There had to be close to five hundred people milling around Expressions. And they all seemed to be talking about her. Annie knew she should be flattered.

Instead, all she could think about was getting out of here. Killian loved these events, as evidenced by the fact that he and the ever-present Ryan were now surrounded by dozens of art lovers all discussing the finer points of Annie's work.

Annie had endured the crush of people she didn't know, saying things that she didn't fully believe, for as long as she could. Then she stole away to this secluded little corner of the gallery to hide and thin—

"Excuse me?"

Annie look down into the most kind twinkling green eyes she'd ever seen. She didn't even have to force the smile that lifted her lips. "Yes?"

One thin, blue-veined hand came to perch on Annie's arm. "You're the artist, aren't you? Miss Justice?"

Annie put her hand over the woman's small fingers. "Yes, I am."

"Miss Justice, my name is Serafina Stowe."

Serafina Stowe. Double Ss. Annie's mind's eye refocused as the colors slid into place, outlining Serafina in a beautiful Kelly green—the perfect match for her eyes.

Kelly green was a good color. Warm and friendly. Happy and alive. With a color like that, Annie couldn't help but like this little woman.

"Miss Justice, I have a message for you. From my husband, Cletus."

Annie looked behind the woman. "Oh? Is he here?"

The woman's fingers trembled on Annie's arm. "No, dear. He's not with us."

"Not…" Annie focused on the woman's face. Was she saying what Annie thought she was saying? "You mean he stayed home?"

"No, I mean he *went* home." Sweet joy mixed with loss in her smile. "Cancer, I'm afraid."

It was hard for Annie to speak around the lump in her throat. "A terrible disease."

"Yes, but as my dear Cletus used to say, anything that takes us home is a chariot of gold."

Now Annie smiled. "He sounds like a wonderful man."

"Oh, he was. But he died before he could make his fondest dream come true."

"I'm so sorry, Mrs. Stowe."

Those clear eyes—eyes of a teenager, not an octogenarian—sparkled. "Oh, not to worry, dear. *You're* going to make it happen."

Annie stared at the white-haired woman smiling up at her. Amazing. The woman seemed so vibrant and intelligent…but clearly she was just this side of crazy.

Annie glanced around, praying for someone—anyone—to interrupt them. But suddenly the throngs intent on talking with her seemed nonexistent. It was just her and a crazy woman.

A *sweet* crazy woman, mind you. But crazy was crazy. "Mrs. Stowe…"

"Please, call me Serafina."

"Serafina, I'm sorry. I have to—"

Thin fingers tightened on Annie's arm, and the woman's gentle smile didn't falter. "Cletus wanted to have a special stained glass window made for our little church. It's too small to afford such an extravagance, but my dear Cletus saw to it that part of the money from his estate would pay for the window. And when I heard about you, I knew. You are the artist to do it."

Dan, where are you when I need you? Some brother you are, abandoning me like this. "Why me?"

"Because the window has to be special."

Annie considered this. "I like to think all my windows are special."

"No, dear. You don't understand. Cletus's window must help people, even those who've known God all their lives, see Him—or some aspect of Him—in a new way. *That's* why I came to you. Because the paper said you see things others don't." She patted Annie's hand. "Yes indeed, God led me to you. So you can let people see who He really is."

Something stirred deep inside Annie. Excitement. Because she was realizing that Serafina wasn't crazy at all. Rather, she was just this side of brilliant. What better vehicle to illuminate some hidden aspect of God than stained glass? The bold colors, the rich hues, the near magic of blended textures...

Annie could almost see it taking form in her mind. To create something that actually let people see God with new eyes?

Now *that* would be a masterpiece.

Get real. What makes you think you can do that?

Annie pressed her lips together, trying to force the all-too-familiar voice of doubt back to the recesses of her mind. But doubt was having none of it.

Okay, maybe someone could...but you? Come on!

Yet even as she tried to ignore the questions, she found herself wondering... What if her idea didn't connect with anyone? What if she let Serafina and the church—and *God*—down?

No way. It was too risky.

She opened her mouth to refuse but didn't get the chance.

"Who's your new friend, sis?"

Annie resisted the impulse to close her eyes and hide. Great. *Now* her brother shows up? She turned to face Dan, who had Kyla in tow. Shelby peeked from behind him. Ryan was next to her.

Hail, hail, the gang was all here.

Well...almost.

Annie looked past them. "Where's Jayce?"

Shelby grinned. "Are you kidding? He's at the buffet, piling a plate to the ceiling."

"Are these friends of yours, dear?"

Annie sighed. No avoiding it. She turned back to Serafina. "No. Well, I mean yes, but no." She shook her head, wishing she could get her scattered thoughts to fall in line. "Serafina Stowe, meet my brother and sister, Dan and Kyla Justice. And this is Dan's wife of a few months, Shelby."

"And I'm Ryan Evans, Mr. Molan's assistant. I run the gallery with him."

A bit of an exaggeration, but Annie didn't bother to correct him. She'd had every intention of introducing them, giving Serafina a chance to shake hands, and then hustling her family away. But before she got the chance, Ryan asked Serafina what she thought of Annie's window. Which opened the door for Serafina to tell them about "dear Cletus" and his window. And sure enough, just as she'd feared, dear sister Kyla stood there, listening intently, that bodes-no-good-for-Annie spark in her green eyes.

Serafina sent a look of supplication to Kyla. "I'm hoping your gifted sister will make my husband's dream come true."

Kyla didn't hesitate. "She'll do it."

"What?" Serafina was delighted.

"What?" Ryan was not.

Neither, for that matter, was Annie. But before she could object, Kyla took her arm and led her to the side. Ryan followed on their heels.

Her sister spoke first. "Annie, you're supposed to do this. I just know it."

"For your information, Sister-Mommy Dearest, I was about to decline the commission."

Ryan's mouth thinned. "Good. I hardly think doing a piece for a tiny church will do your career any good."

Annie wasn't sure she agreed with Ryan, but she didn't argue. "I don't want to do it."

"Right." Kyla crossed her arms.

Ryan scowled. "Really, Miss Justice, I think your sister knows her own mind. If *I* don't think she should do it—"

Annie jerked a look at him, but he just went on. "And she doesn't want to do it, then it's settled."

As much as Annie didn't like the implication that Ryan had any say in what she did and didn't do, she still didn't argue. Better to stick to her guns than show weakness when her sister was trying to get her to do something.

"Besides," Ryan went on, "there are far better projects for

Annie right now that will showcase her talent as it deserves to be showcased."

Annie frowned at that. "What projects?"

Ryan clapped his hands. "I've been waiting to tell you and Killian, but a couple of developers are here, and they just talked with me about having you create decorative windows for a new office complex they're going to put up."

Kyla fixed her gaze on Annie, and she felt the heat filling her cheeks.

"Killian will be delighted!"

Ryan's excitement was painfully clear. But Annie didn't share it. Making windows for an office complex was about as challenging as walking across the street. But Serafina's window? Creating something that helped people see God in a new way?

That was an incredible challenge. She *wanted* to do it. More than she'd wanted to do anything in a long time.

And Kyla knew it. "Annie, be honest. You're afraid, aren't you?"

Of course she was. She'd be crazy not to be.

"All the more reason to stay away from this project," Ryan urged.

But Annie knew that wasn't true. "I'm almost always afraid when I start a new project. Creative insecurities are part of the craft."

Her sister lifted her shoulders. "*Well* then?"

Annie held up a hand to forestall further comment from Ryan. "Kyla's right."

Ryan turned on a heel and went off in a huff.

"He'll get over it."

Annie nodded, then walked back to Serafina. Stopped. Swallowed. "I'll do it."

Serafina's delighted squeal as she hugged Annie—combined with the pleasure in Kyla's and Ryan's eyes and the respect in Dan's—was almost enough to still the voice of doubt within her.

Almost.

Okay, God. If what Serafina said is right, then You got me into this mess. She returned the older woman's hug. *Please...just don't let me blow it.*

NINE

*"We cannot truly face life until we face the fact
that it will be taken away from us."*

Billy Graham

*"The thought of my suffering...is bitter beyond words.
I will never forget this awful time."*

Lamentations 3:19–20

SEPTEMBER 11

He shouldn't have come.

Jed dug his fingers into the wood of the pew. It took all his willpower not to jump up and run from the room. But he wouldn't do that to Ken.

Ken won't care. He's gone.

Jed stared at the closed casket at the front of the sanctuary. Then at Ken's wife and kids, who sat huddled together, faces stricken with grief.

They were so alone, though the sanctuary was full to overflowing with those mourning Ken's death.

Jed's grip tightened.

He tuned out as the pastor droned on about eternity and being together again. Why talk about eternity when today was so full of loss? What difference did *eternity* make?

"From eternity to eternity I am God."

Jed grimaced. Stop it. Not now. He really didn't need that pabulum in his head now.

"No one can oppose what I do. No one can reverse my actions."

He almost came out of the pew at that. Heat suffused his face, constricted his chest.

Oh yeah? I can. And I do! I oppose it. How could You let this happen? He ground his teeth. *That man trusted You. Said You never let him down. So I guess this proves what a fool he was, doesn't it?*

The thought stopped his rant cold.

Ken, a fool? Did he really believe that?

Jed squeezed his eyes shut. He wanted to close it all out. To forget where he was and why. To block out the memory of that morning, meeting everyone at the firehouse. Of the building and the fire trucks draped with black bunting, mute testimony to the devastating loss.

But even as he tried to force the memories away, images of Ken filled his mind—images so real Jed could almost reach out and touch him. As though he were right there beside Jed, eyes shining with kindness and understanding, smile comforting.

Ken Hall a fool? Hardly.

So where does that leave you? If he wasn't a fool, then how could he buy into all the God crud? And look where it left him! Dead! Gone! If that's not a fool, what is?

"Mr. Curry?"

Jed almost jumped out of his skin. He opened his eyes and found himself face-to-face with Ken's widow. A quick look told him the funeral was over.

More than that, the casket was gone. As were the people.

He was the only one left sitting here.

Jed jumped to his feet. "Oh, I'm sorry." How had he missed them removing the casket? All those people leaving?

A soft hand on his arm stopped the words. Jed met the woman's gaze and felt his heart break.

The same gentle care he'd always seen in Ken's eyes shone in

Amy Hall's as well. "Mr. Curry, thank you for coming."

He managed a shrug.

"I...I have something for you." She held out a large padded envelope. "Kenny said if anything should happen to him, he wanted you to have this."

Jed frowned. "Are you sure? He hardly knew me."

She smiled through her tears. "Your time together may have been short, but Ken told me he felt a real connection to you. He cared about you." She patted the package and her eyes held his. "Please take it. Don't let Kenny down."

No. Not in a million years.

He reached out for the package. It was heavy. Like his heart. Jed looked around. "Can I...are you supposed to go somewhere?"

She took his arm. "To the graveside. The car is waiting. And yes, I'd appreciate it if you'd walk with me."

Jed put his hand over hers, where it rested on his arm. Together they walked from the room.

Two hours later, Jed was back at his apartment. The package from Ken lay on the kitchen table.

He avoided it as long as he could, but Amy's soft voice kept echoing in his mind: *"Don't let Kenny down."*

He grabbed the envelope, tearing it open. *I won't. Not like Someone else...*

The angry thoughts froze as Jed stared down at what he held in his hand.

A Bible.

Engraved on the cover in silver was a name: Kenneth Hall.

His throat thick, Jed lifted the cover. Ken's name was inscribed inside. He flipped through the pages...notes dotted the margins.

Notes from a dead man.

One scribbled comment caught Jed's eye. It was written in the margin next to Ecclesiastes 4. *Two people can accomplish more than twice as much as one.... If one person falls, the other can reach out and*

help. But people who are alone when they fall are in real trouble....
Two can stand back-to-back and conquer...

Blah, blah, blah.

Then Jed read Ken's note: *"Need to remember this when life*
doesn't make sense. Don't try to face it alone. Find someone to share
the struggle. And share it with God. He'll have the answers."

Humorless laughter gurgled up from within Jed, and he
slammed the book shut.

This was crazy. Ken Hall may have been a good man, but he
trusted in a God who let him down. So why should Jed pay any
attention to anything the man had to say? "Find someone to share
the struggle"?

Fat lot of good that did Ken.

No, Jed's way was better. He would handle this like he did
everything else—like he handled his father leaving. Like he handled
his parents' divorce. Like he handled having a stranger come to
live in his home, calling his mother "darling" and him "son."

By himself.

No sharing. No praying.

And definitely no God.

TEN

"He is blind who thinks he sees everything."

CHARLES HADDON SPURGEON

"For we walk by faith, not by sight."

2 CORINTHIANS 5:7, KJV

SEPTEMBER 22
6:30 a.m.

"Give yourself time, boy."

Jed turned his back on the huge picture window overlooking the Pacific Ocean and faced his executive producer. He'd made a point of being in Silas's spacious office at 5:55 this morning, knowing the older man would blow in, as he did every morning, hours before everyone else. He liked working in the early morning silence.

"You get more done that way," he always said, "with no one to bother you."

So Jed was there, ready and waiting for his boss's arrival at six. On the dot.

Silas was nothing if not punctual.

The man hadn't looked at all surprised to see him. He marched into his office, leaving Jed to follow in his wake. Plunking down in his plush leather chair, Silas launched in on all the reasons Jed needed to put Ken's death—and the effects of that awful day—behind him.

"Business as usual, my boy. That's what you need right now."

Jed had listened as long as he could, then stood and paced as he listened some more. Finally he'd ended up staring out the window at the dark skies and surging waves.

A storm was coming. How appropriate.

As much as Jed wanted to, he couldn't afford to stand here, to let himself get lost in the simple beauty of nature. Time deep in thought was not what he needed. What he needed was to stay too busy to think. Whatever it took to keep his mind off the one thing it wanted to focus on. The one face that kept filling his memory—

"E J?"

Patience wasn't Silas's long suit, so Jed knew his stubborn silence only stretched his mentor's tolerance to the limits. But there was one thing his executive producer hated even more than waiting.

"Ernest Jediah, you're being a fool."

Ouch. When Silas used Jed's full name rather than his professional moniker, it was a clear signal the man was not pleased. "I know."

The older man's busy eyebrows arched, then twitched, dancing like caterpillars on a tightrope. Silas planted his hands on his mammoth desk and pushed himself to his feet. He paced in front of the desk.

"Let me get this straight. You have one of the hit shows of the season—"

"I know that, Silas, but—"

The man's hand sliced through Jed's objection. "Please. Don't interrupt."

This time it was Jed who buried his hands in his pockets. "Sorry." He moved to lean against the wall.

Silas recommenced his pacing. "Now, where was I?"

Jed crossed his arms. "I have a hit show."

"Ah. Yes. You have the hit show of the season—"

Jed couldn't help himself. "I thought it was *one* of the hit shows."

Silas's narrowed eyes pierced him. "Interrupting. Again."

"Sorry. Again."

"All right then, last week's episode was the hit of the week. An audience share that made the network execs downright giddy."

Jed held back a comment about how unsettling *that* image was.

"As for *this* week's episode, well, I don't have to tell you. Watching those firefighters, seeing the cost the way we did—" Silas cleared his throat—"well, it was more powerful than anything you ever put out." The older man's pacing halted, and the question in his stillness was clear: *Am I right, or am I right?*

Jed's confirming nod seemed to be reply enough. The pacing resumed. "Okay, so here you sit, a bona fide success. Your show's just been picked up for another season—" Silas stopped midpace and faced Jed, the benign half smile on his thin lips utterly belied by the glare shooting from those pale blue eyes—"and you're telling me you're out of ideas?" He angled his head. "Do I have that right?"

"Silas, I—"

The glare intensified.

"What I mean is…well…after what happened…"

One caterpillar brow raised.

Jed let loose a heavy sigh, then stared down at the area rug that almost covered the floor of the spacious office. Silas loved that rug. Custom made. New Zealand wool.

Always the best for Silas. What was it he said? "Surround yourself with the best."

At Jed's low words, Silas studied him, then leaned back against his desk. "That's right, boy. And that's what you are. The best. Knew it the first time I saw your work. Wouldn't have spent all these years on you if it wasn't so."

Jed raised his head. "I know, Silas. I owe you. Big time."

A hand waved Jed's words away. "Not the point, boy. It's not what you owe me." Pale blue eyes met brown and bored deep. "It's what you owe yourself. You've got talent, E J. Don't let it go to waste because of an unfortunate accident."

Unfortunate.

Ken was dead, and that was…unfortunate?

No. Madness, maybe. Unacceptable and wrong, definitely.

But unfortunate? That word didn't even *begin* to encompass what had happened. A flood of emotion crowded Jed's throat. Sorrow. Anger. Loss.

And shame.

He had spent the couple of weeks telling himself he had nothing to be ashamed of. He hadn't done anything wrong. And last week, as he and Andy did the final edit on the show, the shame practically burned a hole in Jed's gut. A man had died. A good man. And there they were, watching it happen over and over, acting like it was just another show.

Yes, Jed had made the episode a tribute to Ken—and firefighters in general. Yes, he showed the episode to Ken's widow before agreeing to use it. And yes, when the segment finished playing, she had put her arms around Jed and hugged him, tears streaming down her face as she gave permission to use the footage. But for all that, it seemed wrong. Wrong to benefit from the loss of such a good man.

Jed had mentioned his reservations to Andy on the drive back to the office from Ken's house. Andy stared ahead, silent, for a full two minutes. A response Jed knew well. When there was a lot at stake, Andy thought things through. Finally he spoke.

"I think Ken's story is worth telling."

Jed couldn't argue with that. And so they let it play. And as Silas said, it was a hit. The response even more so. More than any of them had dreamed. Phone calls. Letters. E-mails. More poured in every day. Along with donations. For Ken's family. For the fire station. For a newly established "Ken Hall Fund for Firefighters and Their Families." All of which showed that what he and Andy had hoped for when they'd started out was happening.

Everyday Heroes was capturing hearts.

Jed had known from the start that the concept was good. So much on the networks wallowed in the ugly side of life, Jed was convinced that people were ready for something different. Something that celebrated goodness. Then he and Andy hit on the idea of *Everyday Heroes*—follow people who help others, who put themselves on the line every day. Watch them, listen to them, give them the chance to open up and remind us what is good and noble about not only them, but ourselves as well.

The first episodes featured a policeman, an inner-city teacher, a doctor who worked with children with AIDS, among others. With each episode, the stories deepened—and audience share grew. When the fire station had agreed to let them come in, Jed warned Andy that this episode would be intense. More than any of the others. Odds were good there'd be a fire, which meant they would follow the men into hell—or the closest thing to it on earth. So when it happened, Jed wasn't surprised. Nor was he surprised by the danger and risk.

But the men themselves? They were a surprise. When fighting fires, they were as skillful and courageous as it got. But at the station, they were more like crazy frat brothers. One minute they tormented each other, playing practical jokes and throwing verbal insults like a bunch of kids hyped on turbocharged Kool-Aid. The next minute they sat and talked, late into the night, about anything and everything.

They were a family.

Jed knew after one day with these guys that this episode was going to be the best yet. And he'd been right.

But at what cost?

The emotions he'd almost quashed flamed to life again with the new influx of guilt, and Jed gritted his teeth against the pain. But some of it must have shown on his features, because Silas did something Jed couldn't remember him ever doing before.

He gave Jed a break.

The older man's glare faded, and he looked away. Out the window to the ocean, sparkling in the morning sun.

"Look, I know this was hard on you, son."

There was an almost paternal kindness in the older man's tone. Silas moved back to his luxurious leather chair, for which Jed was thankful. It gave him a few moments to recover from the shock of not receiving the chewing out he'd expected.

"Take a day or two and think about it. You've got a little time. Not a lot. You've got to get going on next season's episodes. But enough to take a break and get your head back where it belongs."

Jed pushed away from the wall. "On the block?"

Only the thinning of Silas's lips showed that he'd heard the bland comment. "In the game. Remember, 'Our doubts are traitors, And make us lose the good that we oft may win, By fearing to attempt.'"

Jed started, and Silas's mouth actually almost gave way to a smile. "What's the matter, boy? Think you're the only one who can quote Shakespeare?" He picked up a pen. "Now get out of here. *Some* of us have work to do."

ELEVEN

"The evil plan is most harmful to the planner."

HESIOD

*"While their hatred may be concealed by trickery,
it will finally come to light for all to see."*

PROVERBS 26:26

I t wasn't fair!
Things had been going so well. Exactly as they should. And then this. This—tragedy.

It was wrong. He'd tried to prevent it, for all the good that had done.

He'd never imagined it could be this hard, this draining. What was the point of investing so much of yourself if it destroyed you? His hand lifted to his aching eyes. They stung, as though he'd been weeping. But of course he hadn't. Crying was for losers. And he was *not* a loser.

Still...how was he going to fix things? How would he get it all back on track? Of course, he'd faced obstacles before. You didn't get anywhere in this business without learning to either evade or scale obstacles. And learn he had. He always triumphed. Always found a way past the resistance and, often by sheer force of will, got the results he wanted. The results he deserved. Circumstances...people...it was all the same.

All meant to bend to his will.

Little wonder, then, that he always emerged on top. Exactly where he should be. But this time…

He slammed a fist on the table.

How could things go so wrong?

His fingers ached and eased open. He felt the fingers with his other hand. Fortunately nothing was broken. But as hard as he'd hit the table, something could've been. Stupid, stupid.

See what happens when you let things get to you? Just relax. Think it through. You've made it this far. Nothing's going to stop you now.

It was true. He had his goal in sight. One more show…one more and he'd be so well established that nothing would unseat him. His position would be assured. His power would increase. And he'd have it all. Everything he'd worked for. Longed for.

Everything he deserved.

A star. That's what he needed. Just one, and all would be well. He stood.

Time to stop worrying and start doing. He needed a star, so he'd find one. And she'd be perfect. Because he'd chosen her.

Anything else was unacceptable.

TWELVE

"The heart has eyes which the brain knows nothing of."

HELEN KELLER

"You are God's field."

1 CORINTHIANS 3:9

SEPTEMBER 24

Sheriff's deputy Dan Justice sat at his desk, staring at the computer screen in front of him.

He guessed he should be glad no more threatening e-mails had arrived in his sister's in-box. Trouble was, the cybercrime unit hadn't been able to trace the two Annie had forwarded to him. Too bad she'd deleted the first e-mail she received. It might not have made a difference, but Dan figured the more the guys at cybercrimes had to work with, the better.

He picked up one of the printed posts and read it again. The effect was the same as when Annie had first given it to him: rage. Hot, blind rage. He wanted to crumple it into a ball and slam it down the throat of the creep who had invaded his sister's life.

He tossed the paper back onto his desk and stood to refill his coffee cup. *Sorry, Lord. I know that's not exactly a loving response...*

"As surely as I live, when I sharpen my flashing sword and begin to carry out justice, I will bring vengeance on my enemies."

The words rang within him, and Dan took a slow drink of coffee. Okaaay...so maybe God understood better than he realized.

He went back to his desk, staring at Annie's e-mail again. No notes of any kind for a little over a week now. That could mean a couple things.

One, whoever sent the threats had given up.

Or two, he'd changed tactics.

As much as Dan preferred the first, he figured the second was more likely.

And, he thought, fingers tightening around his coffee mug, *more dangerous.*

Jed jabbed his spoon into his cereal bowl, stabbing a floating square of Shredded Wheat. Who would believe it? Here he was, at his prime intellectually—or so they said—and his stupid brain just decided to call in sick for the day.

He'd spent all of yesterday immersed in thought, reading, brainstorming by himself and with Andy, and what did he have to show for it? Nothing!

The ideas for previous episodes of *Everyday Heroes* had come so easily. They flowed so fast and furious that Jed had to scramble to keep up with them. But now?

It was as though the Shredded Wheat was floating between his ears rather than in the bowl.

Muttering, Jed picked up the bowl and tossed it into the sink. He went to jerk the bottle of OJ out of the fridge, then turned to grab a glass—and promptly sloshed half the container of juice on the large envelope he'd received in the morning mail from Silas's assistant, Mildred.

"Perfect! Just perfect." He slammed the container on the countertop and tipped the envelope into the sink, letting the juice drain off.

He didn't need to open the envelope to know what was inside. Newspaper articles, clippings, magazine articles—whatever she or Silas spotted that they thought would help prime the stalled creativity pump in Jed's head.

Like it would do any good.

He wiped the envelope with a paper towel, then slit it open and looked inside at the soggy collection of papers.

Fine. He didn't want to read them anyway. He was about to upend the whole mess into the trash when he caught a head-line—and stopped, midtoss.

What was that?

He reached inside the envelope, snagging a newspaper clipping between his forefinger and thumb. Easing it out of the clumped mass of paper, he held it over the sink. It was the front page of the "Lifestyles" section of...did that say what he thought it did?

He shook the rest of the juice off, then dabbed at the clipping with a dish towel, careful not to tear it. Yes. He'd read it right. The clipping was from the *Mail Tribune*. The local paper from Medford, Oregon.

His hometown.

Jed had left the Rogue Valley years ago, right out of high school. You didn't break into TV by living in Medford, Oregon, so he loaded up his old beater of a car and headed south to find his dream.

And to escape what his life had become.

No, don't go there.

Too late.

Like something straight out of a Stephen King novel, the specter of his past pushed free from the small corner of his awareness where he kept it captive. As it rose, memories pelted him, like cinders sent flying when a fresh log was tossed on a dying fire.

Angry voices. His father's. His own.

Tears. His mother's mostly.

The image of his father's back as he walked away. For good this time. The sound of his own voice railing at his mother, screaming out his rage and fear: "You didn't love him enough. He never would have left if you'd loved him more!"

Years of despair. Of loneliness and longing. Of watching out the window, willing himself to believe. To trust that his father would come back.

And then the death blow, struck when Jed was in junior high.

"Jediah, this is Amos. We're going to be married..."

Jed's breakfast threatened to resurrect. He grabbed a glass off the counter, filled it with cold water, and slugged it back. It helped calm his stomach.

But not his anger.

Amos Elhanin. The man who destroyed his life. His family. Bad enough that he'd tried to replace Jed's dad, but he brought all that God garbage with him too. Suddenly Jed had lost not only his father, but his weekends as well. His mom hauled him to church every Sunday, rain or shine. Bought him a shiny new Bible. Set up family devotions...

Yeah, and you bought into it, didn't you? Hook, line, and sinker. Memorized Scripture like it would disappear if you didn't etch it on your brain.

"I was young." Jed knew he was talking to himself, but it felt good to break the piercing silence. "And stupid."

Really, really stupid. So much so that he'd started to believe not only in Amos's God, but in Amos. He took Jed fishing. Went to all Jed's sports events.

And he prayed. That was the one thing Jed still saw when he thought of Amos. The man on his knees. Praying. For his wife. For his son.

His son.

"God, be with my son."

Not his *step*son. Amos never called him that. Just...*my son.*

The man did everything real dads were supposed to do. Everything Jed's own dad had never done. And little by little, Jed found himself liking it. Even loving it.

Until that day. That Saturday, during Jed's senior year, when his dad finally came back.

September 14, 1985. Jed's eighteenth birthday. Football season *and* a Saturday. So, of course, Jed and Amos were outside, doing their best imitation of the LA Rams, Jed's team. Amos yelled at Jed to "go long," and Jed raced to the end of the yard, jumping for Amos's pass, missing by a mile.

"Yeah!" Amos chortled. "Now them's some *hands,* son!"

"Maybe if you weren't aiming for Meadowlark Lemon, I could catch the thing. This is football, Amos, not basketball!"

Their joking filled the fall air as Jed turned to hunt down the stray football—only to find it being held out to him by a man standing at the edge of the grass. Jed looked at the man, thanks poised on his lips—and froze.

The hair was gray where once it had been dark brown. The face was worn and strained where once it had been smooth. But the eyes…his dad's eyes were the same.

Jed would have recognized them anywhere.

He stood there, wanting to say so much. Incapable of saying a word. A hand on his shoulder jerked his attention to the side.

Amos.

By the time Jed looked back at his dad, the damage was done. His father's eyes had gone cold, hard. He looked from Amos to Jed, then turned.

For the second time in his life, Jed watched his dad's back as he walked away.

His voice finally came to life. "Dad!"

But the man didn't break stride as he crossed the street and got into an old beater of a car. Jed ran after him, pounding on the driver's side window.

His dad didn't look at him. Just started the car up and drove away, leaving Jed standing there in the street.

When Amos came to comfort Jed, he turned on the man. Railed at him. All the anger, the hurt, came back in a rush. He pushed Amos away and ran into the house.

They never played ball again. Didn't talk. Didn't do anything. Jed refused. And though he still saw and heard Amos praying for him, he didn't care. Because it didn't mean anything.

God was a joke. He had to be. Because no God of love and

mercy would let Jed's dad come home at that precise moment—a perfectly timed opportunity to show him he'd been replaced.

The day after graduation, Jed packed up his beater and left his family—and their antiquated beliefs—behind. He left his mom a note, telling her he was going to LA. He knew she'd be upset. He didn't care. He was doing what was best *for him.*

And he'd been right. Hadn't he found his dream? It had taken a lot of years and a lot of work, but everything was finally going great. Better than he'd ever imagined.

Still, seeing the name of his hometown like that did something to him. Stirred up something deep inside.

He carried the still soggy clipping to the table, sat down, and read.

The article told about an elderly woman getting lost in the mountains outside Medford. Jed knew that area. He and his dad used to hike there all the time growing up. And after his dad left, Jed spent more time up there than at home. He'd even found one spot in particular he really liked.

But as great as that area was for hiking, it sure wasn't the place for some old woman. Especially one with Alzheimer's.

Enter search and rescue. And, he flipped the page, one team in particular...

Jed stopped reading and straightened in his chair even as his pulse started dancing. He studied the picture of the woman and her search dog. The animal was huge, almost as big as the woman. As for her, well, that was one pretty woman. And there was something in her eyes. Something...hidden.

Something that Jed knew, without a doubt, he could uncover.

He laid the paper down and leaned back in his chair.

Fans of *Everyday Heroes* were gonna love these two. And even more important, the network was gonna love Jed for finding them.

THIRTEEN

"Surprises are foolish things. The pleasure is not enhanced, and the inconvenience is often considerable."

JANE AUSTEN

"You chart the path ahead of me."

PSALM 139:3

SEPTEMBER 25—A CORNFLOWER DAY (GREEN AND BLUE)
Oregon and Ireland.

Though thousands of miles apart, they shared a common trait: climate. And that was just one more thing Annie loved about Oregon, because that meant she had something many others throughout the states did not: daffodils in September.

And red clover. And roses. And poppies. And cornflowers. And irises. And glads... You name it, Annie had it in her garden. And it was all in glorious, hue-drenched bloom.

She sat back, wiping a hand across her brow. Though early morning, it was plenty warm. And working in the garden always had a way of making her sweat. She'd had no idea when she was little, watching her mother tend her pansies, what hard work gardening was.

But it was worth every drop of sweat, every aching muscle. For there, in her yard, was a blanket of dancing colors.

Her colors.

When she bought her ranch-style log home nearly five years

ago, she'd known that one day she'd plant a garden. But the idea to plant a garden this way, with greenery and blossoms that reflected the colors she saw in letters and numbers, hadn't occurred to her right away. Not until after she'd lived in the home for almost a year. It was then, as she was building a fire in the river rock fireplace in the large family room, that she realized something was missing.

Color.

To be more precise, her colors.

Oh, she had them in several pieces of stained glass she'd done for the doors, for the crescent window overlooking the valley, but that wasn't enough. She needed something more. And no matter how hard she looked, she couldn't find any prints or paintings or decorations that felt right.

Then she received a bulb catalog in the mail. The moment she looked at the pictures of flowers, she knew. This was it.

She'd debated whether to plant the front- or backyard, then settled on the front, lining the walkway to the main door. That way the flowers could greet any visitors.

Kyla helped her with the initial planting during one of her visits. They'd even put in a little pond for water lilies and cattails. What started as a small section of flowers had spread, making her front yard a virtual showcase. She had flowers almost year-round now, both outside in the garden and inside in overflowing vases.

Finally, her colors were everywhere, and she loved it.

The lyrical tones of her cell phone piped up, startling Annie so she jumped, almost sending her garden stool flying. She yanked the offending phone from her jeans pocket and flipped it open.

"Annie? It's Bree."

The moment Annie heard her friend's voice, she remembered. Kodi's vet appointment! "Did I miss it?"

Laughter danced over the circuits. "Nope. You've got fifteen minutes."

Annie looked down at her muddy clothes and sighed. "It's a good thing you guys love me. I'm a mess."

"We don't love you. But we love Kodi, so we put up with you."

She made a face at the phone. "Ha ha. See you in a few."

Flipping the phone shut, she took one last longing look at her garden, then ran to the house to grab the two things she'd better not forget: her car keys and her dog.

"You found 'em again, eh?"

Annie held Kodi's head steady as Dr. Matthew Harding aimed the light from his otoscope to peer down an ear canal.

"Kodi found the woman, Matt. You know that."

He clicked off the scope, then gave Kodi's ear a scratch. "Indeed I do. You've got a regular star here, you know."

"Hmm…" As the vet made notes in Kodi's chart, Annie lifted the dog from the exam table down to the floor. "*She* certainly knows it, with all the attention she's been getting lately. I swear, this dog must have gained five pounds, what with all the extra biscuits she's been getting from people we see."

"Well—" the vet turned—"you *were* in the paper. Not just our paper, mind you, but the *Oregonian* and *LA Times*. Big stuff, Annie. That makes you a bit of a celebrity."

"Goody gumdrops."

Dr. Harding chuckled. "Look at it this way, it's good PR for your search and rescue group."

That it was. And for that reason alone, Annie had tried not to get frustrated with all the attention the last few days—her phone ringing day and night with people wanting interviews.

Annie wasn't sure why this particular rescue had caught the media's attention—though she suspected it was Bertha coming to give her "wolf" a hug that did it. Two pictures had run with the story in the papers: one of Bertha delivering a kiss to Kodi's snout and one of Annie and Kodi. Annie loved the first, tolerated the second—and could only hope interest waned sooner rather than later. "So did our girl here girl pass her six-month checkup?"

"With flying colors, as usual." Dr. Harding fished a doggy treat out of the jar on the counter, then held it out to Kodi, who lady that she was, took it with gentle care—then snarfed it down. They both laughed.

Kodi padding along beside her, Annie headed out to the reception area to pay for the visit. "Hey, Bree."

Brianna Heller, one of Annie's closest friends, looked up, her blue eyes twinkling. "Hey there, Miss Celebrity."

Annie groaned. "Please, not you too."

"Are you kidding? We put the article up on the wall!"

Annie followed Bree's pointing finger, and there it was. Tacked to the corkboard, where pictures of staff members' family shared space with shots of the clinic's four-legged patients.

"I understand you're leaving Kodi with us for a grooming session?"

"Shh!" Annie covered Kodi's ears. "She doesn't know she's staying."

Bree knew as well as Annie how Kodi carried on when she was left at the clinic. Annie had yet to hand the dog off without Kodi leaning against her, whining as though she were being tortured. Not because they treated her badly. Quite the contrary, they loved Kodi and treated her like royalty. But, as with most German shepherds, Kodi was, plain and simple, a big baby.

Annie handed her debit card to Bree, then stepped closer to the pictures on the corkboard. Most of the pictures were typical photos, but there were two—stunning shots of a beautiful towheaded girl—that Annie recognized right away as quality photography.

"You're getting better with that camera all the time."

Bree ran Annie's payment, then held out a pen for her signature on the receipt. "High praise coming from a real artist."

Annie took the pen. "Hmm. Of course, you have a beautiful subject. I swear, Amberly just keeps getting prettier." She scrawled her name, then tucked the receipt in her pocket.

"She was just asking me this morning when she gets to see Kodi again."

Annie's lips twitched. "Kodi, huh? Not Auntie Annie?"

"What can I say? My daughter loves animals more than

people." She waggled her brows. "Takes after her mother."

Annie leaned her elbows on the desk. "So did you talk with Mark about taking a break?"

She and Bree had gone to lunch last week, and after listening to Bree relate all she'd been dealing with at the clinic lately, Annie told the woman to run, not walk, home and tell her husband she needed a vacation.

"Actually, I did. We're going camping for a week with the Conrads up around Diamond Lake."

"Oh, you'll all have a blast."

Bree grinned. "I'll get my exercise keeping up with the kid, that's for sure. By the way, how's the window for that sweet old lady coming?"

Annie grimaced. "Don't ask. That's why I was lost in my gardening when you called. I was trying to find some kind of inspiration."

"Tell you what, I'm taking my camera with me. How about I take some shots for you? I've been playing with perspective and depth of field, and it would be fun to watch for shots that are something…different."

Annie tipped her head. "You mean, something where you see things in a new way?"

"Exactly."

A tinge of excitement stirred in Annie's chest. "That'd be great, Bree. You sure you don't mind?"

"Hey, you know me. I'm happiest when I'm with my family and I've got my camera in my hands."

"Well, you'll get both! And take some shots of Amberly for me too. You've got a real little beauty there."

"And so have you." Bree leaned over the counter and offered Kodi a doggy biscuit.

"She's already had—"

Too late. Casting her mistress a triumphant sideways glance, Kodi plucked the cookie from Bree's fingers and all but inhaled it.

"Pig dog," Annie muttered under her breath as she handed

Kodi's leash to Bree. "You're gonna weigh a ton if you keep this up."

Kodi's tail wagged in happy agreement.

"I get to go for my own checkup today, Bree, so Killian's assistant, Ryan, is going to pick up the beast for me. I tried to get Killian to do it, but you know what he thinks of Kodi."

"Let's see, what was it he said last time? A walking fur ball?"

"Besides, he does have an excuse. Kind of. He's just getting back to town from Hollywood."

"You mean Hollyweird, right?"

Annie grinned. "He was off doing another consultation with some home makeover show."

"Must be nice to be so popular." Bree held another cookie in front of Kodi's suddenly attentive nose. "Now quick, slip out the door while I distract her."

Annie did as she was told, opening the door and slipping out. Nary a whine nor whimper followed.

No wonder she liked bringing Kodi here. Even the receptionists were geniuses!

The sun was just starting to dip behind the mountains when Annie finally made it home. She'd waited more than an hour and a half for her doctor's appointment. By the time she'd seen the doctor, her normally low blood pressure was nowhere to be found.

Robin, the nurse, who knew Annie's blood pressure history as well as anyone, angled a look at Annie as she removed the cuff. "Still hate waiting, huh, Annie?"

Fortunately, the rest of the checkup went well. But then Annie had a number of errands to run, so by the time she got home, she was tired and frazzled and ready to collapse on the couch. Arms loaded with grocery bags, she'd just slipped the key into the front door when she heard the phone ringing.

"Great. Just great."

Juggling the keys and the bags of groceries, she shoved the door open—and was accosted by an even more exuberant than usual Kodi. Nothing got her worked up like a grooming session. "Yes, yes, you're beautiful."

But Kodi was not to be placated. The dog circled around Annie's legs, wagging that massive black head back and forth and talking up a storm with that throaty, deep-chested rumble of hers: "Aroww-row-*row!*"

Translation: *"How could you leave me! And how could you let that awful man pick me up!"*

Annie knew even without the shepherd's accusatory glare that she'd committed a canine cardinal sin: she'd left Kodi at the vet. And she'd almost compounded the sin by asking Killian to pick the dog up to bring her home.

Kodi did not—emphasis on *not*—like Killian. Nothing Annie did or said made a difference. Killian showed up, and Kodi immediately went into sulk mode. Which, when it came down to it, was only fair, because Killian was about as fond of Kodi as the dog was of him.

Annie didn't understand—or like—the mutual abhorrence. Fortunately, Kodi didn't frequent art galleries, so it wasn't hard to keep the two far apart. And equally fortunate, Killian had Ryan to turn to when Annie asked him to come anywhere near the dog.

"Kodi, come on, girl. Give me a break…" Annie tried to dodge the dog and succeeded in nearly taking a header when Kodi zigged back in front of her and nudged her snout at Annie's elbow.

"I *can't* pet you right now! I'm trying to answer the phone. *Move,* you big moose!" Annie angled a hip into Kodi, shoving her out of the way, then plopped the grocery bags on the counter and snatched the receiver, gasping out a hello.

There was a pause, then, "Miss Justice?"

Annie frowned. She didn't recognize the voice. "Yes?"

"This is E J Curry. I'm with *Everyday Heroes,* the reality show on television?"

Great. She'd almost taken a nosedive over her dog for a sales call. "I'm sorry, I don't watch much TV, so I'm not interested. Bye."

She set the phone back in the base, then turned to more

important matters. Such as getting her ice cream into the freezer before it melted.

The phone rang again.

"What is this today? Grand Central Station?" She tossed the ice cream into the freezer, pushed the door shut, and reached for the phone. "Hello?"

"Miss Justice, it's E J Curry again."

Ooooh. A pushy one. Annie leaned back against the counter, lips pursed. Okay, fine. She had a little time to play. "So what does that stand for?"

"I'm sorry?"

She nudged Kodi out of the way. The dog was practically standing on top of her for some reason. "E J. I assume it stands for something?"

He paused. "Ernest Jediah."

Oh my. Talk about a perfect setup. "Don't you find it a bit of a disconnect?" She allowed herself a smile at the silence that met her question.

Perfect. Objective accomplished. Maybe he'd give up and go away.

"Excuse me? I'm not sure I understand."

Or not. Okay, she'd keep at it a little while longer. "A disconnect, Mr. Curry. Being earnest. In your chosen occupation. Actually, in a couple aspects, being a salesman *and* working in reality television."

She wasn't sure what response she expected. Maybe that he'd just hang up on her seeing as she was being such a brat. Still, she told him she wasn't interested, and he called back, so really, who was to blame?

But he didn't hang up. Instead, he gave a deep, rich chuckle.

And a whine. Not from the man, but from Kodi. She pawed at Annie, looking for all the world like she was trying to reach for the phone. Annie shooed the dog away.

"No," the man finally responded, "not at all. Because try as I might, I can't help but be Ernest in pretty much everything I do."

Hmm. Clever guy. But then, he *was* a salesman.

She turned to upend the grocery bag on the kitchen island, then grabbed at a can of orange juice as it tried to roll off the island, nearly tripping over Kodi in the process. What was *wrong* with that dog? "That's fine, Mr. Curry, but as I said, I'm really not int—"

"Miss Justice, I'm not a salesman."

"Oh?" This was a new one. She settled the OJ into the freezer beside the ice cream. "So what do they call you guys nowadays?"

"The director."

This time it was she who fell silent. "Excuse me?"

"I'm the director of *Everyday Heroes*. And I'm calling because I'd really love to feature you and your dog on the show."

Kodi barked. Annie frowned. "Feature us?"

"Right. Are you familiar with the show at all?"

She shook her head, then grimaced. *Dummy. Head shakes don't work over the phone.*

"Let me guess, you're shaking your head."

Annie started. "How did you know that?"

"Well, I could say I heard the rattle, but I was just guessing."

Before she could come up with a response caustic enough, he went on, explaining the show. Annie had to admit it sounded interesting. She might even try to catch an episode to check it out. Still...

Another paw came to rest on her leg. Annie brushed it away. "Will you knock it *off?*"

"I'm sorry, I meant that as a joke."

"No, not you, Mr. Curry. It's my...oh, never mind. Look, what does your show have to do with me and Kodi?"

"Everything!"

Were all directors this dramatic?

"You and your dog are news, Miss Justice. Folks loved that story about the woman you found. I can send you dozens of letters to the editor from papers across the country. I mean, the way you found that poor woman—"

"Kodi found her."

At hearing her name, Kodi's ears perked and she whined.

"Well, yes, of course, But you were part of the process, right?"

She turned her back to her precious pup. "Kodi does all the work. I'm pretty much along for the ride, Mr. Curry. Sorry. Nothing heroic in what I do."

"I disagree, Miss Justice. Please, I'd really like to come film you for one of our episodes."

Kodi slid her head under Annie's hand, those brown eyes full of supplication. Annie scratched the dog's ears. "Film us?"

"Right. I'd come in with the camera and follow you guys for a week or so."

"Follow us where?"

"Everywhere. That's the point. We'd see you at home and at work. See how you and the dog interact—"

"The dog has a name, Mr. Curry."

The chill in her reprimand must have startled him into silence. Good. It was about time he was on the receiving end of the discomfort in this conversation.

"Of course. I'm sorry. We'd like to see how you and Kovi—"

Annie gritted her teeth. "Kodi."

"Sorry! Oh right, Kodi. How you and Kodi interact. And with any luck, you'd get called out on a search—"

Okay. That did it. "Mr. Curry, I don't exactly consider it lucky when we get a callout. After all, it does mean someone is lost."

"Sure. Right. Sorry. I didn't mean—"

"As for having you follow us around at home, I'm sorry, but that's my private life."

"Yes, but—"

"And on a search? You'd just get in my way. So while I'm flattered—"

"You mean in Kodi's way, right?"

"—that you'd...you'd—" Annie frowned. "Excuse me?"

"You meant we'd get in Kodi's way. Because she's the one doing the work. You're just along for the ride."

Annie pursed her lips. Was he teasing her? Or just being a smart aleck? Either way, she didn't think she liked it.

Or him.

"As I was saying, though I'm flattered that you'd want Kodi for your show—"

"And you."

Would the man ever let her finish a sentence? "I...what?"

"I want you."

Heat rushed into her face. Good thing there weren't any cameras on her now!

"Well, okay, I don't want you—"

Oh yeah. That made things so much better.

"—the show wants you. You and your dog." He sighed. "What I'm saying is you two are a team. We want you both."

"Hmm."

"It'll be good for you and Kodi."

"Oh?" Annie looked down at the shepherd now sprawled at her feet. Make that on her feet. "Good for us, huh? How is that?"

"You'll be famous."

Annie pulled her feet free. "We already are, Mr. Curry, in our own little way. And I don't care to be any more famous than that."

"Well then, think of what it could mean to your organization. Media attention is always a good thing for groups that depend on donations."

Kodi barked again, twice this time. Annie grabbed hold of the dog's collar and ushered her to the front door. "I suppose that's true, but I'm not sure the people who watch reality TV are exactly your typical SAR donors."

She pulled the door open and shoved the dog outside, then closed the door against her rumbling *Aarrooowww!*

"You'd be amazed, Miss Justice. These people don't just love watching what our heroes do; they want to take part. Help out. Believe me, your organization would benefit."

Annie went to pull a coffee mug from the rack on the wall. SAR could always use more donations, but was she prepared to give up her life for a couple weeks to accommodate these people? And what about the window she was working on? Having someone watching her every move wasn't exactly conducive to creativity.

No, this was not a good idea. "I'm sorry, Mr. Curry. But I'll have to pass."

"But—"

Wow. It felt good to have the decision made. She even smiled into the receiver. "Thanks for calling. I'm sure you'll find someone far better than Kodi and me for your episode."

With that, she dropped the phone back in the base, then took her mug to fill it with coffee she'd made earlier that morning. Fortunately, she'd learned long ago that if you turned the heat off immediately after brewing a pot, you could nuke it all day long and it would still taste fresh. She slid the mug into the micro and hit the *reheat* button, then went to let her still complaining dog back inside.

"So what was *that* all about?"

Kodi went to stare up at the phone where it rested in the base. "I told him no."

The dog whined.

"Look—" she pulled the doggy cookie container across the counter, then fished a cookie out—"I can't imagine anyone wanting cameras following them around, can you?"

She held the cookie out, just above Kodi's nose. The shepherd, who was already sitting pretty, took her cue and gave one affirming bark. Annie tossed her the cookie.

"That's what I love about you, girl. You always know the right thing to say."

FOURTEEN

"The conditions of conquest are always easy.
We have but to toil awhile,
endure awhile, believe always, and never turn back."

MARCUS ANNAEUS SENECA

"Endurance develops strength of character."

ROMANS 5:4

Well...*that* went well.

Jed listened another few seconds to the dial tone buzzing in his ear, then clicked the phone off. He sat there, tapping it against his leg as he thought.

Okay. So she wasn't as receptive as he'd hoped. No problem. He'd met resistance before. That just meant he had to really go to work now.

Setting the phone back in its cradle, he went to the kitchen table and picked up the newspaper.

"Who are you, Annie Justice?"

"Women speak two languages—one of which is verbal." Hmmm...if there was one thing the Bard understood, it was human nature. Jed sat down, laying the paper out in front of him, and read through the article again. Taking his time. Looking for the woman in what she did—and didn't—say.

"I like helping people. It's an amazing feeling seeing a family reunited when they feared the worst. Especially when kids get lost. Seeing the fear fall away, seeing parents' faces change from terror to

relief, that's what makes this all worthwhile."

Annie Justice cared about others.

"These mountains, this wilderness, it's as much a part of me as my DNA. Oregon is heaven on earth to me, but I'm not fooled. For all its beauty, it can be a hazardous place for the unprepared."

She loved Oregon.

"Kodi's a great rescue dog; it's as though she can't be at peace until she finds whoever is lost. But she's more than that. She's my best friend. I trust her, not just with my life, but with others' lives too. And she's never let me down."

She loved that dog of hers.

Jed frowned. Annie trusted her dog…the animal had never let her down…

He laid Annie's picture in front of him and studied it. Yes, he'd been right. There was something hidden in those eyes.

Hurt.

Distrust.

And a heavy dose of defiance.

This woman was going to be a challenge. He tapped a finger on her newsprint chin. "Okay, Annie, you won this round. But you're about to learn something, lady." He carried the paper to his desk, jerked open the drawer, and pulled out a pair of scissors. Four quick cuts later, the picture was free from its newspaper prison and tacked to the wall above Jed's desk. Right at eye level.

He sat in his chair and met the woman's gaze straight on. "You're not the only one with a stubborn streak."

SEPTEMBER 26—A DAFFODIL DAY (GREEN AND YELLOW)
Annie crouched over her worktable, staring at the paper in front of her.

White. Clean. Empty.

Just like her brain.

"Argh!" She pushed away from the table and paced. What was wrong with her? Why couldn't she come up with any ideas for Serafina's window? She'd even welcome a *bad* idea at this point. But every time she sat down to sketch, her mind drew a blank.

Ideas—good, bad, or otherwise—were nonexistent.

Lord, why did You let me agree to this? And why won't You help me?

A glance at the clock had her teeth clenching. Ten-thirty. She'd been sitting here for three hours! Enough was enough.

Besides, it was past time to check on Kodi. The dog had been in full-on snooze mode when Annie was ready to come to the studio, so she just left her at home. Good thing the studio was only across the yard from her house. Kodi's middle name might be "trustworthy," but it never paid to leave a shepherd alone for too long. Smart dogs got bored easily. And when smart dogs were bored, they got destructive. The last time Annie forgot that, she found a doorjamb chewed into toothpicks and the carpeting from one room shredded into dental floss.

That memory quickened her step as Annie left the studio and hurried past her garden to the house. She loved having her studio in a separate building from her house. It helped her leave work behind when she was done.

Once inside, she roused Kodi, laughing at the dog's quick transition from sleep to dancing excitement when she realized she was going for a walk. Annie pulled Kodi's leash from the hook near the back door. She calmed Kodi enough to clip the leash in place—then jumped when the buzzer from the gate cut through the silence.

Sometimes she really hated that buzzer.

Kodi trotting along at her side, she went to pull the front door open…and froze.

Roses. A mass of them. Vivid tones of peach tinged with red filling the doorway. The flowers' heady scent enveloped her, almost taking her breath away.

"Sorry 'bout that ma'am. Didn't mean to startle you."

Aha! A human hid behind the flowers. Annie stepped to the side so she could see the deliveryman. "Can I help you? And how did you get through the gate?"

"It was open, so I just drove up to the house. I hope that's okay."

Great. She must have forgotten to close it when she came home the night before. Better not let Dan hear about it. He'd been after her since the e-mails to make sure she "secured" her home.

"You're Annie Justice?"

She nodded. "Yes…"

"These are for you. Where would you like me to set them, ma'am?"

"For me?" Annie bit her lip. It had to be a mistake. Too bad, because they were beautiful. "Are you sure?"

"If you're Annie Justice, then I'm sure. Now please, ma'am, these things are heavy."

"Oh! Bring them in." She led him to the kitchen island, and he set the huge vase down, grunting his relief.

"Thanks, ma'am."

She inspected the beautiful blooms, then cocked her head. "There's no card?"

"No, ma'am."

"But…who are they from?"

He shrugged. "You'll have to call the store for that information. I just deliver."

Annie buried her nose in the petals and inhaled. This had to be what heaven smelled like.

"Is this where you want the rest of them?"

Annie eyed the man over the roses. "The rest of what?"

"The flowers. I've got a truckload of 'em, ma'am."

She stared at him. Did he say a truckload? No, she must have OD'd on the fragrance and was hallucinating.

"Ma'am?"

"Show me."

He frowned. "Show you?"

"The flowers. Show them to me."

The man turned and led her outside to the back of his delivery van. The doors were open, and when Annie looked in she saw a veritable ocean of roses in a rainbow of colors. Mouth agape, she turned to the man standing beside her, pointing first at the flowers, then at herself. He grinned and nodded.

Turning back to the roses, Annie finally managed to dredge up her voice. "Sure. Put them all in there."

Fifteen minutes later the van drove away, the deliveryman having effectively transformed her kitchen into a botanical garden. Annie stared at the beauty surrounding her. She closed her eyes, letting the scent fill her senses.

Opening her eyes, she walked from one huge bouquet to another, fingering the petals, drinking in the variations of hues and tones. It was wonderful. And overwhelming.

She'd seen roses all her life, almost every day. Rosebushes adorned her yard, and she always had vases of the lush flowers during blooming season. But she'd never seen them in such abundance. Never been immersed in them. As if she'd fallen inside them, become part of them...

Annie jerked to a stop.

Immersed. Surrounded. A part of the beauty.

There was something there. She couldn't quite tell what...but something. Grabbing two of the vases, she headed for the door, bumped it open, and made her way to her studio. She set the flowers in the middle of the worktable, then went back inside the house for more.

When the worktable was covered with flowers, Annie pulled a large sheet of white paper in front of her. Lifting her pencil, she focused on the colors, the fragrances, surrounding her.

Then put pencil to paper and let the images flow.

Candy came the next day.

Along with a bone.

Annie was just about to head out to her studio when the gate buzzer sounded. She looked at the clock. Ten-thirty. Just like yesterday.

Kodi raced to the door, barking and circling, certain that whoever was there had come to adore her.

"Whaddya think, girl?" Annie grinned at the dog. "More roses? Or maybe this time it's a car."

She wanted to see for herself. So rather than hit the button to open the gate, she opened the door and made her way down the long driveway to the gate. When she saw what awaited her, her mouth dropped open.

Another deliveryman stood there. But what he held in one arm was far better than a car.

Chocolates. Godiva chocolates, to be exact. A huge box of them.

The man's other arm was laden with what had to be the largest dog bone she'd ever seen.

Annie wasn't sure who was salivating most—her or Kodi.

As with the flowers, no card was attached. She carried the gifts back inside, her heart tapping out a mix of disquiet and delight. *Who*, she wondered as she handed the bone to Kodi, was sending all these things? And why?

She watched Kodi carry her treasure to her corner of the kitchen, then lifted the lid from the chocolates. Oh, good golly, where to begin...

Three delectable bites of heaven later, she went to the phone and dialed. She didn't even let Ryan get a full hello out. "Is Killian there?"

To his credit, Ryan didn't miss a beat. "Sure is, Annie. Hang on."

No sooner was Killian on the line than Annie blurted out, "Did you send me flowers?"

"Hello to you too."

"Killie, did you?"

"From the tone of your voice, I'm not sure I'd admit it if I did. But no, I didn't. Why?"

She plunked her elbows on the counter. "Someone sent me flowers. And candy." She paused for effect. "*Godiva* chocolates."

For a second she thought he'd hung up on her. Then, just

as she was about to ask if he was still there, he broke the silence. "Flowers *and* chocolates. My, my. How *will* you survive such trauma?"

Annie really wasn't in the mood for Killian's sarcasm. "Look, I know I should be delighted, but there's no card—"

"Ah. Mystery explained. You don't know your benefactor's identity, hence you aren't in control."

Wow. He was in a mood today. "This is not about being in control."

"Yeah, okay. And selling art isn't about making money."

"*Killian.*"

"Listen, so someone appreciates you. Enjoy. Now if you'll excuse me, I hear my mother calling."

"Your mother died five years ago."

"Then it's about time I answered her, don't you think?"

The dial tone buzzing in Annie's ear told her he didn't expect a reply. Too bad. She had a great one.

Or would have had if she used words like that.

She went to sit on the floor beside Kodi. "You know what, girl? You just may be right about Killian."

Kodi's tail thumped the floor, and she angled Annie a look over the bone.

Annie gave the dog a gentle push. "Don't look so smug, you brat." She stood and brushed the dog hair from her pants. Of course, she'd be covered again in no time. Such was life with a double-coated dog. "You know I don't really agree with you. Killie's a nice guy, down deep." Her lips twitched. "Waaaay down deep."

She snickered, then picked up the box of chocolates—no way she was leaving unsupervised Godiva in the house with Kodi—and headed for her studio. Enough time wasted thinking about Killian's snarkiness and the mystery gift giver. What she needed was a serious dose of art and gourmet chocolates. That would put her in a good mood in no time.

Or a sugar coma.

Right now, she'd welcome whichever hit first.

❖   ❖   ❖

The jangle of the phone sent Annie's pulse into overdrive.

She bolted out of the easy chair where she'd been dozing—dodged the suddenly barking Kodi, who'd also been startled from a deep sleep—and grabbed the cordless, almost growling a greeting. "Hello?"

"Annie?"

At Ryan's uncertain tone, Annie sank back down onto the chair. Poor guy. Between this phone call and the last, he would think she was a total grouch. "Sorry, Ryan. What can I do for you?"

"I was just calling to see how our window is coming."

"Our window?" What was he talking about?

"You know, the commissioned piece for Mrs. Stowe."

Of course. That window. The bane of her existence. "It's not."

"Excuse me?"

Annie fought to keep her tone even. "It's not. Coming."

"It's not—?"

Suddenly she heard what sounded like a scuffle, and then Killian was on the line.

"Annie?"

"Killian."

At her flat tone, he snorted. "Well, don't *you* sound cheery?"

Annie massaged her temples. "What do you want, Killian?"

"And so polite too."

She scowled. He was right to sound miffed. She was being a twit. "I'm sorry, Killie. I was asleep when Ryan called."

"Asleep? This time of day? Shouldn't you be working on the window?"

Shouldn't you two find something other than my window to fixate on? Annie trudged into the kitchen, pulled a glass from the cupboard, and turned on the faucet. "Yes, I should. But as I just told Ryan, it's not coming."

"Not coming? What do you mean 'not coming'?"

Two gulps of cold water didn't make her feel any better. "The window. The scene. The wonderful, creative way of making people see God in a new light!" She plunked the glass down on the counter. "It's just…not there, Killie. I'm as short on ideas as I am on time."

If she'd hoped for encouragement, she was in for a disappointment. "Annot Christine, get over yourself!"

Annie held the phone away from her ear, staring at it, then pulled it back in place. "I beg your pardon?"

"Yes, your art is inspiration. But it's also just plain work. And that's what you haven't been doing lately. Working. You've been running around, messing with training for these searches and whatnot, and letting yourself be distracted from what really matters. Your art."

"Killian…"

"You saw how people reacted at your showing. They love your work, woman. But they won't wait for you forever. You've got a window of opportunity here, and you need to grab it with both hands."

Annie leaned against the counter. Her head was pounding. "But no pressure, right?"

"Pressure? Of course there's pressure! What did you expect, that your calling would be easy?"

No. She hadn't expected that.

She just hadn't expected it to be quite this hard.

"Listen, I'm sorry, Annie. I don't want to nag you—"

Too late.

"—but you've got to get it together, my friend."

He was right. Yet again. But she just wasn't in the mood to admit that. "Killian?"

"Yes?"

"I'm hanging up now."

He didn't miss a beat. "Good-bye. And get to work."

Annie thumped the phone on the counter, then glared down at Kodi. "Get to work. Did you hear that? Get to work."

Kodi's head wagged to and fro. "Arrowwww!"

"That's right. Get to work, he says. Well, I'll show him! You know what I'm going to do?" Annie stomped to the front door and pulled it open.

Kodi stared at her for a moment, then walked through the door, padding outside and heading toward the studio. As she watched the dog, Annie felt her anger melt away. Laughing, she went out too, pulling the door shut behind her.

"What else?" She followed Kodi to the studio. "I'm getting to work."

Mission accomplished.

Jed couldn't hold back a grin as he exited the post office into the bright sunlight. Okay. So he was being smug. And with good reason.

Genius. That's what he was.

Pure genius.

Sure, the flowers and chocolates had cost him a small fortune. But unless he'd seriously miscalculated—which he seriously doubted—they'd worked their magic. Miss Ice Maiden's edges ought to be thawing by now. When this last delivery hit her door, well, good ol' Will said it best: "If you want to win anything—a race, your self, your life—you have to go a little berserk."

And so he had. But it was worth it because the payoff would be getting what he wanted.

Annie Justice and her dog. On his show.

Needless to say, Jed was staying close to his cell phone. This was one call he was not going to miss.

FIFTEEN

"What a man really wants is creative challenge...
so that he may have the expanding joy of achievement."

FAY B. NASH

"If we are out of our mind, it is for the sake of God."

2 CORINTHIANS 5:13, NIV

SEPTEMBER 28—A CATTAIL DAY (GREEN AND AUBURN)
It was no use.

No matter how many sketches she did, how many ideas sparked, they all fizzled. Annie couldn't count the number of times she'd filled her trash can with crumpled pieces of paper.

This window was going to be the death of her. Either that, or the death of her career.

She glanced at the clock. The mail should have arrived by now, and she could use a break. She stood, calling to Kodi. The dog bounded toward her, delighted with the chance to go for a walk, even if it was just to the mailbox.

They walked down Annie's long driveway, and she put Kodi in a sit-stay as she opened the gate and went to the box. She sorted the pile of mail as she walked back, closing the gate behind her and giving Kodi a release command.

"Junk mail, bill, bill, junk mail..."

Wait a minute. What was this?

Annie lifted the envelope. Looked like a card of some sort. But there was no return address.

And no postmark.

Tucking the rest of the mail under one arm, Annie opened the envelope. Hmm. No card, just a folded piece of white paper. She pulled it out and unfolded it.

She recognized the print right away. The message hit her a second later.

THE DOG WILL DIE. AND ITZ UR FAULT.

Annie dropped the paper and stepped back from it like it was a snake about to strike. Kodi dropped her head to sniff at the paper, and Annie grabbed the animal's collar, jerking her back. "Kodi, no!"

The dog yelped like she'd been mortally wounded—her typical drama queen reaction to discipline. Annie fell to her knees and threw her arms around the animal, hugging her close. "I'm sorry, girl."

Annie's voice was as shaky as the rest of her.

How had this person found her address? Her phone number was unlisted. Her address wasn't published anywhere that she knew of. Not even on the Internet.

The awareness that someone who wanted to hurt Kodi knew where she lived was almost more than Annie could take. She surged to her feet. "Come on, Kodi. Let's go call your uncle Dan."

She'd only gone a few feet when she heard the driveway buzzer go off. Spinning, she stared at the gate, ready to take on whatever threat awaited her or Kodi.

The UPS man stood there, eyes wide.

Annie blinked, then looked down at her watch. Ten-thirty, on the dot. Just like the last two days. Chin set, Annie marched to the gate. Kodi obviously sensed Annie's growing anger, because she padded right next to Annie, practically Velcroed to Annie's leg.

Annie didn't even try to stop the dog as she jerked the gate open and grabbed the two large envelopes and three yellow roses from the deliveryman. "Who sent these things?"

If the poor guy's eyes were wide a moment ago, they were huge now. "I don't know. I just deliver them."

"Can you track them?"

His nod was quick and jerky. He looked like a rabbit on speed. "Yeah. Sure. All you gotta do is go on-line and type in these numbers." He held his pen out to her. "Sign here, please."

Annie stared at him for a minute, then took the pen and scribbled her name.

The man kept his gaze fixed on Kodi as he slipped his pen back in his pocket. "That's a good-sized dog."

"Yes, she is."

He shifted, clearly nervous. "I'm, uh…I'm supposed to tell you to open the blue envelope first, then the red one."

"Okay, thanks."

The man beat a hasty retreat to his truck, and Annie carried the envelopes inside. She slammed them down the kitchen island.

Enough really was enough.

Blue one first, eh?

Not on your life.

Grabbing a steak knife from the silverware drawer, she picked up the red envelope and slit it open, spilling its contents on the island. A parchment document and three photos fluttered out. Trepidation tripping along her nerves, Annie picked up one of the photos.

A black and tan German shepherd looked out at her, the name "Gonzo" written across the bottom of the photo. The other two photos were of shepherds as well—"Raven," who was mostly black like Kodi, and "Dove," who was all white.

Annie laid the three photos side by side on the island and thought her heart would break. All three dogs had that shepherd grin on their fuzzy faces, but there was something in their eyes…something deep and compelling. Something timeworn and trial tested, but trusting in spite of it all.

Annie picked up the document that came with the photos. "THANK YOU!" was emblazoned across the top of the paper. *Thank you? For what?*

Frowning, Annie read on.

> A donation has been made in your name to the LA German Shepherd Rescue Foundation. Thanks to your generosity, three beautiful German shepherds who were rescued from shelters the day before being euthanized will be supplied with food and shelter for an entire year! Gonzo is a handsome three-year-old boy who was once abused and neglected but now is with us, waiting to find a new home with a family who will love him. Raven and Dove were rescued from a puppy mill. Though they were neglected and mistreated, their spirits remain strong and they lavish love on all they meet. And because of you, all three will know a year of security and care.

Tears washed Annie's frown away.

Okay, no way this envelope came from the same person who'd been sending her the gifts. Everything about it was different. She touched the three photos, then looked down at Kodi, who sat beside her. Dropping down to a crouch, Annie circled Kodi's strong neck and hugged. Kodi leaned in to her, as though consoling her mistress's jumbled emotions.

Annie pressed her face against Kodi's fur. How could anyone hurt such beautiful, tenderhearted animals? She would never understand that.

Not in a million years.

Kodi whined, and Annie let her go with a shaky laugh. "Sorry, girl. Didn't mean to blubber all over you."

She stood and picked up the document again, turning it over. There, on the back, was a Post-it note.

Okay, now that you've opened the second envelope first, please open the first one second.

Annie stared. Read the note again. Then stamped her foot. Kodi jumped and barked, scolding her.

"Well, I'm *sorry!* But this is driving me nuts. *Who* is sending this stuff?"

And how did that person know her so well?

Grabbing the blue envelope, Annie slit it open. Inside was a folded envelope and a DVD. A note card-size envelope was taped on the DVD case. Annie pulled the envelope free and opened it. The enclosed ivory note card was elegant in its simplicity.

The writing inside was bold and masculine.

Miss Justice, the flowers and candy were an apology for bothering you. Sponsoring the dogs is to honor you and Kodi for all you do for others. No strings attached. I promise. But I'd really like you to see what we're about. Please watch the tape. If you still don't want to do the show, just mail it back to me in the enclosed postage-paid envelope, and I'll leave you alone. But I'm hoping you'll reconsider.
—E J Curry
Director, Everyday Heroes
Ordinary People with Extraordinary Spirit
Changing the World

Annie looked from the note to the DVD to the pictures of the dogs then back to the DVD. She glanced down at Kodi, who cocked her head. The message was clear.

Why not?

"Okay fine." She picked up the DVD and took it to the living room. "I'll watch it."

Kodi came to settle at her feet while Annie started the show. The first episode was about a police officer, and by the middle of the show, Annie had to admit she was drawn in. There was something so noble in the officer...and in the way the voice narrating handled everything. The narrator's insights were both moving and challenging. When the episode was over, Annie actually felt...good. Then another episode began—this one about firefighters. It didn't take long to be enchanted by the men working together in such a hazardous environment. One man even talked openly and honestly about his faith.

Later in the episode, when the firefighters went running toward the window of a burning building where a child was trapped, Annie could hardly breathe.

She perched on the edge of her chair, hands clutched together as she watched and prayed. Of course, she knew the show was taped, not live, but she couldn't help it. She was so afraid something was going to—

The explosion hit her with an impact that was almost physical. She stared at the screen, tears streaming down her face. As the camera panned the destruction then went dark, the narrator's voice came on again.

"A good man died that day. A man who lived his life to serve others and a God he believed in. A lot of us are struggling right now, wondering how that God could let a man like this die so needlessly. But we can know this much: Ken Hall lived a life worth honoring. As do his brothers at the station. These men put everything on the line for us. For you. For me. And though they never ask for thanks, that's what we're giving them tonight. So thanks, guys.

"And thanks, Ken. Rest well. You deserve it."

The screen went dead, and the only sound in the room was Annie's blubbering. She blew her nose and pushed out of her chair, retrieving the DVD from the player. This E J was right—the show was good. And uplifting. And she could see why they wanted to feature someone like her and Kodi.

But…

A show like this wasn't just about honoring people who put themselves on the line for others. It was about ratings as much as about doing good. And when that kind of agenda was present, things could get complicated.

She had Serafina's window to work on. She needed to focus to do that. Besides, what if these TV people came and there wasn't a callout? How exciting would *that* be? "Okay, folks, here we have a K-9 search and rescue dog sleeping in the house…in the yard…in the art studio… Wait! Watch for it! Yes…she's rolling over!"

What was she supposed to do? Sit around hoping someone got lost? No—no way. And having strangers underfoot wouldn't exactly be conducive to creativity. Nuh-uh. No thanks.

She looked down at her snoring dog, then took the DVD back to the kitchen, put it in its case, and slipped it into the envelope. She pulled a sheet of stationery from her desk and wrote her reply: *"Thanks, but I'll pass. Annie Justice."*

She set the envelope on the island, where she'd see it and remember to get it in the morning mail.

And though Mr. E J Curry might be disappointed, he'd just have to accept one immutable fact: She and Kodi were *not* star material.

That decided, Annie reached for the phone. Time to do what she should have done a half hour ago instead of watching that tape.

Call her brother and turn the threatening note over to him. Then pray he caught the creep. Before any other surprises found her.

SIXTEEN

*"It's the constant and determined effort
that breaks down all resistance,
sweeps away all obstacles."*

CLAUDE M. BRISTOL

"I will give them singleness of heart."

EZEKIEL 11:19

SEPTEMBER 30

Jed usually liked surprises.

Usually.

But this surprise was far from pleasant.

His cell phone hadn't rung. And he didn't understand it. He'd been so sure Annie Justice would call when she received the envelopes.

How could she *not* call? His plan had been perfect!

He eyed his cell phone.

He'd checked the battery. Fully charged.

Signal? All bars present and accounted for.

The ringer was on. The volume was cranked. There was only one reason it sat there, silent as a tomb.

She wasn't going to call. He should have accepted that after the first twenty-four hours. But he'd kept telling himself she just needed time.

"Hey, you got a package."

Jed turned just in time to catch the envelope Andy tossed his way. He could tell by feel that it was a DVD. Frowning, he turned it over and read the postmark.

His frowned shifted into a scowl. So much for his so-called genius. Man! He'd pulled out all the stops on this woman. He'd been so sure he'd win her over.

Face it, Curry. You've lost your edge. First Ken, now this. If you can't even convince some woman from the sticks to let you film her, it's time to give up.

"Bad news?"

He didn't answer Andy. Just tossed the package on the counter.

"You're not going to open it?"

"What for? She wouldn't have sent the disc back if she'd agreed to do the show."

"She…" Understanding lit Andy's features. "Annie Justice."

"Right." Jed grabbed a coffee mug, went to the coffeemaker, and poured—but what filled his mug could hardly qualify as coffee. He grimaced and was about to dump the thick black liquid when Andy peered over his shoulder.

"Day-old sludge, bud?"

Jed's fingers tightened on the mug. "It's fine."

"Yeah—" Andy took the carafe and dumped the rest of its contents—"if you like drinking used motor oil." He started a fresh pot of coffee, then picked up the package, tore it open, and upended it on the counter. A folded letter and a DVD slid out.

Jed turned away. So Miss Playing-Hard-to-Get had sent a note, had she? Well, he didn't need to read it. Any more than he needed Andy to tell him what was and wasn't good. Coffee was coffee, right? Just heat it up and drink it. He slid the mug into the microwave and jabbed the *Beverage* button.

Andy scanned the letter, then waved it in the air. "Her stationery even has a German shepherd at the top."

Jed grunted, removing his now steaming brew from the microwave, and tossed back a swallow of the thick black concoction. Only fierce determination kept his throat from tossing it back.

Fighting the overwhelming urge to spit the gritty mess into the sink, he forced it down, then pasted a satisfied smile on his stiff features as he chewed the grounds now coating his tongue.

Andy eyed him. "You are seriously warped, my friend."

Jed shrugged and started to turn, but before he could make his escape, Andy shoved the note in front of his face. The hand-written words danced their defiance: *"Thanks, but I'll pass…"*

"Nice handwriting."

Andy just stared at him.

Keeping a stubborn grip on his nonchalance, Jed lifted the coffee mug to force down another drink, but apparently Andy had had enough. He plucked the mug from Jed's hand, shoved the letter in its place, then marched to the sink and dumped the evil glop where it belonged: down the drain.

"You don't drink crud, man—" Andy poured some of the freshly brewed coffee into Jed's mug and handed it back to him—"and you don't accept defeat. You fight, man. Stare it square in the eye and wrestle it to the ground. But give in? That's just not your style."

Jed looked down at the note. Andy was right. So Annie Justice was a harder sell than he'd anticipated. Did that mean he was beat?

No way.

So his plans hadn't worked so far. Did that mean he'd run out of ideas for convincing her?

Hardly.

In fact, thoughts were swirling through his mind right now. Fueled by Andy's words, the thoughts swept doubt out of the way, pounding it into the ground as they circled, coalesced…and created a truly intriguing idea.

That familiar surge of adrenaline hit him. Oh, man. Forget intriguing, this idea was *great*.

No doubt about it. Annie Justice was as good as signed.

He lifted the mug and took a sip, then paused as the rich, robust flavor filled his senses. Ahh…now *that* was coffee.

"Better?"

Jed's concession slipped out on a smile. "Definitely." He pulled his cell phone out of his pocket. "Now if you'll excuse me, I've got some calls to make."

Andy leaned back, resting his elbows on the counter. "I know that look. You have a plan."

Jed took the letter and tacked it to the wall above his desk, right next to Annie's picture. He studied that picture, then turned back to his friend. "'Action is eloquence,' my dear Andrew."

Andy's exaggerated sigh drew a smile to Jed's face. "If you try to tell me *that's* Obi-Wan Ke—"

"Nope. That's Shakespeare."

"And it means?"

"It means, my man, that you're right. I have a plan. And I owe it to you."

"Now, don't go gettin' all mushy on me." Andy pushed away from the counter. "Just tell me what you need me to do."

Jed punched a number into his cell phone. "Get packed."

"Packed?" Andy crossed his arms over his chest. "To go where?"

"Heaven on earth, ol' bud." Jed grinned. "Heaven on earth."

Dan Justice stood on the sidewalk, staring from the building in front of him to the white sheet of paper in his hand.

He'd been hoping against hope he was wrong. Praying he was wrong. But there was no denying it any longer.

"So, were you right?"

Dan turned to the man next to him. Frank Weeks was a solid cop. He'd been working in the cybercrimes unit for a couple of years and was as close to a computer genius as Dan figured he'd ever meet. "I was right. The letter Annie received in her mailbox was on Expressions stationery."

Killian's stationery.

Frank pulled the gallery door open. "Well then, let's check it out."

As they went inside, Dan schooled himself to stay calm. There had to be an explanation. One other than the obvious.

Killian looked up from where he was standing, studying a painting on the wall, and his brows arched up above the rim of his glasses. "Well, well. Deputy Dan, as I live and breathe. What brings you to my humble gallery? And who's your friend?"

Dan introduced the two, then held the paper out to Killian. "This is what brings us here."

Killian took it, a frown pinching his brow as he read. "Is this some kind of joke?"

"Hardly." Dan shoved his hands in his pockets. "Annie's been receiving threatening notes. First on e-mail, and now this was put in her mailbox." He kept his attention trained on Killian's features. "Notice anything about the paper?"

Killian looked up, an odd light in his eyes at Dan's tone. Then he studied the paper…and his frown deepened. He held it up to the light.

When his gaze met Dan's, there was a hint of something there. Anger? Fear? Dan couldn't quite tell. "Killian, is that Expressions stationery?"

"It is." Killian tapped the bottom right-hand corner of the sheet. "That's our watermark." He handed it back to Dan. "But if you think I had anything to do with this, you're mistaken."

Dan folded the paper and slipped it into his shirt pocket. "You've never been fond of Kodi."

"Dan, get serious!"

"That's quite a temper you have there, friend."

Killian nailed Frank with a glare. "Yes, I have a temper. And no, you are not my friend." He turned back to Dan. "Do you really believe I'd do anything to hurt Annie? I adore her. What's more, I *need* her. She's my star artist. You know as well as I do that anyone could have walked into my office and taken some of the stationery. It's right there, on my desk."

Dan looked past Killian, toward the office at the back of the gallery. "You have a computer?"

"Of course."

Frank cocked his head. "Is it password protected?"

Killian blinked. "Do you speak English? I have no idea what you just said." He waved his hand again. "Ryan deals with the computers, not I."

Dan pursed his lips. That was convenient. Gave Killian plausible deniability.

"Look, just go back there and ask him yourselves."

Dan nodded. "We will. You mind if we look around your office a bit?"

"Look around until you both turn old and gray. You won't find anything, because I didn't send that horrendous note." Killian's tone was decidedly wounded. "Now if you'll *excuse* me, I have crates to unpack."

With that, he spun on his heel and stalked away.

"Testy sort, isn't he?"

Dan inclined his head. "He is that. But then, I would be too if someone accused me of terrorizing a friend."

"You think he's innocent, then?"

"I wish I knew." Dan headed for the office. "Let's check out the computers."

As Killian had said, Ryan was there, sitting at the computer. He looked like a startled owl when Dan and Frank came in.

"Dan! What are you...? Is everything okay?"

Dan explained what was happening, and horror filled Ryan's features.

"Who could do such a thing?" His mouth fell open. "Oh, now wait a minute. Surely you don't think Killian is involved?"

"That's what I'm here to find out." Frank looked at the computer. "Is the system password protected?"

"Sure." Ryan grabbed a piece of paper and jotted the password down. "Killian wouldn't have it any other way."

Dan frowned. "Killian wouldn't?"

"Are you kidding? I was here all of a week when he had me sitting here, learning everything I could about computer protection and security. He's a great instructor, you know. Taught me everything I know."

"Killian did." Frank glanced at Dan. "Taught you about computers."

"He's a veritable Bill Gates." Ryan handed the paper with the password to Frank. "Here, feel free to get on and check things out. But I haven't noticed anything out of the norm. And I'm on this system almost every day." He scooted his chair back and stood. "Now I'd better go see if I can soothe Killian's ruffled feathers."

"You ask me, those feathers needed some ruffling."

Ryan cast a quick look over his shoulder at Frank. "Easy for you to say." He opened the office door. "You don't have to work with the man every day."

"Thank heaven for small favors."

Dan managed a tight smile at his friend's mumbled comment, but his gaze followed Ryan as he hotfooted it to the back rooms of the gallery. Right now, there was only one favor he begged from heaven.

Find the creep threatening Annie.

Because for all his efforts to convince himself these notes were just a prank, Dan couldn't escape the sense that something was coming. Something bad.

Something with his little sister smack dab in the middle of it.

SEVENTEEN

*"Don't let us make imaginary evils,
when you know we have so many real ones to encounter."*

OLIVER GOLDSMITH

*"Woe to those who go to great depths
to hide their plans from the LORD,
who do their work in darkness and think,
'Who sees us? Who will know?'"*

ISAIAH 29:15

It wasn't working.

He'd done all he could, tried every avenue available, all to no avail.

Fine, then. So be it. Annie would not listen to him? Would not surrender? Then he would go after her. It would be inconvenient. Take him away from all he needed to be doing. And yet…

If this was what it took to secure her, then he was willing. So much to be gained if it worked out as he planned. So much to benefit him.

And her. There was good in this for her. She might not see it, not at first. Then again, who knew? If he painted it just right, put it in the proper packaging, she might well see it as a gift. A blessing.

Yes, that pleased him. Being a blessing. That fit with who he was. With the benefactor he longed to be.

Good. It was settled. He would go to her. It was the right thing to do. The only thing to do if he wanted to win.

And he did want that.

More than he'd wanted anything in a very, very long time.

EIGHTEEN

"Want to make God laugh? Tell Him you've got plans."

ANONYMOUS

"'Stop right where you are! Look for the old, godly way, and walk in it. Travel its path, and you will find rest for your soul.'"

JEREMIAH 6:16

OCTOBER 2

Jed and Andy arrived at the Medford airport while it was still dark.

That's what happened when you booked a flight at the last minute. You got stuck on the red-eye special. They loaded everything into the rental car and followed the map they'd found on-line to Annie's home on the outskirts of Central Point, a small town just outside Medford.

The operative word there being *small*.

Andy stared out the passenger window as they drove down Pine Street, Central Point's main drag. "Good grief—" he glanced at Jed—"what'd we do? End up in Mayberry?"

"Come on, Andy. You're just used to LA. It's not that small."

"Yeah, well…it's not that big either."

"Maybe not, but you've got to admit that ten minutes to get from the airport to the other side of town beats an hour and a half in traffic any day."

"Hmm."

Trust Andy to be succinct. Jed fought a yawn. "You have the map?"

Amazing what you could find on the Internet these days. They'd typed in Annie's name and address, and up popped a map leading them right to her home. Jed wasn't sure if that was cool or scary.

Maybe a little of both.

"Yup, right here. And that's the road we want." Andy pointed at the T intersection, then to the left. "Turn here."

Jed looked up at the street sign. "Old Stage Road, huh?" As remote as they were, he wouldn't be all that surprised to see a stage ambling down the road toward them.

"Yee-haw, dude. We're in the Wild West."

Jed raised a brow and shook his head. "There are cities here, Andy."

"Hey, compared to LA, this is Hicksville, man."

"Compared to LA, most anything is."

"Yeah, well..." Andy looked around at the hills. "Let's just say I'll be happy to get back to my concrete and bright lights. It's dark out here. I mean, we're talkin' dark!"

Jed couldn't argue there. They'd apparently outdistanced any streetlights, and since the sun hadn't seen fit to make an appearance yet, blackness surrounded them. He leaned forward, looking out the windshield. "Yeah, but look at the stars. You don't see stars like that in LA."

Andy crossed his arms over his chest and slumped down in the seat. "I prefer my stars with two legs, thank you." He tipped an imaginary hat. "Arnie, how's it goin'? Tom Hanks, long time no see."

"Anybody ever told you you're a funny man?"

Andy grinned. "Sure!"

"They were lying."

"Ha-ha-ha." Andy propped his feet on the dashboard. "So let me get this straight. We're going to stake out Annie's place, follow her to some public setting, then arrange a way to meet her in person."

"No."

Andy shot him a look. "No?"

"*We're* not going to do anything. I am."

"Riiiight. Because once she meets you, she'll be so over-whelmed that she won't be able to refuse you anything."

Jed scowled. "Don't be an idiot."

"Oh, *I'm* the one being an idiot." Andy nodded. "Whatever you say, bro."

"Look, if I can just meet this woman, get to know her a little, earn her trust, then there's a chance she'll agree to do the show."

"But you're not going to tell her who you are."

Jed stared straight ahead. "Not right away…"

"And if she asks your name?"

"I'll give it to her. Jed."

"Jed. Just Jed. No last name."

"Andy, the whole point is that she get to know me without knowing who I am."

Andy's gaze went to the roof of the car. "Do you hear your-self? This is crazy, man. You're going to lie to this woman to gain her trust? How is that supposed to work? And you don't think she'll want to rip your face off when she finds out who you really are and why you're here?"

"No way. She won't be mad. More like flattered that I'd go to so much trouble."

Andy fell silent, which Jed counted as a true blessing. Sadly, it didn't last long.

"Look, I've been with you on a lot of crazy things. And I admit, they've all worked out, but—"

"Well, there you have it. And this one will work out too."

"—but *this* one? It's just nuts, Jed. Worse, it's wrong."

Irritation ruffled Jed's nerves. "Wrong? What do you mean wrong?"

"I mean wrong, as in not right! As in lying and deceiving and playing games with people's lives."

"Whoa, bud. I'm not touching this woman's life."

"Then how about her heart?"

Enough. Jed jerked the steering wheel and pulled to the side of the dark road. He met Andy, glare for glare. "Her what?"

"Come on, Curry. Don't be stupid. You're playing in dangerous waters. Women see things differently than we do, and you know it."

"*Things? What things?*"

"Men. Relationships—"

Jed held up a forestalling hand. "Relationships? Pal, you are way off the mark here. This is not a relationship. Not even close. I'm just going to meet the woman. Spend a little time with her."

"Get her to like you. To trust you."

Jed slipped the car back into gear and pulled onto the road. "Exactly. See? Nothing like a relationship."

"And once this nonrelationship is established, you'll tell her the truth."

Uh-oh. Andy wasn't going to like this. "Sort of."

His friend's narrowed gaze did not bode well. "There is no 'sort of' with the truth, Jed."

"I know. But it's nothing to worry about. I'll just tell her I didn't know it was her when I met her. That it was all circumstantial. I was here to visit my mom, went for a walk, and met a nice woman. How was I supposed to know she was the Annie Justice I'd called and talked with?"

"Because there are so many Annie Justices who live in the area and have big, black German shepherds."

He ignored Andy's cutting sarcasm. "I'll tell her that once I realized it was her, I didn't want to ruin things by saying who I was. Not until we had a chance to get to know each other. You know, to be friends."

"And she'll buy this load of twaddle? What, is her IQ the same as her shoe size?"

"She'll buy it because she wants to. Because by then she'll like me and trust me."

Andy leaned against the passenger's door. "Well. You've got it all figured out, don't you? I'm along for the ride…why?"

"To annoy me?"

Andy didn't reply to that, so Jed went on. "You're here so that when Annie agrees to the taping, we don't have to wait to get started. That's it. Plain and simple."

"Simple." Andy nodded slowly, but Jed could tell it wasn't because he agreed. "Tell me something, Curry. Why this woman? I mean, it's not like she's the only person we can feature on the show."

Jed wished he had a good answer for that, but he didn't. When it came right down to it, he didn't know *why* he was so interested in Annie Justice. Sure, her story would be perfect for *Everyday Heroes*. And viewers always loved seeing animals do amazing things. But if Jed was honest, he had to admit that his interest went far deeper than even he understood.

Fortunately Andy saved him from having to come up with an answer.

"There it is. That's her place."

Jed pulled over, and the two of them studied the wrought-iron gate blocking the long driveway.

"Man." Andy shook his head. "No way we're gettin' through there unnoticed."

"Well then—" Jed glanced around, spotted a driveway on the other side of the road, and pulled in. He jockeyed the car around until they were situated where they could see the driveway—"we'll just sit here and wait for her to come out."

"Sit here. In the car."

Jed nodded. "As long as it takes."

"Anyone ever tell you you're a genius, Jed?"

He eyed his buddy. "No."

Andy reached down and pulled the lever to lay the seat back, then crossed his arms over his chest. "I didn't think so."

October 2—A Clover Day (Green)
Light.

It held unimagined power. Like the breath of life from the Creator, it flowed through the windows of Annie's studio, a stream of warmth caressing the textures, embracing the colors.

Pieces of stained glass hung in the windows—an array of colors. When the sunlight hit them, it enriched the hues, lifted them free, and carried them from the glass to infuse the room with a shimmering rainbow.

And what better place to have a rainbow than in her studio, the perfect haven for creativity? Cubbyholes covered one wall, holding different sizes and styles of glass sheets. Her paints, powders, and brushes were hung on Peg-Board on the back wall, just above a light table. In the center of the room were her work tables—one for sketching, one for piecing together the windows. Large drawers held cutters, pliers, and other tools, as well as a variety of lead came, copper foils, acids, and more. Opposite the cubbies were grinders and soldering tools. Filter masks hung from hooks on the wall.

But what made her studio most effective was its design. Large and open with windows—both plain glass and leaded—on all sides, natural light had free access from every angle. From the first rays of dawn to the last sigh of sunset, light permeated the studio.

Usually, watching the dance of colors, the blend of light and shadow, was all it took to set Annie's pencil dancing.

Here's hoping, she thought as she balanced her coffee mug in one hand and held the door open for Kodi with the other, *today is a usual day.* Heaven knew she needed one.

Annie made her way through the darkness of the studio. She loved this time of day, the twinkling before dawn, when darkness still cloaked the world. Fortunately her night vision was strong, so she could navigate without turning on any lights. Kodi padded behind her, making her way to her dog bed. As Annie eased onto her stool, Kodi pawed her bed into submission, circled twice, then dropped with a deep-chested groan onto the cushion.

Oh, to be so content, Annie thought with a smile. She cupped her hands around her coffee mug and took a sip of the hot, robust coffee. She could just see her pencils laid out, sheets of white paper before her on the worktable.

Okay, Lord. I'm ready whenever You are.

The morning silence enfolded her like the strong, warm arms of an old friend. She lifted her face to it, letting her eyes close and prayers fill her heart. Prayers of praise and worship, of supplication. Asking God to meet her here. To show her the work He had for her. To use her art for His purposes and glory. And as she prayed, deep inside the excitement sparked and grew.

Dawn was coming.

In mere seconds it would arrive, the first rays turning the darkened room into an almost sacred place as light emerged—tentative at first, then exploding with abandon, pouring through the glass Annie had chosen, the windows she'd formed. And as Annie watched the display, images would spark to life in her mind and break free, traveling through her pencil onto the page. It was in those hushed moments that she had the powerful, humbling sense of God's hand upon hers, guiding her fingers, whispering encouragement and inspiration as her sketches took shape.

It was time. Annie knew it as surely as she knew her calling. She opened her eyes, watching the new day scatter color across the floor, coaxing out the rich tones of the wood. Textured and beveled glass caught the growing light, wrestled it, then cast it on the walls, where it flickered like a frustrated fairy.

The splendor never failed to fuel her imagination.

Annie set her mug on a coaster, then leaned forward on the stool, took up a pencil, and waited.

And waited.

And waited.

Okay…so it *almost* never failed.

"Aargh!" Annie flung the pencil back onto the worktable. It bounced and rolled across the table and dropped over the edge, landing on Kodi's head.

Kodi jumped up, barking an alarm, though Annie wasn't sure if it was at the offending pencil or at her. "I'm sorry, girl." Annie slid from her stool and paced the studio. "I just wish I knew what was wrong with me!"

For days now she'd been trying to come up with a concept for Serafina Stowe's window, but all she had to show for her efforts was a trash can full of wadded-up sketches. That, and an ever increasing frustration.

She'd thought she had a good idea that day with the flowers. Was so sure she was on the right track. But try as she might, the images wouldn't flow. Something was missing. What, she didn't know—but it was something important. Something she had to figure out if she was going to fulfill Cletus's wish.

Why had she ever agreed to do this? How was a window—stained glass or otherwise—supposed to help people see God in a new way?

She turned and almost tripped over Kodi. She opened her mouth to yell at the dog, to tell her to get back on her bed, then stopped. It wasn't Kodi's fault she was in this mess. She had no one to blame but herself.

Well, herself and Kyla.

Come to think of it, *she* got her into this mess. She should call Kyla and tell her to do the window.

Annie squatted beside Kodi, and the shepherd scooted as close as she could, laying her massive head on Annie's chest, her nose just touching Annie's chin. Annie scratched the dog's ears. "'Annie, you're supposed to do this,'" she mimicked, "'I just know it.'" She took hold of Kodi's face and looked into her eyes. "Why didn't you stop me, girl? Make me tell my sister to take a leap?"

"Aroow-roo-row!"

Annie laughed. "Yeah, you're right. You weren't there." She patted the dog's head, then stood. "That'll teach me to leave you home, huh?"

"Arrroww!"

"Well, how 'bout I make up for it by taking you for a walk? Maybe go to the doggy park and throw Frisbees?"

Kodi's big ears perked and she circled Annie, tossing her head back and forth and wagging her tail.

Annie headed for the door. At least she'd come up with one good idea today. That was something.

Not much, mind you. But something.

Jed and Andy had been waiting for about an hour when Jed made a discovery.

Car windows do not make good pillows.

He shifted for the twentieth time, trying to find a position in the driver's seat that didn't kill his neck.

No such luck.

He stretched his legs to the side but only succeeded in kicking Andy.

"Man, would you knock it off? I'm *trying* to catch some z's here."

Jed sat up. "Sorry. I just can't get comfortable."

"Yeah, well seeing as this was your genius idea, I'm not feeling too sorry for you."

Jed rubbed the weariness from his eyes.

"Sun's comin' up." Andy's comment was swallowed in a yawn that stretched his mouth wide.

"About time. Here's hoping she's a morning person."

They fell silent then, watching the sunrise color the sky. Andy leaned forward, resting his elbows on the dashboard and peering out the windshield.

"Now that's some kind of artwork."

"What?" Jed craned his neck.

"That, you doof. The sunrise. One second it's pitch-black out there, then wham! Color everywhere." Andy leaned back, stretching his arms above his head. "Kinda makes you think, doesn't it?"

Jed turned his head away. "Don't start."

"I'm just sayin', something like that doesn't just happen."

Flicking the door lock up, Jed shoved the door open and stepped out into the cool morning air.

"You know—"

Jed shot a glare over the car at Andy, who'd gotten out on his side and stood there, arms folded on top of the car as he studied Jed.

"—I've taken you for a lot of things, Curry. Reckless. Crazy. Talented. Determined. But there's one thing I've never taken you for. Until now."

"And that is?"

Andy's arms slid off the car. "A coward."

Jed's eyes narrowed. "Excuse me?"

"Face it, pal. Ever since Ken was killed, you've been on the run."

"On the run? From who?"

"That's what I'm trying to figure out. At first I thought it was God, but you've been avoiding Him for as long as I've known you."

"*Andy.*"

Apparently he didn't catch the low warning in Jed's tone. Either that, or he just didn't care.

"So now I'm wondering if what you're really running from is yourself. What is it inside that pushes you so hard?"

What was pushing Jed now was Andy. His words. They were hitting him a lot harder than he liked. He turned away, falling back on the only defense he had at hand. "'You cram these words into mine ears against the stomach of my sense.'"

"Nuh-uh. Shakespeare isn't gonna get you out of th—"

The sound of metal on metal caught them both by surprise, and they spun to look across the road. The gate across Annie Justice's driveway was opening.

"Quick! Get in!"

Andy scrambled around the car and jumped inside just as Jed turned the key and revved the engine. As they watched, a dark blue Jeep rolled through the gate. Though Jed couldn't see the driver's features, he was sure it was a woman. And that a huge dog was sitting next to her, in the passenger's seat.

Annie Justice and Kodi. It had to be.

The Jeep turned onto Old Stage Road and headed toward town. Jed waited a moment, then put the car in gear, following at a safe distance.

Andy finally broke the silence. "Look, man, I'm sorry. I don't mean to push."

Jed shrugged. "Let's just focus on the job, Andy."

His friend nodded, and they fell into a strained silence. But as Jed drove, careful to keep Annie's vehicle in view, he knew the conversation wasn't over.

It never was.

No matter how much Jed wanted it to be.

NINETEEN

*"Each of us may be sure that if God sends us on stony paths
He will provide us with strong shoes, and He will not send us
out on any journey for which He does not equip us well."*

ALEXANDER MACLAREN

"Beware, the Lord is about to take firm hold of you."

ISAIAH 22:17, NIV

OCTOBER 2
8:00 a.m.

"Wow."

Andy's hushed exclamation pretty well summed it up. Jed
had known from the picture of Annie in the paper that she was
an attractive woman, in a cute and spunky kind of way.

But the real thing was far more impressive than he'd ever
imagined. More...alluring.

Andy let go of the branch he'd been holding, and it snapped
back to swat Jed in the face.

"Hey! Watch it!"

"Sorry."

Funny, Andy didn't sound sorry. He just sounded irritated.

"I'm not used to hiding in bushes and spying on people."

They'd followed Annie to a Dairy Queen. When she pulled
into the parking lot, Andy had looked from the fast-food joint to
Jed. "What? She gonna buy the dog a burger?"

They pulled to the side of the street, watching as Annie parked and got out of the vehicle. She clipped a leash on Kodi and hefted a backpack, and the two of them turned and headed right for Jed and Andy's car.

"Duck!"

The two men slumped down, but they needn't have worried. Annie and Kodi walked past their car, heading for a bridge that would take them over a large creek.

Andy punched Jed's arm. "Park, before we lose her!"

Jed pulled into a parking spot, then they hopped out and hurried after their quarry. Fortunately, Annie's destination was just on the other side of the bridge: a large, fenced-in dog park. Once inside the enclosure, she set the backpack on a picnic table and pulled out a number of Frisbees.

Jed and Andy strolled along the path, but as soon as Annie turned her back to them to throw the Frisbee, they ducked into a stand of tall evergreens.

"I feel like an idiot!" Andy hissed.

"You look like one too." Jed pulled a piece of tree out of his friend's hair and held it out for him to see.

Andy snatched it and flicked it over his shoulder. "I've had enough of this. Either you get out there, or I will."

"Fine. Just wait until she won't see us—" Jed almost swallowed the rest of the sentence when something smacked the trees just to the left of them. He saw a Frisbee stuck in the branches not five feet away. A quick look toward the dog park revealed that Annie was heading for the gate, coming to retrieve the toy.

"Go get it!" Andy shoved him.

He shoved back. "What?"

"The Frisbee, you nitwit! Get it and give it to her!"

Jed considered telling Andy to take a leap, then decided it was time to do what he'd come here to do.

Meet Annie Justice.

◈   ◈   ◈

"Arroww-roww!"

Annie looked down at Kodi. "Hey, I never said I was good at throwing Frisbees."

"Rowww!"

She nudged the dog with her hip, slipping past her out the gate of the dog park. One of these days she would actually learn how to throw a Frisbee. She ended up chasing the silly things more than Kodi did. "Now where did that thing go?"

She was pretty sure it flew over the fence somewhere toward the middle. She started toward the trees, only to be met by a tall stranger walking toward her. She glanced around them, startled. What was someone doing out here this early? If he'd been dressed for running, that'd be different. But it was as though he just appeared out of nowhere.

Her steps faltered as he drew closer. She studied the trees to the right of them lining the bike path, judging how far she was from Kodi and the gate. Then she looked back at the man approaching her.

And frowned.

Odd.

He looked familiar.

"Mornin'." He held out the Frisbee as he reached her. "This belongs to you, I believe?"

Annie studied his features. Had she met him before? If so, she couldn't recall where. But those eyes, the way his smile lit his face...

She shook off the sensation and managed a smile. "Actually it belongs to the monster." She nodded toward Kodi, who was up on her hind legs, front paws on the fence, watching them with that puckered, half-worried expression she got when she wasn't sure what was happening.

Annie knew how the dog felt.

The man's chuckle, a low rumble of sound, was rich and appealing. Annie looked at him again. She had seen him before; she was sure of it. But where?

"Looks like she's afraid you're going to leave her there."

"Fat chance. If she saw me leaving without her, she'd be up and over that fence." Annie took the Frisbee from him, staring at it as her mind scrambled to place him. Compelling number nine eyes—the color of Belgian chocolate—with just a hint of gold flecks. His smile was open and relaxed, as was his stance.

Maybe he was just a nice guy out for a walk.

"Well, she's a beauty. And she's lucky to have an owner who loves her as much as you do."

A really nice guy.

She held up the Frisbee. "Thanks, again. I'm afraid I'm pretty awful at throwing these things."

The man glanced back at the trees, his mouth quirked in a crooked grin. "I noticed."

There was that smile again. Annie liked the way his eyes crinkled at the edges when he smiled. There was something... comfortable about him.

"Tell you what—"

His voice startled her from her thoughts, and warmth filled her cheeks. "Hmm?"

"I'll make you a trade."

Careful, Annie. He may seem familiar, but he's still a stranger. She shuffled back a step. "A trade?"

"You let me pet your 'monster' over there, and I'll teach you how to throw the Frisbee."

She should say no; she knew she should. It wasn't smart to give an opening to some guy she didn't know—no matter how familiar he seemed. No, she needed to just give him the ol' "Thanks, but no thanks" and walk away.

That decided, Annie opened her mouth. "Sure. Sounds good."

What? What was she saying?

"Okay then. Lead on."

She looked at the man. "Right." Nodded. "Okay. Good."

Stop rambling, Annie. You sound like an idiot. Just turn and start walking.

She did as her brain bid, and the man fell in step beside her.

"By the way—" he held a hand out to her—"I'm Jed."

Jed. J. A deep raspberry halo shimmered into focus around him. She took his hand, intending to drop it as quickly as she could. But her hand fit into his so well and there was such warmth and strength in that grip that she held on for a heartbeat.

Then two.

Her eyes widened. *Oh...my gosh...*

The knight. He was the knight. From her dream. Not exactly, of course. But his features, that smile, those eyes...even his color. They were all so similar that Annie almost couldn't breathe.

His gaze dropped to their joined hands, then traveled back up to her face. "And you are?"

"Oh!" She let go of his hand, then turned to unlatch the gate into the dog park, frantic to hold on to something solid.

This couldn't be happening.

"Kodi. No, I mean, that's *her* name. The monster, that is." She puffed out a breath. "I'm Annie." Pulling the gate open wide, she waited as he followed her in, then entered the park. Kodi was right there to greet her.

"Kodi, huh?"

Normally, Annie would have made sure she stayed between Kodi and a stranger, but this time she found herself stepping back. Why?

Maybe that same sense of familiarity made her confident they'd be okay together. That Kodi would recognize him as...what? As a figment from her dreams?

Oh, Annie, you're losing it!

She stepped forward. "Hang on—"

But Jed was already holding out his hand, letting Kodi sniff it. And before she knew what was happening, Kodi was up on her hind legs, paws planted on Jed's chest, licking his face as though he were a long lost brother.

"Whoa!" Jed laughed, giving Kodi a hug, then taking her paws in his hands and nudging her back on all fours. He slanted a smile at Annie. "Now that's a friendly dog."

Annie took hold of Kodi's collar and tugged at her. But the animal was almost wiggling herself into a frenzy trying to reach Jed again. "I'm so sorry!"

"It's okay. Really. I like dogs." He took the Frisbee from Annie's hand and jogged off, Kodi on his heels, barking and grinning like a canine fool.

Annie followed more slowly, mind numb, utterly and completely speechless. But her mind raced with one pointed question: *God, what in the world are You up to now?*

An hour later, Annie watched as the Frisbee she'd just thrown sailed across the dog park, Kodi racing after it in hot pursuit. She turned amazed eyes to Jed. "You, sir, are a miracle worker."

"You just needed some pointers on technique, that's all. Face it, Annie, you're a natural."

An unladylike snort escaped her. "Hardly. I can't count the trees and bushes I've assaulted with rampant Frisbees. And poor Kodi spent more time picking them up off the ground than catching them."

Speaking of Kodi, Annie turned just in time to see the shepherd leap into the air and snag the still soaring Frisbee, then turn and come loping back. Annie held her hand out, and Kodi came to press the Frisbee into her palm. "Good girl."

Kodi's response was to crouch, ready for action.

"Does she ever get tired?"

Annie laughed, launching the Frisbee again, delighting in its smooth flight and in Kodi's unadulterated joy as she chased it. "I think I've seen her tired once, after we were on a callout all day." She smiled at Jed. "But she may have just been trying to make me feel better."

"Callout?"

For a second, Jed's question surprised Annie. She felt so comfortable with him that it was like they'd known each other forever, heard each other's stories at least a dozen times. But the curiosity puckering his brow reminded her that not only did she not know anything about him, he had no clue who she was or what she did.

"Kodi and I are involved in search and rescue. A callout is when someone gets lost and the sheriff's department calls us to help find them."

Interest sparked in Jed's eyes. "Very cool." He knelt as Kodi loped back to them, holding out his hand for the Frisbee. She came to him without hesitation, sitting and offering the Frisbee as sweet as you please.

No doubt about it. Annie's dog was in love.

Not that she blamed the beast. Jed was an appealing guy. Or as appealing as someone could be when you'd only known him for an hour.

"So…do you live in the area?" As silly as it was, Annie had to force herself not to cross her fingers.

Jed glanced up at her, then straightened. "I grew up here, went to school here, but no, I don't live here any longer."

She should have known. Pushing aside the sharp pang of disappointment, Annie reached down and took the Frisbee from Kodi. "Okay, girl, that's enough. Time to head home."

Kodi trotted alongside her as she walked to the picnic table. Jed followed, standing next Annie as she loaded everything in her backpack. He reached out for the pile of large papers and spread them out on the table.

"Did you draw these?"

She glanced at the sketches she'd made of Kodi. "Yes."

Jed picked one up, looking at it in silence. Just when Annie was about to crawl out of her skin, he turned impressed eyes her way. "You're an artist."

Just that simple. Complete acceptance of who and what she was. No question in his statement whatsoever. "I am."

"And a good one."

Warmth started somewhere down in her toes and traveled to the top of her head. "Thanks." She took the sketches and slipped them into the backpack. "So you're just here for a visit?"

Jed gave a slow nod. "Sort of. I'm actually going to be in town for a little while."

She perked up at that, though she did her best not to let it show. "Oh?" She zipped the backpack shut and lifted it, ready to slip it over a shoulder. "Well, that's nice."

Jed reached out and took the backpack. "Actually—" he slipped it over his shoulder—"what was nice was this."

Annie tried not to react to his steady gaze or the sincerity in his tone, but she couldn't keep a hint of warmth from brushing her cheeks. She clipped Kodi's leash onto her collar, then led the way to the gate. They exited, and Annie hesitated. If she were sensible, she'd just ask for her backpack, tell him it was nice to meet him, then say good-bye and go home.

If she were sensible. "Lead on."

Understanding shone in Jed's eyes. He didn't seem any more eager to part than she was. "I'll walk you to your car if that's okay."

"Sure. Fine. Uh…" She bit her lip. "I'm parked over there."

They walked in silence for a few moments. Then Jed's voice broke the silence.

"You're parked by the Dairy Queen?"

Annie glanced at him. Why was he talking so loud when she was right next to him?

"Me too." The volume increased again. "So I'll just walk over there with you."

What on earth? "Okay."

"To your car."

Annie started to ask Jed if everything was okay, but the question died in her throat when something suddenly rustled in the trees along the path. Kodi jerked to a halt, her hackles rising, and issued a deep growl. Annie just had time to tighten up on Kodi's leash before a form burst through the needle-laden branches of the trees and came stumbling out.

At that point, two things happened simultaneously.

One: Kodi crouched, ready to jump between Annie and what seemed to be a homeless man stumbling toward them. But the shepherd didn't get the chance to protect her mistress because *two:* Jed's arm circled Annie's waist, and tucking her close against him, he sidestepped, putting himself between her and the man.

Almost without missing a stride, Jed swept Annie past the still staggering man, and she dragged Kodi along. The shepherd strained at her leash, pulling behind them, still growling. But that didn't impede Jed's progress one iota.

He all but carried Annie across the bridge over Bear Creek, not slowing until they'd crossed the street and stood in the parking lot. Only then did he look down at her—and two bright spots of red blossomed in his cheeks as he apparently realized he still held her close against him.

His arm dropped away, leaving Annie a bit breathless. Said breathlessness, she told herself in her best stern schoolmarm inner voice, was because of their hurried pace. It certainly was *not* because of the unexpected pleasure that had flooded her at being tucked in the protective circle of Jed's arm.

Certainly not.

She stepped back, smoothing her jacket. "Well…" She looked down at the ground, suddenly quite fascinated with the blacktop. "That was…um…interesting."

Jed rubbed a hand behind his neck. "I'm sorry, Annie. I didn't mean to manhandle you—"

"I didn't mind." Oh, good grief. Could she possibly sound any more desperate? "I mean, I appreciate you grabbing me…"

Okay. Yes. She could.

"That is, I appreciate *why* you grabbed me."

Stop, Annie. Just stop talking. Now.

But she needn't have worried about Jed's reaction to her babbling. He was too immersed in apologizing to notice that she'd just made a total fool of herself.

"I don't usually do that. You know, grab women I've just met. Or women I've known a long time. I'm not usually a grabber—" He clamped his mouth shut, eyes lifting to the sky. "What I'm saying is, and…uh, that guy—"

"He was probably homeless. They tend to camp behind those trees along the creek."

"Right, that homeless guy caught me by surprise. I just wanted to make sure you didn't see him." His eyes widened a fraction. "I mean, you know, that you didn't have to deal with him coming up and asking for a handout. Or whatever."

Silence fell between them for a moment, and they stood there, staring at each other.

The laughter started with Annie. It was just a ripple at first, a giggle triggered by her frayed nerves and the images that flitted through her mind as she pictured what they must have looked like as they hotfooted it over the bridge, poor protective Kodi in tow. When Jed's deep chuckle chimed in, the ripple expanded into full-blown laughter.

They leaned against Annie's Jeep, laughing until they were weak. Kodi paced back and forth between them, and the worry puckering her black brow—probably that her mistress had gone right 'round the bend—just made Annie laugh even harder.

When she could finally breathe again, Annie laid a hand on Jed's arm. "Thanks, Jed. I needed that."

Gold lights twinkled in those laughing brown eyes. "You needed someone practically hauling you off your feet and dragging you and your dog across a bridge?"

Annie giggled again. "Well, that too. But no, the laugh. I needed the laugh."

"Yeah." Jed leaned his head against the Jeep. "So did I." He stared at the sky, then closed his eyes. "It's been a tough couple weeks."

The rough emotion in those simple words tugged at her heart, and before she could stop herself, she put her hand on his arm. "I'm sorry."

He looked at her, and it was as though a cloud drifted across his features. Something was troubling him, and Annie wanted to help. More than she'd ever wanted to help anyone before.

"Jed, what can I do?"

Raw emotion flickered in the depth of his eyes, and his jaw tensed.

She'd offended him. Or upset him. Oh, why hadn't she just kept her mouth shu—

He stilled her inner recriminations when he took her hand in his. "'Lady you bereft me of all words.'"

The ragged edge to those soft words tore at her, confusing her even more. Who was this man? And what was going on inside him?

He squeezed her hand, then released her, but the warmth of his smile echoed in his voice. "Thanks, Annie. This was great. Really. I mean, I know you don't know me from Adam, but I enjoyed spending time with you and Kodi."

She didn't even try to hide her agreement. "Me too." She tipped her head. "I mean, I enjoyed spending time with you."

He straightened, his expression sobering. "So, what do you say we don't let it end here?"

"I'd like that."

They shared a smile. "Great. How about coffee?" Hesitation puckered his brow. "You do drink coffee, don't you?"

"More like mainline it."

"Perfect. So how about we meet for coffee tomorrow? You name the place and time."

"Melello's. Behind Costco. Twelve-thirty."

Approval shone in his eyes at her ready reply. "It's a date."

She unlocked the Jeep, letting Kodi jump in and settle down. Jed held the driver's door open for her, waiting as she buckled her seat belt and lowered the window before closing the door. "See you tomorrow."

"Tomorrow." Amazing what a wonderful word that was. Annie hadn't ever realized it before.

She started the Jeep, backed out of the parking spot, and **waved** out the window as she pulled onto the street. As she **turned the** corner on the main drag, she took one last look in the rearview mirror—and felt her heart jump.

Jed stood there, hands in his pockets, watching her. And even from this distance she could tell that his face bore a broad, goofy grin.

The very same grin peeking back from her reflection.

"I gotta admit it, you're one smooth dude."

Jed swiveled. "Andy! What the *heck* did you think you were doing back there?"

He held his hands up. "Hey, it's not my fault. If I'd known you were going to play Mr. Frisbee Coach for an hour, I would have snuck out and gone back to the car. But I had no idea how long you'd be or if it was safe to come out, so I stayed there. And you know how late we got in last night. And how early we got up…"

Jed eyed him. "You fell asleep."

"I fell asleep." Andy hunched his shoulders. "So when you hollered like that, it scared the bo-diddly outta me. I jumped up so fast I got dizzy, but I knew you guys were comin' so I tried to get outta sight."

Jed fished in his pocket for the car keys. "And stumbled right in front of us."

"What can I say. I'm a master of timing." He gazed after Annie's Jeep. "So you're meeting her again tomorrow, eh?"

Jed wasn't so sure he liked Andy's tone. Like he thought Jed was doing something wrong. "Yeah. I'm meeting her. That's the plan, remember?" He punched the remote, unlocking the car doors.

"So we're still working the plan?" Andy pulled the door open and slid inside the car.

Jed followed suit, glancing at his friend sideways as he started the engine. "What else would we be doing?"

Andy rested an elbow on the glass of the passenger side window. "I dunno, man. You just seemed kind of…involved out there. I mean, if you coulda seen the look on your face when you watched that woman drive away."

"It was an act."

Doubt lifted Andy's brows. "Pretty convincing act."

"That's the point, isn't it? To be convincing? To get her trust so I can convince her to do the show?"

Andy propped his feet on the dashboard. "Whatever it takes, huh?"

Jed clenched his teeth. "That's right."

"No matter who it hurts."

He shoved the car into gear. "Nobody's gonna get hurt, Andy."

"Uh-huh." He slumped down in the seat, closing his eyes. "I'll bet you even tell yourself you believe that."

"I *do* believe it."

Though slow in coming, Andy's reply was succinct. "And that, my friend, is the most disturbing fact of all."

TWENTY

*"Twenty years from now you will be more disappointed
by the things you didn't do than by the ones you did do.
So throw off the bowlines. Sail away from the safe harbor.
Catch the trade winds in your sails. Explore. Dream. Discover."*

MARK TWAIN

"'You don't understand now...someday you will.'"

JOHN 13:7

OCTOBER 6—A DAFFODIL DAY (YELLOW)

He should be asleep. Why wasn't he asleep?

The grating sound of a buzz saw with a sinus infection reverberated through the room, and Jed cast a baleful glance at Andy's sleeping form. The fact that he'd forgotten to buy earplugs didn't help. But if he was fair—which he really didn't feel like being at this point—he'd have to admit that Andy's snoring wasn't the problem.

Jed rubbed his gritty eyes, then went back to the vigil he'd been keeping for the last four nights: staring out the hotel window at the darkness, the weight of exhaustion pressing him down, totally—infuriatingly—wide awake.

He lay his head back and closed his eyes. Willed himself to fall asleep. Instead, images and sounds filled his head. As if a miniscule movie projector were tucked at the back of his cerebellum, a scene jumped to life on the screen of his closed eyes. The same scene he'd been seeing for weeks.

Fire. The house. Ken's triumphant smile. *Never lets me down…*

Jed pushed himself out of the chair, going to the bathroom sink. He turned the faucet and scooped water over his face, letting the cold slap him, shocking the last remnants of the images from his mind.

He had to get a grip. So what happened was bad. Fine. It was over and done with. It wasn't his fault. Wasn't anyone's fault. It just was.

All he had to do was convince himself of that.

Yeah. Right.

Wiping an arm over his dripping face, he made his way back to his bed. Sitting on the edge, he leaned down, reaching under the bed and pulling out the book he'd slid there the first night they arrived.

Ken's Bible.

With those words *"Don't let Kenny down"* embedded deep in his soul, Jed hadn't been able to leave the Bible anywhere. He'd thought about it. A lot. Maybe he'd give it to someone who'd actually read it.

But every time he considered the options, the conclusion was the same. Ken gave him the Bible.

So though he'd held true to his word and hadn't cracked the cover again, Jed carried it with him wherever he went. Of course, he was careful to keep it out of sight.

Last thing he needed was Andy seeing him with this thing. Jed squinted through the darkness, making sure his friend was still asleep. Even if he hadn't been able to see the rise and fall of Andy's breathing, the buzz saw would have been evidence enough.

The guy was dead to the world.

Envy slithered through Jed, and he pushed it aside. He'd be able to sleep again soon. Shoot, a few more nights like this, and he'd flat pass out. That'd get him a little rest.

He looked down at the book in his hands. The feel of it was so familiar. When he was a kid, how many nights had he spent poring over these pages, reading, pleading, seeking the magic words that would make his world right again?

But there were no such words. And when Jed had finally accepted that, he thought the disappointment would kill him.

He slid the book back under the bed, then sat there, staring at the floor. And he knew. The time had come. He couldn't put it off any longer.

He stood, tempted to launch the last of his pillows at Andy's head. Jed had spent half the night throwing pillows at Andy, trying to get him to turn over. They lay scattered, some on top of Andy, some on the bed, some on the floor. They'd done the job for a short while, but the rat always ended up back where he started: on his back, mouth hanging open, doing his level best to shake the plaster from the walls.

Nah, no more pillow bombs. He'd let Andy sleep.

Better that than having to answer his questions when he saw Jed leaving without him. But no way was he taking Andy along.

No, this part of the trip he had to do alone.

A quick shower later, he was on his way out the door, jacket in hand, when Andy's croaky voice stopped him. "Where you sneakin' off to?"

Jed leaned his forehead against the door. He'd almost made it. "Out."

"Yeah. I can see that." Andy pushed himself to a sitting position. "Out where?"

"Just…out." He looked over his shoulder. "There's something I have to do."

Andy studied him, curiosity—and just a tinge of suspicion—in his features. Then he shrugged. "Okay. Whatever. I'm gonna go get some breakfast. Guess I'll meet you back here."

Relief infused Jed's tone. "I'll see you in an hour. No more." It better not be more. He wasn't even sure he could stand an hour.

He pulled the door open, but Andy's voice halted him again. "Jed?"

He glanced back.

"Don't do anything stupid, okay?"

Too late.

He stepped outside, pulling the door shut behind him.

Why do I do this to myself?

Jed leaned his arms on the steering wheel of the rental car, staring straight ahead. He didn't need to look at the house beside his car. He knew it—the layout, the colors of the walls, every stick of furniture, the location of every door, every creaking board and cracked window. If he closed his eyes, he could picture her there, smell the eggs and bacon as she cooked breakfast, hear her hummin—

"So are you going to just keep sitting out here sulking, or are you going to come inside?"

He spun to the passenger side window and broke into a huge grin. "Mom!" In a flash, Jed was out of the car and had her wrapped in his arms, hugging her close.

"You're squashing me, dear. Dear? Dear!"

Laughing, he set her free, and she swatted his arm as she stepped back. "I couldn't quite believe my eyes when I looked out the front window and saw you sitting there. Why didn't you tell me you were coming to town, you horrid boy? And how long can you stay?"

He draped an arm around her shoulders as they walked toward the house. "It was a last-minute decision. As for how long, I don't know. Another week, maybe."

It better not take much longer than that. He was running out of time.

His mother pulled the front door open, and Jed tensed. "Don't worry, dear. Amos is at work."

Well, he'd set a new record. It had only taken him five minutes to be a jerk this time. "I'm sorry, Mom."

She waved his apology away. "Never mind. I'm just happy to see you. It's been too long." She linked her arm in his and led him to the living room. At least...he thought it was the living room.

"Wow." He looked around, taking it all in. "You've remodeled."

That was an understatement. What used to be a small living room adjacent to an equal sized dining room was now one spacious, open room. The back wall was no longer a wall, but more of a frame for huge plate glass windows looking out on—

"Is that a deck?" He turned to his mother. "Since when do we have a deck?"

His mom laughed. "Since last year, which you'd know if you came around more often. Amos and I decided it was time to make some changes." She sank onto the stylish new couch and patted the cushion beside her. "Do you like it?"

"Yeah—" he nodded as he sat beside her—"I do. It fits you better."

Pleasure suffused her smile. "Change can be a good thing."

He knew she was talking about more than the remodel, but he didn't want to get into that. Sure, Amos was a nice guy. And yes, he treated Jed's mother like she was precious to him. But did that make breaking up your family right?

They aren't exactly the ones who broke up the family, Jed.

He ignored that. Instead he let his gaze rest on the Bible sitting nearby on the coffee table. "Some things never change, Mom."

She knew what he was saying. He could see it in her eyes. And though there was a tinge of disappointment there, he also saw a depth of love. "Oh, my sweet boy. Don't you understand? 'Our doubts are traitors and make us lose the good we oft might win by fearing to attempt.'"

His mouth twitched. "*Measure for Measure.* Act 1, scene 4. Subtle, Mom. Real subtle."

"Why, Ernest Jediah—" her wide, wondering eyes would have done any two-year-old proud—"I cannot fathom what you mean."

"Uh-huh. Fine. So long as you realize 'I am not bound to please thee with my answers.'"

"*Merchant of Venice.* Act 4, scene 1." She pressed her lips together, acute and loving anxiety in those clear eyes of hers. "'If you go on thus, you will kill yourself: and 'tis not wisdom thus to second grief against yourself.'"

Torn between the familiar fun of their game and his equally familiar resistance to the message underlying her words, Jed laid his hand over hers. "'I pray thee, cease thy counsel, which falls into mine ears as profitless as water in a sieve.'"

"*Much Ado about Nothing,*" she whispered, and he nodded.

"Act 5, Scene 1." She plucked at the couch cushion, her inner struggle playing out on her delicate features.

Jed wished he could assuage her worry, but only one thing would do that. And as much as he loved his mother, as precious as she was to him, he could not profess a faith he no longer embraced.

After a moment, she turned her hand, weaving her fingers with his. "I don't mean to push you, Jediah."

"I know, Mom. I know you're just worried about me."

"I am. I don't know how anyone deals with struggles, with pain, without God. I know the difference it makes to have Him there, to feel His strength and grace, even when I don't deserve it. Especially when I don't deserve it."

It was on the tip of his tongue to promise he'd be open, that he'd take another look at God, seriously consider if he was wrong. But he couldn't make the words come.

He'd lied too much already. He wasn't going to lie to his mother as well.

When she finally broke the silence that had fallen between them, it was with a soft whisper. "I know I can't make you believe. That faith is something you have to find within yourself. Just don't be upset with me for hoping it happens sooner rather than later."

Jed let out a soft sigh. "And don't you be upset when I don't need belief the way you do."

The smile that touched her lips was both loving and sad. "'Fools must eat the bitter fruit of living their own way. They must experience the full terror of the path they have chosen. For they turn away from wisdom—to death. They are fools, and their own complacency will destroy them.'"

Jed's mind churned. It had been years since she'd stumped

him, but for the life of him, he couldn't recall ever hearing those words. He tugged at her hand. "Okay, you got me this time. I haven't got a clue which play that's from."

A hint of pink kissed her cheeks. "That's because I cheated, sweetheart."

"You? Madame Teacher of the Year? Cheated? Okay, so give it up. Where's the quote fro—" His gaze drifted past her to the Bible on the coffee table. "Ah. Let me guess."

"Proverbs 1:30–32. Sort of."

He gaped at her, and she laughed, holding her hands up. "I know, I know, I'm the one who always told you don't quote someone unless you can do it with precision. But in this particular case—" she laid her hand on his cheek—"application mattered more."

He patted her hand where it rested on his face. "I'm just glad you didn't really stump me."

"Of course I didn't." She lowered her hand to her lap. "Silly boy. You were the best student I had in thirty years of teaching Shakespearean studies."

He lifted her hand to his lips. "Only because you were a wonderful teacher, Mother mine. No one could make Shakespeare come to life the way you did."

She offered a tremulous smile, then drew a steadying breath. "All right, then. On to other things. You just sit back there, relax, and tell me everything. What's my only son been up to these last ten months, and when will I get my grandbabies?"

"Mom!"

Her eyes twinkled. "Oh, I'm sorry, dear. You're absolutely right. That was inappropriate. What I meant was, when will I get a daughter-in-law?"

"Mother!"

"Well, I'm sorry, Jediah, but you're not getting any younger. Nor, for that matter, am I."

"Ha. You're just as young and beautiful as you always were." And she was. To him.

"Please, just tell me your job isn't the only thing in your life. Surely there's a woman out there somewhere who interests you."

He hesitated and knew immediately it was a tactical error. His mother clapped her hands and scooted closer. "Who is she?"

"No one." He scooted back. "I mean, not really. She's just...someone I know for the show."

"Someone pretty?"

"Pretty enough." More than that, but he wouldn't give her the satisfaction of saying so.

"And she likes you?"

Jed prayed the heat flooding his face was just an internal thing, but he should have known better.

His mother's mouth dropped open. "Ernest Jediah, are you blushing?"

"What?" He shifted, looked away. "No. Shoot, no. I don't blush."

"Mmmm." His mom pursed her lips, then stood and headed toward the kitchen. Jed jumped up and followed her.

"Where are you going all of a sudden."

"To get sustenance." She blinked her eyes at him over her shoulder. "I have a feeling this is going to be quite a tale."

Jed followed his mother's bustling form. Quite a tale. Yes, that was fair. Trouble was, the ending wasn't finished. True, he had done everything he could to make Annie like him, to earn her trust. Trouble was, it was taking more than he'd expected. More effort. More time.

More of himself.

And with each passing day, it got harder to keep going. Especially when Annie looked at him with those clear eyes. Eyes so full of warmth and trust.

Trust he didn't deserve.

Trust, he feared more and more each day, he would lose when she found out who—and what—he really was.

TWENTY-ONE

*"None of us knows what the next change is going to be,
what unexpected opportunity is just around the corner, waiting...
to change all the tenor of our lives."*

KATHLEEN NORRIS

*"He thwarts the plans of the crafty,
so that their hands achieve no success."*

JOB 5:12, NIV

Normally Andy hated waiting. For anything.

But most especially for coffee.

Today, though, it felt good to just stand here. To inch forward behind the other devotees. His order perched on the tip of his tongue, just waiting to be set free.

He drew deep the fragrance that was distinctive Starbucks, then, thus consoled, looked around him.

How could a town this size have one—O-N-E—Starbucks? It's not like there weren't coffee huts on almost every corner of this Podunk town. Dutch Bros. Human Bean. Great Awakenings. Safari. You couldn't turn around without running into another coffee stand. But Andy was a Starbucks man, and nothing less would do. So he'd hit the road. Jed had the car, so that left him afoot, but he hadn't worried. Not a bit.

This was Starbucks he was lookin' for. Had to be half a dozen of them within walking distance.

Or not.

He'd been walking for what seemed like miles when he finally saw it. Paradise. Well, okay, Barnes and Noble, but he knew—where Barnes and Noble resided, Starbucks couldn't be far behind. Sure enough, his perseverance paid off, and Andy pushed the doors open and walked with new reverence to join the others in line.

The woman in front of him fidgeted. Stepped to the side. Then back in line. Then to the other side. Andy was just about to ask if she was okay when she turned to offer him an apologetic smile. "Sorry, I don't like being in crowds. But Starbucks is worth the trauma, huh?"

"Erk!"

What he'd intended to say was "Absolutely. So glad to be here. Can't wait for the coffee." But what came out was vastly different. One choked sound. *Erk.* That, and nothing more.

Because there, standing right in front of him, was Annie Justice. In living color.

Stunning, arresting color.

Andy coughed. Choked. And coughed some more.

Concern drew her brows together. "Hey, are you okay?"

"Uh-huh." He cleared his throat. "Oh yeah. Yes, I'm fine. Really. Just—" He turned from those wide hazel eyes to stare at the wall. "Hoo! Yeah. I'm just glad to be here." He looked at her, managing what he hoped was a fair facsimile of a smile. "You know. *Here.*"

Annie's giggle flowed over him, like silver bells tinkling out merriment. "I understand. I've had mornings like that." Humor arched one brow. "You just may be even more desperate than I am this morning. Would you like to go in front of me?"

Andy waved aside the offer. "Nah, I wouldn't want you to have to be surrounded by people any longer than necessary. It won't take long."

It better not, anyway. Because if it did, he'd make himself crazy with the thoughts racing through his head.

I shouldn't be talking to her! What if she remembers me from the dog park? No, wait. She didn't see me there. Okay, good. But wait.

What if Jed's idiotic plan actually works? Then when she sees me when I come to film the show, she remembers me? Puts two and two together? Figures out what a lying dog Jed really is…?

"May I take your order?"

Andy jumped and looked around. He was at the counter. Annie was nowhere to be seen. He stuttered out his order, then glanced around again.

Annie was just pushing the door open to head outside. She looked back at him and waved.

Andy's hand lifted as if of its own volition. *Stop that! Put your hand down. You want to make her remember you?*

"Sir?"

He jerked to face the girl at the register. "What?"

"You…need to pay for your coffee, sir."

"Oh. Right." He pulled his wallet out, dumping money on the counter. "What did I order?"

"A mocha breve, double shot, with extra whipped cream."

Andy glanced back at the doorway. "Better make that a double."

"Sir? Double what?"

He grabbed a ten and handed it to her. "Everything. Caffeine. Syrup. Whipped cream. Just pile it on." He grabbed the ten back from her and handed her the credit card Jed had given him for unexpected expenses. "And put it on this card."

Jed would yelp, but that was tough. He owed Andy.

Big time.

"Are you listening to me?"

Jed was stretched out on his bed, flipping through the TV channels. "Sure. You met Annie. You freaked out. You drank coffee." He studied Andy, who was parked on the very edge of his bed, foot tapping out a rapid-fire rhythm on the floor. "Lots of it."

"She's a nice lady, Jed."

"Yes, she is."

"And what you're doing still doesn't bother you?"

"No, Andy. It doesn't."

Andy stood and paced. After the third time of him blocking the screen, Jed punched the power button and tossed the remote aside. It was like trying to watch TV through one of those carnival games where you shot the ducks swimming back and forth.

"You realize we're running out of time, right? We've got to start filming soon if we're going to have all the footage we need. I mean, we've got to get shots of her doing everyday stuff as well as on a search or during training—"

"Say that again." Jed sat up.

"What?"

"That's it!"

"*What's* it?"

Now it was his turn to stand and pace. "Tomorrow we go back to the airport—"

Relief flooded Andy. "Oh, thank heaven. I can't believe you're actually going to listen to me for once."

"—and rent a car for you."

Andy's relief melted into confusion. "Am I driving somewhere?"

"You're driving everywhere. Everywhere that Annie goes." He slapped Andy on the shoulder. "You're going to follow her and film her. Doing everyday stuff."

"Without her permission?"

Jed waved the concern away. "That's in the bag."

"What bag? Where?"

"Just trust me on this. Get out there and get some everyday footage. That way it'll be ready to go when Annie finally signs on the dotted line."

Andy stood still and crossed his arms. "I think you've gone totally crazy, my friend."

"Yeah? Well, they thought Da Vinci was crazy too."

"Da Vinci was an artist."

"And what would you call me?"

Andy didn't miss a beat. "A liar." He held up one hand,

ticking off the words on his fingers. "Make that a sneak, a fake, a deceiver, *and* a liar."

Jed would have been hurt if he hadn't been so convinced Andy was right. "Gee, thanks, pal."

"I calls 'em as I sees 'em."

"Call 'em whatever you like." Jed hopped back on the bed, grabbing the remote. "Just get me my footage."

"Yes, master. Anything else, master?"

"Yeah." Jed waved the remote at his sarcastic friend. "Move. *The Andy Griffith Show* is on."

Andy did as he was bid. "You're gonna regret all this, Jed. You wait and see."

He didn't reply. He didn't need to. Because all he saw was a future full of promise. And once their show was on the top and signed for another season, Andy would see it that way too.

After all, that's what this was all about. Winning. Getting the prize. And he almost had it. He could tell. Annie was almost ready to trust him.

So nothing, not even his best friend, would stop him now.

TWENTY-TWO

> *"Life is all about timing.... Have the patience,*
> *wait it out. It's all about timing."*
>
> STACEY CHARTER

> *"These things I plan won't happen right away.*
> *Slowly, steadily, surely, the time approaches when the vision will be*
> *fulfilled. If it seems slow, wait patiently,*
> *for it will surely take place."*
>
> HABAKKUK 2:3

OCTOBER 8—A CATTAIL DAY (AUBURN)

Annie's feet pounded the pavement as she ran.

She schooled her breathing, keeping it even, not too shallow, not too deep. Oxygen was the key to running without injury.

That, and not tripping on her moose of a dog.

"Kodi—" she panted between gritted teeth—"quit running into me!"

The dog tossed a glance up at her, nudging against Annie's leg as she did so. Fortunately, they'd been through this little dance often enough that Annie didn't miss a step.

If only she could say the same about her relationship with Jed.

Relationship? Good grief, they hardly knew each other, and she was calling it a relationship?

She really was pathetic.

Still...she and Jed *had* spent time together every day since they met. That first coffee together was such a success that they'd continued on into lunch. The next day brought dinner and a walk. The next, breakfast and a drive. She had yet to convince him to go running with her, but that was okay. That gave her some time alone to try and sort through her jumbled emotions.

Which was exactly what she was doing now.

As much as she'd enjoyed her times with Jed, something was nagging at her. It took about a mile before she figured it out. Then it hit her like a brick.

She'd told Jed all about herself—growing up, her family and siblings, Kodi and search and rescue, her art, even her synesthesia. It was safe to say he knew pretty much everything about her. But what did she know about him?

Zilch.

Come to think of it, every time she tried to find out anything about his life, even his work, the conversation would take a detour right back to her. Not that she'd been conscious of that fact while it was happening.

Until now.

The gate to her driveway came into view, and Annie slowed her pace, reaching into her pocket and drawing out the remote. She punched the button with perfect timing, and she and Kodi sailed through. She hit the button again, and the gate eased shut.

Walking up and down the driveway to cool down, Annie made a decision. It was time to mine the depths that were Jed...Jed...

Good night! She didn't even know his last name!

Definitely time to garner some information from the man.

"Come on, Kodi. Time to get a drink."

Annie led the way into the house and made sure there was plenty of fresh water in the shepherd's bowl. She was just pouring herself a glass of orange juice when the phone rang. Fascinating how pleasant that sound had become. Mostly because she was fairly certain who she'd find at the other end of the line.

She was right.

"Mornin', sunshine. How 'bout I take the prettiest woman in town to breakfast?"

"Mm, that'd be nice, Jed." She lifted one foot and planted it against the kitchen sink, stretching forward, working the kinks out of her hamstring. "But I can't. Kodi and I have training today."

"Really? Where?"

She switched legs. "We're going up in the woods near Crater Lake to do some wilderness training."

"Well...how 'bout I come along?"

"Are you sure? I mean, it can be a long day with lot of work. Besides, don't you spend enough time outside already, with your work and all?" She bit her lip, waiting to see if he'd take a swing.

"Hey, spending time with you is plenty of excitement."

Strike one.

"Obviously you lead a boring life, sir." She pulled a chair out from the kitchen table and sat down. "You probably leave work at 5:00 p.m. on the dot, go home and fix a nice, healthy meal, and hit the hay by ten."

"Sounds good to me."

Annie pondered that a second. Not really confirmation, but not really denial either. In fact, it was pretty much like most of Jed's responses. Noncommital.

Strike two.

She hunkered down in the chair. "So you're more of a morning person, huh? Good thing you're a...a..." She put as much innocence into her tone as was humanly possible. "Oh, my memory is getting so bad! What did you say you did for a living?"

"Right now? I'm living for the next time I get to see you."

Annie let her forehead fall to the table. Strike three.

"So where shall I meet you and what time?"

"Meet us here. You can ride up with us."

"It's a plan. See you soon. And Annie?"

"Mm-hm?"

"I'm really looking forward to seeing you and Kodi in action."

She hung up the phone, then sat there, sipping her OJ and running the conversation through her mind again and again. Was Jed hiding something from her? What did she really know about him?

Stop it, Annie! She stood, taking her glass to the sink. One thing she knew for certain: Jed Whatever-His-Name-Was just happened to be one of the nicest men she'd ever met. He'd tell her about himself when he was ready.

Until then, she'd just enjoy his company.

Jed turned to Andy, not the least disturbed by the storm clouds in his friend's expression.

"We clear on the plan?"

"It's a stupid plan."

Jed sighed. "Stupid or not, are you clear on it?"

"What's not to be clear? I follow you to the training area. I park someplace Annie won't see me. I follow you guys without getting caught. I break the law by filming Annie without her permission."

"You're not breaking any laws, Andy."

"Sez you."

Jed looked at his watch. "We'd better go. Follow me to Annie's. I'm riding with her from there. But I'll keep you in my sights so we don't lose you." He held the door of their hotel room open. "Ready?"

Andy pushed up from the chair, hitching his equipment up on his shoulder. "No."

Jed nodded. "Good. Let's go."

"You want me to get lost?"

Annie clipped Kodi's leash onto her collar. "Jayce, I'm always ready for you to get lost."

He sidled up next to her and laid his head on her shoulder. "I love you too, Auntie dearest."

Annie nudged him away with her elbow, holding out Kodi's leash for him. He took it, kneeling in front of the dog, taking her face in his hands, massaging her cheeks, talking in a high-pitched voice. "Whaddya say, girl? Huh? Shall I get lost? Wanna find me, Kodi? Wanna come chase me down and drag me home?"

Annie eyed the boy. "You are one warped puppy, Jayce."

His grin was equal parts playful scamp and adoring nephew. "Hey, Kodi likes it when I talk this way." He turned back to the dog. "Don't you, widdle girl?"

Kodi answered with an enthusiastic swipe of her long tongue across his face.

"I have no problem with the tone, brat." Annie pulled Kodi's shabrack out of her backpack and slipped it inside her belt. "After all, I taught you to talk that way to get Kodi psyched for working. But the words, son, now those concern me."

Jayce looked past Annie. "So where'd Mr. Wonderful go?"

She poked at him with one booted foot. "You should be so wonderful when you grow up."

"Grow up?" No one could sound as mortally offended as a teenage boy. "He-*llo*? Like fifteen isn't grown up?"

"Sorry! How about when you're as old and ancient as I am? That better?"

Jayce huffed, only slightly mollified by her self-denigration.

"Anyway, my poor, decrepit brain forgot Kodi's tennis ball in the Jeep. Jed went back after it. Can't have training without the reward, now can we?"

"Not if you want a happy puppy, we can't. Ah, there's the dreamboat."

Annie turned, and Jed waved as he approached. Having him there, walking toward her with that smile on his face…it seemed the most natural thing in the world. Like he'd been a part of her life forever.

Clearly, she had lost her mind. Either that, or she was twitter-pated. Utterly and completely twitterpated.

It was the only thing that explained her trust in a man she'd just met. But trust him she did. She had a hard time believing any of this was happening. Whatever "this" was.

Kodi danced in circles when she saw Jed, wagging that big head back and forth and greeting him with a hearty "Arrrooowww!"

That was another reason not to worry. If anyone was a solid judge of character, it was Kodi. And she adored Jed.

"Hey, Jed, toss the ball!" Jayce's call pulled Annie from her thoughts.

"You got it." He cocked his arm. "Go long, Jayce!"

The boy jumped up and ran, Kodi racing alongside him, barking encouragement. Jed pitched the tennis ball, lobbing it high in the air, and Jayce jumped for it, giving a whoop when he snagged it with one hand. The boy did a little victory dance, then came trotting back toward Annie.

He and Jed reached her at about the same time, and when Jayce reached out to punch Jed's arm, she shook her head. Those two were cut from the same cloth. They'd talked pretty much nonstop on the hour-long drive up here—mostly about football. God bless testosterone.

Annie studied the clearing and the forest surrounding it. They were just south of Crater Lake, and though the weather was on the chilly side, at least it wasn't raining or snowing. Just cold and overcast. Perfect weather for what they were going to do. "Okay, you two. Time to get to work."

She pulled the shabrack from her belt and knelt to slip it on Kodi. Fastening the vest into place, she looked up at Jayce.

He grinned. "Runaways?"

"Go for it." Annie gripped Kodi's collar, holding her back as Jayce jogged toward the trees.

"Runaways?"

Annie nodded, keeping her eyes fixed on Jayce. "They're warm-up exercises. Jayce finds a place just beyond the clearing to hide, then we send Kodi after him. She finds him, and we heap praise and hugs on her."

A whistle sounded. Jayce was ready. Annie crouched beside Kodi, hands on either side of her collar. "Okay, Jed. Just make sure you don't get between me and Kodi."

He nodded. "You want me to stay here?"

"That's not necessary, just stay behind us." She paused. "Are you looking for someone?"

Jed's head whipped back toward her. "What? No. Why?"

Annie shrugged. "I don't know, you seem to be looking around a lot."

"It's just really beautiful out here, and I don't want to miss anything. So where did you want me?"

She chuckled. "Just stick close, okay?"

An easy smile played at the corners of his mouth. "With pleasure."

How did he *do* that? Make her pulse jitterbug with no more than one or two words? *Concentrate, Annie.*

Right. Concentrate. She could do that.

She leaned forward a fraction and felt Kodi's muscles tense beneath her hands. She infused her tone with high-pitched excitement. "Okay, Kodi, Jayce is out there. *Find* him!"

The dog shot forward, running full tilt to where she'd seen Jayce disappear into the trees. Annie and Jed trotted along behind Kodi.

"How long will it take?"

Annie grinned. Kodi was already running back to her. She gave an alert, planting those paws on Annie's thighs. "Good girl, Kode. Show me!"

Kodi spun and galloped back, Annie and Jed following behind her as she led them to Jayce. Annie clapped her hands. "Good girl! Good find! What a smart doggy you are!"

Kodi almost wiggled herself in half, then vaulted after the tennis ball Jayce threw. The shepherd snagged it, carrying it back, head held high, and gave the slobbery prize to Jed.

He chuckled. "Pretty pleased with yourself, aren't you, girl?"

"That's the whole idea," Annie said as Jed threw the ball. "This exercise isn't supposed to be hard, but to prime the pump."

"Get the dog ready to work?"

"Exactly. I mean, just imagine how excited you'd be about working if you started out with a session of praise and hugs."

"Depends on who's doing the hugging." He waggled his brows.

"Ha ha." But for all her mockery, Annie couldn't help feeling a surge of warmth at the look in his eyes. She turned back to her nephew. "Okay, Jayce, let's go again."

Before I do something to embarrass myself.

Several runaways later, the real search was on.

Annie and Jed waited with Kodi as Jayce, the designated search subject, made his way to a hiding spot deep in the woods. He radioed them when he was set and gave Annie her boundaries on the map.

"So he doesn't tell you where he is?"

Annie smiled. "Wouldn't be much of a search if I knew where he was."

"Oh." The word was as sheepish as Jed's expression. "Right."

Annie squeezed her powder bottle, watching the dust as the breeze carried it away so she'd know which direction to grid in before sending Kodi. That done, she took hold of Kodi's collar, pointing in the direction they needed to go. "Find him!"

Kodi was off.

She and Jed followed, keeping their steps purposeful but relaxed. Running was fine for warming up, but you had to pace yourself on a real search.

"Question."

She kept her focus on Kodi as she responded. "Go for it."

"Why didn't you have Kodi sniff something of Jayce's? You know, a shirt or something with his scent on it?"

"Because she's not searching for Jayce's scent."

Jed stopped, one foot lifted to step over a fallen tree. "Huh?"

Annie laughed. "Kodi is a Wilderness Air Scent Dog. That means she's searching for *any* human scent, not just Jayce's." At Jed's creased brow, she held out her hands. "It's like this. When a human is alive, his body sheds forty thousand dead cells a minute. We call those *rafts*. When someone dies, the bacteria breaking down the body creates a by-product."

"A by-product."

"Right. Gases and vapors that can be smelled by a human at a closer range. But dogs? If the air currents are right, they can pick them up at a substantial distance."

She understood his deep laugh even before he explained it.

"I know someone who definitely gives off plenty of gases. My camer—uh, buddy, Andy."

Annie swatted his arm. "Not those kinds of gases, you goof. These gases are indiscernible to us, but if a human is in the area, they're present. At least a third of the cells emitted from humans are lighter than air, which means they stay suspended for a while, like smoke."

"Now, that I smell." Jed lifted his face to the breeze. "Wood smoke. It's everywhere."

"Right, because folks who live around here heat with wood. And though their homes are quite some distance away, the smoke is carried on the wind. Well, that's what the human scent is like for air scenting dogs. It emanates from people in a cone shape, growing larger and more spread out the farther it goes from the source."

"Okay, so is it affected by the weather, like smoke is?"

Annie's mouth quirked. "See there? I don't care what everyone else says. I think you're a smart guy."

This time Jed punched her arm.

"That's exactly what happens. On calm days, with the sun overhead, smoke and human scent rise up from convective currents. So calm, sunny days are actually harder for air scenting dogs. The scent rises straight up, so Kodi would nearly have to trip over it to hit on it."

"And days like today?"

"Perfect. The air currents move uphill as the sun heats the ground." Annie lifted her hand, pointing to a trail that led off to their left. "Kodi, check it!"

The shepherd ran up the trail, circled, and came back, then continued on ahead of them.

"So you tell her where to search?"

Annie rolled her shoulders, keeping the muscles loose. "Sometimes. I'll let her range at her own pace, in her own way, but if I see something I want her to check out—a path or a culvert, whatever—I'll direct her."

"Man." Jed shook his head. "I can't believe all the stuff you have to know and keep in mind. Weather, time of day…"

"It all matters."

Jed held a branch out of her way. "So how do you remember all of this?"

"Training. Twice a week. We've done it for years, and we'll keep doing it as long as we're in SAR."

"No wonder you're in such good shape."

Annie giggled and flexed her arms. "Hey, walking is one of the best exercises in the world. Look how strong and healthy people were back in Bible days. They walked everywhere. I mean, Jesus and the apostles must have walked hundreds of miles every year. I bet they were like the Jack La Lannes of their day."

"Jack La Lanne? You're comparing Jesus to Jack La Lanne?"

Annie couldn't tell if Jed was amused or horrified. "I'm comparing his physical condition to Jack's. I mean, think about it. Jesus was a carpenter. A number of the apostles were fishermen. These guys were strong and fit. Add all that walking, and I'd wager they were as well developed physically as they were intellectually."

"Intellectually?"

No confusing that one. Disdain dripped from the word like old dishwater from a sodden sponge. Annie glanced at the man beside her. "Well, yeah. They spent all that time with Jesus talking and studying. Learning from the best teacher in history." She shook her head. "That must have been amazing."

"I think it's amazing we still talk about those guys."

Annie cocked her head. Those guys? Was she reading him right? If so, they had a problem, because he sounded like he was talking about a bunch of idiot frat brothers rather than the apostles. "Well, of course we do. They're among the most influential men in history. They brought truth to nations and died for what they believed in."

At the sight of a large fallen log just beyond them, Annie signaled to Kodi. "This way!"

Jed watched the shepherd respond, sniffing all around the log, her tail wagging her delight at what she was doing.

"She seems to enjoy this."

Annie smiled. "She wouldn't do it if she didn't." She glanced at him. "About the apostles, you sound like you don't think much of them."

"And you sound like you actually respect them."

Anxiety gnawed at Annie's gut. Jed sounded so…annoyed. "Sure, don't you?"

"Annie, come on. Look what they did! They walked with Jesus, a guy who was supposed to be the Son of the living God."

Supposed to be?

Oh, no. No, no, no…

She couldn't believe she hadn't asked Jed about this. Annie swallowed the growing panic inside her.

Jesus, please don't tell me You've let me fall for a man who doesn't believe in You!

"Like you said, they talked with Him, were close to Him. They had to be His closest friends. And what do those crumbs do when things get hard? They run. Like petrified rabbits." He kicked a rock, sending it flying. "I'd never do that. Not to someone I was supposed to believe in. Care about."

Such depth of emotion in his tone, his suddenly stiff demeanor. Anger. Pain. Betrayal. It seeped through Jed's words—and his mood—like a black stain on cool white cotton.

And it lifted Annie's spirits to the skies.

If he was this upset, this angry at what the apostles did to Jesus, then he must believe in Him. Of course, she'd ask, just to be sure. But later. Now wasn't the time for that discussion.

Kodi ranged to the left and disappeared in the trees. Annie watched her as she and Jed walked along, making their way through the silence as carefully as they did the forest.

She gave herself a little time by scanning the terrain, looking for spots where she should send Kodi deeper, areas where someone could hide—such as in the middle of bushes, which would hold the scent in.

She paused, checking the drainage they were crossing against the map, then looked at Jed. "You know, I've heard that a lot. People saying they'd never do what the apostles did. But we do, Jed. All the time."

Denial thinned his mouth. "Not like they did."

"Exactly like they did. Don't you see? We're with Him every moment of every day, and yet when something we think is too hard comes our way, what do we do? Pitch a fit. Turn and walk away. Doubt Him."

He considered her words for a moment, but she could tell he didn't like them. "I'm sorry, Annie. I just don't see it."

"Most people don't. They look at the apostles and see weak men. But you know what I see?"

"What?"

"Myself."

The minute the word slipped past her lips, something clicked, deep inside.

Myself...I see myself...

Annie's mouth opened on a gasp. Of course! Oh, it was perfect!

"Hey, are you okay? I'm sorry. I didn't mean to upset you."

"No, it's okay." More than okay. It was wonderful! Ideas raced through her mind. Oh, for a pencil and paper to sketch them! Annie wanted to dance, to jump up and down and yell it out to the world.

I've got it! Oh, I've got it!

Kodi ran past them and out of sight to the right. Annie knew she should follow, but instead, she spun toward Jed, propelled by the pure euphoria of excitement, and threw her arms around his neck. He stumbled backward, his arms enclosing her as she pressed a grateful kiss to his cheek.

"Whoa! What did I do to deserve this?"

Jed's laughing question jarred her from the excitement of discovery, slamming her full bore into the mortification of self-consciousness.

Oh, good heavens! She'd just thrown herself at the man!

She pulled back, but he tightened his hold on her. "Come on, now. Tell me what I did." Mischief twinkled in those brown eyes. "So I can be sure to do it again."

Face on fire, Annie eased from the warm circle of his arms. "I'm sorry, Jed."

His mouth quirked. "I'm not."

What was *wrong* with her? And where was Kodi? Annie listened. No sound. Suddenly, the dog bolted from the trees, heading straight for Annie. "Good girl, Kode! Did you find someone?"

But instead of alerting, Kodi dog ran past them, still hard at work.

Which was more than Annie could say for herself.

"So…what wonderful thing did I do?"

Annie turned to Jed. "I just had an idea about a window I've been working on. Something I haven't been able to figure out." She overcame her chagrin enough to smile. "And I owe the solution to you."

"Wow. Well, let me know any time I can help, 'cuz the payment is great."

Thank heaven her laugh was only slightly self-conscious. They started walking again.

Jed tugged his sleeve back and checked his watch.

"Getting tired?"

He lowered his arm. "Nah, I'm good."

She restrained a smile. Typical guy. Wouldn't admit it if he were about to drop. "It's okay if you are, Jed. We've been out a couple hours now, and this isn't exactly easy terrain to navigate."

"Yeah, well, *you're* not tired."

The smile escaped. "I do this all the time. Kodi and I run every day."

"So what you're saying is that you're in great shape and I'm a wimp?"

"A *what?*" She hooted. "The last thing I'd call you is a wimp."

Interest sparked in his eyes. "Oh? Why is that?"

Annie pushed branches out of their path, holding them back out of the way. "With those shoulders and muscles—?" Oh, good heavens! She couldn't believe she'd just said that. Sure, she'd thought it a number of times, but to say it right out loud like that? She must have lost her mind. She wasn't sure if it made her seem more stupid or desperate.

Either way, Jed didn't seem in the least bothered. In fact, utter delight painted his features. "Please, do go on."

"Ohh, you!" She let the branches snap back into place—and smack into his chest.

"Aaahh! Medic!" He flopped back against a tree, milking the melodrama for all it was worth. "I've been wounded!"

"Not yet you haven't. But keep it up and I'll be more than happy to oblige." Annie hesitated when Kodi came loping out of the trees. But again, no alert. Kodi just eyed Annie and then, reassured that her mistress was still close by, bounded away, nose to the ground.

"Man, this takes a lot of patience."

Annie sniffed. "Almost as much patience as putting up with you."

Jed slung a companionable arm around her shoulders. "Ah, c'mon. You know you think I'm wonderful."

"Hmpf."

He gave her a squeeze. "Right?"

She tugged away from him, but he wouldn't let her go.

"Almost as wonderful as I think you are." The teasing in his tone had vanished, replaced by a low warmth that made her tingle.

Her heart tripped. She couldn't make herself look at him, so she just stared at the ground. "You...you think I'm wonderful?"

He slid a finger under her chin, coaxing her to meet his gaze. The affirmation she saw there sent her spirits soaring.

"Wonderful, and beautiful, and talented…"

With each word, his head lowered a fraction. Annie let her eyes drift shut—

Then jerked them open with a yelp when something nailed her from behind.

Kodi!

The dog was alerting, and Annie hadn't even heard her coming back! She'd actually forgotten for a moment why she was out here! Shame flooded Annie as she scrambled to her feet. Censure wrapped itself around her heart, making her throat ache.

Kodi barked, poised to jump on Annie again, but this time she was braced. Kodi raised up, planted her huge paws on Annie's midsection, then dropped back down on the ground. "Good girl, Kodi. Show me, girl! Show me!"

As the shepherd bounded into the trees, Annie ran after her, not even looking back to see if Jed was following. Because if she did, she'd lose it.

For the first time she could remember, she'd forgotten what she was doing. Forgotten she was out here for a reason—one that could mean life or death for someone. Her only saving grace was that this was a training exercise and not the real thing. That helped.

But not much.

Because she knew, deep inside, it wouldn't have made a difference. With Jed looking at her like that, saying things like that, with his arm holding her close against him like that, Annie did something she always swore she'd never do. Something that absolutely terrified her.

She got lost.

Jed scrambled to his feet, racing to catch up with Annie as she crashed through the woods, calling encouragement to her dog.

"Good, Kodi! Show me!"

He could hardly believe the way she'd stood there, letting Kodi jump up on her. She'd told him that was how the dog...what had she called it? Oh yeah, alerted. But he'd figured it was a nice, gentle thing.

He'd figured wrong.

Kodi had been worked up big time, and when she jumped up on Annie, she planted those moose paws with some serious force. He'd half expected Annie to go flying. But she planted those little feet of hers and took the hit without flinching.

Amazing.

That was the word that kept hitting him whenever he was with Annie. Whenever he thought about her.

Just...amazing.

So it only made sense, didn't it, that he'd gotten a bit caught up in the role? That he'd been mesmerized by those eyes of hers?

That he'd been about to kiss her?

Oh, man. He'd almost kissed her! Andy would have his head. And he'd be right.

Winning Annie's trust was one thing. Kissing her? That had to be a serious breach of ethics or something. And even if it wasn't, it was stupid, plain and simple.

He wasn't out here looking for a relationship. Or even a date. All he wanted from Annie was for her to do his show. That's it. So he needed to get with it. Get the woman's signature on the dotted line, get the episode in the can, and get gone. Back to LA, where he didn't have to think about anyone else.

Just him.

Alone.

The way it was supposed to be.

Excited barking split the air, and Jed saw Kodi licking Jayce's face. The teen pushed the dog away and pulled the tennis ball from his jacket pocket. Annie and Jayce praised Kodi to the skies.

It was like a celebration, a party, and everyone got to take part. Everyone but him. He held back, watching. Picturing what this would look like through the camera. How he'd capture Annie's expression and Kodi's ecstasy, how he'd pan from handler to dog to victim...

Yeah, this is what he needed to do. Keep his distance. Stay focused on the goal. Far smarter than focusing on the woman. And safer. Focusing on the goal would get him what he wanted. The show. Another season. Success.

And focusing on Annie. That'd get him one thing and one thing only.

Lost.

TWENTY-THREE

> *"The wise man in the storm prays to God,*
> *not for safety from danger, but deliverance from fear."*
>
> RALPH WALDO EMERSON

> *"And everyone who calls on the name of the Lord will be saved."*
>
> JOEL 2:32, TNIV

OCTOBER 8
5:00 p.m.

"Finally!"

Brianna Heller and her husband, Mark, stepped back, survey-ing their handiwork. They'd gone camping a number of times before, but this new tent had almost beat them. Of course, they'd arrived later than planned, which didn't help. Bree had started to think they'd still be trying to construct the tent by firelight. She'd come *this* close to suggesting they find a nearby Motel 6. Of course, *near* in this case meant sixty miles away.

Mark's strong arm encircled her waist, pulling her close. "We make a good team, you know that?"

Bree rested her head against his chest, listening to the steady beat of his heart. "Yes, we do."

"You think you'll be able to rest up here?"

She sighed. Mark worried about her so. She loved him for it but wished he didn't feel the need. "Honey, I'm okay."

"Okay, my Aunt Fanny."

She rubbed her cheek on his chest. "You haven't got an Aunt Fanny."

"You know what I mean."

Yes, she did. She loved her job at the veterinary clinic, but one of their best technicians had moved away, so everyone was taking up the slack until they hired someone new. That meant extra work and extra hours. That alone would have been stressful. But lately it seemed that one animal after another was coming in with serious issues. Recently Bree had assisted Dr. Harding as he put down two dogs and a cat. All three had been coming to the clinic for as long as Bree had been there, so it was like saying good-bye to cherished friends.

The Saturday she assisted with the second dog—a darling, albeit ancient, little poodle mix named Fritz—Brianna ended up in tears. They started when Fritzie stopped breathing and continued all through her lunch with Annie.

"I'm sorry," she kept saying as she blew her nose. "I don't know what's wrong with me."

"You're exhausted, that's what." Annie's hazel eyes held an unusually serious glint. "Bree, you take what you do to heart. And it's been tough lately. Too tough." She handed Brianna a handful of paper napkins since Bree had run out of Kleenex. "I'll tell you what you need to do. You need to go home, let Mark hold you, and then tell him you need a vacation. No ifs, ands, or buts. Get away for a while." Annie reached for the dessert menu. "In the meantime, I'm buying you something sinfully rich and chocolaty to get those endorphins flowing."

Bree hadn't argued. She called work and told them she was going home sick. When she got there, Mark was waiting for her.

"Annie called, and I think she's right. You need a break. I've already talked with Ernie and Jane Conrad about a camping trip together, and they said they'd love to go. That way they can watch Amberly for us once in a while to give us couple time, and we'll take Ethan to give the two of them time together."

Bree considered arguing for all of a second—she didn't get

paid vacation, and time away meant less income for the month, not to mention what they'd spend while vacationing—then she gave in. Mark was determined, and budging him when he was like this was next to impossible. Besides, Jane and Ernie were two of her favorite people. And their son was about Amberly's age.

She smiled. "Amberly will be delighted that Ethan is coming. I think our little girl has a crush on him."

Mark groaned. "Oh man, I thought I had *years* before I had to worry about Angel and boys."

Brianna smiled at her husband's nickname for their little girl. He'd called her that from the day she was born. "Don't kid yourself. I knew she'd be a heartbreaker the second she opened those beautiful baby blues."

"Yeah, well so long as I'm always her best guy."

Bree pressed a gentle kiss to his lips. "Hers…and mine."

"Mommy—" a little hand tugged at her pant leg, pulling her back to the present—"tell me a bedtime story."

Brianna reached down to gather her little girl in her arms. "You bet, Angel. There's nothing I'd rather do."

"You two go ahead." Mark pulled his jacket on. "I'm going to go see the ranger about firewood before it's too dark to see anything."

Bree watched her husband walk down the path. Even after nearly ten years of marriage, the way Mark moved still made her heart jump.

"Mommy, why are you staring at Daddy?"

Bree took her daughter's hands and swung her around in a circle. "Because I love him so much."

Amberly squealed, and when Bree stopped spinning, her daughter flung those little arms around her legs, hugging her tight. "He loves you too, huh, Mommy?"

"Yes." She kissed the top of her little girl's head. "Yes, he does. And you know what that means?"

Amberly's eyes widened. "What?"

"That I'm the luckiest woman in the world."

❖   ❖   ❖

He should go inside.

It was stupid to just keep sitting here. Going over and over the last few days in his mind. He wasn't accomplishing anything. Except making himself feel terrible.

And crazy.

Jed shoved the car door open and stomped up the stairs to the hotel room. He needed a shower. A really hot one. To wash away this...this...ugly feeling slithering through him.

He dug the key card out of his pocket as he walked. What *was* this feeling?

"Suspicion always haunts the guilty mind."

Fine. Even Shakespeare was working against him now. But the quote fit, because that's exactly what he felt.

Guilty.

But why? What did he have to feel guilty about? He was just doing his job.

Your job is to lead women on?

He ground his teeth. No. And he wasn't. All he was doing was giving Annie time to see him for who he was.

A fake? A phony? A liar?

To. Earn. Her. Trust.

In a liar?

"Shut—" Jed jabbed the key card into the slot and shoved the door open—*"up!"*

Andy looked up from the camera lens he was cleaning, inquiry lifting his brows. "So? How goes the campaign?"

Jed ignored his friend.

"Not the way you'd expected, eh?"

And his friend's stupid questions.

Andy leaned his elbows on the table. "What's the problem, Jed? Things not as simple as you thought?"

Jed turned and started for the bathroom. He didn't need this.

Didn't need his best friend prodding him, scraping already raw nerves. Not when his own traitorous mind and gut were flaying him already. He needed time alone to get his head straight.

Pity one didn't always get what one needed.

Andy didn't even break stride. He followed him right into the bathroom. "Jed? What's going on? Did something happen?"

Jed planted his hands on the counter and stared at his reflection in the mirror. Just stared. Hard.

"Oh, no."

His eyes closed at Andy's hushed exclamation.

"Ah, Jed. Tell me you didn't do what I think you did. Tell me you didn't go that far…"

Enough! Jed turned, letting his pointed glare speak for him.

Andy didn't flinch. Just met his glare head-on with one of his own. "Annie Justice is a nice woman. A good woman. She doesn't deserve what you're doing."

Jed turned up the glare.

"Okay, okay, fine." Andy took a step back out of the bathroom. "I understand. Sometimes you just gotta be alone with your thoughts."

Jed slammed the door in his buddy's sanctimonious face. But the door couldn't shield him from Andy's voice.

"And your guilt."

When Jed came out of the bathroom, he walked over to Andy's equipment.

"Hey, don't touch the merchandise."

"Is this everything you've taped so far?"

Andy stood, ever protective of his gear. "Yeah, that's it. Why?" Hope sparked in his eyes. "You change your mind?"

"Do you remember that guy we worked with a few years ago? He moved out here to take a job at the local TV station? You guys were pretty good buds."

The hope dimmed. "Sure. Vince Caruthers. Why?"

"Because I want to go see him tomorrow."

"And again I ask, why?"

"To talk him into letting us use their editing equipment. Think he'll do that?"

"Probably—"

Jed's glare stopped the *Why?* he knew was coming. "We're going to take a look at what you've got so far and put together a clip to send to Silas."

The dark clouds returned to Andy's brow. "You think that's smart, huh?"

"I think it'll keep him excited about the project."

For one blessed moment, Andy was silent. "You're heading down a bad road, bud."

"It's the road that will take us where we want to be, Andy."

The sadness in his friend's eyes almost convinced him he should listen to him.

Almost.

But a voice deep inside reminded him why he'd done all this in the first place. All that he'd lose if he didn't push forward.

And that voice, by far, was the most persuasive.

TWENTY-FOUR

"I trust everyone. I just don't trust the devil inside them."

TROY KENNEDY-MARTIN

*"What a difference between our sin and
God's generous gift of forgiveness."*

ROMANS 5:15

OCTOBER 10—A SILVER LACE DAY (SILVER)
3:30 p.m.

"I am persuaded you've abandoned your calling."

"Killie, do we have to talk about this right now? I'm up to my elbows in ground meat."

"Good heavens, whatever for?"

"Burgers, Killian. I'm having guests for dinner, and I'm making burgers."

"*What?*"

Annie almost dropped the phone from where she had it pinned between her ear and her shoulder. "Killie! You're going to break my eardrum."

"You're entertaining? Why aren't you in your studio, working on that window? You said you finally knew what to do with it—"

"Because I do."

"That the concept was coming together."

She let out a huff. "Because it is."

"So why are you wasting time with guests? That window

won't create itself, Annie. I swear, this irresponsible streak of yours is just getting worse. It's that search and rescue foolishness, that's what it is."

Irritation wasn't something Annie felt often, especially with Killian. But it hit her then, quick and heated. "This has nothing to do with search and rescue, and you know it."

"No, I don't. Ever since you went on that last search, you've been distracted. What else could be pulling your attention away from your work like this?"

She started to tell him he was wrong, to deny being distracted, but the words died on her lips. Because Killian was right. She was distracted. But it wasn't search and rescue.

It was Jed.

She'd been spending time with him rather than in her studio. And when she *was* in her studio, even when she was working on the window, his image filled her mind. "Oh…"

"See?" Killian's triumph rang out. "You have to admit I'm right, don't you?"

"No."

"Annie, don't be stubborn. You just said—"

"Killian, stop."

He did, but she heard the frustrated exhalation as he did so. Unfortunately, she had the feeling that hearing what was really distracting her wouldn't make him any happier.

"It's not search and rescue. It's…well…"

"Yes?"

His impatience zinged through the phone lines, slicing through any desire on her part to be tactful about this. "It's a man, Killie."

Silence.

"I've met someone. Someone who—" her heart trembled at the admission she was making—"has come to mean a great deal to me. He's been the distraction. Nothing else."

She waited for his response, but he didn't say a word. She strained to hear. He was still breathing, wasn't he? Had he passed out?

"Well. So. A man."

A flicker of apprehension coursed through her. He sounded so distant. So—controlled.

"I owe you an apology, Annie. I misunderstood."

Okay. Things were fine. He understood what she was saying and accepted it.

"I thought your art was important to you. I apologize for being such a fool."

Okaaay…maybe *accepted* wasn't the right word.

"Killian."

"No. It's fine. Really. I was foolish enough to believe the only thing that could pull you away from your true calling was your absurd fascination with finding lost people."

Absurd fascination? *"Killie…"*

The warning in her tone didn't seem to faze him one iota. In fact, if anything it added fuel to the fire. "First you let these crazy e-mails and letters distract you, and now you say you've met a man."

Whoa. "How do you know about the e-mails?"

"Your brother told me."

Annie shook her head. What? Since when did Dan confide in Killian? "When?"

"When he…when I ran into him in town the other day. He just mentioned it in passing. It's not important."

"Of course it is."

"Fine. You want to get caught up in some mystery, go ahead. You want to get married and grow fat having babies. Fine! Now that I know art is just something you do when it's convenient—"

"Killian Alba Molan, shut *up!*"

He did so. Probably because Annie had never yelled at him before.

When she could speak past her anger, she did her best to sound calm. "I'm going to set the phone down for a second. Don't hang up. I'll be right back."

She didn't wait to see if he did as she asked. She just leaned close to the counter and let the phone drop there. Then she swatted the kitchen faucet with her elbow, washed her hands and dried them, the motions quick and abrupt.

When her hands were clean—and her pulse had slowed to a more normal rhythm—she lifted the phone to her ear. "Are you still there?"

"Your wish is my command."

At the hint of a smile in the words, relief eased the tension in her neck and shoulders. "I'm sorry I yelled."

"I'm sorry I was a jerk."

"Me too."

"You too what? You're sorry you were a jerk as well, or that I was a jerk?"

Her lips twitched. "Yes."

He laughed. "Fair enough. Look, Annie, I'm happy for you. You just...took me by surprise, that's all. I didn't know. And I confess I was a little hurt that you have this—this person—"

"His name is Jed."

"—this Jed person in your life now and you didn't tell me."

She drew circles on the counter with a finger. "I know. I'm sorry, Killie. Things have been kind of crazy."

"Just tell me you're being careful. You know. About those notes."

Her heart warmed. "I am."

"And *please* tell me you're working on the piece."

"I promise you, I am." Not as often as she should, but that would change.

"Good. Thank you. Now I'll leave you in peace. Go grill your dead meat."

"Hamburgers."

"A delectable treat, I'm sure. One that chickens and turkeys worldwide will praise to the skies."

Annie grinned. "Killie, you're a nut."

"Which is why you love me."

That it is, Annie thought as she hung up. *That it is.*

4:30 p.m.

God, what a gift you've given me.

Annie stood in her backyard next to the grill, watching her family tease each other, listening to the harmonies of their laughter. *Lord, I can never thank You enough for blessing me with these special people. So many families struggle to get along. But mine is so comfortable together.*

A shadow flitted through her heart, its whispers all-too familiar. *Pity you're not like the rest of them. That you so often watch them from the sidelines of the gathering. Like now...*

She pushed the thoughts away. She wasn't watching from the sidelines at all. She had a job. Overseeing hamburgers on the grill, ensuring they were cooked just right. Medium-well for Jayce, shoe-leather well for Dan, just this side of medium for Shelby, and for Annie? She licked her lips. Cooked just enough to brown the outside, but leave the inside nice and rare.

She liked her burgers to moo when she bit into them.

Yet another way in which you're different.

Annie was just about to tell the whispers to shut up when a deep voice drifted over her shoulder. "You are one lucky duck, sis."

Annie turned from the grill and pursed her lips at her brother. "Why? Because I cook such yummy burgers? No, wait, that'd make *you* a lucky duck since I'm cooking them for you."

"Burgers schmurgers. You're lucky you've got me to watch out for you, of course."

She turned back to the dismissed patties. "No argument from me on that."

Her suddenly somber tone pulled a frown from him. "Did you get another note?"

"No, thank heaven." Annie sprinkled seasoned salt on the burgers. "No notes, and according to you, no e-mails." She slanted a questioning look his way. "Any ideas who my pen pal is?"

Dan's gaze grew guarded. "Not really. We've been checking some things out, but so far we haven't found anything conclusive. Who knows? Maybe the perp's moved on."

"I hope so."

Dan rubbed her back, his touch comforting. "Don't worry, Annie. We're keeping a file of everything. And we're keeping an eye on you too."

She smiled at that. "You can see me from Sanctuary? Now that's some kind of eyesight."

"I didn't say I was keeping an eye on you, brat. I said *we* were."

"And who might we be?"

"Good men. And that's all you need to know." He watched her slide the spatula under her burger and lift it to the plate. "That's not done enough."

She shrugged him away. "It is for me."

"Livin' dangerously, kid."

"Thus speaks the man whose job requires him to wear a gun."

"Thus speaks the man who knows better than to consume raw meat...or to take up with a total stranger."

Ah, so that's what this was about. She turned to face him. "Dan, Jed is only a stranger because you haven't met him yet. Didn't Jayce tell you he was a nice guy?"

"Jayce is a sharp kid, but he's still a kid." Dan crossed his arms over his chest. "You, on the other hand, are seasoned enough—"

"Seasoned?" This horrified reaction came from Shelby, who'd just come to join them. "What a terrible thing to say!"

Dan didn't let his wife derail his train of thought. He just tugged Shelby into his arms, resting his chin on her head as he finished. "—to know better. Come on, Annie. What do you really know about this man?"

"Oh! Annie! The burgers are getting burned."

"They aren't the only ones," she muttered, turning at Shelby's warning and lowering the flames.

A hand settled on her shoulder. "Sis, you know I want you to be happy."

Her anger fizzled. "I know."

"I just want you to be careful too."

"I hate to say I agree with this big lug," Shelby added. "But

I do worry sometimes that you trust too easily, Annie."

Another country heard from.

It wasn't that Annie didn't appreciate their concern. She did. Truly. But she wished they'd at least wait until they met Jed before judging him.

As though sounding an agreement, the doorbell chimed. Annie lifted her gaze to Dan's. "Judge him for yourself, bro. He's here."

Dan glanced at the house. "So go let Mr. Wonderful in."

Shelby put her hands on her hips. "Avidan Justice, don't you—either of you—" she expanded the glare to Jayce—"*dare* call him that. Remember, he is your sister's friend and this is her home."

Dan's hands went up. "I surrender. Really. I'll behave."

Yeah right. Like Annie believed that for a second. Especially when she heard her big brother mutter as she walked away, "Let the games begin."

Jed stood on the front stoop and went through the drill again.

What is the plan? To get Annie on the show. Why are you here? You are here for a purpose. How will you achieve that purpose? Keep your distance; stay focused.

After that episode in the woods, Jed had stayed clear of Annie for the rest of the weekend, steeling his resolve. When she called him this morning, inviting him over for a barbecue with her family, he knew it was a bad idea.

So why did he agree to come?

Good question.

Still, now was as good a time as any to put himself to the test. He would not weaken. Would not let emotions blur the lines here. He'd hold fast to the wisdom of William:

"And this word 'love,' which graybeards call divine,
Be resident in men like one another
And not in me: I am myself alone."

I am myself alone.

Bingo.

Now if he could just remember that.

A sweet fragrance caught him, and Jed looked again at the flowers lining the walk to Annie's front door. It looked like one of those English gardens they showed on the travel channel. There were even little benches for sitting and enjoying the beauty and a pond complete with cattails.

Clearly this was the home of an artist.

It wasn't just the flowers that showed that either. Jed turned back to the stained glass insert in the door before him. He'd been fascinated when she told him about her art. Even made her promise to show him her studio, where she created. Too bad he couldn't sneak Andy in here with him...

He fingered the textured glass, imagining her hands holding it, shaping it. *Did Annie make this? It's really—*

The door opened, and she stood there, welcome lighting her eyes and smile.

—beautiful.

He followed Annie inside, looking around her home as they walked through. Warm. Welcoming. Creative. Just like the woman herself.

"That's quite a garden you've got out there."

She glanced over her shoulder. "You like it?"

"It's beautiful. Your color choices really work well together."

There was pleasure and playfulness in her grin. "Of course they do. They're my colors."

Ah, yes. The synesthesia. She'd told him about that. He'd gone back to the hotel to research it and found it was like everything else about Annie.

Utterly fascinating.

She headed for a sliding glass door. "We're out in the back and the food's almost ready. Some come on out."

Jed started to follow her, then froze. What...?

Annie glanced back at him, then followed his stunned gaze.

She came to pat Jed's arm. "It's okay. That's my brother."

"Your brother is a sheriff."

"Sheriff's deputy, actually." Pride and love were evident in her tone, which she raised a notch as she looked at her brother, who'd stepped inside and met his stare. "And don't let the glower worry you. He thinks he has to give you the third degree to make sure you're not some kind of closet crazy man."

Glower was an understatement. The man scrutinized Jed like he was some kind of escaped convict or a suspected serial killer. Good thing he hadn't done anything to earn this man's ire.

Right. Nothing but lie to his sister. I'm sure that wouldn't bother him a bit.

Shivers crawled up Jed's spine, then scampered back down.

"I thought you were going to change out of your uniform now that you're off duty."

Dan didn't look at Annie. He kept his focus fixed on Jed. "That's what I came inside to do."

"Hmm." Her skepticism was thick. "Right when Jed arrives, huh? My, my, will coincidences never end?" She sighed and turned back to Jed. "Meet my big brother, Dan Justice. Dan, this is Jed…"

When she hesitated, Jed looked down at Annie and found twin spots of red in her cheeks. A condition that only worsened when her brother arched a brow at her.

"You were saying?" Though Dan's question was directed at Annie, his steely gaze had shifted to rest on Jed.

"Um…" Annie grabbed Jed's shirt front and tugged him down to hiss in his ear. "Quick! What's your last name?"

"Cur—uh, no, wait." Why hadn't he thought up a name before now? Then it would've been ready when he needed it. And he wouldn't be standing here, looking like the proverbial deer in the headlights.

Oh brother! Here's hoping they chalked his stumbling over his own name to being intimidated by Big Brother. Which, just for the record, he was. Dan Justice cut an imposing figure, and having him stare at Jed like that—like he wanted to dissect him and find out what made him tick—was far from comfortable.

Annie's elbow made pointed contact with his ribs.

"Oh! Uh, Current. Jed Current." He held his hand out to Dan. "At your service."

Dan's grip on Jed's fingers was solid.

Rock solid.

So much so that Jed could feel his fingers going numb.

"Sis, you'd better go check the burgers."

Annie glanced from her brother to Jed, worry evident in those golden brown depths. He inclined his head. "Go ahead, Annie. We'll be out in a minute."

"Are you sure?" She looked at the men's still locked hands.

Jed managed a smile through the pain. "I'm sure."

As Annie left, Jed faced Dan head-on. From the spark in that man's eyes, it was obvious he knew what he was doing. So Jed did what any real man meeting a woman's older brother for the first time would do.

He whimpered.

Well, okay, only inside. On the outside he kept his grip equally firm and his gaze locked on Dan's.

After another beat, Dan finally let his hand go. Jed eased it behind his back, hoping no one noticed as he flexed life back into the fingers.

"So, Jed."

Uh-oh. Jed recognized that tone of voice. Annie's brother was in cop mode.

"Tell me about yourself. Where are you from? What do you do for a living? How much did you make last year?" His lips stretched into a tight smile. "What are your intentions toward my sister?"

Jed decided it was time to take the bull by the horns. "Don't I get my rights read to me first?"

Something flickered in Dan's steely eyes. Jed hoped it was respect and not impending violence. "Your rights?"

"Hey, I watch cop shows. You have to read me my rights before you can interrogate me."

"No interrogation, Jed. Just a few friendly questions."

"Aha. Well do me a favor, will you?"

"What's that?"

"Warn me before you get unfriendly. I'll need time to put on a flak jacket."

Dan's stern features melted, but only a fraction. "You're quick on your feet, I'll give you that." His brows lifted a fraction. "Of course, con men usually are."

Jed told himself his temper flared because Dan was pushing him. No way it had anything to do with the fact that the term *con man* hit a little too close to home.

"Listen, pal, Annie's your sister. I get that. And you're protective. I get that too. But you need to get this: The only thing at this little barbecue that's gonna get grilled is the burgers. I'm here because Annie trusts me. So bottom line, the issue isn't do you trust *me,* but do you trust your sister? If you do, then give me a royal break on the cop routine, and let's go join the others."

"And if not?"

Jed straightened. "Then you're not near as smart as Annie says you are."

Dan stared at him, those blue eyes like ice, and Jed felt his pulse jump. Okay, maybe he went a bit too far.

And maybe, he thought, feeling the sweat pop out on his brow when Dan's gaze narrowed, *he went more than just a bit. Maybe he went so far he wasn't going to make it back.*

At least, not without an ambulance.

TWENTY-FIVE

*"Discussion is an exchange of knowledge;
argument is an exchange of ignorance."*

ROBERT QUILLEN

"'Come now, let us reason together.'"

ISAIAH 1:18, NIV

J ed tensed, straining to keep his features neutral.

He refused to meet death with utter panic on his features. So he firmed his jaw and forced a calm he was far from feeling into his gaze.

Okay, Deputy, bring it on. I'm ready for you.

Yeah right. Oh well, at least when that fist hit him, the pain would only last a moment. Then he'd be out cold.

Dan reached out and clamped that big hand of his on Jed's shoulder. "Fair enough."

"It is?" Jed cleared the squeak from his voice. "I mean, yeah. It is."

He and Dan eyed each other, then they both broke into low chuckles. Jed shook his head. "Oh man! I thought you were gonna belt me."

"And have Annie come down on me like two tons of bricks?" Dan grinned and pulled the sliding glass door to the backyard open. "Hardly. But I have to tell you, when I realized she didn't even know your last name…" He followed Jed outside, letting out a heavy sigh. "Leave it to Annie to spend as much time with a guy as she spent with you and not know his last name."

Was Dan implying that his sister was some kind of scatterbrain? If so, then the man didn't know her. He glanced at Annie. Did she hear her brother's comment? From the way she looked away and from the heightened color tingeing her cheeks, Jed figured she had.

He didn't hesitate. He went to slip an arm around her slim shoulders. He liked the way she could just tuck up against him.

A little too much.

"You know, Dan, my last name just never came up." He smiled down at Annie, and the look in her eyes made him feel ten feet tall. "I mean, it's like we'd known each other forever. So I don't think either one of us thought to ask." He gave her a wide-eyed look. "Come to think of it, what's *your* last name?" Everyone laughed at that, and Annie's hug spoke volumes.

Trouble was, Jed wasn't sure he should listen. He was already having enough trouble following the plan.

Dan looked as though he was about to ask another question, and Jed steeled himself, but he needn't have worried. A blond woman stepped around Dan, offering her hand to Jed, her smile as warm and welcoming as Annie's.

Well...almost.

"It's nice to meet you, Jed. I'm Shelby, Dan's wife. And I believe you've met this rascal?" She inclined her head to Jayce, who was playing tug–of-war with Kodi.

Jed waved. "Yup, we've met."

The rest of the evening flew by, and Jed found himself having a good time. Annie's family seemed so comfortable together, though he did notice the way she held back from time to time, watching the others rather than taking part in the rapid-fire teasing. Jed couldn't help but wonder why. Still, there was no doubting the love they all shared. And Dan and Shelby seemed a perfect match.

Just like his folks used to be.

Come on, Jed, at least be honest with yourself. Your parents never got along that well.

It didn't even bother him when the conversation turned to

God. Much. Of course, he'd been wholly unprepared for the shift in topic. Sure, he knew Annie was a person of faith. But the conversation had hardly been conducive to religious application. Jayce was sharing a debate they'd had in class at school about the death penalty.

"It was wild," the kid said around a mouthful of chips. "I mean, half the room was for it, half was against. First time I've ever seen when no one was undecided."

Annie considered her nephew. "Where do you stand?"

Jayce's blue eyes crinkled. "At first I was against it. It just didn't seem right for someone to decide someone else should die. No matter what that person did. But then one of the girls in my class started talking about God and His justice—"

Jed almost choked on his burger. What *was* it with the people around him? How did they get from the death penalty to God?

"—and what she said made a lot of sense. She even showed how the Bible supports it."

Jed couldn't help himself. "Whoa. The Bible? The book that talks about love and forgiveness and all that? Supports the death penalty?"

"Actually—" Dan set his plate of food on the arm of his Adirondack chair—"I agree with Jayce's friend. If you read Romans 13:1–7, it seems pretty clear God gives the government the right to punish those who do wrong. And when Paul says the government doesn't bear the sword in vain…" He shrugged. "I don't think that's referring to a slap on the wrist."

Dan's wife leaned her elbows on her knees. "But is he saying it's okay to kill someone?"

"I think he is."

Jed stared at Annie, his mouth falling open. "You support the death penalty?"

There was a wry twist to her mouth. "I know, Miss Wouldn't-Hurt-a-Fly. But yes, I do."

"So you think it's okay to kill someone?"

Jayce sounded just this side of stunned, and Annie shook her head. "No, not quite. I'm saying I think there's biblical support for governments to put to death those who've committed heinous crimes against society."

Shelby wasn't convinced. "What about the Sermon on the Mount? 'You have heard that it was said, "Eye for eye, and tooth for tooth." But I tell you, Do not resist an evil person. If someone strikes you on the right cheek, turn to him the other also.'"

"But that's not talking about government."

Jed leaned back in his chair, watching Annie, fascinated. This was a side of her he hadn't seen before.

"I mean, think about it," she went on. "Jesus Himself said He didn't come to abolish the law, but to fulfill it. And in the whole 'eye for an eye' section in the Sermon on the Mount, Jesus isn't arguing against the standard law of a life for a life."

"He's not?" Jayce looked almost as surprised as Jed felt.

Annie leaned forward. "I don't think so. I think He's addressing our personal desire for vengeance, not the government's responsibility to exact punishment and justice. Jesus didn't deny the power and responsibility of the government."

"Right," Dan chimed in. "He was telling individual Christians to love their enemies and turn the other cheek. But He also says we're to submit to those in authority, such as the government."

"Well," Jed finally jumped in, "it's no surprise you're for the death penalty. I mean, you're in law enforcement."

Dan took Shelby's hand in his. "Yes, but I'm a Christian first. If I felt Scripture really spoke against capital punishment, I wouldn't support it. I'd still do my job, but I'd do what I could to change the laws."

Shelby traced his fingers with her own. "But you don't think Scripture speaks against it?"

Dan shook his head. "I don't. In fact, I think it mandates that the government use capital punishment to preserve public justice and order."

Jed waited for the explosion. This wasn't just a discussion between family members; it was between husband and wife. And he knew what happened when these kinds of disagreements cropped up.

People got mad. And marriages dissolved.

"I think you're wrong."

Jed tensed. He couldn't believe Shelby had said that in front of everyone. Dan looked up at his wife and tugged at her hand, drawing her out of her chair and into his lap. He circled her with his arms, and she nestled against him.

"I know you do, hon. And I think you're wrong."

She rested her head on his shoulder. "So we keep reading and studying?"

"Absolutely. And who knows? God could always change your mind."

A smile played at Shelby's lips. "Or yours."

Dan grinned. "You do believe in miracles, *don't* you?"

"Okay, you guys!" Jayce hopped up and carried his plate to the trash can. "PDA alert!"

Dan and Shelby laughed. Then he stood, setting her on her feet. "So, sis—" Dan directed a look at Annie—"what's for dessert?"

"Cake. And coffee's inside if anyone wants it."

Jed just sat there, staring.

That was it? I think you're wrong. I think *you're* wrong. Hug, kiss. What's for dessert? Where was the yelling? The anger? The seething resentment?

"What's up, Jed? You look like you're about to fall off your chair."

He met Dan's laughing eyes. "I just…I've never seen people disagree without…you know, *disagreeing*."

Shelby circled Dan's waist with her arms. "It's not that hard when you keep in mind that your relationship is more important than any disagreement."

The words hit him square in the chest. He nodded, then stood and glanced at Annie. "You said there's coffee inside?"

"Help yourself. It's in the kitchen."

He did so, grateful for a reason to grab some alone time. All this togetherness was starting to get on his nerves. Not because it wasn't real, but because it was.

And he didn't entirely understand it.

He lifted the cup to his lips, wandering into the living room, then stopped.

Flowers. Vase after vase of them. Perched all around the room. Well now, that was interesting. Annie kept his flowers.

"Are you hiding in here?"

He turned. Annie stood behind the couch, watching him. He indicated the roses with his coffee mug. "Did you grow all these?"

She chuckled. "Nope. Someone sent them to me."

He let a tinge of jealousy show. Not a lot, just enough to get the point across. "From anyone I should know about?"

"They're not even from someone I should know about."

Ouch.

"They're from some guy from a reality TV show." She came around the couch, the ever-present Kodi on her heels, and sat down. Jed sank onto the cushion beside her as Kodi circled and settled at Annie's feet with a deep doggy sigh. Jed couldn't help but smile. He understood that sigh. Kodi was content so long as she was with Annie.

Jed understood that as well.

Stop it! That's not the way to focus on the plan, you twit.

"The man's name was J T, or J P, or E T..." Her shoulders lifted, eloquent in their dismissal. "Whatever. He wanted Kodi and me to be on his show."

"Sounds exciting."

"Not to me."

Spoken with such conviction. That was not a good sign. "So you weren't interested? At all?"

She leaned back. "I do what I do with search and rescue because it's what God calls me to, not because I want recognition. Or to be on TV. Besides, I can't have some stranger following me around and getting in my way while I'm trying to work." She laid a hand on Kodi's head. "And with my luck, Kodi wouldn't like him. She'd end up snapping at him; he'd probably be a city boy so he'd overreact and say she bit him, and I'd get sued." She shook her head. "No thanks."

Annie folded her knees under her, and Jed tilted his head, taking in the picture she made.

Did she know how striking she was? Not just because she was petite and beautiful, or because of those clear eyes that seemed to see right to your soul, but because of the air of inner strength that rested on her.

You were right, Andy. The camera will love this woman.

The camera? Who cared about the camera? *He* loved—

"Hey, you two. I thought you were getting us dessert."

They both jumped, and Jed wanted to run over and kiss Shelby for interrupting them. For stopping his Benedict Arnold of a mind before it could say those words.

He stood, pulled Annie to her feet, and plastering his best "let's be social" smile on his face, held out his arm. "Our public awaits, my queen. Shall we retire to the royal gardens for tea and crumpets?"

Annie laid her hand along his arm. "The royal gardens, you say? Indeed, milord, I fear what awaits us is far more the royal pains."

"Royal pains? I resemble that remark."

Annie stuck her tongue out at Dan. "And so you should after all you've put Jed through tonight."

Cleary unrepentant, her brother grinned at Jed. "Did I put you through a lot tonight?"

Annie felt Jed's voice growl deep in his chest. "Heckfire, nothin' ah couldn't handle, Shuruff."

She fought back a laugh, knowing what Dan's reaction would be. Three...two...one...

"I'm not a sheriff."

Bingo. Okay, time to get this train on a new track. "What say we go into the kitchen for cake?"

"Finally!" Jayce licked his lips. "And hot chocolate."

Jed's hand engulfed hers as they walked, sending warmth up her arm, filling her head to toe.

He leaned his head close. "You have those little marshmallows?"

"Of course."

He tugged at her hand, and the pressure of his hand on hers both soothed her and made her heart trip just a little. "Well then, dear lady, 'now go we in content.'"

"You're in for a treat, Jed." Jayce was already in the kitchen, pulling mugs from the cupboard and setting them on the center island. "Nobody makes better hot chocolate than Auntie A."

As they made their way to the kitchen, Annie couldn't help noticing that, for once, Kodi wasn't beside her.

Rather, the dog was walking beside Jed.

It was clear: Kodi adored this man. Annie had to admit she wasn't far behind her dog. For all of her protestations to Kyla about dating, she'd never had much time for relationships with men. But Jed…he was different. Special.

He stepped aside, letting Annie enter the kitchen in front of him. Kodi bumped into Annie trying to get into the room in front of her.

"You big moose!" But she wasn't really mad. How could she be when Kodi was the one who'd brought her and Jed together?

Kodi sat near the counter, sniffing the floor just in case someone had been thoughtful enough to drop something for her. Annie went to lift the lid on the doggy cookie jar. Kodi started dancing around the kitchen.

"Arroww-ow!"

"Hang on, you crazy beast." She drew out a handful of cookies.

"Wow, *some*body must have been good." Jayce's eyes were round. "Look at all those treats."

Annie took the cookies, doing her best not to trip on the dancing Kodi, and set them on the dog's cedar bed in the corner of the kitchen. Kodi hopped on the bed and dug in.

Jayce leaned against the wall. "So what'd she do to deserve all that?"

Annie brushed the crumbs off her hands. "That, dear boy, is between me and my dog."

"Yeah, well it must have been something pretty great."

Annie found Jed watching her and a smile filled her features as fully as joy filled her heart. "Oh believe me, it was."

TWENTY-SIX

*"Art attracts us only by what
it reveals of our most secret self."*

JEAN-LUC GODARD

*"For we are God's masterpiece.
He has created us anew in Christ Jesus,
so that we can do the good things
he planned for us long ago."*

EPHESIANS 2:10

Annie hesitated, fingers curled on the large silver door handle. Oh, how she'd been dreading this. But she'd avoided it long enough. Time to buckle down and face the music.

She opened the door and walked inside, immediately taken as always by the elegant ambiance that was Expressions. Killian's gallery wasn't just a place where artists showed their work; it was a place where art dwelled. Where it breathed and lived and touched anyone who entered.

It still amazed her to see her own works displayed here, in an alcove with her name over the entrance. Whatever hassles she had to endure from Killian, she needed to remember how much she owed him.

"Well, to what do I owe this surprise?"

She drew in a deep breath, then turned to face her less-than-pleased friend. "Hey, Killie."

"Keep your heys to yourself. Where's my window?"

She bit back the sharp response. *"Serafina's* window is in my studio. I'm working on it."

"Oh? You mean you've actually carved out time in between jaunts to the mountains and trysts with the new man in your life?"

"Killian, be fair."

Ryan came up from behind them, stepping past Killian to put his arms out and give Annie a warm hug. When he turned back to Killian, he kept one arm around Annie. "You know you don't mean the awful things you say to Annie, so why on earth do you even say them?"

Killian's features darkened for a moment, and Annie thought he'd surely blow a gasket. Then as suddenly as they appeared, the dark clouds dissipated from his features. He waved his hands in the air. "Oh, fine! You're right, Ryan. Of course, you're right." He brushed Ryan aside and drew Annie into a tight hug.

She wasn't sure if she should be relieved or just a bit frightened by the sudden change. Then Killian took hold of her shoulders and set her at arm's length.

"I'm sorry, Annie. I've been a real jerk about this. I just…" He dropped his hands. "I don't know. I guess I was jealous."

Surprise struck her mute for a moment. "Jealous? Killie, of what?"

"I think I can answer that." Ryan put a hand on his boss's shoulder. "Killian has considered himself your primary support and encouragement for a lot of years, Annie."

She gave a slow nod. "Because he has been."

"Right. But with someone new in your life now, someone with a romantic connection, that's going to change."

She stared at Ryan, then at Killian. "What? Why? Surely you don't think our friendship will change just because I fall in…in…"

The expression on Killian's face said it all. He did think that. And if she was honest with herself, she'd admit he was right. For all of Killian's persnickety ways, she'd leaned on him for years. But now it wasn't Killian she wanted to talk with when she was troubled or happy or even just thoughtful.

It was Jed.

She went forward to take her friend's hands in her own. "Oh, Killie, I'm so sorry. I didn't think…"

He looked down at their joined hands, then back up at her. "I know, Annie."

"I don't know what to say."

"You don't need to say anything." He squeezed her hands, then let her go. "I understand. Completely. But understanding doesn't make it any easier to accept." As though unable to endure the tenor of their conversation another moment, Killian spun on his heel and headed toward the back of the gallery. "Now, if you'll excuse me, I must get back to unpacking the shipment that came in today."

Annie barely got a good-bye out before he vanished into the back rooms. She stood there, staring after her friend, as miserable as she could remember being in a long time.

A hand on her shoulder told her Ryan was still there.

"He'll be okay, Annie. He still has your art. And no one can replace him in that."

"No. He can't."

Ryan nodded. "Right. Everything will work out if you just give him time."

"Ryan, get in here! I can't do this by myself, you know!"

At the bellow from the back room, Ryan's smile turned a shade longsuffering. "The master calls, and I must answer."

"How do you stand it, Ryan? I mean, I love the man. But he can be a total pain sometimes."

Ryan crossed his arms. "Killian's a genius at what he does, and I need to learn from him. I can put with up a lot from geniuses."

"I'm glad someone can."

He started toward the back rooms. "Give us a call when you're done with our window, Annie."

Our window.

Apparently, Annie thought as she turned to leave the gallery, Ryan was already learning way too much.

TWENTY-SEVEN

"Do not be afraid of tomorrow; for God is already there."

ANONYMOUS

*"You will have courage because you will have hope.
You will be protected and will rest in safety."*

JOB 11:18

OCTOBER 11
1:30 p.m.

"'Nother story, Mommy."

Amberly's request was delivered by way of a huge yawn, and Brianna stroked her little girl's hair back as they lay together in the chaise lounge chair. It was a beautiful autumn day. The sky was clear, and the sun was just warm enough to make them drowsy.

She fought not to echo her little girl's yawn. "Are you sure, sweetie? Wouldn't you rather take a nap? You seem awful sleepy."

Amberly forced her heavy eyelids open. "No, I'm not. Please?"

"Okay. Do you want to hear about another angel, or shall I tell you about some of the animals in the woods around us?"

"Angel." Amberly snuggled up against Bree, her eyelids drifting shut. "I love stories 'bout angels." Her eyes flew open. "Oh! I know! Tell me 'bout Noah's angel."

Noah's angel? "I'm not sure I know about that one, honey."

Amberly sat up. "Sure you do, Mommy. You told me all 'bout him. Michael, the ark angel."

Bree clamped down the giggle trying to escape. "Oh, *that* ark angel." She'd correct her daughter later. What mattered most right now wasn't correct pronunciation, but this precious time they had together. "Michael was the strongest, most courageous of all angels…"

Amberly's fidgeting stilled, and soon her breathing was deep and even. Bree cuddled her daughter close.

Mark and Annie couldn't have been more right. This was exactly what she needed.

Annie sat on top of the picnic table, sketch pad in her lap, pencil flying as she transferred images of Jayce and Kodi from reality to the paper.

Good thing Jayce had asked to stay with her over the weekend. He was the perfect model for helping her get body positions and movement down before she tried to create them in glass. It was one thing to look at photos and books and another entirely to watch the way someone moved, the interplay of bone and muscle, the flow of athletic grace.

Jayce waved at her, and Annie nodded, unwilling to stop the sketching, even as he trotted toward her, Kodi at his side. She'd filled several pages already, but she needed more. Serafina's window was coming together, piece by piece. But there was still so much to do. So much to figure out. Too much of the pattern, the images, were vague impressions in her mind. She needed to get as much as she could out of her head and down on paper.

"Drink break," Jayce gasped.

She realized he was dripping sweat and jumped off the picnic table. "Oh, Jayce, I'm so sorry!"

He swiped an arm across his wet brow. "Not to worry, Auntie A. Buy me a mondo Dr. Pepper and I'll forgive you."

"Deal." She gathered her sketch pad and pencils and slipped them into the backpack as Jayce clipped Kodi's leash in place. "And do me a favor?"

Her nephew grinned at her. "Sure. What?"

She hiked the backpack onto one shoulder. "Don't tell your folks I almost ran you into the ground at the dog park, okay?"

Jayce's blue eyes sparkled. "Well, I don't know…"

"I'll buy you a burger and fries to go with your pop."

Ah, nothing like food to bribe a teenage boy. Jayce licked his lips. "Toss in a chocolate sundae, and you've got a deal."

"Done."

"You know what?" Jayce led Kodi from the dog park and fell into step beside Annie.

"What's that?"

His grin spread from ear to ear. "I'd have settled for just the burger and fries."

"Yeah? Well, *you* know what?"

"What?"

She poked him with her elbow. "I'd have bought you *two* burgers and *four* sundaes to duck another lecture from your dad."

Jayce raised his gaze to the skies. "Now she tells me!"

"Live and learn, grasshopper." She tossed an arm around his shoulders. "Never give in too soon."

TWENTY-EIGHT

"Nothing is easier than self-deceit.
For what each man wishes, that he also believes to be true."

DIANE ARBUS

"Both hands are skilled in doing evil."

MICAH 7:3, NIV

He watched them, excitement curling deep in his gut.
He'd been right. Right to come here. Right to come after her.

She was the one. The one he'd been searching for. The one who would make everything right again.

The only question now was how…

How to get to her. She was surrounded by family at all times. Protected, as one so precious should be. But that wouldn't stop him.

He had to have her. And have her he would.

The notes had set the stage. Now that he'd found his star, all he had to do was put his plan into action. Tomorrow.

"Tomorrow and tomorrow and tomorrow…"

He could hardly wait.

TWENTY-NINE

"In the midst of our dark and foggy times,
all sorts of voices are shouting orders into the night,
telling us what to do, how to adjust our lives.
Out of the darkness, one voice signals something
quite opposite to the rest—something almost absurd.
But the voice happens to be the Light of the World,
and we ignore it at our peril."

PAUL AIELLO JR.

"I am overwhelmed, and you alone know the way I should turn."

PSALM 142:3

OCTOBER 13
8:30 a.m.

He had to tell Annie the truth.

Jed hated the idea with every ounce of his being. Would sell everything he possessed to not do it. He'd sat here in the restaurant, mainlining coffee, for the last two hours, trying to devise a way out of it.

All of which told him he had to do it.

Not because of any supposed guilt. Not because it was, in some biblical sense, the right thing to do. But because he cared about Annie. More than he'd imagined possible after knowing her for so short a time. It was as though everything inside him had been waiting for her to bring it to life. Pushy, demanding, impossible life.

He slurped another swallow of coffee, not caring that it nearly scalded his tongue, then focused on the TV above the bar. An old black and white western was on. Jed had never really liked those old movies, but suddenly he was nearly overcome with a longing for life that simple. A life where there were no grays and the good guys and bad guys were clearly delineated.

What part would you play in such a world? Certainly not one of the good guys. Jed swirled the coffee in his mug.

No. Certainly not.

He'd never considered himself a bad guy before. He'd always been sure his hat was pure white. But now…well, there was no other way to see it.

He was covered in black. What had he *done* to himself?

No, that wasn't right. He hadn't done this. Annie had. She'd ruined everything.

He'd been so content alone. So sure utter avoidance was the safest way to deal with the roiling waters of relationships—waters that upended his parents' marriage, drowning it in churning anger and hurt.

And now? He couldn't close his eyes without seeing her face. Couldn't listen to music without hearing the melody of her laughter. As for fathoming one more day—let alone an entire future—alone, without her?

Yeah. Right.

So quit whining about it, Curry. Work through it. What are your options?

Options. Okay. As he saw it, he had two: Walk away before he got in too deep. Or tell her the truth.

If he took the first option, Silas would never let him forget how he'd wasted his time and the backers' money. His career would suffer. The show would suffer.

Jed plunked his coffee mug back on the table with a bang. Who was he kidding? *He'd* suffer. Before he got in too deep? He was there, man. And beyond. He was so deep he'd never get out. Forget option one.

Which left him where he was about two pots of coffee ago: He had to tell Annie the truth. Best case scenario, she'd understand. She was a loving, giving woman. She'd see he had no choice. He needed her for the show, and the only way that would happen was to get her to trust him. So he'd come to her, pretended to be someone he wasn't, lied to her, deceived her…

Jed rubbed his throbbing temples. Oh, man. This was not going to be pretty.

"Got a headache?"

He glanced up to find Andy standing beside the table. Jed pushed out a chair with his foot. "Take a load off." He nodded toward the TV. "Your favorite kind of show is on."

Andy turned. "Westerns? Outstanding!" He grabbed the chair and shifted it to the side so he could watch the TV, then laid a tape on the table and eyed Jed as he sat down. "You were up early."

Jed leaned forward to stare into his mug. People read tea leaves, right? Maybe he could read the coffee grounds to find out what he should do. "I had a lot on my mind."

Andy didn't comment. Just perused the menu, signaled the waiter, and ordered the "Hungry Man's Feast": pancakes, eggs, hash browns, bacon, OJ, and coffee. "Oh, and can I have one of those big cinnamon rolls too, please?"

Jed grimaced as the waiter walked away. "How can you eat all of that?"

"How can you not?" Andy pulled one of the empty chairs close and propped his feet on it. "I take it you're not eating?"

The grimace deepened. "I'm not hungry."

"Uh-huh. I've heard a first course of crow can do that to a man."

Jed didn't dignify that with a response.

"So what's up?"

He met Andy's assessing gaze. "Don't you want to watch your western?"

"I've seen this one before. Now spill. What's up?"

"Anyone ever tell you you're too perceptive by half?"

"Yeah. You."

The waiter returned to fill Andy's coffee mug. Andy stopped him when the cup was half full. "We'll need more creamer too."

The waiter glanced at the table, then moved the little pitcher of cream in front of Andy—who upended half the cream into his mug, then set it down. "Like I said, we'll need more."

With wide-eyed assent, the waiter moved away as Andy lifted the sugar and sent a stream chasing after the creamer. He stirred the concoction, then took a long, appreciative drink. "Ah." He smacked his lips. "Perfect."

Jed cocked his head. "No actual coffee beans were injured in the creation of this drink."

"Hey, it's better than the sludge you call coffee."

"If you say so."

"I do, and you know I'm always right. Speaking of which…" He nudged the tape he'd set on the table toward Jed.

"What's this?"

"Something I put together for you." Andy's eyes stayed fixed on him. "Something you need to watch."

Jed set the tape beside his coffee mug. "Sure. I'll get to it soon."

"Get to it now."

He frowned. "It's that important?"

Andy didn't respond. He didn't need to. Jed saw the answer in his steady stare.

It was that important.

"Okay, let me finish my coffee, and I'll go back to the room and check it out."

That must have satisfied Andy, because he turned his focus to the TV. Good. Jed didn't feel like answering any more questions.

"You're going to tell her, aren't you?"

Jed opened his mouth to tell Andy to mind his own stinkin' business, but something entirely different came out: "I've got to. It's gonna drive me nuts if I don't."

"Good."

"That it's driving me crazy?"

Andy inclined his head, though his gaze was fixed on the TV.

"Yeah, that too. Proves there's hope for yo—"

Jed jumped when Andy's hand shot out and grabbed his arm. "What are you *doing?*" He tried to pry Andy's hand loose, but the younger man's grip just tightened.

"Jed!"

"Will you let go of me?"

"*Jed,* look!"

He turned to glance up at the TV and froze.

Annie.

Annie was on the TV. And Kodi.

Andy scrambled for the TV remote, leaning on the bar as he turned up the volume just in time to catch Jed's voice.

"...most riveting episode of *Everyday Heroes* yet. Don't miss it."

Stark realization sapped the color from his face. Jed could feel it just drain away as he stared at the screen. Though the commercial had ended, he couldn't look away.

"Oh man..."

Andy's groan echoed the sick feeling coursing through Jed. "They used it. I can't believe they used it."

"Of course, they used it!" Andy punched the TV off and dropped the remote on the bar. "I *told* you not to send that to Silas. Any executive producer worth his salt would do exactly what Silas did. *Use* it! What are we going to do now? They're advertising a show we haven't filmed yet!"

Jed reached numb fingers into his shirt pocket and tugged his cell phone free. He hit speed dial and waited. Silas answered after the first ring. Jed didn't even say it was him. He just blurted the only thing he could think of to say.

"Silas, are you out of your freakin' *mind?*"

"Jed, my boy! I take it you've seen the ad, eh?"

"Silas—"

"We're getting great reactions so far. The execs figure we'll pull some serious demographics. Well done, boy. Well done!"

"No! Not well done!"

"Now, don't start doubting yourself. Believe me, I've learned to trust those instincts of yours. You were right on the money—and the network execs have cleared a spot just for your show during sweeps week."

With every word Silas's exhilaration—and Jed's dread—mounted. "Silas, what are you talking about?"

"The promo you sent, boy! That wonderful, killer promo! The suits loved it. Everything about it. The woman. The dog. Said to run it just as it was."

Jed's stomach clenched. He met Andy's "I told you so" gaze as Silas went on.

"So, when do we get the whole show? The execs are nervous that it's not in the can by now."

The waiter returned to the table, Andy's breakfast spread out on plates balanced along his arms.

"Silas…"

"But I told them with you at the helm, there's no need for worry."

"Yeah, well…"

The waiter slid Jed's water glass closer to him as he set down the last plate. Jed scooted his chair back. Andy's breakfast took up the whole table.

"You've never let me down, son, and I know you won't start now."

Jed closed his eyes. How could he have been so stupid? Why hadn't he listened to Andy, just this once? "Silas, there may be a problem."

Silence. "Problem? As in inconsequential, doesn't-really-matter, the-show's-in-the-bag problem?"

Jed swallowed. "Not exactly. More like we may not get Annie for the show—"

"Unacceptable!"

The word blared through the phone lines, raking Jed's already raw nerves. "Silas—"

"Don't want to hear it, son. It's not just your reputation on the line this time. I stood up for you. I convinced the powers that be to not only fund your little expeditions, but to put you in a primo slot for sweeps. Blow it now, and we're both finished."

"I appreciate that—"

"*Stuff* appreciation. You can't tell me one little lady with a dog can get the better of you. Now get out there and *get* that show. The clock's ticking! Sweeps wait for no show! Not even a hit!"

Click. The line went dead. He punched the *off* button on his cell phone, then lowered it to the table.

Andy looked up from his breakfast. Apparently he'd recovered from his shock enough to take sustenance.

LOTS of sustenance.

"Trouble in paradise?"

"You have no idea."

"No?" He leaned an elbow on the table, propping his chin on one hand. "Let's see, despite my fervent objections and dire predictions that you'd regret it, you sent the promo of Annie to Silas because you knew he'd love it. Well, guess what? You were right. And so was I. He loves it. You regret it." He lifted his fork and stabbed a chunk of cinnamon roll. "Sound about right?"

"I really, really hate you."

Andy grinned around a mouthful of food. "Yeah. Lots of people feel that way about we geniuses."

"*Us* geniuses, genius."

"Whatever."

Jed cupped his hands around his now cold coffee mug. "Man, I couldn't have messed this up worse if I tried."

"Agreed."

He ignored that.

"So I take it they think the show's in the can?"

Jed nodded.

"And they expect it to be ready for sweeps."

It sounded as bad when Andy said it as it had when Silas said it. Jed rubbed his temples. "So, Mr. Genius, how do I get out of this?"

Andy dabbed at his face with a napkin. "The second thing you do is take that tape I gave you back to the room and watch it."

"And the first thing?"

"That's easy. You do what all men since the beginning of time have done when they've gotten themselves into serious trouble."

Jed was afraid to ask, but he couldn't help himself. "What?"

Andy reached across the table, lifted Jed's cell phone, and held it out to him. "You call your mother."

THIRTY

"More things are wrought by prayer than this world dreams of."

ALFRED, LORD TENNYSON

"'It is not my heavenly Father's will that even one of these little ones should perish.'"

MATTHEW 18:14

OCTOBER 13
10:30 a.m.

"Mommy, lookit! Another squirrel!"

Bree focused the camera on her little girl and waved. Amberly was too busy running here and there along the path to want more of a response than that. Just something to show her that Mommy was listening.

And Bree was getting some great shots. Annie would be thrilled.

"You're a really good mother, you know that?"

Now that needed a more expressive response. Bree lowered her camera and pressed a kiss to her husband's cheek. "Thanks, hon."

It was a beautiful morning. They'd gone on a long hike this morning, just the three of them, soaking up the sun and beauty around them, Bree taking one picture after another. There were so many wonders out here. All you had to do was look.

As for Amberly, she scampered along the trail like one of the dozen squirrels they'd seen as they walked.

"Oh, to have that much energy," Bree moaned.

"Look at it this way—" Mark slanted her a smile—"you probably won't have to fight her to take a nap."

"Wouldn't that be nice?"

Getting Amberly to slow down long enough to take a nap was always a challenge. To say the least.

When they returned to their campsite about a half hour later, tantalizing fragrances met them.

Ernie waved a burger flipper at them. "Hey, you wanderers! Come and get it!"

Jane handed them plates, and Bree looped her arm in Jane's. "Now this is what heaven will be like...the men cooking and serving us."

"And angels dancing." Jane nodded toward Amberly, who bounced around, waving her plate and singing a silly, happy song.

Bree looked over their daughter's head at Mark. "Oh, yeah. She's ready for a nap."

"You're kidding me." Mark turned to Ernie. "Bree thinks I'm wrong, but you just wait. She'll run down any time now."

Their friend regarded Amberly, who'd given up her plate so she could hold Ethan's hands while they twirled in circles. "You're dreamin', pal."

Mark just smiled.

It was probably ten minutes later when Bree realized she didn't see her little girl anywhere.

She jumped up from the camp chair where she'd been relaxing. "Do you guys know where Amberly is?"

Jane scanned the area. "I thought she was here..."

Mark held up a hand. "Relax, everyone, and follow me."

They looked at each other, then did as Mark suggested. He led them to the tent and pulled back the flap. Bree stepped in front of Mark and peered inside.

There, cuddled up on the sleeping bag, her thumb in her mouth, was their little dynamo, fast asleep.

Ernie clapped Mark on the back. "Remind me never to doubt you again."

Brianna leaned back into her husband's arms. "You do know your daughter, don't you?" He hugged her tight, and she patted his arm. "Hey, you wanted a little time to fish, so why don't you go ahead and do it now?"

"That's a good idea." Jane smiled at them. "We can watch Amberly if you'd like to go with him."

"No——" Bree fell in step beside her husband as they headed back to the Conrads' campsite to finish eating—"I'm not that keen on skewering worms. How about you, Ernie? You want to go with him?"

"Not this time. I promised Ethan that his mom and I would take him out in the boat to fish this evening."

"Well then——" Bree picked up her plate and settled back into her chair—"looks like you've got some solitude time, hon."

"You don't mind not going?"

"Well, not so long as you promise to spend time with your adoring girls by the campfire tonight."

He gave her a smacking kiss. "It's a deal. I'll be back in a few hours."

Jane looked at Brianna as Mark went to gather his gear. "Just an hour?"

Bree smiled. "More like three or four hours. But that's okay. He doesn't get much relaxation time alone."

"Neither do you, from what I hear." Jane stretched her legs out in front of her. "You know, if you wanted to take a nap too, I'd be happy to watch for Amberly in case she wakes up and wanders out of the tent."

"Thanks, but I'm not sleepy. I do think I'll go read for a while after I eat though."

"Okay. Just let me know if you change your mind."

They chatted for a while as they finished eating, then Bree headed back to their tent. She unzipped the flap and slipped inside.

Amberly was still sound asleep.

Bree stroked Amberly's forehead, smoothing the blond curls away from her daughter's soft skin. Was there any sight more precious than a sleeping child?

She piled pillows for a backrest, then pulled her book from her backpack and settled in. But after dozing off three times, she finally surrendered.

Apparently Jane was right. Amberly wasn't the only one who needed a nap.

She lay back and cuddled her sleeping daughter close. With a contented sigh, Brianna let her eyes drift shut, listening to the soothing symphony of nature. Echoes of familiar laughter told Bree that Jane and Ernie were at their campsite as well.

Her eyes popped open. Drat. She needed to tell Jane that she was going to take a nap. But she was so comfy here... Besides, with her arms wrapped around Amberly, she'd know if the little girl stirred or woke.

They'd be fine. Ethan was at the next campsite, which pretty well guaranteed that even if Amberly woke, she'd make a beeline for Jane and Ernie.

Still...it couldn't hurt to be sure. There was someone even better than Jane and Ernie she could talk to—and she wouldn't have to move to do it.

So, even as Brianna's heavy eyelids lowered, she sent a plea winging heavenward: *Father, please watch over Your children as we sleep.*

OCTOBER 13
11:00 a.m.

Jed couldn't move.

Couldn't think.

About the only thing he could do was the one thing he didn't want to do: feel.

Emotions assaulted him, a tsunami slamming into him, pounding him into so much rubble as he sat there, staring at the image frozen on the TV screen. Two people, laughing together, eyes fixed on each other's face, expressions clear evidence of what was happening between them.

Jed tore his gaze away, leaned his head back, and closed his eyes. He didn't know. He should have. Of course he should have. But he'd been so focused on his goal that he hadn't realized—

Liar.

The word rang within him as clear as truth. His hands gripped the arms of the easy chair cradling him, and he forced himself to look again. To study the glimmer in the eyes. The brilliance of the smiles.

Okay, God. You win. I'm sorry. I blew it. So act. She's Your daughter. Do something here! That's who You are, right? What You're all about? Forgiveness. Restoration. Setting the captives free? So come on, God. Set me free.

He waited. Senses alert for any hint of absolution.

The stark silence condemned him further.

Then ushered in exactly what Jed did not need: "'I called you so often, but you didn't come. I reached out to you, but you paid no attention. You ignored my advice and rejected the correction I offered. So I will laugh when you are in trouble! I will mock you when disaster overtakes you—when calamity overcomes you like a storm, when you are engulfed by trouble, and when anguish and distress overwhelm you...'"

Jed leaned forward, elbows planted on his knees. *Stop it. Just...stop.*

But the inner echo wasn't listening. The recitation went on, the words weighted and sorrowful—just as his mother's voice had been when she quoted these verses to him mere days ago: "'I will not answer when they cry for help. Even though they anxiously search for me, they will not find me. For they hated knowledge and chose not to fear the LORD. They rejected my advice and paid no attention when I corrected them. That is why they must eat the bitter fruit of living their own way. They must experience the full terror of the path they have chosen. For they are simpletons who turn away from me—to death. They are fools, and their own complacency will destroy them.'"

Complacency? He wasn't complacent! Anything but!

Now. But before this moment? Before seeing what you just saw?

No arguing with the truth.

Jed lifted the TV remote and, for the third time, hit play. Like a longed for dream—and a shattering nightmare—the scenes unfolded: him and Annie at the dog park, him and Annie walking together, him and Annie with Kodi.

Andy's mastery of the lens was painfully evident. Every detail, every nuance of expression, every movement, was faithfully recorded. Jed couldn't miss the changes in the way he and Annie looked at each other. The shift from stranger to acquaintance, acquaintance to friend, friend to...

He turned away.

Coward.

He didn't even flinch. Yes. Absolutely. Oh, not all the time. He could face outward dangers with the best of them. Had been immersed in physical dangers all his career, getting as close as possible to the core of the storm, the fire, the disaster—whatever crisis they were filming. Anything for the show.

Everything for the show.

But this. His eyes defied him, drifting back to the screen, taking in the way Annie touched his arm, the shine in her eyes as she looked at him.

He'd been a coward to the core when it came to something like this. And yet all his careful plans, all his innate avoidance, had been useless. Because there he was, live and in color, looking at Annie with that same glow in his eyes. Touching her arm with the same tenderness. And the sound of his voice when he said her name...

Jed hit the power button, watching the screen fade to black. And this time when he lowered his head into his hands, there was no defiance.

Just a desperate inner plea for help.

As Jed sat there, something stirred at the back of his mind. Something someone had told him once...

"Don't face it alone."

Who said that to him? Or was it something he—

Jed stilled. Then was up and out of the chair, going to kneel beside his bed, reaching. His fingers closed around the book, and he pulled it out.

Ken's Bible.

He fanned through the pages, scanning until he found the note he was looking for. There. Written in bold strokes. *"Need to remember this when life doesn't make sense. Don't try to face it alone. Find someone to share the struggle. And share it with God. He'll have the answers."*

He'll have the answers.

Jed stared at the wall. It all sounded so simple, but he couldn't quite buy it. He'd gotten himself into this mess. He was supposed to just dump it in God's lap and expect Him to fix it all? Why?

His gaze dropped to the book in his hands, and he flipped to the first page, settling deep in the chair.

And started to read.

THIRTY-ONE

"A child's world is fresh and new and beautiful,
full of wonder and excitement.
It is our misfortune that for most of us that clear-eyed vision,
that true instinct for what is beautiful and awe-inspiring,
is dimmed and even lost before we reach adulthood."

RACHEL CARSON

"But I solemnly swear to keep you safe."

GENESIS 6:18

OCTOBER 13
11:00 a.m.

The butterfly was on Mommy's nose.

Amberly put her hand over her mouth to catch the giggle. But it was so funny, the way the butterfly tippy-toed on Mommy's nose. Its pretty wings shook. Like a little orange and black angel.

Oh! The butterfly was flying away. Amberly had opened the tent flap to let it inside, but she forgot to close the flap. She wanted Mommy to see the butterfly. But it was flying outside.

She stood up, then looked back at her mommy. Amberly knew she was supposed to stay inside the tent. She wasn't supposed to go outside alone.

But the butterfly was getting away!

Careful to be quiet, she reached for the butterfly. But it ducked and dodged—then spun and circled right out of the tent.

Amberly looked at her mommy. Should she wake her?

No, she'd just catch the butterfly herself. She would be very, very careful and not hurt it. She would bring it back inside the tent and keep it there to show Mommy. Tell Mommy the funny way it walked on her nose. Then she would let it fly away.

Yes. She would follow the pretty butterfly. And she would bring it back to Mommy.

Amberly stepped through the tent flap, letting her soft giggle escape.

Mommy would be so surprised!

THIRTY-TWO

*"Evil when we are in its power is not felt as evil
but as a necessity, or even a duty."*

SIMONE WEIL

"Don't let evil get the best of you."

ROMANS 12:21

OCTOBER 13
12:00 p.m.

Surely the heavens were smiling down on him.

He almost hadn't come this morning. So much to do. Too much chance someone would miss him. But the dark urging had been so strong.

Finally he couldn't fight it any longer. He made his excuses and drove up into the mountains as though the very demons of hell were on his heels.

Maybe they were.

But whatever the motivation, he was here. And heaven knew he couldn't have arranged such precise, perfect timing no matter how hard he tried. To be standing here, watching, at the precise moment his chosen star decided to wander off? And that the mother should be so sound asleep she didn't hear a thing? For him to trail the child in silence, with nothing to give him away, not a snap of a stick or rustle of leaves?

It had to be the work of heaven.

After all, had he not been here, who knew what could have happened to this precious little girl. This one who would make things right again. He watched her, dancing after the butterfly and going ever deeper into the woods. Poor thing. Her mother certainly wasn't watching over her. Foolish woman. With the world so full of predators—those on two legs as well as four—how could she be so careless?

Yes, it was good he was here.

He would take her. It was his right. He was watching over her when she wandered away. So it only stood to reason that she was his. She'd be the perfect star in his drama. All his care and deliberation were about to pay off. Just one more bit of preparation, and he'd be ready.

Excitement surged through his veins. He hesitated, poised and ready to step onto the stage. He held his breath, savoring the moment.

It was time.

The curtain was about to go up.

THIRTY-THREE

"Not only do we not know God except through Jesus Christ;
We do not even know ourselves except through Jesus Christ."

Blaise Pascal

"Then Jesus placed his hands over the man's eyes again.
As the man stared intently, his sight was completely restored,
and he could see everything clearly."

Mark 8:25

October 13
12:00 p.m.

"Up 'n' at 'em, Mom."

Jed rang the doorbell a second time, though he could hear footsteps approaching. She'd probably scold him for being impatient, but he couldn't help it. He needed to talk with her. Now. And not just about Annie.

On the drive over here his mind—and his heart—had been working overtime. He'd read page after page in Ken's Bible, almost as moved by Ken's notes as he was by the text itself. But both worked together, showing him something he'd never expected to see.

Himself.

One cold, hard truth after another struck home. About who he was. Why he did the things he did to himself. And to others.

Like Annie.

Facing what he'd done to her sliced deep, a grappling hook

that dredged his spirit, revealing other long-ignored truths and shoving them in his face. With each new realization, Jed sank deeper into his chair. Finally he couldn't take it another moment.

He grabbed the phone and called his mom.

The sweet sound of her voice had been a salve to his raw heart. When he said he needed to talk, she hadn't hesitated. "Of course, dear. Come right over."

At the sound of the doorknob turning, Jed steeled himself. He would face his mother and say the things he now knew he had to say. He was ready.

But the words he'd prepared died on his lips when he saw who opened the door.

"Amos."

The man smiled, but not before Jed caught the glimmer of pain in his eyes at the flat tone in Jed's voice. "Come on in, Jed."

He stepped past the older man, his mind scrambling to adjust. Facing his mom was one thing. Facing her with Amos beside her...he wasn't sure he could do that.

Amos was the first to break the awkward silence between them. "Your mother's waiting in the living room. She's got coffee brewed and ready."

Jed started to walk past Amos without a word, but his feet wouldn't budge. They seemed anchored to the floor. He kept his gaze fixed on the rug beneath his feet. "So...you special order this rug?"

Amos glanced down, a slight crease appearing between his brows. "Your mother did." His forehead smoothed as they surveyed the room around them. "She always knows the perfect touch to make a room warm and welcoming."

Jed started and looked up. Studied the man's features. As always, his face flat lit up when he talked about Jed's mom. But where that had irritated Jed in the past, this time he found it fascinating. Because he'd seen it before. Not twenty minutes ago.

On his own face when he talked to Annie.

Suddenly Jed knew he not only could do this with Amos present; he needed to. "Why don't you come join us, Amos?"

His stepfather only hesitated a moment, then a smile broke across his weathered features. "I'd like that."

They walked into the living room together, a sight that stopped his mother cold. Jed couldn't help but smile. He dropped into a large, cushy chair, indicating that Amos should sit on the couch beside his mother.

To her credit, she adjusted quickly, her usual calm settling back in place as she lifted the coffeepot to pour Jed a steaming cup. She handed it to him, catching his gaze head-on as he reached out to take it.

"Ernest Jediah Curry, you know I adore you and how happy I am you've come home, but I have to ask: *What* is your problem?"

Jed's mouth quirked at his mother's blunt question. "Settle back, Mom, and I'll tell you. I gotta warn you though—" he took a sip of the coffee—"it's a doozy."

As she sat back, one hand nestled in Amos's big hand, Jed started to speak. Stopped. Started again. Bit his lip. Grabbed for the first distraction at hand—a flowered throw pillow—and plucked at its fuzzy fringe.

Oh, man. Where to begin?

How about with the truth?

Right.

"I did something stupid, Mom."

The least she could do was look surprised. But no. She just tilted her head. "And?"

Amos tugged at her hand, and she relented. "I'm sorry, dear. Go on."

Heaving a heavy sigh, he told them everything, not sparing himself as he spilled it all: how he came to town to meet Annie Justice, plant the seeds that would win her trust, then get her to agree to do the show. About his decision to send the promo to Silas, the man's reaction.

His mom listened, nodding once in a while but not saying anything. He appreciated that.

In fact, he appreciated a number of things about his mother.

This last week or so it was as though he saw her—really saw her—for the first time. The quick wit. The love that overflowed her actions and words. The joy that cloaked her like an old familiar comforter.

She was a woman at peace.

Had she been like this when he was growing up?

Probably.

If he was honest with himself, he'd have to admit he hadn't seen much of anything but anger when he was a kid. His father's. His own. As he thought back on those days, he realized the only one who hadn't been angry was his mom.

Hurt, yes. Sad, of course. But angry?

No.

In fact, he could see now that he and his father had cornered the market on that particular commodity. And he could see something else too.

He could see how much that had cost him. Not just in his relationship with his mother. But with Amos as well.

"So…" He swallowed hard, punching the pillow. "That's it. The whole ugly story." He bent the pillow in half. "But the thing is, it didn't work out the way I planned."

His mom's clear gaze pinned him. "Really."

"Annie's just, well—" he waved the pillow by the fringe—"she's so different from what I expected. Watching her, talking with her, there's something unique about her. Something really special. And when she's working with Kodi…"

Good grief! Was he going to cry? What was *wrong* with him? He shook off the emotions and shoehorned the words from his tight throat. "I don't know, they make me smile, Mom. Like I haven't done in years." He plucked at the pillow again. "Then there's that family of hers. They talk about God so freely, like—" he tossed the pillow in the air—"He's just a natural part of their lives."

"He probably is." She leaned forward, and with a speed that took him unawares, her hand shot out to snag the pillow and jerk it away from him. She set it on her lap, smoothing it. "It's like that for lots of folks."

Jed laid his hand over hers, where it rested on the abused pillow. "I know, Mom. And I know I've acted like a jerk about...things."

He crossed his fingers, hoping she'd let it go at that. No such luck.

"Things?"

He drew a deep breath. "About the whole mess with Dad. I know it wasn't your fault. And—" his gaze moved to the man sitting beside her—"about you, Amos." Jed wanted to look away, but he didn't let himself. "I was too angry to see how unhappy you were with Dad, how much he hurt you. And to see how great Amos is." He shook the roughness from his voice. "Amos, I've never seen a man act with such love before. You treat Mom like she's the most precious thing in your life."

His stepfather was having his own trouble getting words out. "Because she is, son."

Jed gripped it like a life preserver keeping him afloat in surging waves of regret and self-recrimination.

"You deserve a husband who loves you like that. I'm just sorry it took me this long to see that. And I'm sorry I acted the way I did about your faith, Amos. You never really tried to shove it down my throat. You just..."

Jed finally looked away. He wasn't sure he could say this, no matter how true it was. But he had to get it out. Had to let them know. For their sakes. And for his own. "You were just trying to love me too. To be the dad I never had."

His mother's hand cupped his face, and she lifted his gaze to meet her own. "Thank you, Jed."

"Mom...I'm so sorry."

"It's all right, dear. We understand. And so does God. He knows us, inside and out. Nothing about us surprises Him. Not our weaknesses, not our stubbornness. We don't have to earn His acceptance. He accepts us as we are. Thank heaven."

Even with all the regret and guilt chasing through him, he smiled. "You and Annie are so much alike. I think you'd really like each other. You both share such faith—and it stands no matter what. Believe it or not, I remember how that felt, those first days when I had the sense that God's hand was on my shoulder."

His mom's eyes shone. "It always has been, dear."

"I can't say I understand faith the way you two do, and yet…"

"You'd like to."

He nodded.

"Which must have made it even harder to spend all this time talking with Annie about these kinds of things—"

He knew where she was headed. "Faith and God and truth—"

"All the while knowing you were living a lie."

What could he say? Oh, he'd tried to dress it up, but there was no denying the obvious.

Except… "Not all of it was a lie."

Amos and his mom waited as he sorted through his thoughts. "My feelings for Annie. Those aren't a lie. They're as true as it gets."

"What are your feelings for her?"

Oh, man. Was he really going to say this out loud? "I care about her, Mom." The truth of that simple statement speared him, sending regret slicing deep. "I really do. I care about her more every day."

Joy lit his mother's features. "Oh, Jed, that's wonderful."

"No." He closed his eyes. "No, it's not. It's terrible." Misery pried Jed's eyes open, and he bolted out of his chair, pacing as words poured out of him in a tormented torrent. "What have I done? I mean, how do I tell Annie what I feel, how much she means to me, without telling her who I really am? And if I do that, I have to tell her why I really came back to town. And then there's Silas and that stupid clip I sent. How can I let him down when he's done so much for me, believed in me all these years? And it's not just me, Mom. I could end up hurting his reputation. How can I have *that* on my conscience—not like there's much space left there considering everything *else* I've messed up."

Amos rose and put a solid hand on Jed's shoulder, bringing him to a halt. "Sit down, son."

He didn't even argue. He just plopped into the chair. "I just...I don't know. I wish none of it had happened."

His mother considered that. "You wish you hadn't met Annie?"

Jed stilled. No. He couldn't say he wished that.

His mother must have read his answer in his expression, because she patted the back of his hand, an action equal parts comfort and reprimand. "I'm proud of you, Jediah."

His mouth fell open. "You're...what?"

The corners of her mouth lifted. "I'm proud of you. It isn't easy to admit you're wrong. Even harder to take the steps to make things right."

Jed glanced at Amos, whose steady gaze calmed him. "This won't be easy, son. You know that."

Did he ever.

His mother let go of Jed and lifted her coffee cup to take a sip. "Just do what's right, dear. God will take care of the rest."

Jed marveled at the woman sitting next to him. "How do you do that, Mom?"

"Do what?"

"How do you listen to your only child spill his guts, telling you the awful things he's done? If I were in your shoes, I'd be so disappointed. But here you sit, and all I sense from you is acceptance. Compassion." He halted. This was getting ridiculous. He wasn't the kind of guy who got choked up. Ever. But ever since the day Ken was killed, he'd felt like some kind of emotional basket case.

Like right now. He couldn't even get a sentence out without wanting to lay his head in his mother's lap and weep.

When he finally could speak again, his voice was rough. "Such *love*."

At his mom's silence, he looked up. Tears glistened in her eyes. She tried to speak but couldn't.

Maybe it was genetic.

Amos slid his arm around her shoulders, and she leaned her head against him. Jed understood. She drew strength from his love.

Finally she straightened, her shrug elegant in its eloquence. "'My crown is in my heart, not on my head; Not decked with diamonds and Indian stones, nor to be seen—'" she squeezed his hand—"'my crown is called content, a crown that seldom kings enjoy.'"

"*King Henry VI,*" he whispered. "Act 3, scene 1."

Her smile was a benediction.

Jed didn't need to ask the source of her contentment. He recognized it as the same source that made Annie all she was.

The same Source that had been hounding him since he left home all those years ago.

And while he wasn't ready to give in yet, sitting here in a companionable silence with his mother and stepdad, Jed realized something.

He hadn't been the one planting seeds at all.

Rather, he'd been the soil. And right now, he felt rototilled, fertilized, and planted. And unless he missed his guess, the seeds were taking root. Because every day brought an increasing awareness that something was missing in his life. Something he'd abandoned.

Something he wanted back.

"Are you all right, Jed?"

A mere week ago, Amos's concern would have been an intrusion. Now Jed welcomed it.

"I will be. I know what I need to do."

"You've made some very positive steps already." Jed's mom looked from him to Amos, and the joy on her face told him he'd been right to do this. To open the door not only to her, but to the man who'd made her so happy. "So what will you do now?"

Jed thought for a moment. "As I see it, I've got a couple of steps to take. First, I need to deal with the show. I should be able to get a flight back to LA first thing tomorrow." He sighed. "Silas is going to kill me."

"Could you lose your job?"

"Maybe, but I can't worry about that. I need to put things right. No matter what happens."

"And the second step?"

His mom nudged Amos with her elbow. "I'm betting that has to do with a certain beautiful artist we know."

Amos waggled those bushy brows. "Ah, you mean the woman with a soft spot for lost people and big black dogs?"

"And, God willing, for our boy."

His mother's tender words warmed him, even as apprehension tightened his chest. Yes, it would be great if God was willing. Because Jed had a terrible feeling that once Annie found out what he'd done, *she'd* be willing to do one thing, and one thing only.

Forget Jed Curry ever existed.

THIRTY-FOUR

*"Have courage for the great sorrows of life
and patience for the small ones.
And when you have finished your daily task,
go to sleep in peace. God is awake."*

Victor Hugo

*"I still dare to hope when I remember this:
The unfailing love of the Lord never ends!
By his mercies we have been kept from complete destruction."*

Lamentations 3:21–22

October 13
1:30 p.m.

"Bree?"

She bolted upright, eyes blinking in the bright sunlight. A hand touched her arm even as Mark's voice enfolded her.

"Hey, it's okay. I didn't mean to startle you."

She blinked, reality sinking in. She was stretched out on the sleeping bag inside their tent; Mark was crouching beside her. Slow contentment eased across her lips, and she stretched her arms over her head. "Oh, wow. I guess I fell asleep, huh?"

Mark stroked her arm, his fingers feather light on her skin. "I told you a weekend in the mountains would help you relax."

"Hmm." She batted at him. "Don't sound so pleased with yourself."

"Hey, can I help it if I'm brilliant?"

"Yeah, that's you. A regular Albert Einstein." She sat up on the sleeping bag. "As evidenced by the fact that you married me."

"No argument from me on that one." Laughter danced in his dark eyes.

Brianna glanced around. "Where's Amberly?"

"Probably over at the next tent, with Jane and Ernie."

She shook the remnants of sleep from her head and pushed to her feet. "Did you see them when you got back?"

He stood beside her, uncertainty perched on his brow. "No. You know, I don't think anyone was there." At her start, he touched her arm. "Don't worry, hon. Remember Ernie said he'd promised to take Ethan and Jane fishing a little later today. I bet she wandered over there and begged to go with them. You know Amberly."

Bree did indeed. Her daughter was shameless when it came to spending time with Ethan. Not even having to put a worm on a hook would have dissuaded her.

Brianna made her way out of the tent, glancing to the next campsite as she did. Mark was right. It didn't look like anyone was there. Still, it couldn't hurt to take a look. She lifted her face to the slight breeze as she walked. There was nothing like autumn in the Oregon mountains. Evergreens towered over them, their draping branches granting shade from the still warm sun. Deciduous trees dotted here and there, providing an explosion of color in the midst of the rich fir and pine greens. Temperatures were slightly warm during the day to cool—and even cold—at night. And the night sky…it was glorious. Stars shone in the cloudless sky, a cascade of heavenly lights, and the clear air seemed to carry every heady scent of evergreen and flowers right to their campsite.

Brianna loved it here. Almost as much as Amberly did. She chuckled. Amberly's love affair with the woods and nature was showing no signs of waning. It was great to see her daughter appreciate nature the way she always had, but still, sometimes it made her nervous. She couldn't count the times she'd had to stop her little explorer from following some wonder out of the campsite.

Good thing Jane and Ernie were here to watch Amberly when Brianna fell asleep.

But they didn't know they were supposed to watch her. You didn't tell them you were going to take a nap, remember?

The dark thought quickened Brianna's pace, but when she reached the Conrads' campsite, one glance told her it was empty. As she stood there, looking around, apprehension nibbled at her gut. They *had* taken Amberly with them, hadn't they?

"Hey, Bree. What's up?"

Relief weakened her knees as she turned and watched Jane and Ernie traipse up the path toward her, fishing poles in their hands. So Mark was right.

"Lookit, Bree!"

She just managed to avoid getting hit with the fish hanging from Ethan's small hand. His freckled face was smudged with dirt and wreathed in pride. "I caught it all by myself."

Brianna laughed. Ethan was an absolute towheaded doll. No wonder Angel had a crush on him. She cast an eye at his parents. "All by yourself, huh? Boy, I bet Amberly was impressed."

"Nuh-uh, she wasn't."

"Oh? How come?"

He took his fish to the fire pit. "'Cuz she wasn't with us, silly."

The words jerked Brianna to full attention. She looked at Jane and Ernie. They were studying her, confusion creasing their brows. The three spoke at the same time.

"Amberly's not with you?"

Brianna spun and raced back to their tent. "Amberly!" She looked all around, scanning the suddenly threatening forest around them. "Amberly! Answer me, baby!"

The tent flap flipped back and Mark scrambled out to meet her. "What's wrong?"

Bree tried to still her shaking. "Amberly isn't with Jane and Ernie." She gripped his arm. "Mark, where's my baby?"

"Calm down, sweetheart. When did you see her last?"

"She was in the tent with me, asleep. I put my arms around her... I was so sure I'd wake up if she moved." She clutched her trembling hands together. "It's my fault! I should have stayed awake until you got back—"

He took firm hold of her and gave her a little shake. "Brianna, calm down."

Jane came to touch Brianna's arm. "She's probably someplace close by." She cast a glance at Ernie. "Come on. We'll help you look."

Within seconds they had a plan. Jane and Ernie would take Ethan and walk the circle of campsites one direction; Mark and Brianna would go the other. They'd meet again back at their sites in no more than fifteen minutes.

Brianna started down the circle at a walk, then broke into a run. Her heart was pounding so hard she thought it would break through her chest. Her mind kept pace with her rushing pulse, shooting out desperate pleas to the heavens.

Please, God...please... Don't let anything happen to my little girl!

THIRTY-FIVE

*"Do not lose your inward peace for anything whatsoever,
even if your whole world seems upset."*

SAINT FRANCIS DE SALES

*"Don't be afraid, for I am with you.
Do not be dismayed, for I am your God. I will help you."*

ISAIAH 41:10

OCTOBER 13
3:30 p.m.

Almost time.

Annie could hardly wait. Kyla was scheduled to arrive in about an hour, along with Dan and his crew. As soon as Annie heard her sister was coming down for a visit, she set up the family dinner at her place. She scanned the table. Not a paper plate in sight.

The last two times she'd had the whole crew over, Kyla had given her no end of grief for using paper plates. Well, this time her oh-so-perfect sister wouldn't have a thing to say.

Except maybe "Wow!"

Annie had gone all out. New china and crystal glasses sparkled in the light of elegant candles. The meal she'd prepared was fit for royalty—and took her all day. No wonder she didn't cook like this very often! Who had that kind of time? Certainly not Annie.

In fact, she hadn't really had the time to do it now, what with the window calling to her in her studio. But she'd get right back to it first thing tomorrow.

The sound of the gate buzzer jolted through the room, and Annie jumped. Wow, Kyla must have made great time. She went to the front door, hitting the talk button on the new intercom Dan had installed last weekend. He'd wanted to put in a security camera as well, but Annie drew the line at that. Hopefully Kyla would be able to figure out the intercom gadget on her end. Dan had showed Annie how all she needed to do was lean out the car window and hit the talk button, but Annie still wasn't sure.

"Hey," she called into the device, "you're early!"

A moment's pause. "I am?"

Oops. That definitely was not Kyla. "Jed?"

"Yeah. Hey, when did you get this intercom setup?"

"Last weekend. Hold on, and I'll buzz the gate open." She hit the gate release, then pulled the front door open and waved as he drove up the driveway, the gate closing behind him.

Another of Dan's so-called improvements. Sensors that closed the gate as soon as a vehicle passed through. "Less chance of anyone sneaking through behind the vehicle," he'd said.

Annie didn't tell him she was starting to feel like she lived in a veritable Fort Knox. He was too worried about her to find any humor in the comment.

She went to give Jed a welcoming hug as he got out of his car. "I thought you were my sister."

His chuckle was as appealing as the rest of him. "I think I'm taller."

"Ha-ha. So what's up? Not that I'm not glad to see you, but I thought you were working tonight." She frowned. "Speaking of which, you still haven't told me exactly what it is you do."

He followed her into the house. "Well, right now I'm visiting you."

"Which you said you wouldn't be able to do." She led him to the living room, shooing Kodi, who bounded up to give Jed a greeting almost as enthusiastic as Annie's had been.

He laughed and gave the shepherd an ear scratch, then shooed her to the living room ahead of them. "I know. Look, Annie…"

She turned at the odd note in his voice. "Are you okay?" That sounded far better than the question she really wanted to ask: *Are we okay?*

From the look on his face, he had bad news. But what bad news could he possibly—

Her pulse shifted into overdrive. Of course. The worst kind of news. *It's been fun, but I need to take a step back.* Or *You're a wonderful woman, but I'm just not ready for this.*

Or there was always the kiss of death: *Let's just be friends.*

He sat on the couch next to her and took her hand. "I will be okay. There's just…I have to leave for a few days. That's why I stopped over. To say good-bye."

Annie stiffened. *Here it comes… Oh, Annie, you idiot! How could you let yourself believe he'd feel about you the way you felt about him? Stupid, stupid.* "Leave?" Oh. That was awful. Whining was *not* an attractive quality in a woman. Maybe clearing her throat would get rid of it. "For very long?"

Nope. Still there. Along with the slightest tremble. Well, maybe he wouldn't notice.

He smiled. "Sounds like you're going to miss me, huh?"

Strike two.

"I'm glad, Annie. Because I'm going to miss you. A lot."

It took a second for his soft words to connect, but when they did, Annie melted back against the couch cushions.

He's going to miss me.

A lot.

She didn't even care if he saw the goofy grin on her face. "So when will you be back?"

"In a few days. I promise."

"You'll call me?"

He lifted her hand and pressed his lips to the back of it. "Count on it. And Annie?"

"Mm-hmm?"

"When I get back, we need to talk." His voice, so deep and full of meaning, wrapped around her.

Her grin widened. "Count on it."

He let her hand go and stood. "I'd better get going. I have a lot to do." His brows raised when he caught sight of her decorated table. "Wow. Now that ought to impress your sister. Big time."

She'd told him about the dinner and Kyla's propensity for scolding. "Think so?"

He took her hand again and tugged her up and into his arms. His hug was warm and solid. "Absolutely. You've outdone yourself."

"Yeah, well—" she murmured into his chest—"you should be here to taste the food."

He tipped her face up to his. "Next time. I promise." He delivered a soft kiss to the tip of her nose, then stumbled back when with a low "Roowwoww!" Kodi shoved in between them.

Annie laughed, batting at the pesky pooch. "I think she's jealous."

"Of me?"

"No." Annie grinned. "Of me. This dog adores you."

He chuckled, then took Annie's hand. "Yeah, well, she'll have to accept that I only have eyes for you."

Heart fluttering, Annie let Jed lead her out the door and to his car. He gave her one last hug, then opened the car door. But he stopped before he slid inside. "Hey."

Annie tipped her head. "What?"

He closed the door, facing her. "You never have shown me your studio. How 'bout a quick tour before I go?"

He couldn't have asked anything that pleased her more. "Absolutely."

When they entered her studio, Jed paused in the doorway, his mouth falling open. She was so glad there was still enough daylight to let him see the real beauty of the room.

Annie walked beside him as he wandered the studio, answering his questions about her tools and equipment, showing him the different styles and textures of glass she used, demonstrating some of what she did.

"Is this the window you've been working on? For that woman? What was her name?"

Annie nodded. "Serafina Stowe. That's the one. Actually, I owe this window to you."

"To me?"

She let her fingers brush across a piece of glass. "Remember that day we took Kodi up to the mountains for training?"

"Vividly."

The low, warm tone of his response sent shivers across her. "Well, something you said sparked an idea, and the result will be this window."

He studied the sketches laid out on the worktable, then took in the glass she'd cut and painted then pieced together in a rough puzzle. She had one scene almost finished, and she was holding her breath as he studied it.

His eyes lifted to her, and wonder glinted in their umber depths.

That was when Annie realized she was doing something she'd never done before. Sharing her art. Her calling. Not just the finished product, but the very act of creating.

"Thank you."

She angled a look at him. "For what?"

"For letting me be a part—" he waved his hands over the worktable—"of this." His hands fell to his side, but his eyes held her captive. "Of you."

She didn't know what to say.

As though sensing that the intimacy of the moment was almost too much for her to bear, Jed looked away—and smiled. "Hey, your colors."

She followed his gaze to the window displaying the pieces of glass in her colors and tensed. She'd told him about this window, how it brought her colors to life, but having him stand here, study it… She couldn't help but feel just the tiniest bit odd.

Okay, maybe not so tiny.

"Show me my color."

She started. "Excuse me?"

"My color. The color you see when you look at me. Show me."

Heart overflowing, Annie let him walk her to the window. Once there, she reached up and pulled down the raspberry piece of glass. "Stand over here."

Jed did as she directed, and she went back to the window, then held the glass in the right position for the sunlight to catch the hue and send it out in waves across the room. Jed held his hands out, studying them in the rich flow of color.

"So this is what you see when you look at me?"

She nodded. "It's close. When I see you, or even when I think of you or your name." She bit her lip. "Just so you know, it's not pink. It's more of a deep raspberry. I mean, it may not seem like a manly color, but I don't have any control over...over..."

Jed turned and came toward her, walking through the wash of color, and the look in his eyes stilled the anxiety filling her heart. His fingers closed over hers as she held the piece of glass. With his free hand, he cradled the back of her head and drew her close, then lowered his lips to hers.

Time. Words. Reality.

They all lost their meaning in the wonder of that kiss.

When Jed finally lifted his head, Annie could only press her face against him, breathing him in, letting him hold her steady—though she felt the way his own hands trembled.

His fingers caressed her face, and his breath whispered across her cheek. "I should leave."

She nodded, face still buried in his chest. A deep chuckle rumbled beneath her cheek.

"You'll have to let me go first."

Annie eased away from him, and he took her hand in his. They walked together out to his car, and he seemed as reluctant as she to break the contact of their hands. But he finally did, opening the car door and slipping behind the steering wheel.

He turned the key in the ignition, then looked at her one more time. "I'll miss you."

She couldn't speak around the emotions so just touched his arm, then stepped back and watched as he drove out the gate. When the car was no longer in sight, she walked back inside and dropped to her knees beside Kodi. She gathered the dog in a hug, planting a big smooch on her snout.

"He's going to miss me. A lot."

Kodi's big tail thumpa-thumped the floor, and Annie stood and twirled. Kodi jumped up, bouncing around Annie and barking as she tossed that big head back and forth.

Clearly Kodi approved.

And, Annie thought as she caught her reflection in the sliding glass window and noted the glow on her face, she wasn't the only one.

7:30 p.m.

"Do you think he's the one?"

Annie turned from sliding the last of her new plates into the dishwasher. Three pairs of eyes were trained on her.

Thank heaven Jayce was out walking Kodi. Dan, Kyla, and Shelby were more than enough of an inquisition.

"So? Do you?"

Kyla's question hung in the air, and Annie was almost afraid to answer it. Did she think Jed was the one? Without a doubt. Was she going to tell her family that?

Not on your life!

Not yet, anyway. Not until she and Jed had had more time to figure out for themselves what the future held. Far better to be as noncommittal as possible.

She closed the dishwasher, started the wash cycle, then turned to her questioners. "I haven't known Jed long enough to be able to say that."

"Told you so." Dan poked Shelby with an elbow.

His wife, in turn, pulled a face at him then looked at Annie. "But you care about him, right?"

Annie allowed a nod. "Even so, I want to get to know him better. But it's the oddest thing…"

Kyla was instantly on the alert. "What? What has he done? Tell us and Dan will deal with him—"

"No, no!" Annie put her hands out. "It's nothing like that. It's just…well, he doesn't talk much about his family. Or his job. I mean, I know his mom lives here in the valley somewhere. But every time I ask about his childhood or his job, he changes the subject."

That got Dan's attention. "You don't think he's hiding something, do you?"

"Oh for—!" Shelby stomped her foot. "This is your sister's friend we're talking about here, not Jack the Ripper."

The front door slammed, and Annie heard the tramping of human feet and the scrabble of canine paws on the wood floor. She called toward the sound. "We're in the kitchen, Jayce."

Kodi came loping into the kitchen, a wide doggy grin on her face.

"Annie, do you think he's hiding anything?"

Jayce caught the question as he came in. "Who's hiding something?"

"No one." Annie ignored the suspicious look in her brother's eyes, letting her tone scold him for even thinking what she knew he was thinking—that Jed might be the one sending the threatening e-mails.

"How well do you really know this guy?"

"What guy?" Jayce stared from Annie to his dad. "What are you—you mean Jed? You think he's not who he says he is?"

Great. Now her nephew was getting all protective. "Stop it, you two. Jed is exactly who he says he is."

Kyla pushed at Kodi, who was leaning against her leg and staring up at her with wide, adoring eyes. "But you just told us he hasn't really said much of anything about himself, right?"

Annie pierced Kyla with a glare. "Don't you start now. Try to remember I haven't known Jed that long. I don't think he's hiding anything so much as he's careful."

Dan was not mollified. "Careful? What's that mean?"

Annie shrugged. "I can't explain it exactly, but I get the feeling things maybe weren't great when he was a kid. That there are some issues he still needs to deal with."

"Oooh. Issues." Shelby looked at Dan. "Nobody here knows anything about dealing with issues."

"But *being* an issue." Kyla directed a smirk at her brother. "Now *that* someone here knows intimately, doesn't he, Avidan?"

Dan went to wrap his older sister in a bear hug. "Oh, Kyla, I'm so *glad* to hear you admit you're an issue."

"You know, Auntie K," Jayce joined in, a wicked gleam in his eyes, "that's the first step to getting help. Admitting the problem."

Annie watched her family, loving the way each one's color blended with the others. Dan's marigold provided the perfect complement to Shelby's clear emerald. Kyla's deep pink added a flare of playful contrast, even as Jayce's raspberry tinged her color, deepening it a fraction.

It was like having a living palette right here in her kitchen.

Of course, the palette was exceedingly vocal.

Kodi padded over, sitting beside her, leaning her solid body against Annie's leg. She caressed the dog's ears, listening as the music that was her family's laughter flowed around them, pouring into her heart, filling it with joy. Peace. And anticipation.

Soon.

The promise whispered through her.

Soon another voice would join the chorus. A deep voice. One that made her smile every time she heard it.

One that she couldn't wait to hear again.

THIRTY-SIX

"There is much in the world to make us afraid.
There is much more in our faith to make us unafraid."

FREDERICK W. CROPP

"And so, Lord, where do I put my hope? My only hope is in you."

PSALM 39:7

OCTOBER 13
11:00 p.m.

She couldn't wait any longer. She had to admit the truth.

Her child was missing.

Brianna looked through her despair at her husband's ashen face. She knew he wanted to comfort her, but fear kept him silent. She ran a hand through her hair. "We've been looking for hours. It's going to be cold soon. Really cold." Had Amberly taken her jacket with her?

Bree blinked back tears. "We have to accept it—" the words caught in her throat, but she forced them out—"our baby is lost. We need to call the police."

Mark nodded. He reached for the cell phone and dialed. Then, with a muffled oath, threw the phone. "What good does it do to have these stupid things when they don't have service?"

Ernie stepped forward to lay a steadying hand on Mark's shoulder. "I'll take you to the ranger station down the road."

Mark nodded again, started to follow his friend, then

stopped. He turned back to Brianna...and held out his arms. She went to him, let his strong arms enclose her.

"We'll find her, Bree. I promise you, we'll find her."

She prayed he was right.

11:45 p.m.

Beep! Beep! Beep!

The sound cut through Annie's living room, and several things happened at once. Kyla almost jumped out of her skin; Kodi bounded up, ears cocked; Dan was on his feet, heading for the phone; and Shelby and Annie both reached to pull their pagers from their pockets.

"It's not mine." Shelby glanced at Dan.

He held his pager high. "It's mine."

"Mine too." Annie headed for her purse and her cell phone, since Dan was on her phone.

Kyla frowned at Annie. "You've got to be kidding. A callout? Now?" She craned her neck to see the clock on the wall. "It's almost midnight."

Annie brought her cell phone back into the living room. "Which is when most calls come." She rolled her shoulders, working out the fatigue, starting to get herself into working mode. "You know the drill, sis. People think they'll find whoever is lost, so they keep looking until it's late. Then they get scared and call us."

She dialed the number on her pager and waited for someone to answer.

"Station Seven."

"Hi, it's Annie Justice."

"We've got a callout for the Diamond Lake area. Can you respond?"

Annie looked down at her watch. "We'll be there." She hung up, and Jayce jumped off the couch.

"So what's the callout for?"

"Don't know." Annie dropped the phone back in her purse.

"We don't get the details until we reach Station Seven."

"It's like a mystery, huh?" Jayce's eyes were wide. This was the first time he'd been there for an actual callout. "That's kinda cool."

"Ridiculous, is what it is." Kyla settled back on the couch with a huff. "Going out this time of night, traipsing around heaven knows where—"

"Diamond Lake, is where."

They all turned to Dan, coming back into the room.

Well, this was a definite perk to having a brother who was a sheriff's deputy: getting the details of the callout right away. Annie tipped her head. "Lost hiker?"

Dan's somber gaze rested on her. "Lost child."

Annie stopped. Her two least favorite words. "How old?"

The look on Dan's face said it all. "Five. A little girl."

Lord...

Kyla's entire demeanor changed. "Oh, Annie. A child."

Her sister had heard Annie talk about searches often enough to understand the implications. Finding a lost child could be one of the hardest things to do. With most lost people, there was a kind of pattern to how they wandered. That made them at least somewhat predictable. But with children, there was seldom a pattern. To make matters worse, children younger than six often were too scared to answer a stranger when called.

Seldom anything to help the searchers find the lost before...

Annie laid her hand on Kodi's soft head. Five years old. In the Diamond Lake wilderness. She glanced out at the darkness. Five years old and out there alone...cold...probably terrified...

A moist nudge at her hand pulled her from her thoughts. She met Kodi's brown eyes. "Okay, girl. You're right. Time to get to work." She glanced at Dan. The Diamond Lake area fell in his jurisdiction. "You ready to go?"

He nodded.

"Give me five minutes to change." She was halfway down the hall when she realized Dan was right behind her. She turned to him, taking in the troubled crease on his brow. "What's up?"

"Are you sure you should be doing this?"

Annie cocked her head. "Doing what? Changing clothes? It's cold out there."

"No, Annie. Search and rescue. Are you sure, with what's been going on, that you should respond to this one?"

"Dan…"

"It's not like there aren't other K-9 teams. You guys can sit this one out. Just to be sure."

Annie leaned against the wall. "And what about the next call-out? Do we sit that one out too? Do we just hide out here from now on, just in case there's someone out there who isn't content with just writing mean-spirited notes and e-mails?" She shook her head. "No, Dan. I won't do it. I can't. God called us to this, me and Kodi. And unless He releases us from that call, we'll keep doing it."

He stared at the floor, then nodded. "You're right. I just—"

"You're worried about me."

His shrug was sheepish. "What can I say? You're my little sister." He gave a gruff sigh. "So what are you waiting for? Go change already. Time's a'wastin'."

It actually only took four and a half minutes before she was back at the front door, pulling Kodi's lead from the hook. She looked at her brother. "Ready?"

He planted a quick kiss on Shelby's lips, then joined Annie. "Ready." He looked back at the others. "Wish us luck, everyone."

"We'll do better than that." Shelby slipped her arms around Kyla and Jayce. "We'll pray."

OCTOBER 14—AN ELDERBERRY BLACK BEAUTY DAY
(BLACK AND ROSE)
3:30 a.m.

Annie lay stretched out in her tent, one hand resting on Kodi as the dog snored at her side.

When Annie and Kodi first arrived at the point last seen with the crew from SAR, Dan was on-site already. He'd seen Annie's Jeep pull up, and when she stepped from the vehicle, he signaled for her to come over. As Annie drew close, she heard a cry and suddenly found herself engulfed in a fierce hug.

"Oh! I'm so glad you're here!"

Brianna Heller and her husband, Mark, filled in Annie and the other SAR personnel. When they'd gathered all the information they could, they went back to the command post—a large van equipped with maps, communication equipment, and phones to manage the search on the scene—and waited while the search manager determined the next step.

The search manager pinpointed the different areas for the teams to grid, and everyone who was there headed out. With any luck, they'd find the girl in the next few hours. Unfortunately, it didn't work out that way. Annie and Kodi had trudged back to camp hours later, set up their tent, and tried to grab some shut-eye. But sleep was proving elusive. This was Bree's daughter out there, and that fact ate at her. Hard enough when a child was lost, but to have to look a friend in the face, tell her that her little girl wasn't coming home...

No. Don't go there.

Annie closed her eyes. She might not be able to sleep, but she could do the one thing that would help most of all.

She could pray.

THIRTY-SEVEN

*"There seemed to be endless obstacles...
it seemed that the root cause of them all was fear."*

JOANNA FIELD

*"Give your burdens to the LORD,
and he will take care of you.
He will not permit the godly to slip and fall."*

PSALM 55:12

OCTOBER 21—A BLACKJACK IRIS DAY (GREEN AND BLACK)
1:00 p.m.

The heat beat down, as relentless as time.

Unfortunately neither the weather nor the clock offered an ounce of mercy. Normally, in weather this arid and hot, Annie wouldn't be out here. Wouldn't let Kodi keep working.

But the dog was as reluctant as she to leave the search area.

Eight days.

How could fifty search and rescue members have searched for eight days and seven nights with no sign of the lost girl? Not one sign?

Well, that wasn't quite true. Kodi had alerted three times. The odd thing about the alerts, though, was that they were in entirely different search grids. Amberly would have had to travel some serious distance to be in each of those grids. Annie thought maybe Kodi was alerting on a hunter or a hiker. Air scenting dogs were looking for any human scent, not just the scent specific to the subject.

But each time Kodi led Annie to a location, no one was there. No hunter. No hiker. No lost child.

No sign of *any* human.

It was as though whoever had been there—and somebody had been for Kodi to alert—had erased all her tracks. And done a very good job of it.

The first time it happened Dan was with her and Kodi. Normally her backup would have been a second SAR member. On that particular morning, however, Dan pulled rank, informing Annie and the incident commander that he would be his sister's backup. It would be a waste of breath—and time—to argue.

"Kodi doesn't do false alerts often, does she?"

Annie pulled her attention from her dog to her brother. "She's never done one."

"So…"

She shrugged. "I have no idea what happened." In fact, after the third false alert, Annie wanted to tear her hair out. She wasn't sure what was going on, but she was sure of this much: *Some*thing was rotten in Denmark.

The thought sent a pang through her. Amazing how any hint of Shakespeare brought Jed to mind.

She missed him. How she'd love to just talk with him, to vent her frustration over the way the search was going. Or, to be more accurate, *wasn't* going. He'd been gone what, over a week?

Yes, he left the night the callout came.

"Been gone a long time."

Annie blinked. Had Dan been reading her mind? "What? Who?"

"Kodi." He scrutinized her. "You with us here, sis?"

She was about to inform her brother she was *always* "with it" on a search when the jingling of Kodi's bell sounded. Annie punched her brother's shoulder, just for principle, then turned and watched for the shepherd to appear.

"It's not an alert, is it?"

Annie shook her head. "Ringing's too relaxed. I'm betting she's coming back for water."

Bingo.

The dog trotted out of the woods and came to nudge the water dish at Annie's belt. She filled it and set it down, then pulled a handkerchief from her pocket and tipped the water bottle again, wetting the cloth, and wiping her face.

Dan held out his handkerchief as well. "Man, it's hot!"

Annie stood. "Can you remember the last time it was this hot in October? Especially up here, in the mountains?"

"I remember a few times we hit seventy, even eighty, this time of year. But close to ninety? No way."

Of course, it was better searching conditions—and survival conditions—than October usually offered. "At least we don't have to worry about Amberly dealing with snow."

"Always a silver lining, eh, sis?"

Might as well try to find one. Triple digits were no longer cause for exclamation but rather the norm. During the day, that was. No sooner did the sun set than thermometers decided that, yes, it was autumn, and so they plummeted, dipping low enough to coax almost forgotten jackets out of the backs of closets.

Annie glanced at the brutally blue sky. Two of the elder members of SAR had compared notes on the weather as they ate breakfast that morning. Wilma, who looked as rugged as the mountains around them, commented on the unusual heat. Jasper, a man who had to be in this seventies and yet walked the wilderness with the energy of a teenager, snorted.

"You think this is hot? Eighty-nine degrees ain't *nothin'*! You shoulda been here summer of '46 when we hit 115. Yessir, now *that* was hot."

"You are dreamin', old man. It never hit that up here. In the valley, maybe, but not up here."

Jasper helped himself to more eggs. "Alls I know is there's only one thing you can count on with Oregon weather."

"That you can't count on it."

"Darn you, woman. Stop stealing my lines!"

Annie had laughed along with the rest of the unit. They knew what the two elder members said was true. That was part of the region's appeal. People who lived in Oregon relished its unpredictability.

Most days, Annie counted herself in the relish camp. Especially when she was in the mountains. Nothing like a hike in the woods to refresh the spirit.

Today, though, she hated it.

Hot. Dry. No wind. Conditions custom-tailored to hamper a search. And that's exactly what they were doing.

A soft whine drew Annie's attention, and she put a comforting hand on Kodi's broad head. The German shepherd studied her, a slight wrinkle between those intelligent brown eyes.

"Hey, you're supposed to read the air, girl, not me."

Dan held the ends of his damp handkerchief and twirled it, then tied it around his neck. "You ask me, she's as tuned in to you as anything else around her. Sometimes more so."

He was right, of course. She and Kodi were bonded, big time. They needed to be for what they did.

Besides, Annie loved the big moose. With all her heart.

But that connection could be a problem if Annie's mood was bad. As it was on days like today, when she let her frustration build.

Shake it off, Annie. So you haven't found Amberly yet. It'll happen.

She pushed her damp bangs back off her warm face. "This is going to sound weird…"

"So what else is new."

Annie gave Dan the sister face and went on. "I've just been thinking. I mean, if I didn't know better, I'd swear someone was working against us. You know, planting scent, misleading, moving the girl…"

Dan looked like he was holding something back. Annie planted her feet and stared at him. "Come on, big brother. Let's have it."

"I don't want to frustrate you."

"So why should today be any different?"

It was his turn to give her the brother face. "I'm just wondering, are you sure that's not just sour grapes talking because you haven't found Amberly yet?"

She lifted one shoulder. "I thought about that too. I mean, it's been really frustrating. But I'm telling you, Dan, two of the times Kodi alerted, we were *close*. I'm *sure* of it. Kodi was just too excited, too definite, for there not to have been *some*one there."

"And?"

"And when she led me to the find location, it was the same as it's been on every other alert. Nobody there. And Kodi seemed as confused and upset as I was."

"I don't know what to say, sis."

Neither did she. Because a small part of her wondered...

Was she doing something wrong? Was she hindering Kodi somehow without even being aware of it?

Maybe Dan was right. Maybe you should have stayed home on this one.

She shook her head. Now that was sour grapes talking.

And fear.

Annie wiped the cool handkerchief at the back of her neck. Yes. There was fear. Thanks to those stupid, stupid notes. With each passing day, she'd been less and less successful pushing them out of her mind.

The only saving grace had been that they couldn't follow her out here.

Kodi slurped up every drop of water from her dish, then nudged Annie with her nose again.

"She wants more?"

Annie looked down at her girl. No denying the dog was hot and tired. With a soul-deep sigh, Annie poured more water into the dish, then crouched beside Kodi. She didn't say a word, just put her arm over the animal's shoulders, letting her touch convey the comfort she wanted to give.

When Kodi drained the dish again, Annie picked it up, clipped it to her belt, and stood.

"What say we head back to camp?"

Annie nodded. "It's time. We need a break." She patted her leg. "Okay, Kodi girl. Back to camp."

The shepherd didn't budge.

Dan's brows rose. "Wow. I didn't think she ever disobeyed you."

"You're a dreamer. She's got a mind of her own, and if she thinks I'm wrong—" she indicated the inert animal—"she lets me know."

"So she thinks you're wrong about something?"

Annie planted her hands on her hips, holding Kodi's gaze. The dog's eyes flitted to the side, then came back to her. But for all that she showed submission, she still didn't move.

"She knows what *camp* means."

Dan gave a slow nod. "That you're quitting the search. And she doesn't want to go."

"Apparently not." She kneeled in front of the dog. "Come on, Kode. It's too hot. For you and for me."

And for Amberly. *Father, please, be with her.*

Kodi sat there, eyes wide and intent. And just a shade defiant.

"You could just grab her collar and make her come."

"I could. But I'd rather not." Annie put her hands on either side of Kodi's face and tipped the dog's head so that their foreheads touched. "Kodi, come on. You need rest. So do I." Her voice cracked. "It's no help to Amberly if we miss something or end up hurt because we're tired."

A deep groan rumbled in Kodi's chest—a sorrowful though simple capitulation. Annie couldn't hold back her tears. The dog was giving in, not because she wanted to, but because she trusted her mistress.

If only, Annie thought as she stood and the three of them started back toward camp, she felt the same way.

❖   ❖   ❖

2:00 p.m.

Annie lay in her tent, staring at the nylon ceiling. Kodi was deep asleep beside her.

Good. At least one of them would be rested when they went out again tonight.

Annie had tried to sleep. But her brain wouldn't shut down. It kept running over and over the last few days, second-guessing, telling her how many ways she'd misdirected Kodi, that their failure was her fault.

All her fault.

"You think that little girl is still alive?"

Annie turned her head. Someone was talking beside her tent.

"After so much time in this weather and terrain? I'd say the odds aren't good."

"So I take it the 'Wonder Team' is still out searching?"

"Nah. They came in hours ago. I think they're sleeping."

She didn't recognize the voices, but searchers from a number of neighboring states had been called in so there were plenty of people Annie didn't know. Even so, the snide comments cut deep.

"Like that'll make a difference."

"Man, I thought these two could find anyone."

"Shows you how wrong the media can be, I guess."

Annie heard feet rustling across the dry ground as the voices moved away. She turned onto her stomach and pressed her aching eyes against her forearm. *Don't take it personally. You know how frustrated searchers get when they can't find a child. It eats at them, just like it's eating at you. And then they lash out.*

It doesn't mean anything.

She knew it was true. All of it. But that didn't make the mean-spirited comments much easier to bear.

God…please. Let someone find Amberly. I don't care who. It doesn't have to be Kodi and me.

Liar. You *want to find her. Want to prove you're as good as any-one else. That you belong here.*

Annie's hands fisted. *No. I don't care if everyone thinks we're failures.* I just want Amberly back with her family. Otherwise...

Her throat constricted. Otherwise, she'd never be able to look Brianna in the face again. Never be able to take Kodi to the vet without facing their failure.

Failure that cost a little girl her life.

Jesus...please...

Dark emotions weighed down on her—deep, ugly shades of red, pressing down, as though a heavy hand reached into her tent and pressed, pushing her deeper into the ground. And Annie's frustration only grew when she realized that something else was nagging at her.

Jed hadn't called. Not once! Not to say he was back, not to ask how are you, not to say go jump in the lake.

Annie didn't know what angered her more. That he hadn't called, or that it bothered her so much. With all that was going on in the search, Jed calling shouldn't even matter. But it did.

It mattered a lot.

"Annie. Get up!"

The sharp call, and the sound of a flat palm smacking the fabric of her tent, just about sent both Annie and Kodi through the roof. The dog bolted upright, barking and growling.

If Annie had been able, she'd have growled right along with Kodi.

She settled for a heated mutter. "Darn you, Dan! You scared the *life* out of me!" She jerked the tent flap out of the way and stomped outside, Kodi right on her heels.

"I'm sorry, but we've got to talk."

Annie's anger dissipated as quickly as it formed. Mostly because of the tone of his voice. It held an odd mixture of anger and apprehension.

She rubbed her eyes. "What's up, bro?"

He didn't answer. Just held out a steaming mug of black coffee.

"What's this?"

He lifted his chin. "Drink up. You're going to need it."

She did as he said and took a couple deep swallows. Then, and only then, did he draw a slip of paper from his pocket and hand it to her. The too-familiar type sent her heart plummeting to her boots.

UR STAR SEARCH TEAM IZ A FRAUD. WHY HAVEN'T THEY FOUND THE GURL?

Annie crushed the note into a ball and threw it.

"Hey! That's evidence." Dan went to pick it up, then stuffed it in his pocket.

"Where did it come from?"

He hesitated, and she had the sense he didn't want to answer. But he gave in. "It was in the mail."

"At my house? Did you go back to town?"

"No." The hard note in his words told her how angry he was and that if he ever caught the person who'd been sending the notes…well, Annie just hoped, for her brother's sake, that he wasn't the one who caught the creep.

"At my office. It was waiting on my desk when I got there this morning, so it must have been delivered yesterday."

A chill skittered across Annie's nerves, like a cockroach when the lights went on. She met her brother's grave gaze.

"So he must know I'm not home to get my mail."

"We don't know that for sure."

"Come on, Dan. Why else would he send the note to your office and not to my house?"

"Look, Annie, we're trying to figure all that out. But until we do, I want you to go—"

"No."

"Annie."

"*No!* I'm not going home. I don't care what you say, or what this jerk writing these notes says, or what other searchers say, we are *not* going to quit."

"Lower your voice. People can hear you."

"*I* don't *care!*"

Funny thing was, she really *didn't.* The dark red of her negative emotions had become so oppressive, so all-encompassing, that Annie had been having a hard time seeing much of anything else. It colored everything and everyone, keeping her in a crimson haze that made it hard even to think.

So letting it out felt good.

Really good.

Jackie, a member of the Rogue Valley SAR group, came toward them. "Are you okay, Annie?"

"I never asked to be labeled the 'Wonder Team.'"

Jackie nodded. "I know that."

"I'm not the one who said Kodi and I could find anyone." Her voice raised a notch. "I never asked anyone to interview us or stick our faces in the paper." She looked back at Dan. "I sure as spit didn't ask to become some loony's poison pen pal! It's just the way things worked out. I don't know why. What's more, I don't *care* why. All I care about is that little girl out there. *Someone's* got to find her."

"We will, Annie." Others picked up Jackie's assurance. "You know we won't stop until we do."

"I'm afraid that's not quite true."

Everyone turned to stare at Chuck, the incident commander. A muscle in his jaw tensed, and Annie wanted to scream. She knew that look. She'd seen it before on the faces of other incident commanders who had to deliver news searchers weren't going to like.

"No."

Chuck didn't react to Annie's terse denial. "I just got the word. They're terminating the search tonight."

"They?" Dan stepped forward. "What *they?* Sure as heck not the sheriff's department."

"Some state politician way up the food chain got wind of how long we've been out—"

"—and how much money it's costing—"

Again, Chuck didn't let the sarcasm derail him. "Yes, and the cost. And he convinced the decision makers that, with the decreased likelihood of the child's survival, the expense wasn't justified." He held a hand up to stem the flood of objections. "A rep from said politician's office will be here in a couple hours to join our debriefing. You can express your objections to him. They'll issue a statement to the media around seven."

Annie stepped toward him. "They can't do that. She's alive out there. I know it!"

"I believe you. But if we don't find her tonight, what can we do? When the powers that be say we've got to stop, we have no choice."

"This is crazy. How can money be more important than a little girl's life?"

The coordinator shrugged. "Who knows what motivates politicians?"

Annie spun on her heel, heading for her Jeep, Dan and Kodi on either side.

"Where are you going?" Her brother sounded worried.

"To get my cell phone." With radios for communication out in the field, Annie didn't carry her cell phone.

"*Annie.*"

"Don't worry, Dan. I'm not going to do anything crazy."

"Why don't I believe that?"

She pulled the Jeep door open. "I'm not. I'm just going to place one harmless phone call. That's it."

Dan studied her, clearly not convinced. Annie pulled her cell phone out of the console and gave him a pointed look.

"Oh. I guess you want some privacy?"

She gave him a sugar-sweet smile. "Love that keen sense of the obvious you have, brother dear."

She waited until he was a safe distance away, then leaned back into the Jeep and rustled through a pile of papers on the backseat. *Please…please let it be in here.* She could swear she remembered tossing the paper here when she took the DVD to mail it—ah! Bingo!

Annie read the phone number on the note, punched it into her cell phone, and hit Talk.

Cancel the search? She counted the rings.

Not if *she* had anything to say about it.

3:00 p.m.

"So you think we'll actually get out of Medford this time?"

Jed shuffled another step forward in the security line, trying to ignore the fact that every muscle in his body ached and his eyes felt like someone had poured twelve buckets of sand into them. "We'd better. I can't believe we've been fogged in here for a stinkin' week!"

"Or that we actually stayed in this airport all night last night. The Rogue Valley International Airport." Andy surveyed the building around them. "Right. This place is about as big as a shoe box!"

Jed stretched his shoulders. "They kept telling me we might get on the next flight."

"There *were* no flights after eleven, Jed. That's what I kept trying to tell you. We could have gone back to the hotel—"

"I wasn't taking a chance on missing something. I've got to get this done." He shook his head. "I told Annie I'd be back in a day or two."

Andy hitched his camera case higher on his shoulder. "So call her."

"I told you, not until this thing with the show is settled."

"Then you should have called Silas. That crazy ad has run all week. I don't know how Annie hasn't seen it—"

The ring of Jed's cell phone cut through Andy's tirade. First time Jed was actually glad to have the phone go off and interrupt a conversation. He flipped the phone open. "Hello?"

"Hello. May I speak with Mr. Curry?"

Jed came full awake. He knew that voice as well as he knew his own.

Annie!

But where did she get this number? He'd made sure she only called him at the hotel.

"Hello? Are you there?"

Jed didn't know what else to do. He shoved the phone at Andy. Andy shoved it back. "I don't want it—"

Jed took Andy's hand and put the phone in it, mouthing, "Annie!"

Understanding widened Andy's eyes, and he put the phone to his ear. "Hello? Uh, yeah, this is Mr. Curry's office. Excuse me? You're who? Uh, whom?"

Jed rolled his eyes.

"Oh, yes! Miss Justice. We've been hoping to hear from you. Are we what? Still interested?"

Jed's pulse jumped. Was she saying she would do the show? Before he could stop himself, he nodded at Andy, who frowned in response.

"Well, I'm not sure…"

Jed grabbed Andy's arm and shook it.

Andy jerked free, glaring at Jed, poking a finger in his chest as he spoke. "We've been *thinking* about this and realized we've got some *issues* to deal with—"

His friend's words hit home. Shame rippled through Jed. Man, didn't take long to fall into old patterns, did it? Wasn't he just standing in line, trying to catch a plane to make things right? Then, boom! One phone call and he was off to the races.

Again.

He held his hand out for the phone. Andy studied his face for a moment, then nodded. "Could you hang on a minute? Mr. Curry would like to speak with you."

Jed sucked in a steadying breath and put the phone to his ear. "Miss Justice, E J Curry here." He grimaced. Why did he do that? Why lower his voice to disguise it? Why not just tell her who he was?

Because it isn't something you do over the phone.

"Mr. Curry, do you still want to film Kodi and me for your show or not?"

He couldn't lie about that. "Yes, we're still interested. Very much so."

"Good. Then let's do it."

Jed should be thrilled. Dancing in the security line. Instead, he just felt like gum on the bottom of somebody's shoe.

Really old, cruddy gum.

"Okay. We'll set it up, come do the filming in a week or so." That should give him plenty of time to talk with Silas. And then with Annie. Just thinking about it made his stomach hurt.

"Now."

That made his stomach *and* his head hurt. "I'm sorry?"

"Now, Mr. Curry. Or not at all. Kodi and I are on a search. For a little girl."

Of course. He'd caught a glimpse of something about a lost child on the news last night but hadn't seen enough to realize it was happening here. If Annie was on-site...well, no wonder she hadn't seen the commercial.

"The search area is near Diamond Lake, about an hour and a half from the airport. I can give you directions."

He had to stall her. He couldn't see her without getting things settled first. "Miss Justice, I understand this is a great opportunity for the show, but I'm not sure—"

"No, you don't understand."

The desperation underlying her words stopped him. He dropped all pretense. "What's wrong, Annie?"

Her words tumbled out in a rush. Clearly, she was so focused on whatever was happening she couldn't think beyond it. Which probably explained why she hadn't recognized his voice.

"They're going to cancel the search. They say the girl's chances of survival are minimal after this much time. But I know she's still out there. I know it." She paused, as though trying to rein in her emotions. "Look, if you come in with your cameras, you'll buy me some time. We're close, Mr. Curry. But Kodi and I need more time."

Jed didn't hesitate. "What do you need from me?"

"I need you and your cameras here. Before 6:00 p.m. Tonight."

Clever woman. No politician was going to shut down a search for a child with a camera in his face.

Annie went on. "But make sure you bring cold weather gear. The temperatures drop out here after dark."

"Cold weather gear. Got it." Which they had. In the trunk. They'd bought it when they got to town, just in case.

"So how soon can you get here, Mr. Curry?"

He turned to Andy. "It just so happens, Miss Justice, that we're in the airport right now."

Andy glared at him and gave an emphatic shake of his head.

"We can be there in a matter of hours."

Andy hung his head. "Fine, Jed. Whatever you say."

"Excuse me?"

"That was just my cameraman, asking where we were going." Jed pushed past Andy, heading for the door. Good thing he hadn't checked any luggage. "I'll hand you over to him so you can give him the directions."

"Oh, I know where we're going," Andy muttered as he brought up the rear. "Or where *you're* going. And you won't have to worry about getting cold *there*. Not even a little."

"All right then," Annie said. "I look forward to meeting you, Mr. Curry."

That stopped Jed. Cold. Andy ran smack into him from behind. "Hey!"

Jolted off his suddenly cold feet, Jed shoved the phone at Andy. "Get the directions while I go pick up the car."

He didn't wait for a response, just ran. And as he ran, he talked to God. Something he'd started doing after reading

Ken's Bible, after that last visit with his mother.

And though he knew he didn't deserve it, he begged for mercy. On God's part.

And on Annie's.

Annie closed her phone, then slid onto the leather seat of her Jeep.

Kodi whined, afraid her mistress was leaving without her. Annie just patted the passenger seat, and with one powerful leap, Kodi jumped over her and into the seat.

Well, almost over her.

Once Kodi was settled beside her, Annie leaned her head against the headrest. "Let's see them cancel the search with TV cameras running."

Kodi settled her chin on her paws. Annie smiled. Might as well enjoy the peace while she had it.

Come this evening, some very important people were *not* going to be happy with her. It could very well be the end of her involvement with search and rescue.

So be it.

Just so it gave them time to bring Amberly home.

THIRTY-EIGHT

"This was the unkindest cut of all."

WILLIAM SHAKESPEARE

"My heart is in anguish....
Oh, how I wish I had wings like a dove;
then I would fly away and rest!...
[For] it is not an enemy who taunts me—
I could bear that....
Instead, it is you—my equal,
my companion and close friend."

PSALM 55:4, 6, 12–13

OCTOBER 21
6:15 p.m.

"Make yourself at home, Mr. Bristol."

Annie stood at the edge of the SAR members gathered around the campfire as the sun dipped below the horizon. She loved this time of day. Loved watching the dimming sky, the last gasp of daylight, the dramatic play of light and darkness.

"'It was the gloaming, when a man cannot make out if the nebulous figure he glimpses in the shadows is angel or demon, when the face of evening is stained by red clouds and wounded by lights.'"

"Talking to yourself again, sis?"

She leaned into the arm her brother slipped around her shoulders. "It's a quote, clod. You know, literature."

"Hmm. No wonder I don't recognize it." He directed his gaze to the man standing in the middle of the SAR members—one Mr. Bristol, the promised representative from the politician's office. "Looks like he's in his element, huh?"

"He's red."

Dan pursed his lips. "Red, huh? Not a nice color, I take it?"

She squinted, bringing the color into better focus. "Sometimes it's okay. Pretty, even. Like a deep, red rose."

"I take it the good Mr. Bristol isn't pretty."

Annie gave one curt shake of her head. "Hardly." Indeed, the red outlining Mr. Bristol was harsh, the color of warning and alarm. And try as she might, Annie couldn't make herself like him.

Not one bit.

"Did you eat yet?"

She shook her head again. The evening meal was ready, but few of the unit members had eaten. Annie figured Mr. Bristol's announcement that the search was being called off had killed everyone else's appetite as effectively as it had hers.

She'd promised herself she'd keep her mouth shut during the man's little speech. To extend him that much courtesy—but she couldn't help herself. She stepped closer to the group. "Have you told the girl's parents yet?"

Ah well, so much for promises.

The man looked at Annie. "No. But I will as soon as I'm finished here. Obviously we'll need each of you to show them the proper compassion."

Another of the searchers snorted. "Not exactly compassionate to cut off the search for their child."

Murmurs of agreement rippled through those gathered, and Bristol shifted. "I know this doesn't sit well with you folks."

The searchers were growing more vocal. "There's an understatement."

"Bet it doesn't sit well with the family either. Or the little girl, for that matter."

Annie couldn't stop a perverse spark of satisfaction at the dull red traveling up Bristol's neck. Now his skin matched his color. Sure, she knew none of this was his fault. He was just the bearer of bad news. But with what they'd been through the last week, he was lucky all he was getting was flak.

Someone tugged at her arm, and she turned. A tall, lanky man stood there. "Annie Justice?"

She nodded, peering at him in the dimming light. Did she know him?

"I'm Andy Corwyn. The cameraman for *Everyday Heroes.*"

Relief so powerful it almost buckled her knees hit her. "You made it." She held her hand out. "Good to meet you, Mr. Corwyn."

He took her hand. "Andy, please."

She couldn't help but smile. Andy. Marigold. Now *there* was a nice color—the same as her own. "Andy." She tipped her head, studying his features. "I…I'm sorry, do I know you?"

He licked his lips. "No. You…uh, you don't know me."

He seemed a nervous sort of man. Here's hoping he at least held the camera steady. "Is Mr. Curry here?"

"Yeah, he is. Over by the car." She followed the nod of his head, then started when Kodi gave a joyous yelp and sprinted toward the man.

"Kodi!"

But the dog didn't break stride. Shaking her head, Annie trotted after her, and Andy followed suit.

"Listen, Annie, there's something you should know…"

She looked up at him. He looked so familiar. "Are you sure we haven't met before?"

"Um, no. Well, not really…"

The stammering did it, shoved the pieces into place. Annie stopped. "Starbucks! You were behind me in line."

"Yeeah." Andy drew the word out. "I was."

Annie glanced after Kodi to find her dancing around the man. Thankfully he didn't seem upset.

In fact, he looked liked like he was laughing.

"Listen, Annie, about Jed—"

She spun to face Andy, the stranger her dog was assaulting forgotten. "What?"

"I just, there's something you need to under—"

"Jed. Did you say Jed?"

Even the fading daylight couldn't conceal the misery in the man's features. He looked over her head and shrugged.

"It's okay, Andy. You tried."

At the deep voice, Annie turned. The man who'd been standing by the car had moved closer. Just close enough for her to see his features. the rich raspberry outline...

She was running before conscious thought told her to do so. He opened his arms, lifting her off her feet as he welcomed her into a tight embrace.

He stood there, so solid, so strong, his arms about her forming a warm cocoon of protection. Peace.

"You didn't call." Her reproach was almost lost, spoken into the front of his flannel shirt.

He rested his chin on the top of her head. "I know. I'm sorry."

"Where have you *been?* I really wanted to talk with you."

He was silent a moment, and she pulled back slightly so she could look up into his face. Then pulled back a bit more when she saw how troubled he was.

"Jed? What's wrong?"

He let her step back, but his touch slid down her arms as he captured her hands in his. "I need to tell you something."

She looked from him to Andy Corwyn. Who stood beside Jed. The cameraman for *Everyday Heroes* stood beside Jed. Knew Jed. By name.

"Annie, my middle name is Jed. Short for Jediah."

Okay, fine. It wasn't a bad name. Certainly not bad enough to make him sound like he was about to step in front of a firing squad.

"My first name is Ernest. Ernest Jediah Curry."

It took a second. Then it hit. Ernest Jediah. E J.

Her hands slid from his.

E J Curry. The man who'd sent her all those gifts. And the tape of the show. The director for *Everyday Heroes*.

Oh, Annie…foolish, foolish Annie…

She swallowed hard, her throat suddenly numb. "This…" She met his gaze. "This has all been about the show, hasn't it? That's why you came to town. Why you just 'happened' to meet me at the dog park."

He wanted to deny it. She could tell. And she wanted him to. Oh, how she wanted him to! *Please, Jed, please. Tell me I'm wrong. Tell me you came to town to see your family. That our meeting was an accident. A happy accident…*

But it wasn't. Annie only had to look into Jed's face to know the truth.

She'd fallen in love with a liar.

The lie was there, ready to come out.

Yes, Annie, you're right. I came to see family. I met you by chance.

But Jed bit it back.

He was done with lying. And so he let it all pour out. The whole ugly truth. And as he talked, he followed the emotions stealing across her features. Shock. Anger. And the one he'd feared most.

Hurt.

Stark pain glazed her eyes, settling into her sweet features. Jed cursed himself for being every kind of a fool. But worst of all, for being the kind of fool who would cause such pain to a woman like this.

When he finished his confession, she stood before him, arms limp at her sides. For a heartbeat the pain in her eyes was more than he could bear. He started to reach for her, but she stepped back.

"It doesn't matter."

The cold, even words smacked him right between the eyes. Jed searched Annie's eyes again, and heavy dread descended to the bottom of his gut. Any emotion, good or bad, was gone.

Annie Justice was all business.

"The search is what matters. You're here to film it, right?"

Jed nodded.

"I assume you're both going to follow us then?"

Andy joined Jed in Nod Town.

"Fine. Get your gear and come with me." She spun on her heel, and Jed and Andy scrambled to follow.

As they trotted after her, Andy leaned close. "Well...I think that went okay."

"Are you nuts? She hates me!"

"Yeah—" he shrugged—"but she still likes me. And she didn't sic her dog on you." He inclined his head. "There just may be hope for you after all."

Jed couldn't quite believe that. At least, not where Annie was concerned. He wasn't fool enough to think she was letting him film her for any reason other than to keep the search from being canceled. And he'd respect that. He didn't want to hurt her any deeper, so he'd keep his distance. Stay behind the lens.

He was more comfortable there anyway.

And when they were done, he'd have a great show. The crowning touch of which would be—*please God, let it be so*—when Annie and Kodi found the little girl.

"What do you mean the *camera* crew is here?"

An edge of panic tipped Mr. Bristol's question. Annie didn't let her satisfaction show as she answered him. "It's a crew from that new hit reality show *Everyday Heroes*. You know that show?"

Bristol swallowed. "Yes, of course. Everyone's talking about it. It's all over the TV and news..."

She forced a touch of brilliance into her smile. "Right! That's the show. And they sent a crew here to film me and Kodi during the search for Amberly Heller."

"But...we're calling off the search."

Annie arched a brow. "Oh? Well, okay. Let me just call them over so you can let them know that."

"No, wait!"

"Jed. Andy. Over here. Mr. Bristol has something he wants to say."

To their credit, the two men were at her side within seconds. Andy's camera was even filming as they approached, and Jed gave a running narration. "The searchers have been at it for days, working against time and elements to find little Amberly Heller, a helpless child lost in a vast wilderness."

Bristol opened his mouth to say something, but Jed held up his hand and gave a quick shake of his head. He and Andy drew closer.

"What has the little girl faced already? Weather, certainly. Hunger, dehydration, without a doubt. Treacherous terrain? Count on it. But in these mountains, other hazards lurk. Bears, cougars, and who knows what else that could spell disaster—or death—for a five-year-old girl."

The camera was now about a foot from Bristol's face. He stared into it, his expression quite similar to a turkey trying to swallow a cat. "What? Am I supposed to say something?"

"I understand you have an announcement to make?"

Annie smiled. Jed wasn't giving the man an ounce of mercy.

"No. Not on camera, I don't."

"So you're making a decision that affects this child's future, but you're not willing to say so?"

"I..." Bristol put his hand over the lens. "Can you...please, turn this off?"

"Reality TV, man. We don't cut out the ugly stuff."

This from Andy.

"Please." Bristol looked at Annie. "Let me make a call."

Hope sparked, and Annie put a hand on Andy's arm. "Can you pause that thing?"

"For you? You bet." He hit a button and lowered the camera.

Bristol scampered a few feet away, pulling out a cell phone and making a call. Annie couldn't hear the man's words, but his body language spoke volumes. Within minutes, he returned and stepped in front of the camera.

"Okay, I'm ready."

Andy and Jed exchanged smug glances, then Andy lifted the camera and started filming again.

It took all of Annie's control not to whoop and scream as Bristol, his expression oh-so-serious, told the camera how grateful they were for *Everyday Heroes* and the impact it had on television. "And we are proud to have the show here in Oregon filming one of our own, Miss Annie Justice and her search dog, Kodi."

The man signaled to Annie. She shook her head—no way she was getting closer to this guy. Then Jed came to stand beside her, leaning his head just close enough to whisper. "It's for Amberly, remember?"

Squaring her shoulders, she led Kodi toward Mr. Bristol. Let him shake her hand and tell her how pleased he was that she and Kodi were on the job. Then, still shaking her hand, he turned back to the camera. "And *Everyday Heroes* will be right here, every step of the way, until we bring that precious child home."

He stood there, a plastic smile stamped on his features, his eyes shifting from Jed to Andy. Back to Jed. Then to Andy.

"Are we done?"

He spoke around the smile, and Annie pulled her hand free, turning away so she wouldn't laugh right in the poor man's face. She caught Jed's eye, saw the mirth there as well as he answered the man.

"Yep. That's good." He shook Bristol's hand. "You're a natural with the camera, sir. Really. Great job."

Andy lowered the camera and stood beside Annie. "I'm sorry."

Her laughter died. She looked down at the ground, seeking a response that felt right.

There was none.

"Hey, Annie."

Her brother's voice had never been so welcome. Annie turned, watching him approach. He looked from her to Andy, and she introduced the two. "Andy, my brother the deputy, Dan. Dan, Andy. Cameraman for *Everyday Heroes*."

"*Everyday Heroes,* the TV show?"

"That's the one." Andy studied Dan. "So, a deputy, huh?"

"Are you doing a show with them, Annie?"

She grimaced. "Yes. They're following me on the search."

"Ah, so that explains the commercial I saw this morning. Man! I almost fell off my chair when I saw you and Kodi on TV. Why didn't you tell me?"

Annie knew her brother was speaking English, so why didn't the words make any sense? She caught a glimpse of Andy's expression just before he turned toward Jed—and frowned. Why did Andy look so panicked?

Jed sauntered toward them, and Dan raised a hand in greeting. Annie almost slapped her brother's hand down, then realized he didn't know.

He still thought Jed was someone you could trust.

"Hey, Dan." Jed extended his hand. "Good to see you."

"You too. Wow, *Everyday Heroes,* huh? Great show."

Annie broke up the little lovefest. "What commercials?" She eyed Jed as she asked the question. He stiffened, then shot a quick look at Andy.

Something definitely was up.

She moved to stand toe to toe with Jed. "What. Commercials."

He looked down at her, then sighed. "I had Andy shooting footage of you and Kodi when we were together."

Dan's features turned thunderous. "Are you telling me you didn't know about this?"

Annie crossed her arms in front of her chest. "Not a thing." She jumped when Dan stepped past her, toward Jed, an ugly gleam in his eyes. "Wait! Dan, hold on." She grabbed his arm, felt how tense the muscles were.

Jed's hand eased over hers, removing it from Dan's arm. "It's okay, Annie. Your brother has a right to be angry. What I did was wrong. Morally, ethically, and probably legally. I was so determined to get Annie for the show that I made some bad decisions. I can only apologize and promise you I'll do all I can to make it right." He straightened his shoulders. "But if it will make you feel better, go ahead and take a punch. I deserve it."

Dan's hand closed into a fist, and Annie held her breath. He wouldn't! He was in uniform. If he hit Jed while on duty, he'd be in serious trouble.

Not to mention what it would do to Jed.

A yelp escaped her when Dan's fist shot out—and landed, with minimum impact—in the middle of Jed's chest.

"It will take more than words to fix this, Jed."

He didn't flinch. "I know that."

Dan's hand dropped to his side, and he nodded. "Good enough. For now."

Good enough?

Annie stared at her brother, speechless. *Good enough?* Oh, no it wasn't. Not by a long shot! And the very idea that Dan would think it galled her.

Jed turned to her, but Annie halted anything he might have been about to say by spinning and stalking away.

"Annie, please, wait."

She stopped but didn't face him. Just spoke over her shoulder. "Kodi and I will be going out first thing in the morning. Be ready. And Jed?"

"Yeah?"

"Don't get in our way."

Silence. Then, "We won't. I promise."

Well, that was something. She started toward the tent again, then realized she was alone. Kodi was nowhere to be seen. Annie scanned the near darkness, alarm prickling her—until she spotted the dog a few feet away.

Sitting there. At Jed's side.

Annie's eyes narrowed. "Kodi, come."

The shepherd looked up at Jed, then back to Annie.

"Kodi!"

A piteous whine met Annie's harsh call, but the dog did as she was bid. Pushing to her feet, she cast one more pining look back at Jed, then slunk toward her mistress, like a deathrow inmate taking that last, long walk.

When Kodi reached Annie's side, she took hold of the dog's collar and hustled her toward the tent. "Monster dog," she muttered.

First Jed. Then Dan. And now her own dog.

Traitors, all.

Well, at least there was one good thing about this stupid situation.

There wasn't anyone left to betray her.

Jed was cold.

So cold he was shaking.

The irony was that it had nothing to do with the weather. No, what had him trembling, inside and out, was the sound of Annie's voice as she cried out to God. He'd gone into the tent he and Andy were given, but after nearly two hours of lying there, staring into the unforgiving darkness, he finally got up and came outside.

He'd been standing here for close to an hour. He told himself he'd chosen this spot beneath a tall evergreen because it gave him shelter if it started to rain or snow. But that was just blowing smoke.

He came here because it was close to Annie's tent. And for now, that was enough. Just...being close to her.

He'd been staring up at the night sky, when he heard the sound of footsteps approaching. His heart jumped when he saw who it was. He'd straightened, ready to go to Annie, beg her forgiveness, try to explain—but the sight of her slumping to the ground, then curling into a ball at the base of a tree stopped him in his tracks.

As she sat there, knees drawn to her chest, her agony palpable, Jed fell back against the tree, grateful for something solid to hold him up.

What had he done? How could he have used her the way he did? Lied? Deceived?

How could he ever think she'd forgive him?

"God…please…"

Her ragged words were daggers in his chest. He closed his eyes against the grief in her voice. Emotions squeezed his heart until he didn't think he could bear it a moment longer. Then, breaking through the regret suffocating him, came whispers of memory.

"I don't know how anyone deals with pain without God…"

"That's the business He's in, you know. Helping and healing."

Jed opened his eyes, looking to the heavens. Helping and healing. That's what he needed. Not for himself. He deserved to hurt.

But for Annie.

For her, he'd do what he hadn't done in years. Though he wasn't worthy, didn't deserve to be heard, he would try.

For Annie.

He bowed his head. *Jesus, I know this is my fault. And I don't deserve Your help. But please, Lord, I'm so sorry. Please, help her. Touch her. Don't let her hurt because of me. Please, Lord, give her Your peace—*

"No more!"

Jed started at the low, furious words. Annie was on her feet, and determination hardened her features. For a moment, he thought she'd seen him, and he steeled himself for her fury. But she turned, making her way back toward her tent.

He stood there long after she'd stepped inside and zipped the door shut. Long after the dim light inside her tent went out.

Just stood there. Staring in the darkness. Pleading with God.

Because what he'd seen as Annie walked away told him, more clearly than any words could, that his deception had carried a far higher price than he'd ever dreamed. But he wasn't the one paying it.

Annie was.

THIRTY-NINE

"Long is our winter, dark is our night,
Come set us free, O Saving Light!"

GERMAN PRAYER

"Do not stay so far from me,
for trouble is near,
and no one else can help me."

PSALM 22:11

OCTOBER 24—A RED CLOVER DAY (GREEN AND ROSE)
6:30 *a.m.*

"Whoever invented oatmeal was a genius."

Jim, one of the members of Annie's K-9 unit, looked over her shoulder at the bowl she cupped in her hand. "You trying to tell us there's oatmeal in there, under all that brown sugar and raisins and milk?"

"It's in there." This from Karen, another SAR member, peering across the table at them. "Look at the lumps. Nothing forms lumps like oatmeal."

Annie sniffed her disdain. "You people are trogolytes."

Jim's lips twitched. "I think you mean troglodytes."

"Either way works for me."

He patted Annie on the top of her head. "Sure, Justice. Whatever you say."

Annie realized anyone overhearing their foolish exchange

might think them calloused. To joke over oatmeal when Amberly
was still lost? But humor brought relief. Pulled your perspective
away for a moment, allowing you to regroup, refocus. It brought
you together, where anger and frustration tore apart. Humor was
as necessary to the unit as any piece of equipment or element of
training. Even in the face of searches as unproductive and frustrating as this one.

Especially then.

Of course, the laughter wasn't as much a relief as usual. Because
mixed in with the voices of her SAR compatriots, Annie heard
another voice. A deep, rich voice that used to make her heart trip.

Now it just made it ache.

But she refused to look Jed's way. To acknowledge that either
he or Andy were there. Of course, she knew they were. Was
painfully aware of them sitting there, watching her. Of Jed's eyes
fixed on her, as they had been since that awful day she discovered
who he really was.

He'd tried to talk with her a number of times, but she just
turned and walked way. He was not going to talk his way out of
this. Not now.

Not ever.

Nor was he going to know how much she still hurt. Which
was why she made sure her laughter was as full and light as she
could make it.

"Good to hear you laughing, sis."

Annie turned to find Dan walking toward them. She shifted
over on the bench of the picnic table. "You're out early today."

He yawned, holding his hands around the heavy ceramic coffee mug that accompanied him wherever he went. "I stayed here
last night."

She turned back to her oatmeal. As much as she loved the
stuff when it was hot, even she couldn't stomach it when it cooled
and congealed. "Shelby must've loved that."

"She understands."

"What a control freak you are?"

"I'm sorry, I think you're confusing me with our other sibling."

Annie grinned. "Oh, right you are. That's Kylie's domain, isn't it?" She scraped the last of her oatmeal from the bowl, then set it aside and lifted her coffee. "So you stayed because of me."

His silence confirmed the suspicion. She lowered her voice so only he could hear. "Look, I admit it. This whole situation—the notes, Jed, the search—it's stressful. Maybe enough so that I'm not at the top of my game." She set her suddenly tasteless coffee down and pinned her brother with a hard look. "But I do not—repeat, do not—need a babysitter."

"I'm not doing this because you need me to, sis. I'm doing it because *I* need to. For me."

It was there, plain for her to see, in his eyes. The concern. The apprehension. And suddenly Annie understood.

Dan was afraid of another loss.

She drew in a breath of awareness, then laid her hand over his on the table. "Okay, big brother. No more arguments about it."

He turned his hand up to grip hers tight. "Thanks."

"Present for you, Annie."

She glanced up just in time to see one of the California SAR members drop an envelope on the table in front of her. "What's this?"

He shrugged. "No clue. It was on my truck this morning, under the windshield wiper."

Annie and Dan looked first at each other, then down at the envelope. She picked it up. *Annie Justice* was printed on the outside.

"You want me to open it?"

She shook her head, tore the envelope open, and let the note slide out. She bit her lip, then smoothed out the note so they could read it.

I KNOW WHAIR THE GURL IS. FIND HER. BEFORE IT'S 2 LATE.

Dan's hand on her shoulder helped still the shaking that gripped Annie.

"What's going on?"

She jumped, grabbing the note as she surged to her feet. *Oh, no you don't. No way this is going to end up on TV.* She faced Jed. "Nothing."

He wasn't buying it. "That wasn't nothing. I've seen notes like that before. Plenty of them. None of them good." He directed a look at Dan. "Tell me what's happening."

Dan stood as well. "Annie, Jed's going to be your backup while you're searching. He needs to know what's going on."

"No." She turned imploring eyes to her brother. "It's none of his business."

Dan's hand closed over hers, where she had the note crumpled into a ball. He eased her fingers open. "Yes, it is. If something happens, he needs to know. To protect you."

"I can take care of myself!"

"And to protect himself and Andy."

She resisted a moment longer, then let go of the note. Dan handed it to Jed, whose features darkened as he read. When he looked up, rage glittered in his eyes. "I take it this isn't the first note?"

Dan sat on the table. "No. There are several. And there were e-mails before that."

"So you're taking it seriously."

Dan's eyes were glittering now. "Definitely."

Annie took the note again. "What does he mean, he knows where the girl is? Amberly? How can he know?"

Dan rolled his clearly tense shoulders. "I'm not sure he does. He may just be pulling your chain. Saying what he knows will cause you the most stress."

It was working.

Jed's brow creased. "Dan, you got this just now?"

He nodded. "It was on one of the searcher's cars this morning. When he found it, he brought it to Annie."

Though Annie hadn't thought it possible, the anger in Jed's eyes deepened. "You know what that means."

Annie frowned, both at the fierce question and at Dan's nod. "What? What does it mean?"

Dan didn't answer right away.

"You have to tell her. She needs to know."

Jed's ominous words breathed new life into the fear within her. She looked at her brother. "Know what?"

Dan took the note from her. "This was on a searcher's car, Annie."

She nodded. "I know."

"How did it get there?"

Understanding was immediate—and terrifying. She put a hand on the table to steady herself.

"He's here."

Perfect.

It was perfect. Just the right amount of tears.

Just the right amount of blood.

He looked at the child curled into a ball on the cot, a thin blanket tossed over her restless form. He could have used her blood. Seriously considered it. But one thought held him back.

What if he made a mistake?

He wasn't a doctor. What if he cut her too deep, or couldn't stop the bleeding? Then she'd be dead and of absolutely no use to him.

No, this had been better. Of course, they'd know as soon as they tested it that the blood type was wrong. But until then...

Oh. Until then. The agony Annie would suffer. Agony that would break her heart. Her spirit. Her love for this damnable pastime that wasted her time and talents.

Oh, yes. Annie would suffer.

He could hardly wait to see it.

FORTY

"We turn to God for help when our foundations are shaking,
only to learn that it is God who is shaking them."

CHARLES C. WEST

"'My thoughts are completely different from yours,' says the LORD.
'And my ways are far beyond anything you could imagine.'"

ISAIAH 55:8

OCTOBER 25—A CORNFLOWER DAY (GREEN AND BLUE)
6:00 a.m.

God, what are You doing?

Annie stood just outside her tent, staring at the blanket of
white that covered the ground, weighted the trees, coated the
tents. At the large, fluffy flakes floating down from the muted sky.
There was pristine beauty in the sight, but not even the artist in
Annie could appreciate it.

All she felt was despair.

Bad enough that her brother followed her everywhere like an
extra shadow. That when she and Kodi were out, Jed and Andy
made her nervous as a cat with the way they kept scanning
around them for any possible evil.

Now this.

Father, how could You let it snow? Doesn't Amberly have enough
working against her?

And though only a few inches had fallen, it would make the

work harder on Kodi as well. There would be spots where the powder was fairly deep—hard going for the shepherd, even with her long legs. To make matters worse, the drop in temperature would make much less scent. Like trying to smell an ice cube.

Annie knelt, lifting a handful of the dry, powdery substance. Wonderful. Just wonderful. Kodi would practically have to trip over Amberly to find her.

What next, Lord? What else can happen to keep us from finding Amberly?

"This isn't good, is it?"

Jed's voice fell as soft as the snow, a touch of warmth in the cold. But Annie didn't turn. She couldn't. Couldn't bear facing him and the snow at the same time. She dropped the snow she'd been holding and stood. "No. It's not."

"I just wanted to let you know Andy and I are ready whenever you and Kodi are."

She rubbed one gloved hand with the other. "Okay. We'll head out right after we eat breakfast. In a half hour."

Snow crunched behind her as Jed walked away. The sound tugged at her heart. Everything within her wanted to turn, to call him back. To have things like they were.

But what they'd shared was lost. And not even Annie could find it again.

No matter how much she wanted to.

"I take it that's the infamous Jed?"

Annie spun, her mouth falling open. "Killian!"

He opened his arms to her, and Annie didn't hesitate. She went to him, letting him enfold her in a comforting hug.

"What's wrong, Annie? You look so heartbroken."

She shook her head and stepped back. "What on earth are you doing here? You hate the cold!"

His shoulders lifted, the motion eloquent. "I may hate the cold, but I love you. I told you I'd think about what you said, about how all this—" he waved his hand, encompassing the search site, the tents, everything around them—"fed your soul.

That thought won't leave me alone. So I decided if I'm going to call myself your friend, I need to understand what it is about this that inspires you so."

She took his hand, then looked down. "Killian, what did you do to yourself?"

"Oh, you know me." He pulled the bandaged hand away. "Clumsy to a fault. I had a bit of an argument with a utility knife when I was opening boxes at the gallery yesterday. Ryan called me every kind of fool for not being more careful."

"Good thing he was there." Annie grinned. "You get faint at the sight of blood."

"Yes, well. Enough about me." He linked his arm in hers. "I heard you say you're nearly ready to go out again. So show me where I can wait until you come back."

Annie laughed, and this time it was even sincere. "Thanks for coming out here, Killie. It means a lot to me."

"Me too." He didn't meet her gaze, but there was a small smile on his lips. "Me too."

Stillness.

That's what surrounded them as Jed and Andy walked along, a couple of paces behind Annie. Sounds were both muffled and magnified at the same time. The crunch of their feet on the snow was swallowed almost as soon as it sounded. And yet the steady tinkling of Kodi's bell drifted to them as clear as if the dog stood beside them. From what Annie had told them the first night they trailed her though, the dog could have ranged a considerable distance away.

Jed couldn't imagine it. "Aren't you afraid Kodi'll get lost herself?"

"She'd have to work at losing me."

"Surely she can't see you from that far away."

A smile crooked Annie's lips. "All she has to do is smell me. Remember, a search dog has forty-four times the olfactory sensory cells a human does."

That brought Andy peeking out from behind the camera. "Man! That's a super sniffer."

"That it is, but it makes sense. God created these animals to be scent smart. Twelve percent of their brains are dedicated to scent analysis. That's twelve times the percentage for human brains."

Jed loved listening to Annie talk about all of this. He seldom had to coax her into doing so. She was so passionate about what she and Kodi were doing, the thoughts just poured out of her. "Such as?"

"There only needs to be roughly one part of scent per ten quadrillion for Kodi to detect it. One in ten *quadrillion*. I can't even imagine how much that is, but she can do it. It's as easy for her as breathing."

"She was made to do this."

"That she wa—" Annie stopped so suddenly Jed had to grab Andy to keep him from running right over her. She held up one hand, head cocked, listening.

Jed perked his ears too and caught the sound that must have captured her attention.

Kodi's bell was ringing to beat the band.

He watched Annie, waiting for excitement to fill her features. But it wasn't there. Instead he saw something he didn't understand. Apprehension.

Until, that is, Kodi came flying through the trees toward Annie. The shepherd bounded up to her mistress, and Jed found himself tensing his own muscles as Annie readied for those big paws to punch her thighs. Kodi jumped up, and Annie's praise was immediate. "Good girl, Kodi!"

Jed had to fight not to groan. How did a woman as petite as Annie stay on her feet when that much force hit her?

She's strong.

She was that. In more ways than just physical.

"Show me, Kode! Good puppy, show me!"

Kodi spun and ran, Annie, Jed, and Andy hot on her heels, dodging trees and scrambling over brush and fallen branches. Jed could hear Annie saying something as she ran but couldn't quite make out what it was. He sped up, drawing closer—and his heart constricted when he finally understood what she was saying.

"Please...please be there...please..."

Longing flooded Jed. He ached to comfort her, to *do* something, to give her what she was asking. To ease the burden weighting her features more every day.

And the pain.

"Hey, Jed, you okay?"

He looked over his shoulder at Andy, who'd turned off the camera to navigate a wide stretch of blackberry bushes. "I'm fine."

"You don't look fine. You look...I don't know, like you're having chest pains or something."

Jed forced a touch of humor to his tone. "Look at it this way. If I keel over, it'll make for a great show."

He'd never admit it, but Andy was right. He was having chest pains. Just not the kind Andy thought.

Seeing Annie hurt like this, hearing her fear—it tore at him like the blackberry thorns snagging his clothing. With a deep gulp of the cold air, Jed turned to the place—no, the One—who'd become a haven since that night he watched Annie scream at the darkness. Since he'd poured out his heart, begging help.

And forgiveness.

God, please, help her. This is crushing her heart. Her spirit. She loves You. She's trying to do what You've called her to do. Please, help her.

A long-forgotten peace descended on him, its touch like that of the snowflakes that brushed his face as they tumbled by. Light. Cool. Fresh.

And as he broke free from the blackberries, he realized something inside had broken free as well. The pain was gone. In its place was a growing certainty. God had forgiven him. Restored him. He didn't have to worry about having the right to ask for help.

God was his Father. He would hear him.

And He would answer.

FORTY-ONE

"Never despair, but if you do, work on in despair."

EDMUND BURKE

"He lifted me out of the pit of despair,
out of the mud and the mire.
He set my feet on solid ground
and steadied me as I walked along."

PSALM 40:2

There's something there! Look!"

The excitement ringing in Annie's words was contagious. Before he could stop himself, Jed grabbed Andy's arm. "You getting all this?"

Andy shrugged Jed's hand off. "Quit! You're making me lose the shot."

"Sorry." He knew he should just let Andy do his job, but he couldn't help himself. He hopped behind Andy, peering over his shoulder into the viewfinder. "Zoom in on her."

Andy did as Jed ordered, and the camera zeroed in on Annie's face. Jed could see everything. Every nuance of emotion flitting across her features. The way her eyes shone, the tentative smile that nudged the corners of her mouth. The rapid blinking of eyes that suddenly glistened with tears.

Go, Annie. Find her. You can do it.

The camera panned out, catching Kodi in action. The shepherd sped up, bounding through the snow like a four-legged pogo stick.

Then with a suddenness that took Jed's breath away, Kodi stopped.

"Do you see anything?"

"Jed, back off! You're fogging up the viewfinder!"

He swatted the back of Andy's head, but he stepped back. "Zoom in. Do you *see* anything?" He held his breath, waiting. One heartbeat. Two.

"No."

Jed's stomach plummeted. *No?* That wasn't possible! He saw the way Kodi acted. And there was that certainty inside. "She *has* to be there."

"What is going on?"

Annie's cry of frustration rent the air, and Jed started toward her. Despair was etched in her features, in her stance. He watched her push the emotion aside as she applauded Kodi.

But the dog wasn't fooled.

She looked up at Annie, then circled the spot, shoving her nose into the snow. With a sharp bark, she dug at the offending ground.

"Kodi, it's okay." Annie's voice caught. "Leave it."

The dog's digging grew more frantic.

Jed snagged Annie's arm as she started toward Kodi, apparently intent on stopping the dog.

"Annie, wait."

She shot a venomous glare at him, jerking her arm away, but Jed didn't let go. He tightened his grip. "Look. I think she's found something."

Annie spun back to her dog, and a gasp escaped her. She dropped to her knees and pulled something out of the snow and dirt. Kodi's ecstatic barks filled the air, mingling with Annie's tear-soaked laughter.

"Good girl, Kodi. Good girl."

Jed leaned down and held his hand out. Annie didn't even argue. She handed him Kodi's tennis ball, and he threw it, calling encouragement as the shepherd bounded after her reward.

Annie pulled her radio free and reported Kodi's discovery. Then she picked up a stick and poked at it. Jed leaned close.

It was some kind of material.

"It's a shirt. A little girl's shirt."

Jed couldn't understand the sorrow in Annie voice. Wasn't this a good thing? A sign Amberly was out here?

Annie shook the dirt free and held the shirt out to study it.

All they had to do was take it back, show it to the girl's mother. She'd identify it—

Oh.

He could see the shirt clearly now that Annie held it up. Reddish brown stains. Ragged and torn, as though something had ripped into it. A piece of metal, maybe. Or…

He stilled.

Teeth. Wild animals. His mocking words, designed to strike terror into the politician's heart, came back to taunt him. *"Bears, cougars, and who knows what else that could spell disaster—or death—for a helpless child."*

As Kodi ran back to drop the ball in Jed's hand, Annie clasped the shredded shirt to her chest, then walked to a large boulder and sat down. She lowered her head into her hands, pressing her face into the shirt.

And burst into tears.

Jed turned, but Kodi reached her mistress first. A low whine escaped the dog as she lifted one paw and laid it in Annie's lap, then licked Annie's trembling hands. Annie reached out and touched the dog's head.

It was enough.

Kodi stilled, but she stayed next to Annie, leaning into her as though offering mute comfort.

Jed stood there, looking at the two of them, so vulnerable, so weary…and his heart broke. "Turn it off," he said to Andy, then walked to put his hand in front of the camera lens.

Andy glanced from behind the camera and met Jed's gaze.

"Turn it off."

He studied Jed for a second, then hit the power button and lowered the camera to his side. "I'm gonna go back a little ways."

He looked past Jed to Annie and Kodi. "Give you some privacy."

Jed thanked him with his eyes, then turned back to Annie.

She put a protective arm around Kodi. "What? Show over? Don't think your viewers want to see this part, huh?"

He winced at the bitterness in her tone. He deserved it, but he knew it wasn't really directed at him. "Actually, this is exactly what the viewers want to see."

She swiped her eyes with her sleeve, then glared at him. "So why not keep filming?"

He tried to speak, but his voice didn't want to cooperate. He swallowed. Hard. And tried again. "Because I can't."

His voice was raw, even to his own ears. Annie didn't respond, but he hadn't expected her to. He'd have to make the first move.

She watched him walk toward her, her expression unreadable. He half expected her to bolt. Either that, or set Kodi on him. But she did neither. Instead, she sat there, tears slipping from those beautiful eyes. Waiting.

He reached the boulder and sat beside her. His movements slow and cautious, he put his arm around her. She stiffened, then her resistance left on a small sigh. She sagged against him, turning her face into his shoulder. He gathered her close, tucking her against him.

And let her weep.

This was all wrong!

Annie sitting there, leaning against that lapdog Curry…

It was wrong.

As for Curry, who did he think he was holding Annie like that? How *dare* he take advantage of her when she was weak, hurting? No one had the right to be close to her like that.

Things had been going so well. With each passing day, as he kept little Amberly drugged and asleep, he'd seen Annie's despair grow. The wonderful doubt that touched her features, her actions.

The way her once confident stride grew hesitant.

His careful planning was paying off.

The notes had worked even better than he'd hoped. He didn't like frightening her—after all, doing so risked hindering her creativity just when she needed it most—but it was necessary. And then he heard about *Everyday Heroes*. It was as though providence itself was pointing him to E J Curry, the perfect—albeit unwitting—accomplice. Just the person to hound Annie, make her see that her involvement in search and rescue would only lead to loss of privacy and peace. He'd scanned in the newspaper article on Annie, then e-mailed it to Silas Whittle's assistant, attention E J Curry.

Curry's natural instincts for a story did the rest.

But he hasn't behaved himself, has he?

He pressed his lips together. No, Curry hadn't. What on earth had possessed him to actually come here to meet Annie? And then he had the unmitigated *gall* to become part of her life.

Which made him part of the problem.

Hence, the need for the drama. Which, all in all, was working out well. He'd expected someone to find the shirt sooner. Amberly had been happy to turn it over in exchange for the beautiful new shirt he'd bought her. And a little ground beef had provided the blood—and the motivation for the dogs at the shelter to tear into it.

That it snowed and covered any sign of his tracks was a miracle.

That Annie was the one who found it was more than he could have hoped for.

That Curry was there, ready to console her, was maddening.

Why, every time he turned around, was Curry there? He was making this far harder than it needed to be. And it was getting more difficult to keep Amberly hidden away in the cabin he'd rented. Harder still to keep her in the drama, to not let her grow frightened. She'd been away from her mother for too long. But that was Annie's fault!

Why didn't she just do the sensible thing and give up?

They'd come so close when the search was almost called

off. He'd known just the right person to contact—someone with the perfect blend of power and imprudence—to cancel the search.

And then Annie had to call Curry.

Well, enough was enough. He would just have to up the ante a bit. Do something that would make her walk away.

But what? What would have the proper impact?

He studied the two of them, then looked away. He simply couldn't stomach watching them a moment longer. Better to focus elsewhere.

Such as…

He smiled. Of course.

Annie's precious dog. Without which she would have no reason to be in search and rescue.

Clarity swirled in his mind, then settled deep in his gut. So. His path was clear. More's the pity. He didn't want this. Really didn't.

But Annie wasn't leaving him much choice.

"We're running out of time."

Annie's voice was so low and ragged that Jed almost didn't catch the words.

"She's just a little girl. She can't survive out here much longer." Annie looked up at him, her anguish palpable. "I don't understand what's happening."

Jed knelt in front of her. "Talk to me."

"It's never been like this before. Kodi and I, we've always found the victims we looked for. It was as though God had His hand on us, leading us." She looked at the dog leaning against her. "There've been tough searches. Times when it took longer than I thought it would. But no matter how hard or how long, it always turned out right."

"Annie, it's not your fault. No one has been able to find the little girl."

"But that's just it! We did find her before. Or Kodi did. There was just no evidence to prove that's what Kodi alerted on those times. Now there is."

Jed opened his mouth, but Annie stopped him.

"I know what you're going to say. What the others have been saying. Kodi made a mistake. The stress...my stress is affecting her. But they're wrong. I know my dog. She alerted. On a *person*. This—" she held the shirt, crumpled in her fist—"was a plant. I know it sounds crazy, but someone is working against us, Jed. Someone is moving this child."

She sounded so certain...but if she was right, why wasn't there any sign of anyone. "Annie, there aren't any tracks. How could someone put this shirt here without leaving tracks in the snow?"

Doubt wavered in her eyes, and Jed hated that he'd put it there. *God, please...*

A light went on. "Unless." He stood, looked from Annie's tear-stained face to the ground.

She followed his gaze, then stood and came to join him. "Unless?"

"Remember what the note said? He knows where the girl is? You wondered how he could know."

"Yes, but—"

"Annie, there wouldn't be tracks if someone planted the shirt here before the snowfall."

Her eyes swung to meet his, understanding dawning—and then flaring—in those hazel depths. "That's why we haven't been able to find Amberly. Because she's not out here?"

Jed nodded a slow, thoughtful agreement. "I think you're right. Somebody's been moving her. Positioning her to draw the dogs, then moving her. Playing us."

"But *why?*"

"I don't know." He took her arm, turning her back the way they'd come. "But we need to go back and talk with your brother. Because I don't think we're dealing with a lost child at all—" a sense of urgency gnawed at him, and Jed picked up his pace—"but with a kidnapping."

FORTY-TWO

*"The wicked are always surprised to find
that the good can be clever."*

MARQUIS DE VAUVENARGUES

*"Even when I walk
through the dark valley of death,
I will not be afraid,
for you are close beside me.
Your rod and your staff
protect and comfort me."*

PSALM 23:4

OCTOBER 25
10:00 a.m.

"Okay, then, everyone clear on the new search?"

Annie watched the heads around them bob up and down. But she saw something more than simple agreement in the searchers' faces.

She saw anger.

Anger that someone might have used them all this way. That someone would use a *child* this way.

Anger was good though. Because in situations like this, it erased the frustrations and confusion that had been plaguing them and replaced them with focus and determination. Annie allowed herself a twinge of satisfaction. If there was one thing these people were, now, it was determined. To bring Amberly Heller home.

And to bring her kidnapper to justice.

She was surprised at how quickly Dan agreed with Jed's conclusion. Then again, it was the only thing that made any sense. It explained so much—Kodi's false alerts in different grids, the fact that no one of the more than fifty searchers found any signs. Now Annie understood how that could happen.

Whoever was out there was as fixed on her and Kodi as they were on Amberly.

"Are you going to tell Brianna and Mark?"

"I have to."

Annie understood the regret tingeing her brother's words. He knew telling her friends that their little girl may have been taken was only going to increase their fears. But if he was going to do everything possible to get Amberly back, he had to ask them if they had any idea who had taken their child. And if so, where that person might have taken her.

"You're heading out again?"

Annie turned at the question, nodding at Killian. "Yup. We'll probably be out most of the morning. If not longer."

He touched her arm. "Just be careful. If there's really someone out there, doing what you think he's doing…" He shook his head. "Just be careful."

She patted his bandaged hand, then jumped when someone took hold of Killian's wrist and lifted his hand off her arm.

"So Killian—" Dan eyed the injured hand—"how, exactly, did you say this happened?"

Killian tugged at his hand, but Dan didn't let it go. Annie frowned. What was wrong with her brother?

"I cut myself. Why?"

"Would you mind showing me the wound?"

"Dan!" Annie shivered. "You're being gross."

His glare told her quite clearly she should butt out.

"Don't worry, Annie. I don't mind." Killian jerked his hand

free and tugged at the bandage. He grimaced when he pulled it free from his palm, then held his hand out for Dan's inspection.

"Still pretty fresh, huh? Deep too." He eyed Killian. "Must have bled a lot."

"Like the proverbial stuck pig." Killian's lips pressed together, and he dangled the bloody bandage with the thumb and forefinger of his other hand. "And it's bleeding again, thanks to pulling the bandage off."

"Sorry about that. Tell you what—" Dan reached out and took the bandage from Killian—"I'll get rid of this for you." He turned and called to one of the SAR unit members. "Hey, Jim, would you take our friend here to the first aid station and patch up his hand?"

"Sure. Follow me."

Killian tossed one last glare at Dan, then followed Jim across the site. Annie waited until they were out of earshot, then spun back to her brother. "All right, *Deputy*. What was that all about?"

"Just hitting all the bases, sis."

"If you think for a minute that Killian has anything to do with this—"

The look in his eyes stopped her cold. "Annie, until we know who the perp is, I think everyone's guilty. And when a little girl's safety—" his gaze narrowed—"and my *sister's* safety—are at stake, I don't leave any suspect stone unturned."

She wanted to argue with him, but a voice from behind them halted the angry words perched on her tongue.

"Hey, you ready to go?"

They turned to find Andy standing there, camera at the ready. He'd been filming the briefing, then went to film comments from a number of the SAR members.

Now, here he was, camera aimed at them.

"How long have you been here?"

At Dan's firm question, Andy lowered the camera and held his hand up. "Hey, I just arrived."

"Okay." Dan eyed Annie. "Be careful, okay?"

Her anger faded at the concern in his tone. "I will, Dan. I promise."

As he walked away, Andy hiked his camera back up on his shoulder and started filming. "As I was saying, you ready to go?"

Annie was finally learning how to just relax and talk to the camera lens as though she were talking to Andy. He'd even let her tape a little picture of him on the top of the camera.

"I'm ready."

Jed came to join them, and with Kodi at their side, they headed out to Annie's Jeep. "So some of the teams are now doing evidence searches?"

Annie nodded, opening the door for Kodi to hop in. "We'll still be searching for Amberly, but we're ranging farther because of the likelihood that Amberly isn't just walking. She's being carried to different locations."

It took them about fifteen minutes to reach their designated search area. A rocky ravine. They walked to the edge, peering down. "Lots of shale here." Annie looked over her shoulder at the guys. "And the snow just makes it that much more treacherous."

Jed leaned forward, looking down. "And we're going down there...why?"

"Because we determined this was too far for Amberly to walk. And too hard for her to navigate. But if someone has her and is looking for a place to hide her..." She motioned toward the ravine with her chin. "This is the place to go. Lots of trees and brush down there, which makes it almost impossible to see anything from up here. The descent is treacherous, which keeps folks from wandering by. Unless, of course—" she stepped forward— "you happen to be a crazy SAR person. Watch your footing."

"And her crazy camera crew," Andy muttered as he followed her over the edge.

They made their way down the incline, sliding as much as walking. Annie kept an eye on Kodi, but the dog was faring better than she and the men. Four feet definitely gave a more solid base in terrain like this.

Once at the bottom, Annie sent Kodi out, and she and the men fell into what was becoming routine. She walked just ahead of them, talking, explaining what Kodi was doing or what she noticed.

She looked over her shoulder. "So you still think this is going to make a good show?"

Jed's nod was immediate. "Count on it."

"We're not exactly *Baywatch*, you know."

"No, you're not," Andy called from behind the camera. "You're better."

Annie laughed at that. "You obviously need to get out more, Andy."

"What I need—" he said as he slipped on some loose rocks— "is another latte."

"Sorry, no coffee kiosks out here."

"Well then," Jed joined in. "We're in great shape."

Annie frowned. "How's that?"

"We've got the best K-9 search team in the northwest here. So whaddya say, Annie? Ready to find this little girl and get back to town?"

She glanced at him and saw he was serious. What she saw on his face took her breath away.

He believed in her.

"You can do this. You and Kodi."

Andy joined the chorus. "C'mon, Annie. Forget this creep and his stupid notes. Let's find the girl."

Warmth filled her chest, even as a smile filled her face. "Okay." She turned to follow Kodi. "Let's do it."

He didn't want to do this.

But what choice did he have?

The shirt hadn't worked. After all the trouble he'd gone to getting the blood, hiding the shirt, waiting for them to find it. At first he thought it was working. Thought they believed the child was hurt.

Maybe even dead.

As he watched despair overtake Annie, he'd felt a surge of pure, raw elation.

He was winning.

But then...

Something changed. It was Jed's fault. Curry wasn't doing anything the way he was supposed to. *Why did I bring him here? He's going to ruin everything!*

Too late for recriminations. It was what it was. He simply needed to up the stakes.

He steered his car to a secluded spot, nudging the nose of it into dense bushes and trees. Then glanced in the rearview mirror.

The child had been more of a trial than he'd imagined. Oh, she'd been pliable at first, believing him when he told her he was an angel, sent by her mommy to protect her. But with each passing day, she'd grown more restless. Demanding.

His lips pressed together.

He hated demanding people.

It took time, but he finally accepted that he couldn't control her. Happily, the pills were working. Keeping her deep asleep. She hadn't stirred as he wrapped her in the blanket and carried her to the car. Hadn't moved as he drove. Now, as he watched her in the mirror, he almost thought the rise and fall of her little chest would slow so much it might stop. A thrill of panic shot through him.

Then she took a breath, and the excitement faded.

She was only sleeping. She was fine.

For now.

But such were the caprices of the fates. Plans, no matter how precise, could be foiled. And though he hadn't intended on harming the child, who knew what would be necessary before they were through?

Still, for now, it was enough that she slept.

He slipped from the car, locking it tight, then ran to the edge of the ravine just in time to catch a glimpse of Annie and her lackeys. Good. They were going the way he'd hoped.

He ran into the woods, toward the spot on the edge of the ravine.

Five minutes. That's all it would take him to reach the spot he'd prepared. Five minutes.

And it would all be over.

"She's alerting!"

Annie readied herself for Kodi's jump, then encouraged the shepherd to show her what she'd found. Her heart pounded. Kodi was more excited than Annie had seen her in days.

This had to be it.

Annie ran after her dog, shouting encouragement.

Please, God, let this be it!

It was cold.

Amberly shivered, pulling the blanket over her. But it didn't help. Her teeth started chattering.

She tried to open her eyes, but they didn't want to open.

She didn't feel good.

"Mom…my."

When her mommy didn't answer, Amberly started crying. Where was she? Why couldn't she open her eyes. Where was her angel? He said he would protect her.

Open! She told her eyes. *Open!*

Finally they obeyed.

Sniffling, she saw she was in a car. She pushed herself up, but everything started to twist and spin in circles. Amberly cried harder.

"Mommy!"

She blinked, making her eyes see better. Mommy wasn't here. Neither was her angel. No one was here. She was all alone. And so cold.

She scooted across the seat and grabbed the door handle, crying so hard now she had to rub away the tears to see anything. She turned the handle and pushed. The door flew open.

Amberly slid out of the car, but her legs wouldn't hold her up. She dropped to the ground, then jerked back at the cold snow. She wanted to call her mommy again, but she couldn't talk because of the tears.

She pushed onto her hands and knees and crawled. Around the car. Away from the woods. Crying harder than she'd ever cried before.

"Mommy!"

"Don't lose them!"

"Don't *what?*" Andy's voice grated behind Jed. "I'll be lucky not to lose the camera! This stuff is like running on marbles!"

Jed scrambled over the slippery ground. He'd almost gone down twice now. How did Annie move so fast over this stuff? He looked ahead, then pointed. "I think Kodi has something! Are you filming?"

Andy lurched to stand beside him, pulling the camera to his shoulder. "I've never missed a shot yet. I'm not startin' now!"

As they drew closer, Jed saw Annie running toward Kodi, who was barking and digging frantically at a large pile of lose rocks and shale at the base of the incline.

"Man, that does not look safe…"

He agreed with Andy. "Shoot up, toward the top. I want to see what's above—"

"Crud!"

Jed looked at Andy. "What? What's wrong?"

"There's someone up there."

"What?"

Andy pointed, and Jed followed his finger. But all he saw were rocks and boulders at the top.

"He's up there, I'm tellin' ya. I *saw* him."

Alarm surged through Jed as he scanned the incline. It wouldn't take much to send the whole side of that hill down on top of Kodi. And…

He started running. "Annie!"

She didn't look his way. She was intent on helping Kodi uncover whatever she was digging at.

"*Annie!*"

She jerked her head up, looking at him. He was no more than ten feet away when he heard it. An ominous rumble.

"Look out!"

Andy's yelp hit them at the same time Jed lunged forward, catching Annie by the waist and carrying her out of the path of the falling rocks and shale. Holding her fast, the two of them rolled, the hard ground slicing at them as their momentum carried them.

When they came to a stop, they lay there panting, dust from the rock slide settling over them. Jed had Annie's face pressed to his chest, and he looked down at her. "Are you okay?"

She managed a nod. "I think so."

They sat up and looked back. A pile of rock and rubble lay where Annie had been standing.

The realization of what could have happened slammed into Jed. A half second later, Annie surged to her feet.

"*Kodi!*"

She and Jed scrambled over the rubble on the ground. "Do you see her? Oh, God, please! Do you see her?"

The panic in Annie's voice tore at him, and he started grabbing rocks and throwing them. "We'll get her out, Annie. We'll get her…"

But even as he dug, he knew it was too late.

Kodi was gone.

FORTY-THREE

Rocks.

Rocks piled on rocks.

There was no way a dog could survive being buried under all of this.

Jed grabbed and threw, hands tearing on the jagged edges of rocks and shale. It didn't matter. In fact, the pain helped him disregard his screaming muscles—and the scream trying to claw its way up from his chest.

Beside him, Annie stopped digging. He turned to her, a question poised on his lips, and saw she was shaking, tears streaming down her face, leaving damp trails of denial as she pled with heaven. "Jesus, please…this can't happen. It can't."

Her hoarse whisper cut deep, and still kneeling, Jed grasped her arms and pulled her close. Her fists pounded on his chest, and he took the onslaught without flinching. Outwardly, anyway.

God? This can't be Your answer. It can't…

When her fists finally stopped, her fingers tangled in the front of his shirt, clutching as she sagged against him. He tucked her tight, turning so his body blocked the sight of the pile of rubble.

Voices wrestled within Jed, one screaming that no God who allowed this could be good, loving, trustworthy. The accusations pelted his heart, tearing at it, and he could feel it stiffening, turning as hard and cold as the rocks that lay behind him.

But another voice breathed through him, a gentle whisper calling his rampant thoughts to silence.

Trust.

But how can Annie handle this? You know Kodi was more than just a dog to her.

Trust in the Lord always.

Jed pressed his face against Annie's hair. *I want to, God. You know I want to...*

Trust in the Lord always, for the Lord God is the eternal Rock.

"Jed! Annie! Are you okay?"

Jed turned and saw Andy running up to them—and went still. "Annie."

She pressed against him, shaking her head.

Jed closed his hands on her arms, gave a gentle shake. "Annie, look."

"I can't. I just...I can't..."

He firmed his grip and set her away from him, turning her to face Andy as he approached. Annie gasped, then tore free of Jed's hands, scrambled to her feet, and ran to meet Andy.

And the dog limping along at his side.

Kodi's deep "Arroww-roow-*row!*" filled the air, accompanied by Annie's tear-filled laughter. The shepherd then lavished her mistress's face with kisses when Annie threw her arms around the animal and buried her face in that black neck.

Jed sat back on the pile of rocks, floating on a cloud of gratitude and relief. *Thank You, Lord. Thank You.* He watched as Andy came to stand beside him. "How?"

Andy put one hand out to help Jed up and with the other

held his camera high. "I got it all, bro. Every beautiful second. That dog can *move*. You startled the spit out of her when you tackled Annie, and she did one of the fastest scrambles I've ever seen. She got clipped, but that didn't stop her. She ran a circle away from the rock slide then over to me. I had to stop taping for a few minutes while I held her back though. She didn't seem to care that she was hurt or that the rocks were still falling. She just wanted to get to Annie."

"I know how she felt." Jed knelt beside Annie, one hand on Kodi's soft back. "Is it bad?"

Annie's hands ran up and down the dog's body. Kodi sat, watching Annie with such trust. Only when Annie's hands took hold of the dog's injured leg did she protest—by laying a woeful chin on Annie's shoulder.

"I know, girl. It hurts." Annie looked at Jed. "I don't think it's broken, but there's a bad gash." She unzipped her day pack and pulled out a first aid kit. "I need to wrap it, then we can get her back to base camp so the vet can examine her."

"Get her wrapped up, and I'll carry her." Jed buried his fingers in the dog's thick fur. He still couldn't quite believe she was here.

Annie's hand covered his where it rested on the dog's back. He met Annie's wide gaze.

"Thank you." Her voice was hoarse with tears. "You saved our lives."

The mere thought of losing Annie made Jed's gut churn. He wanted to grab her, hold on to her, but before he could do so, Kodi suddenly turned that big head and emitted a low whine. Ears perked, she stared past Jed, up the incline.

Amberly couldn't talk.

All she could do was cry. And scream. It made her throat hurt. But she was too scared to care.

Her knees were sore and cold, and her fingers hurt so bad. She stopped crawling and curled up in a little ball, shaking.

Where was her mommy? Where was her angel?

She didn't like it here. Didn't like being all alone. It scared her. And made her mad.

She fell back on the cold, cold ground, kicked her cold legs, and screamed again.

He *missed*?

He peered over the edge of the incline, staring, unable to believe what he saw.

The dog was still alive!

How had it escaped the rocks? He'd cut squares from the child's blanket and buried them in just the right spots to position the dog.

He'd taken such care with the planning. How could he have…have…?

Wait. That noise. What was that noise?

Alarm skittered up his nerves, and he turned away from the ravine, staring through the trees.

Back toward the car.

He listened. And the alarm shifted into panic.

No!

He ran.

No!

"Kodi, no!"

What on earth was wrong with that dog?

She'd broken away from Annie and was limping back the way they'd come, along the bottom of the ravine, barking up a storm. How she could run on that injured leg was beyond Annie. But she had to stop her before Kodi hurt herself even worse.

Suddenly Kodi spun, trying to scramble up the incline.

Annie caught up with her, grabbing at her, managing to snag the edge of her shabrack. Kodi fell with a yelp when her injured leg gave way, then scrambled back to her feet and tried again.

"What's wrong with her?"

Annie could barely hear Jed over Kodi's frantic barks. "I don't know! It's as if she hears—" Annie's fingers tightened on the shabrack, and she turned to meet Jed's eyes. "As if she *hears* something."

Jed was already looking up to the edge of the ravine. Annie finally got an arm around Kodi's straining neck. "Kodi, no! *Stand!*"

Every muscle quivering, the shepherd finally obeyed. She fell silent, except for a pitiful whine. Annie closed her eyes, listening.

There!

Her eyes flew open. Someone was crying. No, *wailing*. The piercing, terrified wailing of a child.

A little girl.

"It's coming from up there!" Even as she pinpointed the sound, Annie jerked her radio free and called in to command. "We've found a child." She clamped down on the emotions wanting to surge through her, focusing on giving command the correct GPS coordinates.

"10-4. I'm going to try to get to her from here."

Andy was beside Annie then, taking hold of Kodi's collar. "Go. I'll hold her."

Annie didn't have to be told twice. She ran to Jed's side, and they started up the steep incline.

"Watch it!" Jed's cry came a moment too late.

The rocks beneath Annie's boot shifted and tumbled, and she went down. Hard. But she pushed back up and kept going.

Jed moved in right beside her. "Take it easy, Annie. You can't help Amberly if you get hurt."

She wanted to argue, but she knew he was right. His low, calming voice flowed over her.

"Take a deep breath, and let's climb. Together. We'll get there. But we'll do it smart."

She met his steady gaze and nodded. Together they climbed.

"Amberly!" Annie's cry was as loud as she could make it past the tears clawing at her throat. "We're coming, honey!"

The footing was treacherous, and each step sent rocks sliding and tumbling in their wake. But they didn't stop.

"Look!"

Annie followed Jed's pointing finger and froze.

A little face peered at them, just over the edge of the incline.

Annie's heart seized. "Stay there, honey. We're coming. I promise." *Father, please, don't let her fall. Move her back from the edge!* "Don't move, honey, we're coming."

Amberly scooted closer to the edge, looking down at them with wide eyes. "I...want...my *mommy!*"

The child's hiccupping sobs punctuated her demand, and Annie's heart nearly broke. "I know, sweetie. And she wants to see you. Just stay there, okay? Just stay right there. You're safe now. I promise."

Please, God, Annie prayed as she dug in for a better foothold and pushed forward, *let me be right.*

Trees grabbed at him, branches slapping him in the face as he ran.

It wasn't fair! Everything was working against him!

He hit the edge of the woods—and stopped cold. The passenger's door stood open. Even from here he could see the tracks in the snow. He followed them, looking past the car...

And then he heard her. Annie. Calling to the child. "You're safe now. I promise."

No! No!

He stepped out of the trees, ran to the car, and slammed his hands on the hood. The child was there. On her hands and knees in the snow, looking over the edge. He took in the distance. He could do it. He could get to her—

"Amberly!"

His disbelieving eyes watched as Annie surged up and over the edge, scooping the child into her arms.

Anger. Fury. Despair.

Not fair! Not *fair!*

He crouched low, behind the car, and clawed at the driver's door. Jerking it open, he scrambled onto the seat and jammed the key in the ignition. He slammed it into reverse, then spun the steering wheel to clear the trees as he turned around and floored it.

His tires threw dirt and snow as they spun then grabbed and propelled the car forward, the open passenger's door slamming shut from the violent motion of the car.

He took one look in the rearview mirror as he sped away. One horrible sight met his angry eyes: Jed Curry, coming up over the ridge and putting his arms around Annie and the child.

Jed buried his face in Annie's hair, holding her and the little girl tight. He wasn't going to let either one go.

"Jed."

He shifted his face to answer. "Yeah?"

"I...can't breathe."

"Oh." He let her go. "Sorry."

Annie stepped back, glancing past Jed. "Did you see it? The car?"

"Just caught a glimpse of it." He gritted his teeth. "I didn't catch the plate, but I think it was an old Chevy Nova."

Jed could see the anger in Annie's eyes and the touch of disappointment. He understood. They all wanted to catch the creep.

Annie knelt, setting the shaking child on the ground, running her hands over her arms and legs. "Are you hurt anywhere, honey?"

The girl popped a thumb in her mouth and nodded, her tear-soaked eyes fixed on Annie. "My knees are cold and sore," she said around her thumb. Those big blue eyes blinked, as though the child could barely keep them open.

Annie scooped up Amberly, then directed shining eyes at Jed over the blond head. "How 'bout we take you someplace where we can fix those old knees up?"

"Can I see my mommy and daddy now?"

Annie's smile was glorious. "I think that's a wonderful idea."

Jed drew a breath of relief. At last, the search was over. The lost was found.

And she was safe.

He turned to look down at Andy and realized his friend had the camera on his shoulder, filming it all. A pang pierced his heart.

The search was over.

Time for him to leave.

FORTY-FOUR

*"While we are free to choose our actions,
we are not free to choose the consequences of our actions."*

STEPHEN R. COVEY

*"A prudent person foresees the danger ahead and takes precautions;
the simpleton goes blindly on and suffers the consequences."*

PROVERBS 22:3

Nothing felt as good as this.

Annie watched Bree and her husband hold their daughter, tears bathing their faces even as their laughter brushed the air.

An arm slid across her shoulders, and she turned. Killian smiled at her.

"See why this means so much to me, Killie?"

He gave her a little shake. "I just said so, didn't I? Brat. You want me to grovel?"

"Why not?" Dan came to stand between Annie and Killian. "After all, most men have to grovel at some time or another. Why should you be any different?"

Annie frowned at the hard edge to her brother's words. Was he angry with Killian for some reason?

Dan turned to her then, and his features softened. "You done good, sis."

"Kodi done good. She led us to the right spot. And the SAR unit done good. It was a team effort."

"You play a part too, Annie. Don't ever forget that."

Dan nodded. "Killian's right. You and Kodi, you're a team. And a very good one." He tugged at her hair. "I'm proud of you, little sister."

Pleasure warmed her cheeks, and Annie smiled around the tears that had suddenly sprung to her eyes. "Thanks, Dan. That means a lot."

More than he could know.

She glanced back toward Bree and her family. "Are you going to talk with Amberly, Dan?"

"Yes. Would you mind coming along? Amberly knows you better, and she's comfortable with you. Besides, I think it would help Bree for you to be there."

"I'd like that." She hopped off the picnic table, ready to follow him.

Killian straightened. "As for me, I believe I'll head back home. Glad the little girl is back safe and sound."

Dan glanced at Killian, an odd spark in his eyes. "Sure you don't want to meet Amberly? Might help you understand Annie's work even more to talk with the victim."

Killian studied Dan for a beat, a small smile tipping his lips. "A tempting offer, but no. I've left my work long enough. Poor Ryan is probably overwhelmed. I tried calling him a few minutes ago and he didn't even answer. So I'll more than likely get an earful when I get back."

"Hmm."

Annie glanced at Dan and frowned. He looked like he was going to say something more, but another voice stopped him.

"Annie?"

She turned, heart dropping to the bottom of her stomach. Andy. And if he was there, Jed probably was too. She wasn't ready to see him. But when she turned, Andy was alone.

"Can I talk to you for a second?"

Annie looked from him to Dan, who inclined his head. "I'll wait over here."

She turned to Andy. "What's up?"

"Look, I know things are kind of unsettled with you and Jed."

If he was looking for her to deny it, he was in for a disappointment. When she didn't respond, he shrugged. "Okay, things are really messed up with you and Jed. I know that. But I wanted—" he held out his hand—"to give you this."

She took the business card and read it, then looked at him. "Your card?"

"It's got my home number there too. On the back. You know…just in case you need anything. Someone to talk to. Someone who understands Jed really well." He looked at the ground, then angled a look at her. "And who respects you. A lot."

She pursed her lips, looked from the card to him, then stepped forward to wrap him in a hug. "Thanks," she whispered in his ear. "I hope Jed knows what a good friend you are."

He hugged her back, then let go. She started to turn, but he stopped her.

"He really loves you, you know."

Annie kept her gaze fixed on the ground. "I know."

"And you love him."

She could only shrug.

Without another word, she went to catch up with Dan, glancing around as she did so. "Did Killian leave?"

"As fast as his little legs could take him."

She frowned again. "What's with you and Killian? Are you mad at him about something?"

Dan started to say something, then stopped, shaking his head. "Nah. What could I be mad at him about? Let's go talk to Amberly."

As they walked, Annie pulled the business card from her pocket and read it again. Dan glanced down at it as well.

"Andy seems like a good guy."

Annie nodded. "Yes, he does."

"And Jed?"

"Is off-limits."

At her terse reply, Dan put an arm around her shoulders.

They walked the rest of the way in silence. They'd no sooner reached the family than Brianna threw her arms around Annie. "I can never thank you enough for bringing my little girl home." She stepped back. "Is Kodi okay?"

Annie smiled her relief. "She'll be fine. No broken bones, thank heaven. She's asleep in the tent right now. The unit vet bandaged her leg and gave her a shot of antibiotic and a light sedative so she'd sleep."

Dan stepped forward. "I'd like to talk with Amberly for a minute, if that's okay."

"Of course." ·

Dan set the little girl up on a picnic table. As he eased onto the bench so they were almost eye-to-eye, the child looked at Annie.

"Is your doggy okay?"

Like mother, like daughter. Annie touched Amberly's hair. "She's just fine, honey. She's taking a nap."

"Can I see her?"

"Sure, you can. Right after you talk with the deputy. Did I tell you he's my brother?"

Taking his cue, Dan leaned forward. "Hi, Amberly. I'm Dan."

Those big blue eyes peered up at him. "Hi, Dan."

"Honey, can you tell us what happened when you got lost?" He jotted down notes as Amberly spoke, and listening to that little-girl voice, Annie could picture the child chasing after the butterfly, suddenly realizing she was lost...

"Were you scared?"

At Dan's question, Bree turned away, biting her lip. Amberly tugged at her mother's sleeve. "It's okay, Mommy. I wasn't afraid. My angel was there to take care of me."

Bree and her husband exchanged a surprised look.

Dan's brows creased. "Your angel?"

Amberly's little head nodded. "Uh-huh. He was always with me." Her smile beamed up at her parents. "He was the ark angel, Mommy. He told me you sent him to take care of me. So I wasn't afraid."

"Ark angel?"

Brianna stroked her daughter's hair. "Michael. I told her a story about Michael, the archangel."

Bree sounded so apprehensive. Annie studied her friend's features and knew. The terrible thoughts that had been taunting Annie were beginning to torment Brianna as well. Annie wished she could comfort her friend, put her fears to rest.

But she couldn't.

Bree looked from Annie to Dan. "Is something wrong?"

Dan watched her, his gaze steady. Annie could tell how careful he was being with what he said. "About Amberly's angel—"

"Oh." Brianna clutched her hands together, two bright spots of red blooming on her pale cheeks. "She's loves angels so much. And she's always been such an imaginative child."

Mark stepped forward. "I'm sure Amberly conjured this angel up because she was afraid."

Annie wasn't convinced. "But she said she wasn't afraid."

Dan turned his focus back to the little girl. "Amberly, we need you to tell us if your angel was real, or if he was a pretend angel."

The little girl frowned. "Am I in trouble?"

Bree put her arms around her daughter and hugged her. "Not at all, sweetheart. We just want to know because…because—"

"Because if he's real, we want to thank him for coming to take such good care of you."

Bree's gratitude shone in her eyes as she turned to Annie.

"Oh, he'd like that!" Amberly patted her mother's arm where it was wrapped around her. "Honest, Mommy, Michael came to take care of me. He was real. I talked with him and held his hand, and he took me to a cabin to visit." She looked at Dan. "He was a very nice angel."

The disquiet that had been lurking deep inside Annie burst into full-blown dread. So it was true. The little girl hadn't been lost.

She'd been taken.

By someone posing as an angel.

Annie saw the same horror color Bree's features.

"He told me he was the ark angel—" Amberly twisted to face

her mother—"and he said it the same way I do, Mommy. *Ark angel.*" She grinned, clearly delighted that she'd known something her mother hadn't.

Mark put a protective arm around his wife's shoulders as Dan turned back to Amberly. "So what did you and your angel do together?"

Annie tensed.

"For a while he brought me food and played games with me."

Dan's pencil paused. "What kinds of games?"

"Oh—" she kicked her feet back and forth over the edge of the table—"hide-'n'-seek an' follow the leader, mostly. He showed me where to hide, then went away for a while. And when he came back, he'd find me. Then we walked and walked to a new hiding place."

The child's simple, straightforward words sent chills across Annie's skin.

"What did your angel look like?" Dan slipped off the bench seat. "Was he tall, like I am?"

Amberly shook her head. "He wasn't *that* tall."

"What color was his hair?"

The child's smooth forehead wrinkled. "Shimmery." She shrugged. "It was just his angel hair."

Dan eyed Annie, and she understood. Her experience with search and rescue had taught her how difficult it was to get any kind of details from adults, let alone children.

Her brother nodded to Brianna and Mark. "Can I talk with you two a minute?"

Fear tinged Bree's features. "Can Annie come with us, Dan?"

"Sure. We'll just get someone to watch Amberly for a minute."

Annie turned to the child. "Hey, kiddo, I have some of my art pencils with me. If I brought them to you with some paper, could you draw a nice picture for your mommy?"

The little girl clapped. "Oh, that would be fun!"

Annie trotted back to her tent. Kodi lifted her drowsy head, then lowered it and went back to snoring as her mistress entered. Annie gathered up the art supplies and hurried back to the table, pausing near where Jed and Andy were sitting by the campfire. She called to them, and the two men came right over.

Annie laid the colored pencils and paper out on the table, explaining what Amberly was going to do. "When she's done, would you guys mind taking Amberly to see Kodi? She's asleep in my tent, and I promised Amberly she could visit."

"Happy to do it." Jed parked himself on one side of Amberly, and Andy settled in on the other. Annie smiled to herself.

No one was getting near that little girl.

She followed Dan and the others as they moved out of Amberly's earshot.

Dan studied Amberly's parents a moment before he spoke. "I think it's pretty clear that Amberly's angel was someone real. Do you two know of anyone who would want to take your daughter, or why?"

Mark, his arm forming a protective barrier around his wife, shook his head. "It's not like we have much money or anything. I can't imagine someone doing something like this."

"What bothers me—" the tremor in Bree's voice showed how hard she was struggling to keep it together—"is that he knew about Michael. And that Amberly called him the *ark* angel. How could he have known that, unless—" Her hand went to her throat and she turned to her husband. "Oh, Mark! He must have been there. At our campsite. Watching us, listening when I told her stories."

She hid her face in Mark's chest; and he looked at Dan over her head. "Do you think he'll come after Amberly again?"

Would he tell them what they suspected? That this whole thing wasn't about Amberly at all? That whoever took Amberly had done so to torment Annie?

"I don't think so." Dan spoke with slow care. "I can't explain why, because it involves an ongoing investigation of another case, but I think Amberly just happened to be in the wrong place at the wrong time. She presented an opportunity for this person, and he took it. I seriously doubt he'll bother you or your family again."

"Just get him, Deputy." Mark's tone was hard and angry. "That's all I ask. Just…get him. And make him pay for what he did."

Dan's gaze drifted to Annie. "That, Mr. Heller, you can count on."

The sun was just dipping behind the mountains when Jed went to find Annie. He wasn't sure what he would say to her, but he had to say something. They couldn't go on the way they had since they'd returned with the child.

In silence.

Other than asking him to take Amberly to see Kodi, Annie hadn't spoken two words to him since they got back to camp. He'd hoped, after what she said about him saving her life, she'd forgiven him for his deception. But there had been hints in her actions, in the way she looked at him—or, to be accurate, *didn't* look at him—that said otherwise.

Ah. There she was. At the edge of camp, leaning against a tree, staring up at the sky. Happily, she was alone.

He made sure she heard his approach. Last thing he wanted to do after all she'd been through was startle her. Sure enough, she turned her head. He watched for any sign of change in her expression when she saw him approaching.

Nothing.

No frown. But no smile either.

Jed swallowed. This did not bode well.

He stopped next to her, standing there in the early evening stillness, enjoying just being near her.

The silence ended all too soon.

"You ready to leave?"

He glanced back to where Andy waited by the car. "Yeah. We're ready."

She didn't say anything. Just stared up at the sky, where the moon had just become visible. The blanket of stars would be next. He'd never seen as many stars as dotted the night sky out here.

Say something.

He shifted. *What do I say?*

Tell her how you feel.

He almost laughed out loud at that. *When I don't know what she'll say? You know what kind of risk that would be?*

"It's worth it, you know."

He stared at her. "I—what?"

"The work, the frustration…it's all worth it when we bring someone home."

Ah. Right. "You made it happen, Annie. They would have given up too soon if you hadn't pushed things."

She turned to face him. "I guess, when it comes right down to it, we all do what we have to."

He couldn't bear the raw pain in her eyes. "I'm sorry, Annie. So sorry…"

She looked down and wrapped her arms around herself. "It's getting late. You'd better go."

His gut churned. His heart pounded. His hands shook…

So this was love.

Frankly, he didn't care for it one bit. He'd be better off without it. *And Annie? Would you be better off without her?*

The ache inside threatened to choke him. No. Not in a million years.

"Annie—"

She stopped him with a glance. The merest shake of her head. Their gazes caught, held, and he read in those magnificent eyes the depth of his betrayal.

Without another word, she turned and walked away, the only sound around him the soft crunch of her steps in the snow.

Jed wasn't sure how long he stood there, but it was dark when he finally walked back to the car. Andy got inside, and Jed was grateful that his friend didn't ask. Didn't talk.

The car backed out, turned, and Jed drove it toward the road. But he couldn't stop himself from taking one last look in the rearview mirror. He saw Annie's tent and a shadowed form standing beside it. And the words poured forth, giving voice to his regret.

"'Love is a smoke made with the fume of sighs,

Being purged, a fire sparkling in lovers' eyes,
Being vexed, a sea nourished with lovers' tears—'"
His voice caught, but he forced himself to continue.
"'What is it else? A madness most discreet,
A choking gall and a preserving sweet.'"

Andy leaned his head back against the headrest, pursing his lips. "You know what, bud?"

Jed stared at the road ahead. "What?"

"Shakespeare knew what he was talkin' about."

"That he did, my friend." Jed's sigh was deep and heavy. "That he did."

FORTY-FIVE

*"Show me a man who knows his
own heart and to him I shall belong."*

JEWEL KILCHER

*"And I can't stop!
If I say I'll never mention [him] or speak his name,
[it] burns in my heart like a fire.
It's like a fire in my bones! I am weary of holding it in!"*

JEREMIAH 20:9

NOVEMBER 24—A BLOODSTONE DAY (GREEN AND ROSE)
1:00 p.m.

"Kyla, you don't know what you're talking about."

Annie put on her best angry face, but her sister wasn't fazed. "I'm just saying, it can't hurt to watch the show."

She wished with all her heart that her sister would drop it. She'd had a hard enough time these last few weeks holding on to her anger. Thankfully, sheer determination to never let Jed make a fool of her again won out.

Maybe distraction was the key. Annie wiped her hands on her apron and went to pick up a large envelope off her desk. "Dan, this is for you. From Brianna Heller."

"Oh, no you don't." Kyla propped her fists on her hips. "No changing the subject."

Annie ignored her, handing the envelope to Dan.

He took it. "What is it?"

"Something from Bree. I took Kodi in for a follow-up on her leg, and Bree asked me to pass this on to you." Annie went back to cutting up the turkey.

"Annot, I will not be ignored!"

Wanna bet?

"Annie, have you looked at these?"

She looked at her brother, who was holding the papers he'd pulled from the envelope. "Nope. They were for you, not me."

"All right, you two." Shelby nudged Dan in the side. "Pay attention to your sister."

"Thank you." Kyla sniffed her indignance. "At least someone here has a modicum of manners."

Annie sliced a piece of white meat and set it on the platter. "I'm happy to listen to you, Kylie, when you make sense."

"What's not making sense? This show is about you and Kodi. The least you can do is watch it."

Annie looked to her brother and his wife for help. "Dan, explain to your sister why that's such a bad idea."

He held his hands up. "Sorry, kiddo, no can do."

"What?" Had everyone gone looney?

"I agree with Kyla. You've been moping around for a month, ever since Jed went back to LA."

"Now listen—" Annie squared off with her brother—"I don't push you to talk about things you don't want to talk about."

"Such as?"

"Such as the fact that you still don't have a clue who wrote those terrible notes to me and took Amberly Heller."

His features darkened. "Nice, sis. You know we've been doing everything we can in that case. We just keep hitting dead ends."

She waved a hand in the air. "Exactly. And because I know that, I don't push."

"Yes, *but*—" Shelby joined the chorus—"as frustrated as Dan has been about that case, he hasn't been pathetic."

Annie's brows lifted. "Are you saying *I* have?"

"As pathetic as it gets."

She skewered Shelby with a glare. "You're not helping."

"Actually, Auntie A, we are, if you'd just let us."

Great. Even Jayce was in on the conspiracy. Annie hacked at the turkey carcass with the carving knife. Leave it to her family to turn Thanksgiving into Let's-Fix-Annie Day.

But Jayce wasn't finished. "I mean, you're as miserable as Kodi was when she couldn't go outside. Remember how she moped around after the search while her leg was healing? Whining, looking like we were doing something terrible to her when we were just trying to take care of her?"

Annie pulled a leg loose. "And your point is?"

"That you're just like your dog. You're enjoying being miserable too much to let anyone help you."

Annie turned to give her nephew a piece of her mind when a gentle hand closed around her wrist. "Please, Annot."

She refused to meet Kyla's eyes, but her sister didn't give up. "Just come watch the show. I taped it when it ran last week." She looked at the others in the room. "None of us have watched it. We wanted to watch it together. With you." She tugged at Annie's sleeve. "You have to watch it."

"I don't *have* to do any such thing."

"Yeah." This from Dan. "You do."

"We can buzz through the commercials."

Annie's lips twitched. Her older sister knew how much she detested commercials. Annie stood for a moment, thinking, then set the knife down and turned to her family. "If I do this, will you all let the subject of Jed Curry go?" She narrowed her eyes. "I mean it. No more hints that it's time to forgive him, no more not-so-subtle suggestions to call him. Nothing."

Four heads bobbed up and down.

"Fine." Annie started for the living room. "Let's watch the stupid show."

As Annie sank onto the couch, Kyla popped the tape into the player and grabbed the remote before Annie could. She just smiled sweetly when Annie glowered at her. The theme song for *Everyday Heroes* came on, and it took all of Annie's self-control to stay seated on the couch.

Annie sank back, then stiffened when Jed's voice came over the speakers. Kodi, who'd been lying at her feet, sat up like a shot, big ears perked. She looked around the room, then got up and looked behind the couch.

"She's looking for Jed, isn't she?"

Jayce was right, but Annie refused to admit it. She called Kodi, patting the couch. The dog hesitated, giving one last glance around the room, then hopped on the couch. Annie draped her arm over Kodi's neck and forced herself to listen. To focus on the action on the screen.

Within minutes, she was in tears.

It was...beautiful. The scenes and Jed's commentary captured the heart of their work in search and rescue.

No, more than that. He captured Annie. Her heart. Her passions. Her longings. It was as though she was seeing herself for the first time.

She didn't recall sharing her struggles as a kid, with the synesthesia, with perceiving things in ways others couldn't, but it was there. In her voice, in her own words. As was her love for her family, her passion for her art, her desire to help through SAR.

Every word, every scene was a glimpse into her spirit.

She'd been so afraid the show would turn them into some kind of circus act. She couldn't have been more wrong. The overarching tone was one of respect.

And something more.

Something that tore at Annie's heart as she watched the footage of the search for Amberly. Saw the rock slide. Heard her own voice crying out as she ran to find Kodi. Something nagged at her as the show ended, with a still of the main subjects—her and Kodi.

Annie lifted a hand to brush away the tears on her face, then froze.

What was this? This was different...

The other episode she'd watched went to black after the still of the main subjects. But this time Jed stepped in front of the camera and sat down. He looked right into the lens, and it was as though he were there, looking at her, piercing her with those eyes.

"Hi, I'm E J Curry. But you can call me Jed."

Kodi pawed at the couch, crawling closer to the edge—and the TV—her whine utterly pathetic.

Annie flicked the dog's ear. "Knock it off, you traitor." But her words lacked conviction, even to her own ears.

"Many of you know I created *Everyday Heroes*. I told myself it was to honor people who helped others, who risked their own lives to save others. But something happened while I was working on the episode you just saw."

This time it was Annie who scooted to the edge of the couch, listening, her mouth open, as Jed told the world what he'd done, how he lied to Annie, trying to trick her into being on the show. "But the trick was on me." His smile was so gentle.

So sad.

"As you've just seen, Annie Justice is the most genuine, authentic person I've ever met. She showed me what life should really be. Because of her, I found my family again." He stopped, cleared his throat. "And my God. But here's the kicker. She took something from me too."

Annie wasn't sure when Kyla moved to the couch to sit beside her, but suddenly she was there. Annie gripped her sister's hand.

"Annie Justice took my heart. I've never been in love. Had no idea what it was like. But friends, this is as real as it gets. I love this woman. Will love her all my life." His laugh was broken. "And I lied to her. Tricked her. Betrayed her. I don't know if she can ever forgive me." He looked down at the ground, then back up into the lens. "Annie, please forgive me."

The impact of him speaking directly to her stole the breath from her lungs.

"I know I don't deserve it. Don't deserve you. But I'm asking anyway. Forgive me. You know how to reach me. To tell me if there's a chance for us." He hesitated. "I pray you'll call. But if you don't, I'll understand. Either way, I want to thank you. For my family. For giving me back a part of life that I didn't even know I was missing."

Jed's smile was like sunshine through dark clouds. "Thank you, Annie, for helping me see God again. With new eyes. *Your* beautiful kaleidoscope eyes. I love you."

The screen went black. The room was silent.

Annie stared at the TV, but her focus was on the inside.

Something was missing. Had been missing for weeks, but she wouldn't admit it. Her anger at Jed was gone. And in its place was a deep, empty ache.

Yes, he'd hurt her. But that's what happened when you let someone in, when you gave your heart away. People were human. They made mistakes. They hurt each other. And with God's help, they forgave. Then built new trust on the foundation of His grace.

Annie absorbed that truth, and the one that came right after it. For sitting there, staring at that blank TV screen, Annie finally understood. She'd rather have Jed in her life—would rather have all the joy and pain of loving him—than live another peaceful, empty day without him.

God, what should I do? Annie closed her eyes. *Please, tell me what to do…*

"If you don't find that man right now and marry him," Kyla finally muttered from beside her, "*I* will."

Annie was on her feet, Kodi in her wake, running for the phone.

FORTY-SIX

"When the world says, 'Give up,' Hope whispers,
'Try it one more time.'"

UNKNOWN

"But if we look forward to something we don't have yet,
we must wait patiently and confidently."

ROMANS 8:25

I'm sorry, ma'am, but Mr. Curry doesn't work here any longer."

Annie wanted to pound the phone on the countertop, but the tiny, rational part of her brain told her that wouldn't help.

"When did he leave?"

"He resigned on Monday."

"Well…can you give me his home phone? This is Annie Justice—"

"I'm sorry, ma'am. But I can't."

"Look, I was on his show. He knows me. He *loves* me!"

"I'm sure he does, just like he loves the twenty other Annie Justices who've called in the last three days looking for his home phone number. Good-bye, ma'am."

She set the phone on the counter. *Okay, Annie, think.*

"No luck?" Kyla propped her elbows on the counter.

"He resigned. Can you believe that?"

Her sister's nod was slow, thoughtful. "Yes, actually. I can."

"Me too." Dan plopped down in the chair next to Kyla. "So call him at home."

"I don't have the number."

Kyla's face lit up. "I know, what about his mom? She lives in the valley, right?"

"Right." Annie felt like weeping. "But she remarried, and I don't know her married name."

"Hey!" Dan jumped up. "What about Andy? He gave you his card, right?"

Of course! Annie ran to her purse, upending it on the desk and sorting through the contents until she found the card. "Got it!"

Andy answered on the first ring. "Hello?"

"Andy! Oh, thank God."

There was laughter in his tone. "I've always wanted a woman to react that way. Too bad you're not looking for me. I mean, I'm guessing you're looking for Jed?"

"I am."

"You saw the show."

"Just now. My sister taped it."

"I knew it! I told him you probably wouldn't watch it when it aired, to give you some time. Knowing your brother, I figured he'd hog-tie you if he had to so you'd watch it."

Annie raised her eyes to her brother. "You're almost right. My whole family ganged up on me."

"Perfect. So—" she could tell he was grinning—"you want to know where the man is?"

"You said if I needed anything…"

"That I did. He's at his mom's. He had a flight set up in case you didn't call him after the show aired."

"You know he resigned from his job."

"Yup. He needed to."

"What about you? I mean, you guys are such a great team."

"That we are. Which is why I'm already at work setting up a business for the two of us. Jed's been talking about us doing that for years. I figure now's the time to get it going."

Annie cradled the phone close. "You really are a good friend, you know that?"

"Yeah—" he was grinning again—"I'm a peach. Now go find your man."

Dan stood in his sister's kitchen, reading the note Bree had put in the envelope she'd given to Annie:

> *Dan, yesterday Amberly showed me the pictures she drew when you were talking to us up in the mountains, right after she was found. She said they are pictures of her angel. The one who was with her in the woods. They're not exactly Rembrandt, but I thought they had enough detail to give you some idea what he looked like. Anyway, thought I'd get them to you just in case. Thanks again for all you did to help find our little girl and bring her home.*
>
> *With gratitude,*
> *Brianna Heller*

Dan lifted the drawings and stared at them.

It couldn't be.

"What are you so interested in?" He jumped and turned to find Shelby standing beside him, also looking down at the drawings.

Dan held them out for her to see. "Drawings from Amberly Heller. Of the man who took her. Her so-called angel."

Bewilderment shimmered in his wife's eyes. "Are you seeing what I'm seeing? I mean, I realize it's just a child's drawing, but that could be—"

He stopped her, glancing toward the living room where Jayce sat with Kyla. "I know. In fact, I've known for a little while. Or suspected. But there was never any proof."

"And you think *he* was the one writing those awful notes to Annie?"

Yes. The pieces all fit. Whether Dan wanted them to or not. "I'm sure of it."

"Oh, Dan. Annie will be heartbroken." Her tone reflected the same misery churning inside him. "What are you going to do?"

"Pray for wisdom. Not say anything to Annie until I've got proof." He slid the drawings back into the envelope. "And then nail the jerk."

A half hour later, Annie stood on the doorstep of the Elhanin home, her fingers shaking as she rang the bell.

She tossed a glance over her shoulder. Kodi sat in the Jeep, her nose pressed against the window. Annie was willing to bet the dog's tail was wagging up a storm.

The door opened, and a lovely woman stood there with a welcoming smile. "Annie. I'm so delighted you're here."

Annie let the woman usher her inside, following her to the spacious living room. "You have a beautiful home, Mrs. Elhanin."

"Joyce, please. I can't tell you how happy I was when you called."

Annie lowered herself onto the soft, plushy cushions of the couch. "Joyce." She could see Jed in his mother. They shared the same eyes, the same smile...

"You're as beautiful as Jed said you were."

Heat swept into Annie's cheeks, and she laughed. "I was just thinking the same thing about you."

Joyce waved her hand. "Fiddle. I'm too old to be beautiful." Mischief sparkled in her eyes. "I'll settle for *elegant* or *striking*."

"If you ask me, *beautiful* is right on the money."

They both turned as a tall, broad-shouldered man entered the room. Joyce held her hand out to him. "Amos, come meet Annie."

His brows lifted. "Annie Justice. We saw the show. The episode Jed did on you and your amazing dog."

"Kodi. She's out in my car."

"Well, you should bring her in."

Joyce swatted at him. "They're not here to see us, silly man."

"Ah." He sat on the arm of the couch. "She's looking for Jed."

"I am." Annie took Joyce's hands in hers. "Please, can you tell me where he is? Andy thought he was here."

"No, but I believe I know where he is." Joyce stood and went to pull a photo album from a nearby shelf. "Jed talked with me after the search, before he left for LA." She sat next to Annie again. "He told me what happened. About the little girl. About you." She folded her hands on the photo album in her lap. "I've never seen him look that way when he talked about a woman. Not ever." An easy smile played at the corners of her mouth. "I knew when my son fell, he'd fall hard."

Annie wasn't sure if she wanted to laugh or cry. So she settled for biting her lip. "He's not the only one."

Joyce lifted a hand to cup Annie's cheek. "I know, child. I can see it on your face."

"And a glorious sight it is."

Annie couldn't help but smile at Amos's enthusiasm.

"Here—" Joyce slid the now open photo album from her lap to Annie's—"this is where he is. I'd bet my couch on it."

"Oooh—" Amos put his arm around Joyce—"and she really likes that couch."

Annie giggled as she looked down at the pictures. A child-Jed grinned out at her, holding up a huge fish on a stringer. Beside him was a man that, for a second, Annie thought was Jed as an adult. But that was impossible.

"That's his father with him." Joyce leaned back against Amos. "Jed adored his father. When he left us, my son was devastated. Not even our divorce convinced Jed his father wasn't ever coming back."

"Or our marriage, for that matter."

Annie tried to discern bitterness in Amos's comment, but there simply was none. Only acceptance. And a depth of love.

Joyce reached for her husband's hand, laying it against her cheek. "Amos is such a good man. All he ever wanted to do was be a father to Jed. But Jed's anger was so deep that he couldn't accept love. Not from Amos. Not even from God." She smiled. "Until he met you." She let go of Amos's hand and leaned forward, enfolding Annie in a tender hug. "You opened my son's heart again, Annie. I can never thank you enough."

Joyce sat back, then, seeing Annie's face, lifted the Kleenex box from the coffee table and handed it to her.

Annie managed a choked laugh as she wiped the tears from her face. When she'd gotten herself under control again, she faced Joyce and Amos. "Please, where is Jed?"

Joyce tapped the photo of Jed and his father. "We own this cabin, right on Lake of the Woods. It's quite rustic. No electricity or running water. Those two used to go there several times a year. Jed told me, before he left for LA, that if you didn't call him after the show, he was going away for a while. To a place he used to love. Someplace quiet. To think and pray. I don't know for certain, but I believe that's where he is."

She rose and went to a desk. She pulled out the top drawer, removed a key, then handed it to Annie. "This is for the front door. If he's not at the cabin, I'm sure he's somewhere nearby. Sitting by the lake, most likely." A pert smile tipped her lips. "I believe your Kodi will find him with no trouble at all."

Annie threw her arms around the woman. "Thank you!"

She touched Annie's cheek. "Oh no, thank you. You're giving me something I've always wanted."

"Really? What's that?"

Those eyes twinkled again. "A godly woman who will love my boy as much as I do."

NOVEMBER 24—A BLOODSTONE DAY (GREEN AND ROSE)
5:00 p.m.

Jed sat at the edge of the lake, booted feet propped against a fallen log as he held his fishing pole steady. He tugged the line just often enough to keep the lure hopping, its dance pure tantalization to the fish he could see swimming below it.

This was the life, man. Peace. Quiet. The sun warm enough to be comfortable, the water clear enough that he could watch the two or three good-sized trout about to take the lure. Yeah, he'd have to be crazy to not be content out here.

Fine. Crazy it was.

Heaving a sigh, Jed started reeling in his line, not even caring when one of the fish finally made up its mind and broke the surface, snapping at the rapidly retreating lure.

"Too late, buddy. Just like me."

He pulled the lure from the water, snagged it and hooked it on one of the guides, then tightened the line to keep the hook secure. He leaned the rod against a tree and crouched next to his tackle box, putting everything away.

Might as well pack it in and head back to the cabin. No point staying out here when all he wanted to do was find the nearest phone and call Annie, beg her to see him.

Lord, I'm doing what You said. I'm waiting. On You. He snapped the tackle box shut. *Any chance You could speed things up a smidge?*

A light sound caught his attention, and he tilted his head, listening. What was that…?

Realization hit him smack between the eyes.

A bell.

That was a bell ringing!

He stood just in time to spot a black blur as it broke out of the woods and jumped at him, hitting him square in the chest, sending him flying. He landed in the dirt with a grunt, hands grabbing at the dog perched on top of him, trying to lick him to death.

"Kodi, off!"

The dog scrambled off of him, and Jed pushed to his feet, heart pounding, and drank in the sight of the woman standing there.

"Annie."

Her name was no sooner past his lips than she was in his arms. He framed her beautiful face with trembling hands, staring down at her. "Are you really here?"

Her laughter lifted his heart, sending it soaring. "I'm really here."

Jed slid his hands down, linking them behind her, locking her close as he looked at the woods around them. "But...how?"

Annie's mouth curved. Did she have any idea what a captivating picture she made when she smiled like that? "Haven't you heard? Kodi and I are the Wonder Team. We can find anyone we want to find. And believe me, Mr. Curry—" her voice grew husky—"we wanted to find you."

"Then, you forgive me."

She took his hand and placed it against her cheek. Tears glistened in her eyes. "I forgave you weeks ago. I was just too stubborn to admit it. But these last weeks without you—" She plucked at the buttons on his shirt.

"Yes?"

She flattened her palm on his chest, over his heart, and lifted her glistening eyes to his. "I don't want to live without you, Jed. Not ever again."

She was here. Really here. Looking up at him with eyes that glowed with such warmth, such love, it stole his breath. "Ah, lady—" he let a slow smile work its way across his lips—"'you bereft me of all words, Only my blood speaks to you in my veins, And there is such confusion in my powers.'"

Annie pressed a kiss into his palm. "'Then come kiss me, sweet.'"

He bent his head and did as she asked.

And then, just to be sure, he did it again.

FORTY-SEVEN

*"Everything that happens happens as it should,
and if you observe carefully, you will find this to be so."*

MARCUS AURELIUS

*"Therefore, since we have been made right in God's sight by faith,
we have peace with God because of what
Jesus Christ our Lord has done for us.
Because of our faith, Christ has brought us into this
place of highest privilege where we now stand,
and we confidently and joyfully
look forward to sharing God's glory."*

ROMANS 5:1–2

NOVEMBER 25—A CORNFLOWER DAY (GREEN AND BLUE)

The colors were more glorious than she'd ever imagined.

Annie told herself over and over, as she blended textures and types of glass, that the effect would be all she hoped. But she'd never really let herself believe it would work.

Until now.

She walked from one end to the other, her footfalls muted in the soft carpet of the sanctuary, awash in wonder. That God had used her hands to create this…

Annie touched the tips of her fingers to the window, half expecting the images within to come to life.

"It's stunning."

She didn't turn. She didn't need to. She knew that voice as well as her own. And the awe in Jed's hushed tone sent chills through her.

His strong hands slipped around her waist from behind. "Just like the artist."

She laid her arms along Jed's as they circled her. "It really worked, didn't it?"

"Like a dream."

Annie turned in his arms. "A dream I owe to you."

"I think the idea came from Someone else. He just used me to deliver it."

She studied the window again. "I know exactly what you mean."

A loud clap broke the blessed stillness of the sanctuary, and they moved apart. Annie cast a scolding scowl at the men approaching them. "Killie, was that necessary?"

Ryan lifted his shoulders. "I told him it wasn't really appropriate in this setting."

"Just wanted to get your attention." Killian's words rang with his excitement. "The seraphic Serafina should be here any minute to view your masterpiece—"

"And so I am."

Annie never ceased to be amazed at the strength in the little woman's voice. Annie stood there, tapping the back of a pew as she watched her client make her way to where they stood.

This was the hardest part of being an artist. That suspended moment between the satisfaction of a project completed and the reaction of the recipient.

Jed's hand eased over hers, stilling it. He leaned close, his lips next to her ear. "She'll love it."

She touched her forehead to his. "How do you do that?"

"What?"

"Know me so well after such a short time together?"

He caressed her cheek. "You've been a part of me my whole

life, Annie. The fact that it took us this long to find each other doesn't change that."

Serafina finally stood beside them, then reached up to adjust her glasses on her nose. Those gentle eyes rested on Annie, then drifted to Jed. "Is this your beau, dear?"

Warmth surged into Annie's face, and Jed put his hand out. "Jed Curry, at your service, ma'am."

"A nice strong handshake, but gentle too." Serafina beamed her approval at Annie. "I believe he's what they call a keeper, dear. And if the lovely pink in your cheeks is any indication, you think so as well."

Serafina rested one elegant hand on the back of the pew. "So, the day has finally arrived. Come, Annie. Show me Cletus's window."

"Yes, Annie, let's." Killian started to accompany them, but Serafina halted him with an upraised hand.

"I'm sorry, but no."

Killian's mouth spread into a thin smile. "Excuse me?"

"I said no." Such iron in that soft voice. "I prefer Annie show me. And only Annie."

For a moment Annie thought Killian was going to throw one of his infamous fits right then and there, but he surprised her by bowing his head and stepping back. "Whatever you say, dear lady."

Casting him an apology over Serafina's head, and glad that Ryan had moved in to soothe his boss's ruffled feathers, Annie led the woman to the edge of the pews. "You need to see the window twice."

"Twice?"

"The first time from a little distance, to see the big picture."

Serafina's focus moved to the window. "And the second?"

"You'll see."

They started walking, and Annie kept their pace slow and even.

"Oh my." Serafina's eyes followed the length of the window. "It's...quite large, isn't it?"

Indeed, it was. It actually was more of a wall of glass rather than a window, one that glittered in every hue. The lower edge of the window started just two feet from the floor. The window measured five feet, top to bottom, and fifteen feet from left to right. Colors and textures—waterglass, baroque, cobblestone, iridescent, opalescent, granite, rippled—all flowed and swirled into each other, creating a panorama of the life of Christ.

Annie walked Serafina beside the window, watching the older woman's expression as she studied each image. The nativity…a young Jesus teaching at the temple…Jesus rejoicing, a lamb draped across His shoulders…Peter, his face awash with shame as the rooster crowed…the mocking crowds at the crucifixion…a soldier piercing Jesus' side with a spear; others casting lots on Jesus' robe…Mary, outside the tomb, reaching out to the man she just realized is the resurrected Christ…and, in the last panel, framed by an explosion of brilliant colors, Jesus' face, His features filled with tenderness and joy as He looked down at the open Book of Life.

Serafina lifted one hand, her fingers brushing across the glass. "The details are exquisite, my dear. They're so lifelike. I almost expect them to step from the glass."

The words were clearly praise, and yet, there was an odd note in Serafina's tone. Just the faintest hint of disappointment. Annie started to say something but didn't get the chance.

"Well? Isn't it *glorious*?" There wasn't one iota of disappointment in Killian's voice. "Have you ever seen anything so beautiful?"

The older woman's gaze fell to the floor, her disquiet evident in the slump of her thin shoulders. Annie forced herself to sheath her feelings, and when she spoke, her voice was carefully colored in neutral. "Please, don't worry. You haven't truly seen the window yet."

The woman's soft hands patted her arm. "Oh no, my dear. Really, it's quite lovely. I'm sure you did your best."

"Please." Annie held out her hand. "Come with me."

The woman let Annie lead her closer to the window, where the images seemed life-sized. Annie looked over her shoulder to where Jed stood next to the light switches and nodded. Jed flipped the switch, and lights designed to accentuate the angles of the glass—from both above and behind the window—came on. The glass welcomed the light, amplifying it so that it set the pigments free to wash the sanctuary in a shimmering kaleidoscope.

Serafina caught her breath, and the hand resting on Annie's arm trembled. "Oh! It's so beautiful."

"Now…" Annie guided her to face the scene before them. "Look again."

The woman did so, and her fingers tightened on Annie's arm. She opened her mouth, breathing out her amazement. "It's…" She turned to Annie, eyes misty, voice hushed. "It's me. I'm in the window."

Annie's smile blossomed. "Yes, you are. And so am I, and so is anyone who looks at each scene close up. They see themselves, their faces, in the image." Once again, she led Serafina past the images of the window. "See? You're the shepherd, looking down at the Christ child. You're one of the crowd Jesus is teaching at the temple."

Serafina exclaimed each time she saw her face reflected. She sighed when she was the lamb on Jesus' shoulders, trembled when she was Peter denying his master, and then the soldier mocking the crucified Lord. The tears started when she cast lots, then held the spear. They flowed in earnest when she was outside the empty tomb, reunited with the only One who'd ever loved her with a pure love.

When they reached the last image, and Serafina saw Jesus looking down at her face in the pages of the Book of Life, she turned to Annie. "But how?"

Apparently Killian couldn't stand not taking part a moment longer. "She's a master at her art, that's how." He turned to Ryan. "Do you have the photos of the process?"

Two spots of color bloomed in Ryan's pale cheeks. "I left them in the car."

"In the car? Good heavens, man, use your head. What possible good can they do us in the car?" Killian waved his hand. "Go get them."

The spots took over Ryan's features as he turned and made his way to the front of the church. Killian turned back to Annie. "Please, continue."

It was on the tip of her tongue to scold him, both for the way he'd talked to Ryan and for acting like some kind of circus ringmaster, but she decided now wasn't the time. She turned back to Serafina.

"It took some doing, but I finally found the right mix of mirrored and dichroic glass to use for the faces. When you look from a distance or stand and a certain angle, you see the images painted on the glass. But close up, the effect is like a muted mirror. So you see your own image—"

"And become part of the story." Serafina clasped her hands.

"Exactly."

"Oh, Annie, it's more wonderful than I hoped." She pressed a hand to her throat. "Cletus would be so pleased."

"I'm so glad."

"Hey! Who turned out the lights?"

They all turned to the front of the church, and Annie started forward with a pleased cry. "Brianna! Mark! What are you guys doing here?" She waved at the little girl between them. "And Amberly. It's so good to see you."

"Hi, doggy lady."

Bree winked at Annie. "I heard we had an unveiling of a masterpiece today, so we came to pay our respects to the artist."

"A masterpiece, eh?" Annie laughed and looked over her shoulder. "Sounds like Killian invited yo—" She frowned. Where did he go? "Killie?"

"No, actually, Dan told us about it."

Dan?

Jed leaned on the pew. "Killian said Ryan was taking too long to get the photos and went to get them himself."

A yelp from the front of the sanctuary, followed by the sound of a scuffle, drew their attention. Alarm skittered up Annie's spine, and she turned to call to Jed—but he was already on his way.

They needn't have worried. Apparently Dan had everything under control. He appeared near the pulpit, Killian in tow. "Look who I found heading out the back door."

Annie took a step toward them. "There you are, Killie. I wondered where you...you..."

Why was Jed pushing Killian in front of him? Annie's mouth fell open. Were those *handcuffs* on Killian's wrists?

"Annie, will you tell this barbarian of a brother of yours to turn me *loose*?"

She stepped forward. "Dan, what's going on?"

He didn't answer her. He just poked Killian forward. "Come on, Killian. Let's go meet Amberly."

Killian held up his handcuffed hands. "Fine, fine! Lead me to the child. Though why you think it's so world-shattering important—"

"My angel!"

Annie spun at the delighted cry. Amberly was skipping up the middle aisle, clapping her hands, and looking at—

The shock of discovery slammed into her.

Killian?

"Where have you been, Angel? I missed you."

Dan's gaze hardened as he watched Amberly walk to Killian—then widened when she passed him right by.

Annie caught her breath, and they all spun to look back toward the pulpit area. Ryan stood there, alarm on his features, as Amberly ran to him. She reached for his hands, but he jerked away.

"Get away from me, you little monster."

Amberly pulled back, then turned and ran back down the aisle to her parents.

As Annie fought through the cobwebs of confusion, she realized Dan had spun and was making his way to Ryan, even as Jed grabbed Mark Heller, restraining him.

"*You* took my little girl?" Rancor sharpened his voice as he tried to push past Jed. "Why? We don't even *know* you!"

Jed held the furious man fast. "Mark, if *I* can't belt him, *you* can't belt him. Let Dan handle it."

"After what he did—" He spun, a fist drawn back, and Annie cried out, sure Mark was going to take his rage out on Jed.

"Daddy!"

Amberly's alarm stopped her father cold. He stood there, fist suspended in the air, then let it drop. Amberly put both hands around his. "Why are you mad, Daddy?"

He dropped to his knees, pulling his little girl into his arms. "I'm not mad, honey. Not anymore." He opened one arm and Bree knelt, letting her husband draw her into the hug. "I'm just happy you're safe."

Annie swallowed back the emotions clogging her throat and turned to Serafina. Amazingly enough, the woman watched the goings on with a serene calm. Her smile touched Annie. "Go ahead, dear. I can tell you want to talk to your brother." She looked toward the front of the sanctuary. "And that man."

"Jed—" Dan tossed him a small key—"let Killian loose."

Amazingly enough, Killian didn't say a thing. He just watched, tight-lipped, as Jed set him free, then rubbed his wrists as Annie made her way between the pews to where Jed awaited her. Jed circled her waist with one arm, and Killian fell in step on the other side of her. Together, the three of them walked toward Dan and the man he now held captive.

Killian handed Dan the cuffs. "I believe you need these."

Dan nodded, then jerked Ryan's wrists behind his back and slapped the cuffs in place.

"So you sent the notes, Ryan?" Annie couldn't hold back the angry edge in her voice.

Killian met Dan's hard stare. "And you thought *I'd* sent them? That I was the one who took that little girl?" His eyes widened. "*Kodi?* You thought I would try to kill Kodi, knowing what she means to Annie?"

Regret weighted Dan's words. "I'm sorry, Killian. All the evidence seemed to point to you."

"You thought *he* did it all?"

They all turned stunned eyes to the raging Ryan. Fury blazed in the gaze he aimed at Killian. "*Him?* He's so caught up in himself, he'd never be able to pull something like this off."

Killian spread his hands in front of him, grief in his voice. "How could you do all that, Ryan? Why?"

"Everyone thinks you're such a genius." He all but spat the words out. "But I saw. I know. You made a couple of good calls, but your wonderful success? Dumb luck. *I'm* the one who organized the gallery, who took it to the next level. Me! I should have been a partner *years* ago. But all you ever see is yourself."

"But why Annie?" Killian took a step closer. "Why do all this to her?"

Ryan dragged his gaze from Killian to look at her, and what she saw glittering in the man's eyes chilled her to the bone.

"Because, dear Killian, you said it yourself. She belonged to the art. It was the only endeavor worthy of her attention." He tugged against Dan's hold, leaning toward her, then sagged when she recoiled. "And you needed Annie. Expressions needed her. All I wanted to do was help her. And you."

Killian looked from Ryan to Annie. "You can't possibly believe I wanted this. That I wanted you to do anything like this."

"He didn't."

There was something in Dan's tone that drew everyone's attention. He gave a slow nod. "I should have seen it." He pressed his lips together. "I'm sorry, Killian. I was following the evidence, and it led me to you." His hard gaze fixed on Ryan. "Because that's what *you* intended all along. That day in the gallery when I stopped by about the notes, I thought it was awfully convenient that Killian said he didn't know anything about the computers. Well, it was convenient. But not for Killian." Dan's gaze narrowed. "It was convenient for you. You sent the note on Expressions stationery to lead me to Killian. You used the computer at the gallery to lead me to Killian."

An ugly smirk painted Ryan's features. "Like I said, Killian taught me everything I know. He showed me how important it was to be focused on your goal. To do whatever it takes to accomplish it."

"Annie. Amberly. They weren't the real targets, were they?"

Annie shivered at the cold anger in her brother's tone.

"They were just a means to an end."

"Me."

Dan met Killian's gaze. "You. And Expressions."

Killian turned to slip his arms around Annie, hugging her close. "I'm sorry. I'm so sorry. This was all my fault. If I hadn't said all those things…hadn't put those ideas in Ryan's mind…"

"Stop trying to take credit for my work!"

Killian let Annie go and turned to face Ryan. "You're crazy."

Ryan's harsh laugh cut across Annie's nerves. "Fools often mistake genius for crazy."

"And crazy people—" Dan gave Ryan a hard shake—"mistake delusion for genius. Now you've got the right to remain silent. Do us all a favor and exercise it."

Ryan opened his mouth, but fortunately whatever he was about to spew was halted when two policemen came in the front doors.

"You radioed for help, Deputy?"

Dan took hold of Ryan's arm. "That I did." He nudged the man down the aisle, delivering him to the officers. Annie caught bits and pieces of her brother's explanation: "Charges of harassment…stalking…kidnapping…"

Annie buried her face in Jed's chest; he cradled her against him.

"My dear?"

Drawing a steadying breath, Annie pulled away from Jed. "Serafina, oh, I'm so sorry about all this…"

The woman waved away Annie's concern. "You need make no apologies. I'm only sorry you've been hurt by what that man did." She took Annie's hand in her own. "I don't know the details, of course, but I wanted to reassure you that it doesn't matter what you do, as long as you do it out of obedience. There's only one place you need to belong, and that's in the center of God's will."

Annie blinked back the tears burning at her eyes. "But how do I know…?"

"All you need do, child, is look at what God created through you." Gentle hands turned Annie toward the window. "Truly look, with your heart as well as your eyes. And you'll sense, as we do, God's utter delight in what you do."

"*All* of what you do."

Mark Heller's assertion was rock solid. He stood there, his wife at his side, his daughter in his arms. "I shudder to think what would have happened to our family if you and Kodi hadn't been there when we needed you. That man—" he threw a disgusted look Ryan's direction—"was either a fool or a liar."

"They're right, Annie." Belief in her shone in Jed's eyes.

And in Killian's. "You're doing what you were meant to do, Annie. Don't let anyone, especially me, make you doubt that."

"Hey, sis. I need to go to the station with these guys, but I wanted to check on you first." Concern clouded Dan's features. "Are you okay?"

Annie looked at her brother, then at the others surrounding her. Love and respect looked back, embracing her, erasing any power Ryan's words—or the voice—held.

Peace flowed through her, easing her spirit, lifting her mouth into a warm smile. "Yes, I'm fine."

Jed slipped his arms around her. "I've always thought so."

She poked him with an elbow. "You know what I meant."

"Well—" Dan started toward the front door—"I'm on my way then. Looks like you're in good hands."

Annie couldn't argue with that. And as far as she was concerned, she planned to stay in them. For a very long time.

FORTY-EIGHT

"People are like stained-glass windows.
They sparkle and shine when the sun is out,
but when the darkness sets in,
their true beauty is revealed only if there is light from within."

ELISABETH KÜBLER-ROSS

"For you are a holy people, who belong to the LORD your God."

DEUTERONOMY 7:6

It was nearly nine o'clock that night when Dan finally returned to Annie's home. It was clear he could tell from Annie's expression that she wanted a full debriefing, so they all gathered in the living room.

As they did so, Dan touched Killian's arm. "Look...I'm sorry. I was way off base."

"Not so far. Ryan and I, we're similar in a lot of ways. And I have been the one spouting off about Annie quitting search and rescue—"

"—and talking about how she was wasting her gift," Shelby added.

Jayce nodded. "And I heard you say a couple times that you didn't like Kodi—"

"Fine!" Killian held up his hands. "Ample evidence against me. I get it." He cast a pained look to the ceiling. "I'm *so* misunderstood."

It felt good to laugh in the face of all that had happened.

Kodi followed them into the living room, circling at Annie

and Jed's feet after they sat on the couch, then plopping down with a heavy, contented sigh.

"I have to know—" Annie couldn't wait a moment longer— "what made you so sure poor Killian took Amberly?"

Dan pulled some folded papers from his shirt pocket and handed them to Annie. She unfolded them—and understood.

The drawing was childish but startlingly accurate.

"Obviously it's not a detailed sketch."

Annie studied the drawing. "No, but it's enough. The short, gray and silver hair. Those round glasses. Even the wide smile." She laid the drawing in her lap. "It would have made me think of Killian too."

"Well, trust me—" Killian gave an exaggerated sigh—"next time I hire an assistant I'll be sure he looks nothing like me."

Dan took Shelby's hand in his. "Once we got Ryan to the station, he couldn't talk fast enough. Believe it or not, Annie, he's the one who made sure Jed found out about you."

Jed stiffened. "What?"

"Oh dear." Killian grimaced. "I'm afraid that's my fault. I heard about *Everyday Heroes* on my last trip to LA. You know, when I was a consultant for one of those home decorating shows. Their sound stage was right next to yours, Jed. The crew couldn't stop talking about your show, what a success it was becoming. So I went along with them to watch you working on an episode. I was so impressed that I told Ryan all about it."

Dan nodded. "He must have figured Jed would be the perfect tool for broadcasting Annie's failure. He figured she'd be so distraught when they didn't find Amberly that she'd leave search and rescue, and he'd have what he wanted."

"Annie." There was murder in Jed's one, dark word.

"And her art. Fortunately, he'll go away for a good long time. The penalty for kidnapping is severe, but you add cyber stalking and using the U.S. mail for one of his poison letters...well, he's not going to bother you again, Annie."

Shelby hooked her hands around her knees. "Looks like you're on your own at the gallery again, Killian."

Annie and Jed exchanged a glance.

"Actually, I might not be." Killian looked at Annie, and she nodded. "What happened with Ryan prompted me to do something I've been considering for some time. I'm taking on a partner."

Jed inclined his head. "Maybe."

Annie's family all stared at Jed.

"You?" Kyla's wide eyes showed her astonishment.

"And Annie." Jed took her hand. "The three of us talked it over after we got back from the church today. Killian can't expand if he's on his own. And we believe in his vision to find and feature new talent in the art world."

Annie leaned back against the couch cushions. "That's not all. Andy called a few hours ago and told us he's decided to move out here to 'the sticks,' as he calls it. He and Jed are going to focus their talents on filming some independent projects. And if we go through with this partnership—"

Killian took it from there. "They've agreed I can feature my star artist with at least one major showing a year."

"And he's agreed to add a viewing room to feature promising film projects." Annie leaned into Jed. "Like those that will come from two certain somebodies."

"I love it!"

Annie was caught off guard by Kyla's enthusiasm. "You do?"

"Absolutely. God's taken all the broken pieces and put them together in a beautiful mosaic, blending your love *and* your gifts." She lifted her water glass in a salute. "If you need any help with getting things set up, just call. I know a thing or two about running a business."

Dan lifted his glass of milk as well. "All I can say—" he took Shelby's hand in his and kissed it—"is it's amazing how things turn out when God's involved."

Jayce's gaze went to the ceiling at the mush, but his grin belied the action. "So, I've got a question."

Annie didn't hesitate. "Shoot."

"When's the big day?"

Jed leaned down to scratch Kodi's ears. "The opening? We don't even know if we'll be buying the place yet—"

"Nuh-uh. You know what I mean. When's the big day for you two."

Jayce's question was as unexpected as the warmth that surged through Annie. She slanted a look at Jed. "Well, we haven't been dating all that long."

Jayce wasn't buying it. "Come *on!* You're telling me you two don't think you belong together?"

Annie chewed the inside of her lip. She met Jed's shining eyes, and the answer in those brown depths sent her pulse into double time. "Are...are you sure?"

Jed pulled her onto his lap, hugging her close. The playful action inspired Kodi, who jumped up and joined them on the couch, crawling onto Annie's lap with a resounding *Arroww-oww!*

"More sure than I've ever been in my life." He kissed her, and Annie didn't even care that they had an audience—or that she had a ninety-five-pound dog squashing her and trying to shove her head between the two of them.

When he raised his head, she was so breathless she couldn't speak. She circled Kodi's neck with her arms and hugged the beast. Then she took in the goofy grins on her family's faces, and her heart sang.

Jed winked at her. "It's up to you."

"*Well* then—" Annie pushed Kodi off the couch and sat up— "what are you all doing next weekend?"

Whoops and cheers echoed through the room as her family jumped up and came to hug Annie and Jed. Kodi danced in a circle, tail wagging, head swinging back and forth, and let loose with a series of low rumbles and barks.

Jayce cracked up. "Is that an alert of some sort?"

Annie knelt on the floor and hugged the shepherd close. "If not, it should be. After all, she's found someone very important. We both have."

As Annie's eyes met Jed's, she blinked back joyful tears. All these years she'd spent so much time finding the lost. But now she was the one who was lost.

And she didn't mind one bit.

Funny thing, when she finally let go, finally stopped struggling to find who she was, she discovered the truth about herself. That God knew her, inside out. That He created her to be exactly who she was.

That Jed accepted her that way too—just as she was. No changes. No "fixing" what was different.

Just her. Annie. Quirks, oddities, colors, and all.

Who would have thought it? Letting go set her free. And now, at long last, Annie knew she belonged. Right here. Right now. Immersed in God's love. And in Jed's.

And she knew something else too.

It had been worth the wait.

Dear Reader,

Annie's struggle in this book is a familiar one for me. I've always been a bit of the odd one among my family and friends. As the only extrovert—and I mean off-the-scales extrovert—in a family of introverts, I struggled at times with the differences between me and my parents and brothers. But the struggles didn't last long. Not because I was so smart, but because my family was so loving. They may not always have understood me, but they accepted me. And nothing gives you a sense of belonging like being accepted and loved, quirks and all.

God understands that about us.

As I said in my acknowledgments at the front of the book, one of the perks in writing this story was that I got to follow our Rogue Valley K-9 search and rescue dogs during a training event. I haven't had that much fun in a long time. Watching those dogs do their jobs with such unadulterated enjoyment and focus was inspiring. Seeing the connection between the dogs and their handlers was moving.

But you know what impacted me most? The flat-out delight the dogs exhibited when they found whomever was lost! These dogs went from down-to-business professionals to dancing and twirling party dogs. Of course, one handler suggested they were so excited because they knew they got food rewards when they accomplished their goal. But I think it was more than that. I think these dogs actually have a heart for bringing the lost home.

Imagine, then, the joy our Father must feel when He finds a lost child and brings him or her home. When He finally gets through to a lost heart that He loves and accepts, without hesitation. That we belong.

To Him.

Too often we forget that. We wander off thinking we're on our own when in reality we have the very resources of heaven at hand. All we need to do is turn to the Father and trust Him.

All we need to do is come home.

Consider the amazing words of Galatians 4:4–7: "God sent

his Son, born of a woman, born under law, to redeem those under law, that we might receive the full rights of sons. Because you are sons, God sent the Spirit of his Son into our hearts, the Spirit who calls out, 'Abba, Father.' So you are no longer a slave, but a son; and since you are a son, God has made you also an heir."

Abba. Daddy. God isn't just our Father, He's our daddy. And nothing delights Him more than when we, like the little children we are, run to him, holding out our arms that He may reach down and lift us, tucking us close against His heart.

Do you struggle as Annie and I have, with feeling as though you don't belong? Do you feel at times that nobody really understands you, that you're just…different? If so, rest in this fact: Abba understands. He accepts. He loves. And He's there, waiting for you to come home to Him. He made that abundantly clear in Deuteronomy 7:6–7: "For you are a holy people, who belong to the Lord your God. Of all the people on earth, the Lord your God has chosen you to be his own special treasure. The Lord did not choose you and lavish his love on you because you were larger or greater than other[s]…. It was simply because the Lord loves you…his own special treasure."

Don't wait a moment longer. Accept His love. Rest in His promises.

Come home.

In His Peace,

Karen Ball

READER'S GUIDE

1. What was the root cause of Annie's feelings that she didn't belong? Have you ever felt as though you didn't fit in? How did you resolve those feelings?

2. Consider Mother Teresa's quote from the prologue: "If we have no peace, it is because we have forgotten that we belong to each other." Why do you think people need to feel as though they belong? What gives you a sense of belonging?

3. Psychologists describe an "alienated existence" as a joyless one, an existence that will cost the one living it a heavy emotional price. Have you known anyone who lives like this? What was the emotional price that person paid? Have you ever felt alienated? What was the emotional price you paid?

4. Read Deuteronomy 14:2; Psalm 33; Romans 8:29–31; and Romans 11:16–18. What do these verses tell us about where and to whom we belong? How might these verses make a difference to those who have been wounded by a sense of alienation?

5. What was Jed's primary internal conflict? What was it about his father (or parents) that turned him away from trusting God?

6. How has your relationship with your earthly father (or parents) impacted the way you see, trust, and relate to your heavenly Father?

7. Read John 10:11–18; Romans 8:26–39; and 1 John 4:7–21. What promises do these verses give us about the kind of Father God is?

8. What motivated Ryan to do the things he did? Have you ever had a "Ryan" in your life who tried to manipulate you? How did you respond? What did God teach you through that situation?

9. Consider the following verses: Exodus 20:23; Joshua 24:14, 23; Psalm 106:35–36; Hosea 14; and Ephesians 2:1–10. Is there anything in your own life—ambition, money, family, a relationship—that could become an idol, thus coming between you and God? If so, what will you do to surrender it to the Master?

10. Many of us long to know God's will in our lives but aren't certain we do. How has God shown you His will for your life?

11. Consider the following story. What does it tell you about discerning God's will?

> A man prayed, asking God to tell him what His will was for the man's life. God led the man to a large fallen tree at the bottom of a hill and told him to push the tree. The man did so. He pushed, day after day, and yet the tree never budged an inch. Finally, he cried out to God, "How can this be your will for me? I keep pushing and pushing, and the tree never moves!"
>
> God's reply was simple: "The tree isn't supposed to move. I asked you to push, not to move the tree. My will was for you to be obedient, and in that obedience, to grow strong."

12. Read the following verses: Genesis 6:8–9; Psalm 25:4–5; Psalm 119:105; Proverbs 3:5–6; John 14:23–27; Romans 12: 1–2; 1 Thessalonians 5:12–22; Hebrews 10:16, 23–25; 1 John 2:27. How might they help you as you seek to discern God's will for your life?

"Karen Ball has penned a modern classic and given us two unforgettable characters to root for. This is an author to watch!"

—ROBIN LEE HATCHER, bestselling author of
Firstborn and *Promised to Me*

1-59052-033-5

Gabe and Renee Roman are on the edge—relationally and spiritually. But after years of struggling in their marriage, their greatest test comes in the most unexpected of forms: a blizzard in the Oregon wilderness. Their truck hurtles down the side of a mountain, and suddenly they are forced to fight for survival by relying on each other. But both must surrender their last defenses if they are to come home at last—to God and to each other. Only then will they learn the most important truths of all: God is sufficient, and only through obedience to His call can we find true joy. Can the Romans overcome their greatest obstacle—themselves—in time?

Multnomah

www.mpbooks.com